THE ACCUSER

ARTHUR TOOM

ISBN:
Paperback   979-8-9997193-0-0
Hardback   979-8-9997193-1-7
Ebook (EPUB)   979-8-9997193-2-4

Library of Congress Control Number: 2025917312

Published By **Arthur Toom LLC**
Edited By **Shanna P. Lowe**
Cover Art By **Hanlie Wessels**

Printed in the United States of America

CONTENTS

Acknowledgements — V

1. The Chains of Law — 1
2. The Mountain and the Lily — 13
3. The Historian — 23
4. The Symbols of His Title — 33
5. The Bee Sting — 43
6. The Repose — 59
7. The Task — 71
8. The Tipping Scales — 79
9. The Only Child — 89
10. The Farmer in the Strange Little Town — 99
11. The Evil One — 109
12. The Beast of Burden — 125
13. The Wanderer — 137
14. The Bait — 147
15. The Living and the Dead — 161

16. The Exile   171

17. The Debt Collector   187

18. The Deadbeat   197

19. The Shelter   209

20. The Warden   219

21. The Storm   231

22. The Master of Forms   247

23. The Lunatic   259

24. The Composer   273

25. The Grim Wreath   289

26. The Friend   301

27. The Last Mercy   317

28. The Dancer in the Sun   331

29. The Song of the Lost   345

30. The Survivor   363

31. The Imposter   375

32. The Shadows of the Lowest House   383

33. The Debtor   393

34. The Accused   407

35. The Messenger   415

MAP   431

Glossary   433

ACKNOWLEDGEMENTS

Drew White – Thank you for always being willing to read whatever I put down and for entertaining my wildest ideas. You've been a friend of the highest caliber.

Shanna P. Lowe – Thank you for your dedication, your diligence, and the countless hours you've spent helping turn this dream into something real. I'm incredibly proud of what we've made together.

My Parents – Thank you for always believing in me—for smiling past my failures and reminding me that success is always possible. Your faith has carried me farther than you know.

1

THE CHAINS OF LAW

GALADRATH RESTED ON A large stump, watching as the first of The Sisters began to rise. Before he could see the first sun itself, rays of light crept over the horizon and lit up the morning sky like fireworks. Overhead, clouds of dust and streams of fractured asteroids hung high above him. These were the remnants of the Shattered Children, and the early morning light made them sparkle. He thought of the power it had taken to destroy the heavenly bodies, to sunder the gods that had watched over them for so long.

He tossed his shoulders back and opened the front of his cloak, baring his forearms to the cool morning air. His heavy leather sleeves were obscured by the loops of heavy chains encircling them. There were sixty-seven links in the chains. Each link was expertly crafted, a masterpiece of scrollwork and inscriptions, worth a fortune. Each held a fraction of the power of the Shattered Children, and he knew each one like it was a friend.

The first sun, Sari—the oldest of The Sisters—crested the horizon slowly, light tracing the bushes and brush of dense wildflowers in the clearing around Galadrath. The darkness was slowly washed away and left the vibrant colors of a sea of petals, thousands of flowers waving idly in the morning sun.

"Many thanks for your blessings, Sari, nurturer of humankind. Forgive me for what I must do," Galadrath said to the massive red ball.

Standing up, his white silk cloak almost shimmered from the dawn, the embroidered flowers of the white fabric mimicking the surrounding fields. He bent over and picked a single red bud, not yet opened, and pushed it into the boutonniere of the matching vest he wore under the cloak. The floral palette danced across the white fabric as he began to move slowly through the vast fields of flowers around him.

Galadrath walked for a long time, long enough for the second Sister, Seli, to show her bright yellow light. With both suns rising, he could already feel the heat of the day. It would soon be time for him to complete the task he was sent here to do. He closed his eyes and inhaled the fresh countryside air, filled with natural perfumes and earthy musk. He listened to bustling insects and chirping birds.

Deep in his mind, he heard the links of his heavy chains' constant whisperings. The chorus of sixty-seven servants each spoke with a unique and hushed voice, but they hummed to him in harmony. He clenched his fists and as his forearms tightened, pushing against the heavy chains wrapped around them, and he called to them.

Then it came—the glimpse of terror—as if the chains had been asleep, dreaming some terrible dream, and he had jolted them awake. In an instant, a memory surged through him: a woman, drowning in murky darkness, her piercing scream fading into the void. The vision vanished as quickly as it came, the sliver of memory shoved back into the shadowed recesses of his mind—where the horrors of someone else's past were kept.

Galadrath reached inward and drew on the power of the chains. He pushed his influence outward, letting it stretch as far as it could go—down into the earth, up through the breeze, across the vast fields teeming with insects, plants, and life in all forms. Everywhere his mind touched, the matter greedily answered his presence, eagerly pledging fealty to his will.

He let their voices in—the whispering plants, the calling stones, the murmuring air. They filled him with warmth. He felt like an entertainer standing on a stage, a million voices giving him praise—each droplet of dew, each grain of soil, each breath of wind vying for his attention, singing his name.

The feelings washed away the cold shadows he buried in the back of his mind. It soothed him like cool water over a burning itch, washing away the darkness that clawed the edges of his soul.

Only one did not answer him. Of all the things he could feel, only one did not bend to his influence.

"Come out, boy, where I can see you with my eyes," Galadrath called out.

He turned to face a bush fifty feet away, where he had sensed the hiding child. He could feel the shallow breaths of the young boy even from this distance. In fact, Galadrath could even pull the air from his lungs if he wanted. However, his power could not make the boy obey him like other objects of the world. The matter and energy that made up the child had a mind and will of its own.

"I know you're there. Come out, I won't hurt you," he said, his voice loud and stern.

He felt the earth move under the boy's feet, small bare toes flexing and relaxing with nervousness, carving shallow ruts in the soft dirt. The boy refused to emerge. So Galadrath commanded the bush instead, his power destroying it and drinking it into his body. The energy tingled in his veins and made his limbs feel both light and heavy at the same time. The bush had vanished, crumbled away into nothing instantly.

The boy now sat in plain view, bewildered and afraid. His wide eyes stared at Galadrath, who was slowly walking closer.

"I said I wouldn't hurt you," Galadrath said, crouching in front of the stunned boy.

"You're...You're one of the Many," the boy said.

"I am. Please, call me Galadrath. What's your name?"

"Milo, Milo Pikeman, sir," the boy said.

"No need to call me 'sir,' Milo. Is this your farm?" Galadrath asked.

"Nice to meet you, Galadrath," Milo answered. "This is my father's farm."

Galadrath chuckled lightly.

"Well Milo, I apologize for wandering through your fields. I hope I didn't disturb you. May I offer compensation for the bush and the flower?" Galadrath pointed to the red flower bud on his vest, and then vaguely toward where the bush had been.

"No sir—Mister Galadrath—these are just wildflowers. We didn't plant them. But, mister, I would like to know where the bush went? I've never met a Many before," Milo wondered.

"It's right here," Galadrath said.

He held out his hand, his empty palm open in front of Milo. Galadrath pushed the power still resting in his veins out into his hand, forming it back into a solid shape. Branches of smooth, polished stone slowly grew and wove themselves into the image of a bush. The brownish granite tendrils came to a halt, and the strange, false life that seemed to possess it disappeared. Galadrath offered the stone shrub statuette over to the boy, sighing softly. Absorbing matter took effort and concentration, but the act of expelling the energy was natural, almost effortless.

Milo gasped, mouth hanging open, and carefully took the little stone bush.

"You must be an Architect! I bet you've built whole towns! Whole cities!" the boy yelled in excitement.

Galadrath smiled painfully, shoulders dropping. He sighed, "I'm afraid not, Milo. This is just a trick I taught myself while passing the time. The Architects are capable of much greater feats than I. My calling is much less appealing. Here, take this as payment for the flower."

He slipped a gold coin into the breast pocket of Milo's baggy shirt.

"This is too much! You could buy the whole field of flowers for a gold coin!" Milo said.

Galadrath laughed, his smile cooling as he spoke. "Take it, Milo—you've earned it. But you must promise me one thing in exchange. Tell no one that I was here. That is worth a coin."

"Yes, Mister Galadrath, sir. I promise."

"Thanks, Milo. It was a pleasure meeting you, but I must get to work. Maybe I'll see you again." He paused before reciting, "Blessings of the Sisters upon you, blessings of all the gods, the dead and the living."

"Honor and glory, Mister Galadrath," Milo said.

Galadrath clenched his teeth at the boy's greeting, but he knew he had to return it.

"Honor and glory, Milo," he said, throwing the hood of his cloak over his head.

He turned and walked from the fields, the long cloak folding over and parting between the dense flowers and shrubs, until he found the meandering dirt road heading northeast into town. The shining white fabric of his attire now reflected the yellowish brown of dirt and dust, trailing behind him on his walk. The busy road to the south stretched from the capital, the City of Light, to the large port of Axehead Bay. That road bore all the trade goods of the entire countryside, which would be sent across the vast ocean to far-off lands. Yet, amidst its steady flow of commerce, there was a tiny turnoff—where the roadway's solid sheet of stone met a wagon trail of dirt and pebbles. At its end was the tiny, misshapen town he was headed to.

He read the worn sign welcoming him to the little town. It read "Threshook" in chipped black paint that had been carelessly smeared on a plank, long ago. He had not set foot in the small town for years.

Galadrath continued down the worn dirt road and slowly came to the center of the small town, where the homes and buildings began to cluster closer together. There were few people on the streets at this time of day. Most had work to tend to in the countryside and had already left to begin their toils. The only place that seemed to show any signs of life was the large building across from the town well, from which noises of joy and anger could be heard already in the early morning. The building sat squat, as if the burden of its walls had fatigued the posts they were mounted on. The roof had a shallow pitch and sagged in a few places.

He paused at the entrance door and called on the chains with his mind. Their chorus answered him immediately, and he projected his influence in the world around him. He *felt* each beam of the building, each flake of crumbling plaster, and each old board in the roof covered with new ones. The objects greeted him as he called them to attention. The ground below him seemed to vibrate with anticipation, the air flicking back and forth in a breeze, impatient to please him.

"Thumblethin Inn and Alehouse. It's good to see you again, old friend," Galadrath mumbled to the building.

He pushed the door open, his mind set on edge, ready for anything. It swung open begrudgingly, creaking loudly, and rested on rusty hinges. He entered the room, shutting the door behind him. A few dim candles illuminated the large space, a contrast to the stark sunlight outside. He allowed his eyes to adjust even though he was not really using them. He could feel the space around him without needing to see. Galadrath held the whole structure in his mind, at his beck and call.

No one seemed to mind him. A few faces turned and squinted at him briefly, before they resumed their conversations and drinks. Galadrath walked to the bar and sat on the stool, taking a moment to straighten his cloak out behind him, careful not to crease the silk.

"I'll have some mead, if you have it," Galadrath addressed the bartender.

"You've got it... sir," the man stuttered.

Galadrath produced a gold piece, placing it gently on the bar top.

The bartender returned with a wooden stein of mead. He looked down at the coin and then back to Galadrath.

"I can't make the difference on that coin there... sir," the bartender grumbled.

"You don't need to—if you can tell me where I can find Dietrich Bledfett?" Galadrath asked loudly.

The barkeep stared at Galadrath as if he was trying to read his mind.

"What's a thing like you doing out here in such a pretty dress? And flashing such a shiny coin?" a sarcastic voice drawled from beside Galadrath.

The words belonged to a man with wild red and silver hair, his face was wrinkled and darkened by the suns. He had heavy stubble forming the beginning of an unkempt beard. His pale blue eyes squinted at Galadrath, staring mockingly.

"At first, I thought you might be a lovely lady of the night—lost and confused. But you're just a man in a dress," he continued.

"I apologize if I've offended you, sir. Could I buy a round of drinks for you and your friends?" Galadrath spoke softly.

The man produced a long, crude knife from a sheath on his waist and ran the blade along his own chin, the red stubble scraping against the dull edge. "I think, maybe, I'll turn you upside down and see if I can get more than just a drink along with that apology. We'll see what falls out of that dress. After all, coins are like thieves, they rarely travel alone," the man said.

Galadrath shook his head slowly, sighing. "It's a cloak, not a dress."

"But it has flowers on it. It's very pretty. Makes you look like you should be wearing a bonnet," the man replied. He held out the knife he was still holding and leaned against the countertop, tapping the metal edge of his weapon against the wood.

One of the young men at the table spoke, "Emmett, don't, he's one of the Many."

The warning came too late.

Galadrath pushed his elbows outward, spreading the cloak aside, resting his hands deliberately on the wooden counter. The heavy chains around his forearms clattered and scraped as he dragged them against the edge of the bartop. He stood slowly, his stool vanishing as he consumed it. The man did not notice, his eyes transfixed on the chains rattling against the wood. Galadrath felt the weight of power in his veins, and his focus throbbed as the energy flooded his mind.

The faces in the room turned slowly toward the two men, the grating chains interrupting the dull mix of voices. The tavern quieted, and the chains settled where Galadrath finally pressed them onto the countertop.

The red-bearded man was taller than him, forcing him to look up.

Galadrath stared up at him, unwavering, and watched the man's smirk fade.

"I get the sense that you may have changed your mind? Do I still look like a man in a dress? Do you have a bonnet I can borrow?" Galadrath whispered into the silence.

The man's face sank, his eyes growing wide, and he acted as if he was about to speak. His mouth opened and then shut again. All he managed was a painful swallow.

"Your silence is reassuring," Galadrath spoke as he turned to the room. He shrugged the cloak from his shoulders, making sure the chains around his arms were visible for everyone to see.

"You're the Accuser," the red-bearded man said.

Galadrath nodded.

"Since you all seem to know who I am, maybe you can be of help. I'm looking for Dietrich Bledfett," Galadrath asked.

There was complete silence again.

Moving between tables, Galadrath began pacing throughout the room, inspecting each person. The men seated simply watched, their eyes following him in fear as he made his rounds. Eventually, he stopped at a table in the back corner.

Galadrath pulled the small flower bud from the boutonniere of his vest and handed it to a young man sitting across the small round table.

"Dietrich. You should be proud that your friends did not betray you—only your shallow breaths did," he said.

The young man hesitantly took the small flower. The other four people sitting with him rose quickly and scrambled to the opposite side of the room.

"Dietrich Bledfett, I am Galadrath. I accuse you of high treason against the Kingdom of Thainegom. By law, you are entitled to a trial. If you plead guilty, you will be sentenced according to the severity of your crimes, which are punishable by death. How do you plead?" Galadrath stated in a monotone.

Dietrich lowered his head, his greasy brown hair covering his face. After a moment, he looked up again, scowling at Galadrath.

"Yea' I know your name. This is a farce. It is madness that you can come here and throw these crimes and sentences in the face of any man—and then expect him to defend himself? The king must be very afraid of me, to have sent the Chained Honor, Galadrath the Accuser," Dietrich spat furiously. Then he added with a laugh, "The Grim Wreath."

"I'm not fond of that nickname," Galadrath responded. "People fail to see past a cloak, a few colors, a simple design. No matter, that's of little importance. I did not hear you make a plea. What is yours? Guilty?"

"If I plead not guilty? What joke of a trial do I get?" Dietrich asked.

"The same trial everyone gets by law. Trial by combat. Now, please, make your plea," Galadrath said.

Stalling, Dietrich yelled, "And by law, the Accuser is the combatant who would carry out the trial? So you would sentence me to death by execution if I plead guilty, or to death by combat if I claim to be innocent? Where is the justice in this accusation? You and your station are a farce, a blight on the good name of Thainegom. King Thestus allows this absurdity, unlike the kings before him."

"I never claimed to serve justice. I serve the law. I have accused you. Make your plea." Frustration seeped into Galadrath's tone.

"Not guilty." The young man rose up from the table. He crossed the room to the entrance door, pulled it open, and sauntered outside.

Galadrath flicked another goldpiece onto the bartop. He used his manipulation of air, to land the coin perfectly on the first gold piece he had placed there.

"I did say I'd buy everyone a round," he said, before he pointed at the red bearded man and at one of the men who had vacated the table Dietrich had been sitting. "You two, come with me, I'll need witnesses, and I'll need your names for the records."

"The name's Emmett Brigborn, and that's Justus Kennd," the red bearded man said begrudgingly.

"Thank you kindly. Justus, bring your sword—Dietrich will need it," Galadrath commanded.

The three men followed after Dietrich, who was already waiting in the late-morning sunshine.

"Most men run." Galadrath raised his voice to cover the short distance between them.

"Would I have a chance if I did?" Dietrich asked.

"There is no honor in it."

"I'd rather keep my life and lose my honor."

"You'd end up with neither," Galadrath stated flatly.

Justus handed Dietrich his sword and retreated back to the edge of the street, away from the impending fight.

Galadrath stepped forward and shrugged out of his cloak. The wind picked up, as he willed it to, and helped him shed the garment. It flew away quickly, still open as if it were possessed by a ghost, and came to rest on the railing of the inn. Matching the cloak, his vest was a brilliant shining white, a thousand tiny flowers of warm colors embroidered onto it. Under it, he wore a black silk shirt, heavy black pants, thick leather boots, and two sheathed swords hung from his waist. His infamous chains were bulky in contrast to the rest of his attire, looking out of place. In the bright sun the inscriptions on each link could be made out.

Galadrath could see the reality of the situation dawn on Dietrich. The defiance tapered from his eyes, the realization of his own mortality taking root.

"Gods, living and dead, I don't stand a chance. Earth Mother, soon I'll be buried. Please nestle me in the warmth of your bosom," Dietrich prayed under his breath.

"Draw—and we'll begin your trial," Galadrath urged.

Dietrich drew his weapon, the long blade flashing in the bright light. Galadrath gave a short bow and grabbed his own swords from their sheaths, producing the two lengths of fine steel. He crossed the short distance between them quickly and slashed wildly, drawing out his opponent with one of the swords. Dietrich parried the blow, and the blades clanged against each other loudly. However, Galadrath had already swung his other sword. The precise movement blurred. The energy in his veins propelled the weapon at inhuman speeds, cleaving cleanly through the neck of the accused.

The head and body of the young man fell to the ground with two dull thuds.

"Dietrich Bledfett, you have been accused of high treason by Galadrath Yaralok, tried, and found guilty by combat. Emmett Brigborn and Justus Kennd of Threshook are recorded as witnesses," Galadrath said.

Dietrich's body and head shrank and dissolved, evaporating almost instantly, leaving only the weapon and the clothes he was wearing behind. Galadrath had consumed his matter and pushed the energy back out into the palm of his hand into its purest physical form, an emblem. He closed his eyes for a moment and listened to the memory, the accusation that he had just completed, now stored in the tiny grain-sized crystal. The memory of the event that had just unfolded, perfectly chronicled, flashed before his eyes in an instant. He sighed heavily.

"Farewell."

Galadrath absentmindedly addressed the onlookers, stowing his swords, and draping his cloak over his shoulders once more. He began walking out of town, along the same path he had entered only a short while before.

2

THE MOUNTAIN AND THE LILY

THE SISTERS HAD DANCED their way across the sky, and the shadows were once again growing longer. Galadrath had spent most of the day wandering roads, mulling over the words and the events of the morning. Currently, he was slowly meandering along the lengthy road known as Delia's Stretch.

"The King must be very afraid of me to have sent the Chained Honor..."

Dietrich's words rang over and over in his mind. There was more to this observation than either of them had initially realized. In the capital, Galadrath was treated as a ghost, a monster, something supernatural to be feared. No matter how softly he spoke, no matter how kind he was—polite and passive—everyone he encountered would hold their breath as he passed. His mere presence was an omen of death. Here he was, sent to accuse a man who was not one of the Many—a man who was barely proficient with a sword. The work was beneath him.

He held the tiny speck that made up the emblem, the pure form of matter that had been Dietrich's body. He reached into one of the pockets of his vest, pulling out a small length of paper. On the paper

13

were a few short sentences written down and a delicate drawing of the dead man.

"Dietrich Bledfett, hereby accused of high treason, supported by acts of sedition chronicled by Lord Otto Drumm. The trial is to be carried out by the court of King Thestus, 48th of his name. If found guilty, the accused is sentenced to death," Galadrath read under his breath, the parchment crackling faintly in his hands.

"Acts of sedition, chronicled by Lord Drumm himself?" he grumbled.

With a small sigh, he folded the document carefully, slipping the tiny emblem inside its creases before tucking it back into his coat. His fingers lingered in the pocket for a moment, then dropped.

"Time to go home," he said to no one, spurring himself out of thought and into action.

He clenched his fists, the resistance of the chains biting into his forearms, and drew power from the emblems he carried elsewhere in the hidden pockets of his vest. He pulled energy from one in particular, the blackstone he had owned since he was a young man. It had been used and replenished countless times, but a shred of the original essence still existed within. The dark energy flowed into his veins like icy despair—the prickle of forgotten nightmares itched in the back of his mind.

The energy flowed out of him, seeping out of every pore in the form of a thick black fog. He breathed out. The black gas rolled off of his tongue, hissing out from beneath his eyelids, and enveloped him completely. He felt like he was looking through a pale version of distant memories. An endless mist moved around him across a distorted landscape. He seemed to spend both a moment and also a thousand years opening every door, entering every room, walking down every path he had ever traveled, until he found the door of his own home.

Then the dreary image became reality, the color of the real world flowing back into what he saw before him. At the edges of his vision, he saw the thick black fog flowing off of him, sinking and dissipating as it reached the ground. He pushed the remainder of the energy into the blackstone emblem and let the warmth of the sunshine radiating off of the sandstone walkway heat him up. He had learned the art of Stepping, the ability to move great distances in only one step, when he was a young boy. Even now, years after the first time he had drawn on the power of blackstone, he was still filled with the cold sadness every time he used it.

He heard the faint laughter of his children. Tracing the sound, he looked upwards. His house was not wide, squeezed along the tight streets among other sandstone buildings, but it was taller than most, boasting four floors. He extended his influence outward, the chains still under his command from Stepping. He felt the small feet running back and forth on the roof terrace. He thought of scaring them by Stepping onto the roof, appearing out of nowhere, clouded in black fog, like he had done so many times before. He could snatch them both up before they even saw him, and he knew they would scream and then laugh, but the chill of sadness clung to him. The execution he had carried out was still fresh on his mind and on his hands, causing his heart to thaw more slowly.

Instead, he released his concentration on the chains, the conduits for the power of the emblems now just heavy weights on his arms. Pushing the front door open, he was immediately greeted by his butler.

"Galadrath, welcome home. Administrant Callidron will be joining us for dinner. May I be of service in any way?" the servant said.

"Thanks, Raatel. Nothing will be necessary," he replied. "I'll just help myself to a quick bath."

Galadrath climbed the first two sets of stairs and retreated into a large bathroom. Quickly stripping off his attire, he kept the heavy chains close enough so he could still use their power, and, with a quick flick of his mind, he drew in water and fire from the collection of emblems in his vest. The bathtub filled with steaming water from an invisible faucet. The cool freshness of water mixed with the searing heat of flame in his blood, and as quickly as he tapped the energy of the emblems, he expelled it into the tub.

Lowering himself into the near-scalding water, the tension in his muscles and mind soothed. He closed his eyes briefly, indulging himself in the moment of tranquility before he began to wash the day from his skin. He felt his actions clinging to him like dust, and he pushed his fingers through his hair to knead the uneasiness from his thoughts. When he finished, he dried himself with the aid of an air emblem and dressed himself in a loose-fitting shirt and pants. Refreshed, he ran up the flights of stairs and onto the terrace.

"Who is making all this noise?" he boomed.

"Father!" both children cried in unison. They ran away laughing, to the far edges of the covered area, hiding behind chairs and large potted plants.

"Oh, you're going to make me come get you? First, I'll have to steal a kiss from your mother, since she is easier to catch. Then I'll come for each of you!" Galadrath said in a deep voice.

He smiled between scowls, pantomiming like he was a lumbering giant. He walked awkwardly to a large chaise lounge where his wife lay. She was holding a large feather fan in one hand, absentmindedly waving it in front of her face. In her other hand, she held a golden cup aloft in his direction. Raising an eyebrow, she smiled.

"I've come for my kiss, Heladra," he said sweetly, looming over her.

"Dearest, if you'll cool my drink I'll give you the kiss freely," she replied.

"I've already put away my work things," he grumbled. "I guess I can't afford your lips."

She laughed, slowly putting her cup down on the small table next to where she was reclining, feigning laziness. Then she snatched up the front of his loose shirt, pulling him down.

"*Whooaaaa!* I'm no match for your mother, children!" He braced his fall against the furniture.

Their lips met, and they held them there for a long moment.

"Awww, come on!" his daughter said. "He's supposed to be chasing us!"

Heladra let her husband go, pushing him away as she still gripped his shirt. To the children, she said, "Fine, you can have him, but don't come crying to me when he catches you!"

Galadrath pulled up his hands in front of him, miming claws, and he began to slowly stalk them. He paused at intervals, hiding poorly behind large plants or crouching behind a column in such a way that his hindquarters stuck out. He growled and panted, sniffed and huffed, acting like a feral predator. He slinked around on the balls of his feet as the children laughed and dashed from hiding place to hiding place. Occasionally, they would stop to peek at him, stifling a giggle and hiding almost as poorly as he was.

Then he stood upright, banged on his chest with both fists, howled skyward, and took off running. The children squealed and bolted from their hiding places. His daughter, Radralia, was youngest and slowest, so he quickly scooped her up in one of his arms, gnawing playfully at her ribs to tickle her. Still in motion, he reached his son, Marcanus, and grabbed him in the other. He howled again, a child in each arm, as they laughed and squirmed.

"Now, I've got you both—just in time for The Sisters to sleep. Let's watch the suns set and wish them a good night, so that tomorrow they will be well-rested to dance across the sky once more," he said.

He put them down. Over the next hour, they all leaned against the short column railing of the terrace, watching the dark red sun and the small yellow one slowly sink behind the horizon.

"Thanks for your blessings today, Sisters—for shining down on Galadrath during his journeys this day," Heladra said from behind, wrapping her arms around the three of them.

"Now children, wash up. Your Uncle will be here shortly, and then we eat," she finished.

The children broke free from their mother's grasp and scampered down the stairs.

"Shall we, my glowing lily?" Galadrath smiled at his wife.

"Of course. Better not have Raatel climb all these stairs just to announce our guest," she laughed.

"Did you pick me a flower today?" she asked, leading him by the hand toward the stairs.

He sighed softly.

"No, I forgot. You know any flower would wilt in the presence of your beauty," he said drably, deflecting her intended question.

"But you did pick a flower?" she whispered.

"I did," he replied.

They continued down the stairs in silence, his wife understanding the implication.

"Heladra, Administrant Callidron has arrived," Raatel announced.

Booming laughter followed as the butler finished.

"What! Raatel, I'll never understand you. You call the lady of the house by her name, but you refer to me by title," Teratos Callidron roared.

"I respect her wishes and your title. These are ideals you would do good to take under advisement, Administrant," Raatel chastised him.

The butler stood a head taller than Teratos. His figure was lean and muscular, even in his old age. Curling slightly under his chin, a well-groomed beard covered his rutted and wrinkled face. He looked down his nose at Teratos, while standing impossibly straight.

Teratos's eyes widened as the butler's cool rebuke took the wind from his sails. He pointed to Heladra, and then to Galadrath, as if to urge them to put their servant in his place. Then he guffawed louder than before.

"I suspect you're right," Teratos said. "Maybe you'd take my place in the Court of Lords?"

"Let me pour you a drink while I hold my tongue, Adminstrant Callidron," Raatel quipped.

"I'm not sure if your wisdom exceeds your wit, Raatel, but I have no capacity to judge a man as great as you," Teratos said.

Raatel locked eyes with him before smiling sinisterly.

"Galadrath, where do you find such a wild man? Teratos simpered. "And how did you tame him?"

Galadrath glared grimly at Teratos. The comment overstepped even the farthest boundary of appropriate banter. He knew Teratos would not let the last joke be at his expense; he needed to get the last word.

Heladra cut the tension between them, smiling sweetly at Raatel and taking the drink he had poured. She moved across the room and handed it to Teratos.

"I was looking forward to seeing Maxima," she said. "We have so much to catch up on. When will your wife join us for dinner again?"

"Ah, yes—I know she would have loved to come this evening, but she isn't feeling quite herself," Teratos answered timidly. His bombastic and overbearing presence had been tempered by Galadrath's stare.

"I hope she isn't falling ill. It is a terrible thing to suffer in this summer heat. I'll have to visit her," she answered.

"No, she's not sick, she's just radiant with emotion," Teratos paused, and then said slyly, "Speaking of not feeling herself, where are your children?"

"They'll be down shortly, just washing up. They're excited to see you," Galadrath said.

He had not taken Teratos' subtle hint and answered the obvious remark, but Heldra gasped and covered her mouth with her hands. Galadrath's eyes flicked between his wife and his friend, trying to recall what he had missed.

"Why, Teratos! Congratulations! That is fantastic news indeed! I must go see her as soon as she'll allow me. How exciting!" Heladra squealed.

Galadrath paused a moment longer, not sure what the excitement was about.

Heladra restrained her excitement in a forced whisper. "A child! They're expecting a child, Galadrath, you thick oaf!"

"Ah! Teratos!" Galadrath exclaimed. He turned and grabbed his friend, embracing him in a hug. Teratos returned the gesture, and they both laughed and cheered, rocking awkwardly as they held each other.

"I told you my wife lets me touch her!" Teratos joked heartily.

"I won't believe it until I see the child. Could be that handsome cook of yours'!" Galadrath teased.

"Probably, but I'd love the little bastard either way. We've been waiting too long," the Administrant replied.

"I'm truly happy for you and for your family. You'll have a beautiful child, and you'll make a great father," Galadrath said.

"Thanks, my friend. But speak not a word of this to anyone. I'm not supposed to spoil the news. Maxima wants to share it." Teratos widened his eyes, straining them at each of the occupants of the room in turn, urging them into secrecy.

"I'll take it to the grave, Administrant Callidron." Raatel pursed his lips and placed a finger in front of them.

They all laughed at the serious demeanor of the butler, and he cracked a wry smile.

The patter of tiny feet scrambling down the stairs quieted them slightly, as the two children joined them in the great room.

"Let's sit—I'm sure everyone is famished," Heladra insisted, then asked, "Raatel, please, some light."

"A thousand apologies, Heladra. Even after a lifetime, my eyes haven't adjusted to life in the City of Light," Raatel embellished.

He flourished a hand, and the polished golden sconces on the walls were instantly filled with wicking flames. As twilight faded, the open windows framed the flames that filled the room with a warm glow. He flicked another hand, conjuring a spontaneous breeze that fluttered through the drapes, drawing them shut in front of the windows.

"It makes me uneasy to see how easily you've learned to call to the emblems. You've become quite the Duster," Teratos addressed the servant.

"He's not a Duster, Teratos," Galadrath replied. "Those self-taught criminals are dangerous, a menace. I've taught Raatel myself, and he's got a knack for it."

"It doesn't matter how he was taught. You know as well as I do that anyone who calls on the power of the Many without being sanctioned is a criminal. I don't have to explain it to you—just note that it makes me uneasy," Teratos scolded. "Nonetheless, I'll take it to the grave," he finished, nodding at Raatel and Galadrath in turn.

"Please sit," Heladra cut in with a warm tone.

They all found their seats at the long wooden table, inlaid with swirls of gold and silver. Small chunks of flatbread, topped with spinach and goat cheese, sat ready to be dipped. Polished steel plates—containing garlic, oil and herbs—suspended over small flames, propagated a heavenly aroma throughout the room.

Teratos quickly grabbed one of the chunks, doused it in the oil and began talking. "You're not wearing that gaudy cloak you are so fond of. Did someone finally talk some sense into you?"

"The only flower I need is right here," Galadrath replied, touching Heladra's arm. "However, I did have some fool call me the Grim Wreath today—and another referred to me simply as 'man in a dress.'"

"I'm sure their foolishness earned them appropriate punishment," Teratos replied as he chewed.

"Well, I bought a drink for the one and his friends—and the other I killed," Galadrath stated.

Teratos sputtered, almost choking on his bread. There was an awkward pause, and then he roared with laughter. Galadrath chuckled briefly, raised his glass in a sort of salute, took a drink and began laughing along.

"Surely, you didn't kill a man for calling you names, father?" Radralia asked.

"No, my shining star, he was the man I was sent to accuse. That is why I killed him," he answered softly.

"He was a criminal?" she asked.

"He was guilty, my sweet child," he said.

"Then he was no match for a great fighter like you, father!" Marcanus exclaimed.

Teratos sighed. "No one your father is sent to accuse is a match for him," he said with a faint smile.

"Yes! He is the greatest of the Many!" Marcanus continued.

Teratos howled with glee, and the infectious noise spread to the children, and then even Heladra joined in with a snicker.

Galadrath smiled and waited for the noise to die down. "I appreciate the compliment, my son. Your uncle meant that the people I am sent to accuse are my lesser. That anyone I am sent to challenge, I am meant to defeat," he said.

"Accusers are the greatest warriors among the Many—why wouldn't you be able to beat anyone they send you to fight?" Marcanus asked.

"Let me explain," Galadrath began.

3

THE HISTORIAN

"After the Shattering, when Thainegom was weak from the war, there were few people left to keep the peace. The armies were destroyed, and the countryside was ruined. People were poor and desperate, so they began to prey on each other. The King could not control the amount of unrest, thus he made a new law. He said that any man who was wronged could accuse the perpetrator and settle the matter without the help of the court. Since many crimes had no witnesses or proof, most grievances were settled by trials of combat.

"For a few years, it worked. People were afraid to anger their neighbors, knowing that anyone could justly accuse them. However, there were also those who had lived by the sword and had turned to crime. Criminals accused honest people of false crimes, killing them unjustly for their goods, and were protected by the law. Farmers and tradesmen who were wronged by fighting men could not accuse them and win in combat. So the people recruited warriors of their own. They found honorable men and paid them to accuse criminals on their behalf. Even some brigands and thieves became accusers, using their fighting talents to make money. The King heard of this, and he began the Court's Accusers, hiring these professional fighters to root out and accuse unjust men."

Galadrath paused for a moment, his mind wandering as Raatel began to produce the mezze, a multitude of small plates carrying delicate morsels of stuffed grape leaves, oozing with honey and minced meat mixed with fresh herbs.

"But there were Keepers of the Peace already," Marcanus interrupted. "Why didn't the King just use them?"

Teratos answered, "The King wanted to save face. He was weak, relying on the Keepers to protect himself from being overthrown. His law was weak, so he bought himself loyalty from dangerous men."

Galdrath glared at the man momentarily, then softened his expression as he finished swallowing a bite of pita bread dipped in tzatziki and continued explaining to his son.

"The Keepers were few in number, and many of them couldn't fight as well as these mercenaries. None of them could compete with the Dusters, when they began to surface. Ordinary men who had found shards of the Shattered Children had started unlocking the ability to wield the divine metal. The Dusters were the beginning of the Many, and they were more powerful than any of their countrymen. Some of them became warlords, proclaimed themselves as new kings. Some even claimed to be among the Few. A lot of the King's Accusers died trying to kill these men."

"But the Few died," Marcanus said. "You told me the Lowest House saved the people."

Galadrath nodded and began to remove chunks of meat and vegetables from a large wooden skewer. "The Few did die, but their disciples helped rebuild, namely The Timeless Mother. Without her aid and power, the world would be a much different place, a much darker place. The King tried to recruit any of the Many that he could, but most of them realized they were now more powerful than the King himself. Fearing the collapse of his kingdom, he went to his new allies across the sea, Barkrill, and pleaded with them to send help. They responded by sending ambassadors from the Lowest House.

"Just like the Dusters began to use the divine metals here in Thainegom, the Barkrillen had already discovered something similar after the first war, a thousand years ago. The Lowest House had the most powerful warriors in existence, and they had perfected the Art of Stepping. The ambassadors from the Lowest House quickly rounded up the Dusters. The King outlawed anyone from using divine metal, unless they were sanctioned by the court, and then trained his own army of Many, now known as the Emissaries," the Accuser finished.

Plates rattled as the dishes were passed between them, each person sampling something new.

"What happened to all the Dusters that the ambassadors rounded up?" his son asked.

"They were recruited by the Temple of Light to become Emissaries, and those who wouldn't join were found guilty," Galadrath replied.

"You are an ambassador, aren't you?" Marcanus discerned. "Even though you are an Accuser?"

"Your uncle and I are both ambassadors—we have been for most of our lives."

His son gaped, "So, you grew up in the Lowest House?"

"We did. I was nine when my parents sent me." Galadrath jabbed at his friend, attention shifting to him. "Teratos, you were a little older? Ten? Your parents probably thought you were a little slow."

Teratos bobbed his head, smiling slyly, "Maybe if your parents had sent you later, you'd have become an Administrant like me. If you had spent as much effort completing your studies as you spent trying to avoid them, you could sit at Court with me, instead of standing before it."

"I prefer to look into a person's eyes when I drive a blade into them. There is no honor in stabbing someone in the back with a sharpened tongue," the Accuser growled.

"Everything is always about death and ruin for you, Galadrath. You weren't always like this, answering every question with a cut, your wit only as keen as the edge of your blade. My sharp tongue can cut the bonds of a man, setting him free. It can carve a new idea from rough stone and set it before a king; it can etch a promise of a better future into the laws. We can't simply destroy evil and expect goodness to grow," the Administrant replied.

His words diffused the tension between them as quickly as it had arrived.

"Sorry, the memories of that place always set me on edge," Galadrath said.

Teratos forced out a loud laugh, and turned toward Marcanus. "Speaking of your father trying to get away from his studies... Marcanus, did he ever tell you about how he met your mother?" he asked, turning his attention back to the pearl onions heaped on his plate.

"He met her in a field of flowers, and they kissed and fell in love," Radralia piped in.

Heladra laughed, adding her own account, "We did meet in a field of flowers, dearest, but we didn't kiss and fall in love just yet. I was working on my family's farm, clearing a field to plant. We were digging up stones and all of a sudden your father appeared in a thick cloud of black smoke. I thought he was a Patchwork, and in my fear, I chased after him with a shovel. He ran from me and fell down, tripping on some of the thick wildflower bushes. I came to my senses and saw he was just a boy."

"She was the most beautiful flower I saw in that field. Even as she was about to bash my head in with a shovel, the only thing that crossed my mind was how gorgeous she was," Galadrath added.

"Save the sappy stuff, Accuser, and tell them how you got there," Teratos chuckled.

"Well, it's obvious I had Stepped there. Only moments before I had been sitting in the halls of the Lowest House. Regardless of what your uncle thinks, I was quite good at my studies. I was one of the best students at Stepping, and so I was working on Wandering. See, to be able to Step, someone must use a trinket made of one of the divine metals and draw upon a blackstone emblem. The power of those emblems allows you to see the world like a dream, to see every place you've ever been, to imagine yourself walking through your own memories. Just like in a dream, you can move from one place to the next, and even though they may be two places very far apart, or two different memories in time, it seems to all make sense.

"Then when you want, you can transport yourself to whatever place you picked in that dream, that memory. Any place you can remember, any place you've been, you can appear. Wandering, however, is much more difficult. Wandering is like Stepping, but it leads to places you've never been. Imagine trying to create a memory of a real place you've never been and seen."

"That must feel amazing to be able to imagine a place and go there! Did you imagine a field with mom in it?" Radralia asked.

"It is amazing," Galadrath replied, "but it's also sad and scary. Dark memories hide in the blackstone. And no, I didn't have that wonderful of an imagination to be able to imagine your mother. I was fourteen at the time, so I had already spent five years in the Lowest House. Those cold dark halls are far beneath the island of Barkrill, deep in the almost endless depths of the Scar. It's dreary and depressing. The walls themselves seem to whisper sad songs.

"I wasn't happy there, so I tried to imagine my parent's house—their garden, specifically. My father cultivated the most beautiful flowers, and the memory of their sweet scents mingling with the salty seabreeze was always a comfort to me. But I couldn't just Step to their house and visit them—it was forbidden. Instead, I Wandered to the first similar place I could find," Galadrath finished.

"That's how you Stepped into the field with mom?" Radralia asked again. "And she tried to whack you with a shovel? Then you fell in love and kissed?"

"She did try and whack me with a shovel," he smiled. "We didn't fall in love and kiss just yet. We sat, talked, and walked through the fields. I visited her as much as I could, and we grew to be friends. Every time I had to leave, she'd pick me a flower, and I'd hold onto it until I saw her again. We did that for a few years, until I was finally done studying," he answered.

"And *then* you fell in love and kissed?" she asked impatiently.

Heladra answered, "Yes dearest. Then we fell in love and kissed."

"And then *we* got placed in the ambassadorship to Thainegom," Teratos said, pointing to himself and Galadrath, "to help train and recruit for the Emissaries, working in the Temple of Light! We were just seventeen and had been placed in some of the most prestigious positions known to all of the world. We were rich, almost overnight! We had power and status—people parted before us in the streets! The world was at our young fingertips, and we could go anywhere we pleased—literally anywhere!" Teratos laughed.

"But we were still bound as servants to the Lowest House," Galadrath grumbled.

"We are still bound in service to this day. You wear their chains, don't you? But happiness! Wine! Delicious food! Servants of your own! If this is servitude, please, bind my wrists even tighter!" Teratos boomed, laughing again. He picked up his golden goblet and clinked it hard against the metal pitcher Raatel was walking by with. He bellowed, "To servants and servitude! Honor and Glory!"

Raatel produced another set of dishes as the main course had slowed—a desert of fried dough balls soaked in honey.

Teratos chuckled heartily, his mirth infectious as the children and Heladra joined in with their bright smiles and delighted cheers. Even Galadrath raised his glass, toasting to the warcry of the mighty Thainegom empire. Out of the corner of his eye, he noticed Raatel give a short, almost imperceptible bow in his direction.

"Father," Marcanus began with a hint of caution, "why are you angry that you are a servant?"

Teratos spoke before Galadrath could. "He's not angry at being a servant. Any Barkrillen worth his salt knows that servitude is noble. Being a servant means you are strong enough to care for yourself and still have strength left over to care for others. Serving the Lowest House means being a Pillar on the foundations of greatness, holding up the roof that shelters others.

"No, your father is angry because they had forbidden him to marry your mother. He had to petition for it. But as rare a flower your mother is, I'd say she was worth the wait," Teratos concluded.

"Well worth the wait," Galadrath said, grabbing his wife's hand.

"It was," Heladra said. "I'm just sorry it cost you so dearly. It wasn't right of them to force you to become an Accuser—to punish you for wanting to marry me."

Then with a soft voice, Teratos spoke quickly, as if to sweep her statement away with care.

"No no, you can't blame that bureaucratic triviality for his position. He has a gift, unparalleled by any other. Anyone can jabber on like I do, whisper in a king's ear and laugh off heated statements made by a lord. It is a skill, sure, one that I have all but mastered, but what Galadrath has is talent that can not be taught," Teratos said, then turned his attention from Heladra back to Marcanus. "We are both Pillars of the Lowest House, but your father carries a greater burden than most. He is good at finding people. After all, in his Wanderings, the first person he bumped into was your mother. That's fate as sure as the Sisters shine."

Teratos absentmindedly pressed his honey coated fingers together and pulled them apart, chasing a rogue olive around his plate with his other hand and popping it in his mouth.

"Uncle Teratos," Radralia chimed in playfully, "you do jabber a lot, but it takes a lot to admit that. I would know. I can be very talkative."

They laughed at the blunt truth. As usual, Teratos bellowed the hardest of them all.

"Why didn't you want to become an Accuser?" Marcanus asked Galadrath, nudging his sister to be quiet. "What else did you want to do?"

"I didn't know what I wanted to be. I didn't really put a lot of thought into it. I wasn't really *forced* to become one, but I had a knack for it, and I was promised adventure," Galadrath paused. "If I could wish for something else, I might want to be an Architect—taking the land in my hands like clay and molding it into great cities with massive gardens, bridges and waterways that carry people like lifeblood to and from their own jobs and homes and families." He sat back, cup in his hand, pushing his plate away from himself.

"And you, uncle?" Marcanus asked. "Do you enjoy being the Administrant to Lord Ostiphan? Would you choose to be in service doing something else if you could?"

"He serves only with his tongue, and the only person he makes happy with it is Maxima, when he lifts her with it," Galadrath snarked.

Heladra gasped, and Teratos roared with laughter.

"Galadrath! Behave yourself!" Heladra chastised him.

Teratos returned his attention to Marcanus and replied, "I deeply enjoy my position and the work I manage to do, even if my slippery tongue brings disdain to most. I do wish I served with more purpose. The Court of Lords is tedious at times, and I would enjoy being able to make a more direct difference with my work."

"I don't know how you can stand working in the Court, for such false men. Men of power should be powerful, instead these men have their power given to them by those who are powerful—the people," Galadrath grumbled.

"You work for them, same as I do. You are no better, just because you do their deeds at a distance. Tomorrow they will throw another link on your chain for your service—they will pat their faithful servant on the head, just like they pat their dogs of war," Teratos said, licking his greasy lips.

Heladra raised her eyebrows and grabbed Galadrath around the wrist.

"Another link? How do you know?" she asked in a low voice.

Teratos smiled wryly, "I wasn't supposed to say anything, but Lord Ostiphan has been very pleased with the Chained Honor. He has appealed to the king and the Court, and they have agreed to bestow another trinket on your humble husband." Then his tone turned jokingly, "Soon, our Galadrath will have to wear those chains around his neck, they'll be so long and heavy."

He leaned back with difficulty, trying to give his stomach room to breathe, and gripped his chalice tightly as if it was steadying him.

"Like a collared dog? Or would the chain serve as a noose?" Galadrath chuckled.

"Husband! Do not tempt the gods!" Heladra strained the words through her teeth.

"Like a humble servant, who has been graciously celebrated by his king," Teratos said abruptly.

"Yes, this is great news indeed." Heladra exclaimed, smiling brightly. "It should be celebrated. And your news, Teratos! The best news of all! I wish Maxima was here to join us, on such a joyous occasion."

Then she added, "Raatel, clear the table and help yourself—we'll be retiring to the lounge."

They all stood, each giving a short bow to the servant, before they climbed the stairs to the second floor.

"Off to bed with you two," Galadrath said to the children. "Let's go wash your hands and feet."

"I'll do it dear. Go speak with your friend," Heladra said, and then she herded the children up another flight of stairs, smiling softly at her husband.

Teratos was already making himself comfortable in a stout chair, with armrests that were soft and bulbous. He leaned forward slightly, preparing a hookah positioned at the center of several other chairs. He rested one hand on the large golden vase of the smoking apparatus, while the other hovered above its top, the tip of one hose already in his mouth.

The golden vase began to gather condensation around his hand, the tiny droplets quickly freezing into a frosty sheen. Flames spontaneously ignited around his fingers, and he used them to light the purple, mashed substance in the bowl.

"I see your training in the Lowest House has been put to good use." Galadrath smiled broadly as he walked into the room, watching as Teratos prepared the smoking instrument.

"Being Many does add a great many conveniences to life. There is never a day too hot for someone with ice in their veins, or too cold with fire in their heart. A bath is never chilly in the house of the Many; a room never dark," Teratos said between puffs.

Galadrath sat down across from him, stretching his legs, propping himself on a pillow with his elbow. "Your tongue dances admirably, Teratos. Maybe you should become a poet. Just don't let this flower dull your mind too much," he said, referring to the Nightbloom burning in the hookah.

"There are edges of my mind I wish I could dull permanently," Teratos slurred.

The purple stains from inhaling the strong smoke already formed on his lips. Galadrath picked up one of the hoses and drew in a deep breath, as if to agree with Teratos.

The sweet and peppery smoke of the burning Nightbloom flower filled his lungs, and a pleasant calm washed over him. The nightmares itching at the back of his mind began to rest. He closed his eyes and drew deeply on the hose again, letting the peaceful feeling flow over him.

4

The Symbols of His Title

Galadrath was the last person in his household to wake. The suns had already risen, and he could feel their heat beating down on the outside of the thick stone walls. Giggles and laughter drifted from his family downstairs. He climbed out of bed, washed his face, and dressed in the clothes that were already carefully laid out at the foot of the bed. The black silk of his shirt and pants breathed easily against his skin, and the bright white of the vest and cloak shimmered, even in the dim light of the room. Accusers did not have a standard uniform, but these clothes had become his.

He slowly wrapped the leather bracers around his forearms, before he pulled the chains tight around them. The links were each two inches long and an inch and a half wide, strong enough for oxen to pull up tree stumps. As he coiled them and pulled them tight, he reflected on how he had earned them. Each one carried an inscription with the date and the honorable act, along with the members of the court that had appealed for the award. He did not need to read them—he had committed each act, and they were all burned into his memory.

Once they were fastened around his arms, he pulled on their power. He felt the five emblems that were tucked into the pockets of his vest:

33

earth, air, fire, water, and the blackstone. Matter and energy condensed into its purest form. He pulled on each one in turn, drawing the power into his body. The fog in his head from the previous night's revelry burned away as his lungs filled with a breath that never ended, his arms becoming both heavy and light at the same time. His heart burned and chilled, like a block of ice catching on fire, and the itching dread crept into the back of his mind. Then, he pushed his influence out to the objects until he felt everything around him. A million voices rejoiced as all the matter around him pledged their fealty to him.

Just as quickly as he had drawn them in, he deposited the energy back into their emblems. The voices of the world around him grew silent.

"In service, yield to none," he said under his breath. The Oath of the Lowest House rang in his ears.

He walked softly down the stairs and joined his family for breakfast.

"You look dashing as ever," Heladra greeted him.

They shared a quick kiss.

"And you, my sweet rose, radiant as ever," he replied, then smiled at the rest of his family. "And my children! A wonderful morning isn't it?"

Raatel approached, placing a plate neatly in front of him. The thinly sliced meat, seared onions, and candied dates looked delicious, but the lingering power of the emblems, and the impending meeting, had tempered his appetite.

He picked through the contents of the plate lazily, as he engaged in the morning banter of his family.

"The court sent a messenger early this morning," Heladra said.

She slid the small folded and sealed paper across the table toward him. He opened it, and quickly read through the simple request, finishing with a glance at the royal seal.

"I'm glad Teratos said something last night. This is short notice... it's strange that they would send an appeal for a trinket so quickly," Galadrath said.

"Don't be so skeptical of a good thing, my sweet husband," Heladra chastised him.

"Then I best get going," he said. "I don't want to be late for my own ceremony." He pushed away from the table and stood, giving a short nod to Raatel.

"Delicious as always," he said.

He gave his wife and his children a hug and a kiss goodbye, before he walked out the front door.

The heat of the bright daylight beat down on the paved street. It was quiet, except for the far off bustle of the city. Only one other person was on the street with him, a man who sat a few doors down, huddling in the shade of an awning. He was in rags, with a thick gray beard—dirty and unkempt. He was missing one of his arms at the shoulder, and his head hung low, hiding his face.

Galadrath walked a few steps closer to him and said with a slightly raised voice, "This is not a good place to beg."

The man looked up, staring at him with sorrowful eyes. They spent a moment measuring each other. This amused Galadrath. It wasn't often that someone saw him and didn't react in some fearful way. He reached into one of his pockets, closed the distance between them, and dropped a gold coin in the man's lap.

The man croaked, "Seems to me it is."

Galadrath nodded at him in understanding. "Seems you are correct," he replied.

Galadrath called on the blackstone, and the fog enveloped him. In an instant, he stood in the looming sandstone entrance of the colorfully lit throne room of the City of Light. The large round room was open, the floor littered with loose rows of chairs and benches filled with people of all stations. The low murmur of hundreds of separate conversations filled the open air, and the stale smell of polished wood and bureaucracy mulled over them. The massive hole in the center of the domed ceiling held the Crown of Light—a huge array of mirrors that reflected the light from the suns above into the room like a kaleidoscope. The only beam that never shifted, was the one in the center of the room, shining down steadily on the empty tomb of the Brightcaller, the King of Light, the first of the Few. It was a constant reminder that the Few were dead and gone—that the age of man and the Many had replaced them. King Thestus sat in his throne on the raised semicircle at the far side of the room, a number of the Lords huddled around him, discussing an issue before announcing a verdict into the room.

He stood next to the Court's Herald, the black smoke wafting over him, exuding out of every pore. A woman turned to face him, unfazed by his sudden appearance.

"Chained Honor, pleased to see you," she said.

"The pleasure is mine, Herald Alatolia," he said, bowing slightly.

She returned the bow and wrote his name down in the large ledger she was holding.

"Most of the morning's business has been concluded. The court has asked to speak with you in private. The wait shouldn't be long—please make yourself comfortable," she said.

He thanked her, making note of the impromptu meeting. He stepped aside and found an empty seat in the crowd to the side of the massive throne room. The room was still packed. Many of the nobles of Thainegom were sitting in the rows to each side, closest to the raised platform in the middle of the room.

Galadrath chose a seat toward the back. Many citizens sat in his vicinity, some moving aside for him as he passed, others whispering about him, thinking he was out of earshot. He sat idly, turning his attention to the throne where King Dartan Thestus sat, flanked by the eight Lords of the kingdom seated slightly lower to his left and right. He spotted Teratos behind his own Lord Ostiphan, fulfilling his administrant duties. Some of the lords had as many as three administrants, but Ostiphan only needed one.

He watched as citizens and nobles presented claims and arguments to the Court, each called up in turn. His eyes wandered, seeing boredom on the faces of some nobles. Undoubtedly, they were whiling away the morning hours, present only to be more visible to the king. Others seemed invested, keeping up on the current events of the kingdom or, at least, gathering gossip to impress their peers with.

A man and woman bowed deeply in front of the council before retreating hastily to the back edges of the room, finding a pair of empty seats. Galadrath paid little attention to their plight or the resolution presented by the Court, but he could see on their faces the decision had not been made in their favor.

"Calling Accuser Diatara Slaaterson—on this fourth day of the second month, year seven thousand ninety-two—to receive the title and benefits of Honor, along with the third symbol thereof," the Herald shouted over the low murmur of the crowd.

Galadrath watched as a young woman stood from among the seated folk. She wore loose brown trousers with high leather boots and a fitted tan shirt covered in a small vest. A single red flower was embroidered on the lower edge of the vest. She walked to the front of the room, weaving around the raised podium of the tomb, stopping in front of the raised semicircle of the throne.

He remembered her. She had trained in the Lowest House, and she was also an ambassador and an Accuser. The flower on her vest was an unofficial badge of honor, a symbol to others that she had mentored under Galadrath. In his ambassadorship, he had trained Emissaries and provided guidance for other Pillars of the Lowest House. She was seven years younger than he was, and she had risen through the ranks admirably. He had even fought alongside her in many campaigns across the country and abroad, rooting out rogue clusters of Patchwork haunts. She had been fearless against those faceless and shambling evils that had been festering since the last age.

She took a knee and bowed deeply. King Thestus rose to his feet.

"I, King Thestus, 48th of his name, grant thee, Diatara Slaaterson, the title of Honor. Henceforth you shall be known as the Honorable Accuser Diatara Slaaterson. As granted by this title, you shall gain the benefits and the obligations as listed in the Laws of Thainegom, upheld by this court. Rise Honorable Accuser, and take this trinket fashioned in your style, as a symbol of your title."

She stood as she was approached by one of the Court's Jewelers. She held out her arm, where two links of chain were fastened to the leather wrap around her wrist. The Jeweler quickly looked around the room, stopping in the direction of Galadrath.

Galadrath, too far away to discern what was happening, had extended his influence, feeling for the intent behind the exchange. When he sensed the Jeweler's own influence pressing back against his, Galadrath whispered a silent apology into the wind—and let go.

The jeweler conjured a pure blue flame of incredible heat. The flame itself was not required to mold the metal, but Galadrath was well-versed in the ritual through which trinkets were bestowed on the Many. They would pass their hand through the flame without burning, demonstrating they had both the ability and the skill to master the elements, as well as prove their worthiness of title. Those who had seen the ritual but had not experienced it might see it as a parlor trick, but anyone not exerting control and influence over their own trinkets and emblems would quickly lose a hand.

Diatara completed her portion of the act, passing the outstretched hand slowly through the flame, the intense heat lapping harmlessly around her fingertips.

The jeweler nodded in thanks at no one in particular, took a third link of chain, and fastened it to the others. The metal of the link became liquid on one end and flowed around the two solid links Diatara already had. The jeweler willed it back into a solid once they were joined.

"Honor and Glory!" the king yelled.

The room came alive, a celebratory warcry echoing in the massive stone room. The noise took a moment to die down.

Diatara bowed deeply. The room once again erupted into sound, cheers and hoots filling the space. As she returned to her seat, the voice of the Herald strained to bring order to the court.

"Calling High Honor, Accuser Galadrath Yaralok, to receive the sixty eighth symbol of his title," the herald cried.

The room died down, resuming a buzzing murmur of forced whispers.

He stood and walked toward the throne, intentionally taking the long way around the tomb to pass on the side where Diatara had returned. When he saw her in the crowd, he pointed and waved, making eye contact with her. He bowed a little too deeply in her direction, and she returned the gesture. She smiled widely, and he turned again, starting toward the front of the court.

He took a knee and bowed lowly, his fists resting on the floor in front of him, his eyes pointing to the ground.

As the King spoke his rehearsed piece, Galadrath rose from his bow and acknowledged the jeweler approaching him.

"I'm sorry to have imposed on your work earlier," Galadrath whispered.

"No matter—I was surprised to find such a tight grip of influence in the court. I should have known it was you," the jeweler said.

Once again the flame was produced, and Galadrath complied, offering his own hand to the flame and removing it unscathed.

The jeweler began working, concentrating on the link, drawing in his own power. Jewelers were also Many, as the unique metals that produced the power, couldn't be forged by conventional means. As the link seemed to melt onto the chain, the jeweler whispered as he worked.

"Just like the one I gave to Diatara. Most Emissaries choose to have their trinkets fashioned into bracelets, necklaces, amulets, or earrings. It would seem you have quite the following though, as many Accusers still take their trinkets as links, hoping to one day have chains like yours," he finished.

"Chains like mine?" Galadrath scoffed under his breath.

"Hopefully, no one will ever have to earn them," he added.

The jeweler nodded and retreated back to his place to the side of the court.

"Honor and Glory!" the king yelled.

Galadrath bowed again to the king and turned to face the room.

The room roared with the chant. Fists pumped in the air as the masses shouted the words over and over. He took a short bow before returning to where he was sitting. The herald cried for order, attempting to move the crowd's attention to the next order of business.

Eventually the room died down, and the rest of the items presented to the court moved quickly. Galadrath watched time pass on the walls of the throne room. As the suns moved, the rays of light slowly crawled along the walls. Now they marked noon, the beams in perfect symmetry on the circular walls.

The court ended its session. Some of the people grumbled softly, knowing that they would have to leave but return the next day to handle their business. Slowly the room emptied, large groups shuffling their way out. Galadrath was the only one left sitting, alone in the outskirts of the vast room. Keepers of the Peace, armed and armored soldiers stood around the perimeter of the room. A few Emissaries also lounged at their posts, the wildly colorful silks of their uniforms glittering with jewelry of all shapes and sizes. Most of the gold and silver they wore were mundane, but Galadrath could make out the trinkets they each carried. Ceremonial pendants, rings, bangles wrapped around upper arms, all symbols of their power, as part of the Many.

One of the court pages scurried toward him and beckoned him forward to speak. Galadrath approached the throne once again, weaving through the disarray of empty seats. As he did, a shout rang out. The commander of the royal guard issued an order, and the sentries around the room, including the Emissaries, all moved to leave. Soon Galadrath stood in front of the throne with only the king, the lords, and their administrants remaining in the room.

The low voice of Lord Sigrol Braf penetrated the silence.

"High Honor Galadrath, we've called this meeting to give you a charge—one I trust you can handle with an abundance of caution, one that must be completed in absolute secrecy," he said.

One of his administrants shuffled out from behind him and moved down the stairs at the front of the raised semicircle. The man handed Galadrath the paper, before returning to his seat behind his lord.

Galadrath opened the note. He slowly began to read the words, as if they themselves were dangerous. Several minutes passed as he read them, reread them, and studied the portrait of the man he was being sent to accuse.

Sebbatin Grade, hereby accused of high treason, supported by acts of sedition chronicled by Lord Ostiphan, Lord Sigrol Braf, Lord Gresser Freid, Lord Willen Tireod. The trial is to be carried out by the court of King Thestus, 48th of his name. The accused, if found guilty, is sentenced to death.

"My Lord, I'm not sure I'm understanding this. I know Sebbatin Grade and his respected titles, High Honor and Dead Hand. I've worked with him before. He is an honorable man. I did not think him capable of such an offense," Galadrath appealed.

"It is not your place to question what you think he is capable of doing; it is your duty to act on what he has done," Lord Braf replied.

"My King, this man served both your father and you his whole life. What he did for the kingdom at Marrette..." Galadrath pleaded.

The King stood, urging silence with one hand. He turned and glared at Lord Braf, forcing the lord to sit with only a look.

"I am well-aware of the duties Sebbatin completed in the name of my father, Durium, and I understand the gravity of the accusations that are being brought against him," King Thestus growled.

"I am..." he began again, and paused.

"The Court of Lords has brought evidence against him that I can not refute. It is with sorrow in my heart that I ask you to do this." He sat down heavily, as if the words had taken an immense physical strength to conjure.

"May I ask what evidence was brought against him?" Galadrath asked.

Lord Braf interjected, "It is in the best interest of the crown that this information remain—"

"It is in your best interest to remember I am king, Sigrol!" King Thestus boomed at the lord. "You may sit at this court, but I am still the one who sits on the throne!"

Galadrath flinched at the bitter and violent words. He had never seen the king angry. Unlike Durium, his father, Dartan had always been calm and level headed.

Lord Braf shuddered in his seat, fearing more than just the words of the king. Thestus returned his attention to Galadrath, regaining his calm demeanor.

"Galadrath, I understand your hesitation, but I can vouch for the validity of the claims. We have personal accounts from trusted sources that Sebbatin has met with foreign agents who wish to remove me from the throne. It shakes me deeply to admit that a man I trusted has betrayed me," King Thestus said.

"Thanks, my king. I'll carry out my duty. Just one last question—is Sebbatin still titled?"

Lord Braf reflexively sat forward in his seat to correct Galadrath, but then he slumped back in his chair.

"Yes. High Honor, Dead Hand, Sebbatin Grade holds ninety-one symbols of his title," the king responded sternly.

"Then he won't be hard to find, my king," Galadrath replied.

He folded the note neatly and deposited it in one of his vest pockets.

"Honor and Glory, Galadrath," King Thestus said.

"Honor and Glory!" he yelled.

The court echoed the cry, the voices of the lords and their servants filling the hall with a call to war.

5

THE BEE STING

THE COLD MELANCHOLY OF the blackstone filled him. In an instant, he walked every path he had ever set foot on, opened every door he had walked through. There were always places in the fog that he had known, but he could not go—the memory of a place just out of reach, where he was unable to step to. These holes in the fog of his memories were created by the other Many, in the places where they exerted their influence. Just as his influence had overshadowed that of the jeweler, others could trump his own. He could spend the effort to rip the attention away from them, but the concentration and energy that it took would drain him physically. Even the energy of the emblems, even the power of his chains, could not help him in the battle of wits that it takes to wrench matter free from the attention of the Many.

But he knew he would not need to. Galadrath knew that the absence of something is just as much an indicator as the presence of it. As he searched his mind and the memories of the places he had been, there was an impenetrable blackness over the Park of Marrette. He had been there many times, attending the peace summits between the Lords of Thainegom and the Sons of Dradofir. Now the miles of gardens and statues lay under the influence of a single man. He knew Sebbatin would be one of a handful to be able to call so much of the world to his attention.

The black fog rolled off his body, lightly hissing from his skin, as he stepped to the edge of the darkness.

The suns still sat at their apex, now slightly shifted to the south. He was hundreds of miles north of the City of Light, at the edge of the Park. He stood on a small dirt road, where the paving stones had all but sunk into the soft ground. The dilapidated causeway was uneven under his feet, and the air itself seemed to resist him as he passed into the influence of Sebbatin.

It took hours to walk. He could fly, like the Many often did, but the effort and power it would take to cover so much distance would be exhausting. He could slip silently under the ground, moving through stone and dirt as though it were nothing, but the sphere of influence of the Dead Hand would fatigue him. It took the least amount of effort to put one foot in front of the other.

He eventually passed into the gardens of the Park. The tall trees offered shade from the heat, and the flowers and grasses brought peace to his mind. He pushed deeper into the heart of this place.

He stopped for a moment, picking a single rose. Thick petals of variegated pinks, whites, and reds were spread widely in full bloom. He tucked the flower into his boutonniere.

As he grew close to the center of the Park, his suspicions were confirmed. He saw a massive statue floating high off the ground. As the sculpture spun slowly in the air, he could make out pieces of the stone dissolving into the air, dripping like liquid, and solidifying once more. The rough form of a woman was being honed, worked on by the artist.

Then a voice boomed from far away, the air around him amplifying it to a deafening volume.

"Good afternoon, Galadrath, Chained Honor," Sebbatin said.

Galadrath felt the influence shrink away from him, retreating to a focal point underneath the statue.

"Sorry to have made you walk so far—my mind was elsewhere," the voice of Sebbatin rang, more softly than before. "I've been trying to capture the likeness of this lady for quite some time. Her beauty escapes me, my mind is too feeble to capture her greatness."

Galadrath walked to the center of the large courtyard, where an old man sat cross-legged. The wind roared and whipped in a confined space, exerting the upward force to keep the immense stone afloat. He could see the dust wicking into the column of air flowing spontaneously from the ground, wildly blowing the long silver hair of the sculptor.

"It's good to see you, Sebbatin, God's Bite," Galadrath said.

Sebbatin began to chuckle roughly, and then it quickly became a cackle. "Do people still call me that? Such a silly name. A god with no teeth, maybe," he said.

"A god with no teeth can still shake the core of the great Earth Mother. Better that, than The Grim Wreath," Galadrath said.

The cackle grew into a fit of laughter.

"Why do we let the people give us such strange names?" Sebbatin wheezed.

"We can mold the world as we see fit, but we can't change even one mind," Galadrath smiled.

"True words. A wise man you have always been."

The statue floated to the ground softly and sat down next to the old man. The intense column of air and the light breeze surrounding it all died down, leaving them sitting in the dead heat radiating off the paved stones.

"She's beautiful. Myriad, if my memory serves me," Galadrath said.

"Your memory and your history does serve you well. I'm glad I can do her enough justice to be recognized," Sebbatin replied. Then he waved him closer. "Please sit, I'll make us some tea."

The two men sat comfortably across from each other. Sebbatin wore little clothing in the pounding heat of the day. A loose fitting plain cotton shirt with insignificant sleeves hung sweat stained around his neck, and baggy knee length pants were held up by a salvaged piece of rope. His windblown hair showed matted brown curls at the tips, as his cracked and dirt covered fingers had compulsively twirled them in thought. He had lived long enough to serve two kings, and the wrinkles on his face numbered as many as the roads he had traveled.

His shoulders and calves were browned by a sunkissed life, and their strength was only muted by his age.

"It is strange to see her so far from her home, on the shores of Irah. What made you decide to honor her here, or was this piece commissioned?" Galadrath asked.

"I find it strangely fitting that the woman who brought us the Ashmaker would sit where his deeds brought so much ruin," the old man said, somberly.

"Then wouldn't it be fitting to carve a statue of yourself?"

"You're cruel, even if you are honest. I am merely an instrument, a few threads on the tapestry woven by the Few," Sebbatin replied.

"Then, as one instrument to another, I must tell you why I'm here," Galadrath said.

"Please, the tea first," Sebbatin urged.

Sebbatin molded two small black marble cups out of thin air, and they spontaneously filled with steaming water. He reached into a large, makeshift bag crafted from canvas and leather. He retrieved some loose herbs and spices in one hand, and sprinkled them into the two cups. He reached into the bag again and produced a second handful of rich purple leaves.

"Care to partake? My old wounds are becoming more bothersome. Maybe I'd be a better sculptor if I didn't dull my mind," Sebbatin said, his hand hovering over the cups.

"None for me, I'm on business I'm afraid. I've brought a flower of my own," Galadrath said.

He pulled the rose bloom from his lapel, as he took the cup of tea, and handed over the flower. He saw the old man's eyes widen.

"You've picked a flower for me?" Sebbatin whispered.

"With great pain in my heart, I have," Galadrath said.

Sebbatin plucked a few of the rose petals and pushed them into the mix of leaves already in the cup.

"But why?" Sebbatin asked, exasperated.

Galadrath produced the small paper from his pocket, gulped harshly at the tea, and began to speak.

"Sebbatin Grade, you are hereby accused of high treason, supported by acts of sedition chronicled by Lord Tallus Ostiphan, Lord Sigrol Braf, Lord Gresser Freid, Lord Willen Tireod. The trial to be carried out by the court of King Thestus, 48th of his name. The accused, if found guilty, is sentenced to death," he choked, his stern facade showing his heartache. "By law, you are allowed a trial, if you plead guilty you will be sentenced according to the severity of your crimes. How do you plead?"

The old man sat in shock and horror.

"And the king?" Sebbatin finally asked.

"From his own mouth, just this afternoon," Galadrath forced out the words.

"Then you mean to kill me?" Sebbatin asked.

"As one instrument to another, I do," he said.

They sat in silence, sipping their tea. Eventually Galadrath found himself holding an empty cup, unaware of how much time had passed. He instinctively set the cup down next to him.

"Another?" Sebbatin asked.

"Please."

The soaked leaves at the bottom of the cup vanished, and the cup filled again with steaming water. Sebbatin reached into the bag and sprinkled a fistful of tea leaves onto the water.

"More leaves—seems I won't be needing them," he said.

Galadrath looked up at him, and he met the one faded eye of the man across from him.

Sebbatin began to cackle raspily. Galadrath was unable to muster strength to join the strange mirth.

"Honor and Glory," Galadrath said.

"For you, yes. Maybe even for me. Not for those who put us here," Sebbatin cut the laughter with his statement. He paused, letting his words hang in the air, before his tone shifted, lighter but no less unsettling. "You know I was the first of the Dead Hands, and the only one who's ever been known?"

"Of course. You are a legend."

"Do you know what I said when they called my name? When they called me to serve my purpose?"

Galadrath held his tongue, waiting for the old man to continue.

"Honor and Glory, I said."

A tiny bee landed on the discarded rose laying next to Sebbatin, its abdomen pulsing as it worked to shed the heat. Its fragile feelers prodded the wilted petals, failing to find nourishment.

"Marrette was a mining town, you know," he said. "There, shards fell from the Shattered Children like snowflakes. Some meteorites were as large as a man's chest. This land was covered with them. People flocked from all over, even as the sky still burned and the shards fell. They came to gather the metals. Picking up even a handful of divine metal made them rich beyond comparison."

Galadrath fiddled with the chains on his arms, well aware of where the metal came from. He knew the story and began to interrupt.

Sebbatin lifted a single finger in his direction and croaked, "Let me finish. I'm not telling this story for your benefit. I need to hear my own words."

The Accuser dropped his gaze shamefully as he listened and stared at the bee that had buzzed its way onto the side of Sebbatin's arm.

"What was left of King Durium's armies were sent to secure as much as they could, and the people of Dradofir did the same. After all, this was their land. The tensions rose, but the war was freshly won, and the brittle alliance had to hold. So the peace was maintained, each person was allowed to gather and mine what they could stake claim to. It lasted for years, until the ground was depleted of all its metals. But the city of Marrette stood, it had flourished and become more than just a mine. The people of two great cultures lived happily, peacefully in unison. I know, I lived among them. I worked as a mason for years, no one the wiser that I was a Dead Hand," Sebbatin recalled.

He filled his own cup of tea again, blowing on the steam before taking a sip. He continued to speak.

"I built their houses, their businesses. I played with their children, repaired their schools. We loved each other. But the Sons of Dradofir and the Lords of Thainegom were all greedy. They each felt like the other had taken the lion's share of the fallen shards. So the Sons brought their soldiers and snuck them in a few at a time, dressed as settlers, merchants, farmers.

"One night, they set the whole city to the sword. They killed everyone from Thainegom they could find. They even killed the children of marriages made under the alliance, they killed their own. When the message of the massacre reached the king, his response was simple. He had gotten his precious metal, there was nothing left in Marrette that he cared for, his people all dead. So he called on his Dead Hand. He called my name." His voice began to break, and he stopped to brush the insect from his arm.

He hadn't realized it was a bee, and as his fingers grazed over the little yellow and black body, it stung him. The stinger had found a landing place between the cracked ruts that made up the joints of the old hand. Galadrath watched as Sebbatin placed the teacup carefully on the ground, and without showing any sign of discomfort, dislodged the stinger with an uneven fingernail. The bee had dropped to the ground, now dying. Sebbatin sighed slightly, and pulled the pad of his thumb across the body of the insect leaving a smudge on the stone, and continued his story.

"There is nothing the teachings of the Temple of Light could have given me to prepare me for what I had to do. I pulled on my emblems until there was nothing left of them. 'Honor and Glory,' I said, and then I let go. The Ashmaker would be proud. There was nothing left to bury, no trace of bones, not a brick was left standing. The buildings I had built—the friends I had made—gone. In an instant blazing fury, Marrette ceased to exist. There was nothing left but ash and memories.

"'Honor and Glory,' I said, and came home a hero. The Sons sent messengers, begging for the peace to be restored. The court gave me more trinkets, more jobs, and another purpose. I traveled the world in the name of my king and his kingdom, but I always returned here. I always came back to try to find the honor and glory they spoke of. I built this great park, and stood by as the new alliance was forged. All in the name of a king who now calls me a traitor," Sebbatin finished.

"Sebbatin, how do you plead?" the Grim Wreath asked.

Fear and anticipation covered Galadrath like a morning frost. The hair on the back of his neck stood on end.

"I am guilty of many things. Treason is not one of them. Not guilty," the Dead Hand answered.

Galadrath's heart sank like a stone. He had not expected the man to give in, but now the reality of the situation weighed heavy on his being.

"I'd like to finish her, before we begin," Sebbatin said.

He looked toward the statue.

Galadrath stood and extended a hand. The old man grabbed it, allowing the accuser to help him to his feet.

"I hate to ask, but you won't run, will you?" Galadrath asked.

"There is no honor in it."

"Take your time with her. I'll be in the gardens—let me know when you are ready."

Galadrath wandered the garden for hours. A mild breeze pulled the aroma of the flowers through the air. He listened to the buzzing of insects and the chirping of birds. Every now and then, he would look toward the center of the gardens where Myriad floated. The fine features of the young woman, clad in a flowing dress and pointing outwards with one hand, were taking shape. He passed by great trees, planted decades ago, and walked by other statues—some small-scale likenesses of heroes and leaders. Others were massive, looming over even the tallest trees. The suns were low in the sky when the statue finally rested on the ground again.

He approached the spot where Sebbatin stood beside his newly formed masterpiece.

"She's perfect," Galadrath said.

"You know, I didn't make most of the statues in the park. The king commissioned most of them from his greatest architects. I spent many days trying to learn what I could from them," Sebbatin mumbled, lost in thought.

"You learned well."

"I wonder if there will ever be a statue of me—or you?" the old man asked.

"Not while we're living."

"Soon enough, then," Sebbatin answered.

He opened the drawstring on the top of the large bag. He began to rummage through the contents, grunting a mumbling while the items inside clanged loudly together.

"I never did learn to organize my things," he growled.

He produced a helmet from the bag. The bright silver of the metal showing a blank face, with a stubby horn protruding from the forehead. It looked like a great beast whose horn had been cut off, harvested for its ivory, but allowed to live. He haphazardly dropped the helmet onto his head, slapping it down and shaking his head from side to side.

"Now then, I should probably make quicker work of this," he mumbled again.

The bag ripped open in a blast of air, the contents scattering across the stone paved ground. Galadrath saw a collection of iron tools—those of tradesmen—among the other sundries. Small ceramic pots, a few now broken, spilled their contents: herbs, seeds, water, and wine. A bulk of armor also scattered across the ground. The body armor was made of scales—small metal diamond shapes, each one covered with an inscription detailing how it had been earned.

... holds ninety one symbols of his title.

The old man donned the armor, sometimes using his hands, sometimes floating the pieces around him where he couldn't reach. When he finished, he was covered in his own liturgy, the acts inscribed on the divine metal singing his praise silently.

"I am ready," God's Bite said solemnly.

"Should we... should we go somewhere else?" Galadrath asked sheepishly.

"No, just try not to break my things," he said.

"I'm not sure that's possible."

Galadrath called on his chains and drew in the power of the emblems. He felt the raw energy pour through his body. He pulled and pulled, filling every fiber of his being with fuel from the five emblems. He could hear them whisper to him, the memories that were trapped inside of them, pin pricks of time in his mind.

He exerted his influence in a wide circle around him. The stone pavers beneath his feet became his foundation. He could feel the dirt beneath them, and far below that, he felt the glass fragments of a city destroyed in an instant. The air around him stood at attention, like soldiers waiting for orders. Time seemed to slow, the growing shadows halting all around him.

"Sebbatin, draw your weapons so we can begin your trial," he said.

"I do not intend to die today, Chained Honor. I will not give quarter, nor will I offer an inch of mercy. I will share nothing, and take everything," Sebbatin growled from underneath his faceless helm.

"Do your worst, Dead Hand," Galadrath called back.

Then Galadrath felt the influence of Sebbatin extend around him, trapping him in a prison several miles wide. He could sense the energy flow into his opponent. On the outside, the world became strangely calm. The air grew still, and the birds and the insects fell silent, as if they could sense the impending chaos.

Spears of stone shot from the ground in front of him, instantly stabbing toward him. He poured the energy in his veins into the air, hardening it like iron. The stone spines shattered as they failed to penetrate his invisible armor. More shot out of the ground, this time from all directions, attempting to find a weakness in the fortress of air. The ground beneath him compressed and shot upwards, but his foundation held firm.

Galadrath channeled the air into a blast, a razor slicing into the broken pillars ahead of him. A spray of shattering stone cascaded onto the ground between the two men, but the attack dissipated as Sebbatin pushed it aside. Galadrath shot another blast, carving a corridor through the debris, glancing once more off of the immeasurable power of his opponent.

The ground came alive again, granite tentacles the size of trees surrounded him and began crashing down where he stood. He countered with more blasts of air, shearing them from their roots, crumbling them as they fell toward him. Despite the hardened air deflecting most of the boulders hammering down on him, he was forced to dive out of the way as a partially-intact tentacle shattered on the ground where he had stood.

"I must be out of practice, Accuser. I've not fought one of the Many in years. You must forgive me," Sebbatin laughed.

As Galadrath regained his footing, he heard the crack of displaced air far above him. A block of iron appeared in the sky above him, larger than his home. The block fell toward him, and he knew there was nothing he could do to stop it. He blinked, and a moment later he stood two miles away, beyond the reach of Sebbatin, black fog rolling from his body. He heard the boom of the immense block hammering into the ground where he had stood a few seconds earlier. Then, Galadrath Stepped back to where it had landed, where he still held his influence. He stepped *into* the block. The solid iron he displaced was soaked into his veins, and the hiss of the fog attempting to escape filled the iron prison he was in.

"Clever, but you can't hide from me in there forever," Sebbatin's muffled voice reverberated through the iron.

Galadrath felt as the iron around him began to heat.

When facing a superior enemy you must divide him. Make him send his armies to attack where you are not.

He could not compete with the raw power of the Dead Hand, he would have to attack the mind of his adversary.

He focused his concentration and ripped a hole in the influence of Sebbatin. He stepped out of the cube into the new space he had created, and brought it under his own influence. Once again in the open, he could see the torrential flame heating and liquifying the outside of the cube he had just occupied. The air around him was stifling, the heat and intensity of the flame jet instantly combusted two nearby trees.

Sebbatin turned the furious jet of white hot flame toward him. He retaliated with a gush of water and ice, the slurry meeting the flames with an explosive hiss of steam. He bought himself only a few moments, using the valuable seconds to rip another hole in the influence of Sebbatin. He stepped again, now close behind his opponent. He lashed out with a spear of iron, the weapon jetting out of his hand, materializing ahead of him as it shot into the back of the Dead Hand. The point of his lance thrust against the divine scales of Sebbatin's armor, and threw him forward violently.

The jet of flame disappeared as the Dead Hand's concentration was momentarily broken. Steam was rising all around them in mirages of heat, Sebbatin was thrown into the fog. Galadrath took the small respite to recompose his concentration. The effort it had taken to wrestle the small beachheads from his enemy was exhausting. He felt static grow in the air around him, the hairs on the back of his hands arcing tiny sparks between them.

He grunted, and tore another hole open in the expansive influence of the God's Bite. As he did, fingers of lightning flashed and arced out of the cloud of steam, lashing at the space that he had just created. The bolts crackled in a deafening buzz, and cut gashes into the stone floors, spattering molten slag in every direction.

Sebbatin floated out of the obscuring fog, lifting himself into the air under his command. His long tendrils of hair rose from the bottom of the silver faceless helm, dancing erratically under the influence of the electricity. Instantly, the wind picked up, whipping around them. The steam dissipated as the air became a torrent of movement, the burning trees roared as the cinders of their trunks were caught in the wind, like coals fueled by the bellows of a forge. The Dead Hand floated high in the air above them.

"Stand still long enough for me to kill you," Sebbatin said.

Galadrath could hear the pain in his voice. The blow he had inflicted with the spear had punished the body of his opponent, and would have killed him if it had not been for the armor.

"I'd rather not," Galadrath replied.

"Then I'll give you nowhere to stand," Sebbatin replied from the air.

There was crackling high above them, like fireworks. The unending popping of matter being forced into existence. Galadrath couldn't make out the shapes in the dimming light of the evening, until they began to glow. Thousands of meteorites falling, being pulled down to earth by gravity, and accelerated by the fury of the Dead Hand.

It would have been enough to lay waste to entire armies, to burn fields and raze cities. Sebbatin was a master tactician in warfare, but he fought on a scale that was inappropriate. He used his power like a hammer, wildly and violently attacking en masse. But Galadrath was none of those things, he was a servant of the Lowest House, a ghost among men. He was like the bee sting, needing only the tiniest pressure to break skin.

He blinked, and in a moment that felt like a lifetime, he Stepped through the fog of the blackstone, assessing the boundaries of Sebbatin's influence. It had shrunk, the concentration of his opponent had weakened, and so had his domain.

Pain shot from his arm, as something collided with it. Another blow cracked against his head. His vision faded for a moment, and a rush of sound filled the air as icy hail the size of his fists began to break against the ground. He had anticipated the glowing orbs of flame plummeting to the ground, but they had been a misdirection. The hail caught him off guard.

He forced the wind upward in a cyclone, to scatter the downpour of projectiles bearing down on him. Hail spattered in every direction, and he was momentarily safe from the onslaught, but the impending doom of the accelerating orbs of molten stone and metal was soon to follow.

Then I'll give you nowhere to stand. Galadrath recalls the words of Sebbatin.

Galadrath needed to get close to him, but Sebbatin had flown far out of reach, and if Galadrath pursued him into the air he would be resisted by The Dead Hand's influence. It would be like swimming through mud, every movement he made he would be forced back to the ground. He could step to the small spheres of influence he had wrestled away, but they would surely be bombarded.

Be the stinger that breaks the skin.

It dawned on him. Once again he let the blackstone fill his mind, and he began to wander, high above the battlefield, outside of Sebbatin's influence. He vanished and appeared a mile in the air, still very far away from his opponent, but directly above him.

It was a breathtaking sight, as he looked down. The ground below him was mostly dark, the suns now all but set. The burning trees and flames spreading below him, the swarm of glowing meteorites tracing their paths through the air. Some of them already reached the ground, splashing in small explosions as the molten rocks collided with the surface. They looked like fireflies, willfully plummeting to their deaths.

He began to fall, the air resisted him, but the persistence of gravity made it so he did not have to exert effort. The crackling sound of more stones appearing in the air surrounded him. They flew by him as Sebbatin changed their directions to meet him, trying to hit the falling target. Galadrath nudged himself aggressively and erratically in different directions, making himself unpredictable.

The Dead Hand began to move, flying at breakneck speed, changing direction below him, as Galadrath, now a human missile, fell down toward him. Static once again filled the air around him. Fear grew in his mind in anticipation of the coming attack. He was gaining on his opponent as he fell, but he needed to buy himself more time.

Lighting arced upwards in large thrumming bolts, as Sabbatin concentrated his fire on the human bullet shooting toward him. Galadrath braced his good arm in front of him, using the chains wrapped around it as a conduit. The lightning struck him, and flashed violently off the chains, scattering and arcing as the sustained blast of energy instantly superheated his own divine metal. He pulled the energy into himself as fast as he could. His head was swimming with the influx of energy, and he began to dump the excess into his own emblems as quickly as he could.

Then the full force of the Dead Hand poured into the arc of lightning. It was too much for Galadrath. He could not purge the energy quickly enough as it struck him, and the chains on his arm began to glow as they heated, the leather underneath smoldering and catching fire.

But he was close enough; he had bridged the distance between him and his enemy. The shape of silver armor was brightly lit by the violent cascade of electricity. He focused on the empty space directly below Sebbatin, and ripped one last hole in the influence of the Dead Hand. He stepped into the space, flipping so his back faced the ground. He saw the unarmored inner thigh of the man above him, and with every fiber of his being, drawing focus from the entirety of his mind, he created his stinger.

A lance of focused flame shot out in front of him, the bright beam of heat blasting upwards into the leg of the Dead Hand. The limb was ripped free, burned completely off, the beam hammering into the torso of Sabbatin from below.

He felt the air stop fighting him, the rage it had for him instantly gone. Galadrath conjured a ball of water, encasing himself in the cool liquid. The flames were extinguished, the surrounding heat calming. He slowed his descent easily and listened as the body of the Dead Hand fell past him, striking the ground with a muffled thud. The remainder of the meteorites continued to plummet downward, hammering the surface below.

He floated slowly down, like a lazy raindrop, and landed on his back against the ground. He released the water around him, and the pool splashed naturally into the cracks of the stone pavers. The remaining energy he held in his veins flowed instinctually back into the emblems, and he lay there quietly, relying on his born senses to tell him that he had won—that he had survived. His hair stood on end as the energy Sebbatin had held dissipated across the great expanse of his influence the moment he was killed.

The spike of pain in Galadrath's left arm dulled and went numb as shock set in. The searing pain in his right lingered for a while, his consciousness fading to black.

6

THE REPOSE

GALADRATH WOKE. IT TOOK his mind minutes to adjust to his surroundings. Muted light pushed through colorful curtains, and a light breeze wafted the smells of rich herbs around the room. The soft linen of his bedding was almost imperceptible, as the pain in his limbs commanded his attention. He recognized his own bedroom and the face of his wife, a worried look in her eyes.

"Galadrath..." she said softly.

His vision faded again, his name on her lips echoing in his mind as he fell unconscious.

He dreamed restlessly, unable to distinguish nightmares from memory. Cries of pain—screams of lives ending—haunted his mind. He saw the mangled body of Sebbatin floating inches above a shattered and charred landscape. He saw the body collected in the tattered bag that had once carried the man's valuables. He saw himself stumble onto his own doorstep and collapse into the arms of Raatel. He heard the clang of chains hastily unwrapped, and the cool press of poultice applied to wounds he did not remember sustaining.

He heard a quiet motherly voice hush him as he tried to sit up.

"Don't move too quickly, my love. You're still very hurt," Heladra said softly.

The recent events he had witnessed began to solidify in his mind.

"Sebbatin was found guilty," he said hoarsely.

She offered him a goblet of water, and he drank thirstily.

"Yes, you brought him here with you," she said.

"Did the children see?" he asked.

"Yes. We were eating dinner when you crashed through the front door and collapsed onto Raatel. We were terrified, my sweet," she replied.

Her voice grew harsh and gritty, and she began to sob.

"You could have died, and you didn't even tell us where you were going," she said, her rising voice a mix of worry and reproach. Soon, she was yelling, "You didn't even think to tell your wife you were off to accuse an Emissary, a Dead Hand at that!"

He groaned in pain, trying to prop himself up on his burned arm.

"Sit still! I'm not done with you yet!" she spat.

He slowly reached with his left hand to unwrap the bandage around his right, moving carefully to avoid the shooting pains.

"You want to see?" Heladra seethed. "I'll show you your foolishness."

She unwrapped his arm a little too carelessly, causing him to wince in pain.

He looked at his arm, the skin warped, red, and blistered. White and brown paste covered the skin in blotches, smelling of milk, herbs, and honey. The burns were the least of his concern, however, as meandering blackened scars traced up and down his forearm. He turned it over slowly, taking note of the flecks of colors. Like grains of sand that had been ground from a rainbow, glints of every color were fused into his skin along the black burns. It was something he had seen before on the more reckless of the Many. When one draws in too much energy from the emblems, it threatens to burn its way outward from the body and etches itself into the flesh.

He clenched his fist slowly, watching the muscles in his forearm contract and release under the scars. He remembered the pure ecstasy of the overwhelming energy that had flowed through him, when he had tried to draw in more power than he could possibly hold. He shuddered at the moment of agony when Sebbatin had almost destroyed him. He looked up at Heladra, and saw the pained look on her face.

"They sent other Emissaries to the Park of Marrette. They were afraid a war had broken out. Diatara has been coming by every day to see if you are awake yet. She's downstairs right now. Everyone is afraid, Galadrath, no one knows what is happening," she said.

"Nothing is happening. It's over. Let me go talk to her," he said flatly.

He pushed his feet out of bed and made to stand.

"Slowly, my dear, you are still hurt," she said, helping him to his feet.

He shuffled to the mirror at the end of the bedroom and stared at himself. His forehead was swollen around the cut, the bruise a range of yellows and purples. The rest of his face was gaunt and colorless in contrast, dark circles enveloping his eyes.

"You should eat," she said.

She grabbed a silk robe from the closet and draped it around his bare shoulders. She cinched it around his waist and began to dab his face, and then his feet, with a bowl of cool water. They descended the stairs together, slowly taking each step on the way down.

"Galadrath!" Diatara yelled.

She ran to the side opposite Heladra, and the two women helped him into a chair. Raatel bowed slightly at the opposite end of the room. He removed his colorful apron and quickly ladled a steaming helping of hearty soup, placing it softly in front of Galadrath.

He ate slowly, the others inspecting him as he raised the spoon to his mouth.

"The court is eager to meet with you," Diatara said, "but they understand that you are still recovering. I've been keeping them informed of your condition. They'll be happy to hear you are feeling better. Administrant Callidron has been beside himself, asking for any news."

"Yes, Teratos will want an update," Heladra answered, looking toward Diatara expectantly.

"I should go," the woman replied, clearly receiving the unspoken message.

Diatara stood, bowed slightly, and showed herself out. As soon as she was gone, Heladra scooted her chair closer to him, placing a hand on Galadrath's shoulder.

"I don't like any of this, husband. Sebbatin Grade? Why him? He was King Dartan's right hand—he was a symbol of freedom, an icon of Thainegom. Sentenced to death, I can't believe it," she said with disbelief.

"I'd like to have dinner with Teratos. I'd like to see Maxima too. We still have some congratulations to give," he replied.

"Do you think it is wise? In your condition? Shouldn't you rest?" she urged him.

"Don't mourn me, Heladra. I'm alive, and I'd like to see my friends. Can you send word?" he stated.

She turned to look in the direction of Raatel.

"I still have to visit the market today. I can deliver a message to the Administrant while I'm out on errands," the butler said.

Galadrath nodded at him, and made to stand.

"I think I'll go lay down," he said, making his way to the stairs.

She hovered alongside him, ushering him up the steps. He entered their bedroom, and looked toward the dresser. His chains laid in two straight lines, draped over the edges of the wooden furniture. They sparkled, cleaned and spotless, not a trace of the prior events was left on them. His cloak and his clothes underneath them, on the other hand, bore the marks of what had happened. The pure white silk was charred and torn. He could make out the shredded holes in the cloak where hailstones had narrowly missed him—pockmarks where the lightning had scorched holes in his vest.

"Don't worry, you have so many others. I'll have these tossed out; I can hardly stand the sight of them," Heladra said, tracking his gaze.

He laid down and closed his eyes, listening to the rattling of the chains as Heladra moved them out of the way and collected the destroyed clothing.

Later, Galadrath woke to the sounds of his children unceremoniously opening and shutting the front door from the floor below. He could tell the contents of the room had been arranged and rearranged, as Heladra had kept herself busy, never straying too far away from the bedside.

Missing them, he yelled, "Radralia! Marcanus! Come see your father!"

He heard the squeals and footsteps thundering up the stairs, before his children burst into the bedroom. They ambushed him on the bed, jumping up next to him and wrapping their tiny arms around him.

He laughed through the pain of the reckless embrace, squeezing them tightly against himself.

"We're so happy to see you, father!" Radralia giggled and squirmed against his embrace.

"I'm happy to see you, my shining stars," he replied, trying to stifle the lump rising in his throat.

Marcanus pulled away from him, holding him at arm's length.

"I wasn't afraid. I know you are the best warrior in all of Thainegom," the boy said.

The words flowed over Galadrath with pride. The boy's voice lacked any doubt, not a single grain of hesitation in the words.

"He was a bad man. We knew you could beat him," Radralia's tiny voice scratched.

Galadrath's mind wandered through the foggy memory of his return home, as well as Heladra's recount of him stumbling through the door, carrying the scorched and dismembered remains of Sebbatin.

"The king's men came and took him away—Sister's blessings," his daughter added.

Galadrath could hear the words of his wife, parroted by his daughter. She was too young to fully grasp the gravity of what had happened. Remorse festered deep in his chest. She should not have had to witness such violence at such a young age. It was his fault.

"Sister's blessings," Heladra whispered, repeating Radralia's words for emphasis. She began slowly prying the children away from their father. "We have to get ready for dinner with uncle Teratos, go tend to your schoolwork," she sent them away.

They protested for a moment, but then left sullenly.

Heladra replaced the bandage on his arm and checked the splint on the other, before she helped him dress for the outing. Afterward, he sprawled out on the bed, feigning exhaustion, so he could watch her. She slipped out of the normal dress she was wearing, smiling at him in the mirror. She walked provocatively across the room and retrieved a brightly colored evening dress, covered in golden baubles set with jewels. Short tassels weighed down the edges of wide flowing sleeves.

"Seems you aren't as injured as I originally thought," she said coyly.

"Your figure could raise the dead," he mumbled, trying to hide his prying eyes under his arm.

She tied the cords of gold loosely around her waist and inspected herself in the mirror.

"I'll keep that in mind for the next time I need you to get up early and take the children to school," she said, mustering her most sultry voice.

He groaned heavily, over emphasizing his injuries. She pulled him upright from the bed.

"Oh my arms, so weak," he joked.

They laughed softly with each other and departed from the room, where Raatel greeted them.

"Breathtakingly radiant, as always, Heladra. Galadrath, you look well," he said.

"Poetry for my wife, and a thinly veiled lie for me," Galadrath laughed.

"In good spirits, I see. Enjoy your dinner—I'll see the children to bed," the butler smiled.

The husband and wife nodded slightly in his direction before making their way out the front door. The couple wove their way through the narrow, winding streets. They greeted the denizens of the neighborhood, wandering slowly toward the house of Teratos. The solid sandstone facades of the buildings eventually gave way to brick and mortar of the more common housing. The smells and sounds of the bustling city greeted them, as they made their way from mansions crafted by architects to the squat utilitarian homes of the working class.

Teratos's house was not far, just beyond one of the smaller markets, nestled into the side of a small hillside overlooking the large docks of the port city and the vast ocean beyond. They meandered their way between stalls, seeing if there were any eye-catching wares they could not live without. Galadrath heard a familiar melody over the noise of squabbling merchants and the calls of hucksters peddling their wares. The song was about a love drunk sailor committing foolish acts in an attempt to impress a young maiden. It was a jaunty tune, considering by the end of the song, the sailor is dead and the young lady he was courting never even learned his name.

When the song ended, Galadrath came to face the busker. He placed a gold coin in the man's hand, and the performer bowed deeply with great pageantry.

"Shall I sing one about you, O Honorable Accuser?" the man asked with poise.

"No need," Galadrath replied.

It was no surprise that the musician recognized him. He had become used to the fact that those who wove facts from scraps of legend were often drawn to people of his station.

"Busker, have you written a song about me?" Heladra asked.

"Ah, your beauty is the thing so divine that I dare not diminish it by attempting to capture it in mere words," the man replied, bowing so deeply that his chin almost touched one of his outstretched knees.

She laughed loudly and gave a short bow back in his direction. She glanced at Galadrath, clutching onto his arm. He returned a warm smile, and they continued onwards.

They finally reached the home of the Callidron family. The single story building sat awkwardly between its tall neighbors. It sat like a man who had laid down on a park bench for a nap, forcing others to stand, uncaring for their discomfort. The City was cramped and the streets narrow, so a spacious house that could afford not to have the shuffling of feet on a floor above, was the purest symbol of luxury. Teratos had built it as a metaphor, that all people accepted through his doors were equals, no one dwelling above or below another, but the display of wealth could simply be measured by counting the tiles on the floor of each room. Outside they were met by a servant.

"Mitte, it is good to see you," Heladra acknowledged the butler.

"It is a pleasure, Heladra. And Galadrath, I'm happy to see you are well," the woman said, bowing deeply. She moved to hold the door open. As they entered, Maxima moved to greet them. She swayed gracefully as she moved, and her dress lapped restlessly at her feet like waves in a harbor. It seemed like she floated on some elegant buoy, only her feet betrayed the illusion, showing their gold rings and ankle bands that jingled as she walked. Unlike her home, Maxima wore her wealth unabashedly. Her dark olive skin was gilded with gold from her toenails to her nose. Even her dark brown eyes were flecked with the precious metal.

"Heladra! My heart leaps! It is so wonderful you could join us this day." She swept forward on light feet, and embraced Heladra, kissing the air between them a few times. "Why is it we live so close and see so little of each other?" she asked.

"Was my presence so tedious last time we spent time together that you've forgotten it altogether? It was just last week," Heladra joked.

"I could never forget you! But it does feel like a lifetime ago! I've been meaning to come visit since then."

"Yes, it seems congratulations are in order," Heladra said.

Maxima groaned.

"I should have known Teratos couldn't keep that big mouth of his shut. If the rest of him was as persistent as his tongue, I'd already be surrounded by a raft of children!" she replied.

"I told you—" Galadrath began, nudging at Heladra.

She elbowed him where he stood behind her.

"And Galadrath! It would seem you've accomplished great feats in your short absence!" Maxima said shrilly. She moved from Heladra's hug and grabbed him softly.

"You can hug me, you know! I won't break."

"But I might," he chuckled.

He held his hostess at arms length. She had a flowing head of jet black hair, enriched with herbs and oils. He could smell the perfume permeating from her entire being. Teratos had an eye for beauty, even his servants were among the most beautiful citizens of Thainegom.

"I'm so happy for you, Maxima—and for Teratos. Blessing of Seli upon you; may her rays nurture your growing family. Maxima, you look absolutely divine," he said.

"May she bless the child we await with handsome features like your own. Sister's blessings to us all," Maxima replied.

"Mine, maybe not, but what about Krosse?" Galadrath winked.

"Galadrath! Mind your tongue!" Heladra chastised him.

The cook, hearing his name, appeared from the kitchen.

"Ah! The man of the hour! I've prepared a feast—I hope you have brought your appetite," Krosse said.

"I have been looking forward to it. And where is the father to be?" Galdrath said.

"He'll be out shortly. Business as usual, the court has kept him on a short leash," Maxima replied.

As if summoned by her excuse, Teratos came lumbering down the hallway.

"My guests! Already thick as thieves and not a drink between you. Krosse, Mitte! Drinks!" Teratos bellowed.

The servants scampered in the presence of their employer and began distributing golden chalices among them. While they busied themselves, Teratos stepped forward and grabbed Galadrath from the clutches of his wife.

"My dearest friend! I see you are, as always, victorious!" he roared.

"It was a close victory, and it has cost Thainegom dearly," Galdrath replied somberly.

"Nonsense. Let us sit. A toast! Krosse, bring us some of those tasty morsels you've been hiding from me all afternoon!" Teratos exclaimed.

Teratos shifted his bulk into a nearby seat. He was still wearing the uniform he wore to court—vividly colored and emblazoned with a golden wolf. The cook appeared with a plate of steaming meats, each packed carefully into the shell of a spicy pepper. Teratos scooped one from the serving tray and raised his cup.

"To Galadrath! The Court's Accuser!" he yelled.

They all joined in, raising their cups and exclaiming in praise. Galadrath took a short bow and drank to the toast.

"And to my wife!" Teratos added. "Soon to bear me a son! Or if I'm so lucky, a daughter!"

They all cheered again and sipped at their drinks.

"Galadrath, you must tell me about the trial. I'm sure you will give a testament to the court, but I must know the details! They say half the Park of Marrette has been laid to waste!"

It pained Galadrath to recall the recent memories, but he could not deny his oldest friend. He began retelling Sebbatin's trial, knowing full well that his words would be repeated, embellished, and committed to song.

They sat in awe, quietly filling their plates as the courses emerged from the kitchen. Each of them gasped in turn, interjecting with questions and beckoning the servants over when their cups ran empty.

"Magnificent. Absolutely magnificent, I say," Teratos mused, as the story ended. He wiped his greasy hand on the wide vest of his uniform. "Before we descend too far down the path of revelry, my friend, I must handle just a small piece of business."

Teratos produced a small letter, sealed with the symbol of the court. He slid it across the table toward Galadrath.

"I understand you are still on the mend, but the Court has issued you another service. Mind you, there is no urgency here—take your time, when you are ready," Teratos said.

"Teratos!" Maxima exclaimed. "Can't you let the man rest for a moment! We are here to relax and enjoy ourselves!"

She stood from her seat, reached across the table, and snatched up the letter, tucking it away in the folds of her dress.

"You can have this back when we're finished. No business at my table! Not until I say so!" she said with a flourish.

"I agree. I think you've asked enough of my husband," Heladra stated.

The words seemed to cool the room, and Teratos gave an injured look to those around him.

"Fair enough, more drink!" he called, waving his cup around.

Tensions eased and the conversation lightened. They whiled the night away, sharing stories and laughter. The men gossiped and the woman planned for the arrival of the new child. Eventually, the servants cleared the collection of plates from the table and retired to their own rooms.

The group made their way to more leisurely seating in an adjacent room, and Teratos began to pack the smoking instrument he loved. The men smoked for a while, while the women reclined on the couches and pillows. They talked deep into the darkness of the night, until Teratos's lips were stained with the smoke of the purple flower, and he began to snore lightly.

"It seems we have overstayed our welcome," Heladra said, nodding toward Teratos.

"No such thing. He has been working vigorously and doesn't hold his vices as well as he once did. You'll have to excuse him," Maxima said.

"We should be going," Heladra said.

"Before I forget, he'd never forgive me if I was still holding court documents," Maxima added.

She produced the sealed letter, and handed it to Galadrath.

"Please, take your time. The court can't expect any more from you," she said.

Nodding to her in thanks, he tucked the letter into his shirt.

They made their way out into the cool evening air and down the empty streets. Galadrath threw his head back, his mind numbed from the intoxicating flower, and stared up at the night sky. The stars mingled with the sea breeze, and he felt a calm wash over him. Heladra chuckled softly, as she could feel the stress in his shoulders dissipate. They walked, arm in arm, returning home, nestled peacefully in the bosom of the City of Light.

7

THE TASK

GALADRATH SPENT TWO WEEKS at home, resting in bed. His afternoons were filled with games, studies, and the laughter of his children. In the evenings, he would go for long walks in the surrounding narrow streets.

When he finally became restless, and his injuries had mostly healed, he attended court. He watched as citizens from far and wide came before the king, presenting matters of all kinds. When he became bored with the pleas of the people, and the stuffy nobility that swarmed like flies on dung around the throne, he wandered the halls and atriums of the Temple of Light.

He watched the ranks of initiates struggle with the simplest of tasks. The demands placed on them to become Emissaries were great, to learn to control the power given by the divine metals. Some of them were Dusters, who had found a piece of raw divine metal and discovered the ability themselves. Others were recruited from noble houses, pledging their fealty and lives in service to the throne. Each one had been sanctioned, allowed to train under the supervision of the Temple. Each one had been given a great honor, to be allowed to serve Thainegom as one of the Many.

He had met with a few of the youngest ambassadors from Barkrill. These servants of the Lowest House, like himself, had been sent to join the ranks of their ally. Their stay might not be as lengthy as his, depending on their placement or aptitude. He shared his own skills with them—the nuances of the secrets of Stepping, allowed only to the Pillars of their order. He did not wear his chains, not wanting others to assume he was there in any official capacity. However, like any Pillar, he wore a small black ring that acted as a conduit for the blackstone. The ring was a symbol of the Lowest House, and the young men and women of his order recognized it immediately.

He found great joy in imparting his knowledge, his adventures, and his successes to fellow Barkrillen. They were young and still had much to learn. The Emissaries of the Temple often came to collect their pupils and return them to their formal studies. Some hinted that he should not distract the young minds; others openly chastised him for disrupting the order of the Temple. Each time, he was reminded that he still had a duty—and a pending trial.

He had carried the letter with him on most days but had not opened it. He was a little afraid, a little unsettled that inside his pocket laid the name of another doomed soul. But every day he delayed, every day he nursed his wounds and regained his strength, the accused walked free.

He reached into his pocket and pulled out the court's orders. He ran his thumb across the wax, embossed with the symbol of the king. He folded the paper carefully, cracking the seal open.

Teratos Callidron, hereby accused of murder, abuse of authority, and acts of covert insurrection, chronicled by Lord Ostiphan. The trial to be carried out by the court of King Thestus, 48th of his name. The accused, if found guilty, is sentenced to death.

Galadrath dropped the note as if it were covered by a deadly poison. His eyes grew wide and his mouth hung open.

"Teratos, you fool. What have you done?" he whispered to himself.

He sat there for a long time, watching the instruction of the Emissaries. The class was learning the basics of using the divine metals. They were taking turns bringing the sand and the air of the sunlit atrium under their influence. The group was a mix of children and adults, some as old as he was now, others the age he and Teratos had been when they had first joined the Lowest House.

When he had first trained, it was not in the open air and sunlight. It was in a dungeon, deep in the depths of the Scar that ran through Barkrill. The tiny windows in the walls of the Lowest House restricted light from entering, only the fog and gloom of the endless chasm that had almost destroyed their civilization crept in through the openings. He had quickly become friends with Teratos. They had shared everything, their successes and failures.

He would not have survived the crushing despair of that place had it not been for the laughter and optimism of his friend. He scooped up the piece of paper he had thrown on the ground and held it in his hands.

Now, he would have to kill the man that kept him alive so long ago.

He called on the power of the ring, the Stepping Stone that he had carried with him since he was a boy. The power of the blackstone crawled over his skin, and he watched a few of the students gasp in his direction, as he vanished in a cloud of black smoke.

In his bedroom, Galadrath washed absentmindedly and began to dress. The bright whites and colorful flowers were a stark contrast to his mood. He walked up the stairs to the covered rooftop, where he found Heladra. She admired him where he stood.

"Are you going back to work?" she asked with hesitation.

She had not seen him in his uniform for weeks, and he knew she would be reluctant to let him return to his duties.

"I have to go meet with Teratos. I have some questions for him about my next trial," he answered.

"Who is it?" she asked.

"I can't say," he told the truth.

He walked to the railing of the rooftop, staring out over the buildings toward the center of the city where the palace stood. He picked a white lily from the planters that lined the edge of the rooftop and tucked it away quickly into a pocket of the cloak, so Heladra would not see.

"I know, but I always ask," she said softly. "Hopefully this time it is someone a bit safer. Be careful, my love."

He had tried to be discreet, but as he turned to face her, he could see her eyes on the empty stalk of the plant, where the flower had been. She set her jaw, and pursed her lips for an instant. This was the charade they took part in when he dealt with the secrets of the court. Every word that could not pass on his tongue, she simply read from his face.

"You'll be careful, won't you?" she urged him.

He could sense the fear in her voice. He turned back toward her and embraced her, gave her a kiss, and then planted a second on her forehead.

"I'll be back here before you have a chance to miss me. I love you, Heladra," he mumbled into her hair.

He vanished, leaving her looking longingly at a cloud of rolling black fog.

The throne room was mostly empty. A few guards stood around listlessly, and small groups of court pages sat in the audience among citizens, filling out documents and chronicling the details that would be presented to the court on the next day.

"Herald Alatolia, always a pleasure to see you," Galadrath said.

"And you, High Honor. Court has adjourned for the day. How can I help you?" she said.

"I'm looking for Administrant Callidron."

"You'll find him in the king's library. He's been there most of the day," she stated.

He bowed slightly, and she mimicked the act. He walked out of the throne room, heading down the massive arched hallway, into the inner cloisters of the royal courtyard. He traveled along the winding paths with long steps, quickly making his way toward the library. It took him a long time to find Teratos among the seemingly endless rows of shelves. He walked past the long tables covered in books and scrolls, the titanic stained glass windows casting beams of colored light onto the workspaces.

"Galadrath! You look well! The image of the Court's Accuser is always a welcome sight," Teratos boomed.

A librarian stuck her head out from behind a set of shelves, glaring menacingly at the disturbance.

"You may not find me as welcome as you would hope, old friend," Galadrath said, before he threw down the opened note onto the table in front of him.

"Ah, back to business I see," Teratos said.

His voice was lowered, but still too loud. He glared back at the librarian. The woman slunk out of view, still visibly annoyed at the volume of the Administrant's voice.

"Do you know the man's name that is written there?" Galadrath said, pointing at the note.

"I'm not sure I know the details, but it's not a man's name. Farrah something…" Teratos trailed off.

"It's your name!" Galadrath yelled.

Teratos flinched, shocked at the intensity of his friend. His eyes widened and his mouth opened and shut silently. Galadrath regained his poise, knowing that he rarely raised his voice.

"Open it," Galadrath said.

Teratos grabbed the piece of paper, his hands shaking, and unfolded it. It was undeniable—his name was written plain as day, followed by a regal depiction of his face, and underneath the royal crest, the signatures of the Lords who had condemned him. He placed the paper down carefully in front of him.

"This is a mistake. This is not the trial the court had entrusted you with. I'm not culpable for any such things! Murder? Covert insurrection? Chronicled by Lord Ostiphan? Madness. I am nothing but the finest servant of the court. You can't actually believe any of this!" Teratos argued.

"Do you know how many people have presented the same argument? How many I have found guilty, after they have appealed in the same fashion? You handed me this trial yourself. How could you not know? What have you done, Teratos? What skullduggery have you been a part of that these accusations land at your feet?" Galadrath said through gritted teeth.

The librarian appeared again, this time walking quickly out from between the tall shelves.

"Gentlemen, Accuser and Administrant, I beg of you. Please take your business elsewhere. You are disturbing the peace of the library. I just wish to maintain the sanctity of this place," she said.

Galadrath glared at her. She had overheard their conversation, and he understood that she expected him to carry out the trial right there and then. He could make out the fear on her face, the anticipation of bloodshed, maybe even the destruction of her domain. Afterall, Teratos was hardly defenseless, he was a Pillar of the Lowest House. He carried the symbols of his title and was well versed in their use.

"Teratos Callidron, you are hereby accused..." Galadrath choked on the words.

The librarian's eyes widened, and she turned and ran, careening off of a bookshelf and retreated into the library with heavy footfalls.

"I'm not guilty! Not guilty! Old friend, you can't believe any of this!" Teratos screamed.

He felt the defensive posture of Teratos, as the Administrant exerted his influence. Galadrath drew on his chains and focused his mind. Teratos shot up from his chair and it clattered onto the floor behind him.

He ripped Teratos's influence away. Like a hammer crushing an eggshell, the Administrant's defense was annihilated. In a blur, Galadrath drew one of his swords and placed the edge on the neck of his friend. He knew the man could try and Step away to any of a million places, run and hide across the expanse of the vast world. But the Accuser would follow him through the black mist, and Galadrath knew that his oldest friend would not be able to do so before his head was severed.

"Believe me, trust me," Teratos pleaded softly.

As he swallowed dryly, the lump in his throat scraped up and down on the blade of Galadrath. The accuser's eyes glared intensely at him, searching for a reason—an excuse. They stood there for a moment, each anticipating something more.

"Swear on your oaths, swear on your life, swear on the life of your unborn child. Give me a reason, Teratos. Give me a reason to spare your life," Galadrath spat.

The edge of the sword began to quiver, as the wave of emotion washed over the Accuser.

"I swear on all of it—and on our friendship. Trust me."

Galadrath lowered his sword and breathed out deeply. He pulled the lily from his cloak, tossed it onto the floor, and crushed it under his heel.

"I meant to give you that. I'm sorry to have doubted you. My heart was not in it. This was not my task," he said.

"I'll find out what this absurdity is all about. Just give me some time," Teratos replied. His eyes filled with gratitude. "Thanks for your trust, Galadrath. I do not take what you have done here lightly."

"No one will take it lightly. You have sworn on your oaths, but I have broken mine. I didn't just fail in the service of the court, I have defied it," Galadrath said.

"I can make this right. I'll go before the court. I'll speak with Lord Ostiphan. I'll plead with the king—whatever I have to do I will do to clear my name, and yours," Teratos said.

There was a distant clanging of armor and footsteps. Galadrath was certain that the librarian had gone to summon guards, but they wouldn't find the aftermath that they anticipated.

"Go home, Galadrath. Let me deal with them. I'll explain it was a misunderstanding, I'll make it right. Go home and wait for me. I'll call on you once this mess has been resolved," Teratos urged him.

Galadrath nodded gravely, and then vanished in a cloud of smoke.

He appeared before the planters on the edge of his home's rooftop.

"That was quick," Heladra said cheerily.

As the black fog rolled off of him onto the floor, wafting away in the light breeze, she saw the sword he was still holding. He appreciated how she always tried to make light of his work, to accept him as a man of his station and not a bloodied murderer. But now, he was unable to control his anger. His voice cut through her compassion.

"I was sent to kill Teratos," he growled.

He tossed the blade aside wildly, and it clattered loudly on the tiled floor. He turned to face her, hate and pain in his eyes.

"By the gods, Galadrath," she breathed in sharply.

She covered her mouth with both her hands and began to cry. Tears ran down her face, as she sobbed. He watched her for a moment, his mind and his heart hard as stone. The abrupt violence, and the lack thereof left him reeling in his own thoughts. As she cried, her wet cheeks softened him, her tears washing away the tempest of emotion inside of him.

"I couldn't do it," he whispered.

He walked to her and held her close. Her crying stopped. Still sniffling, she looked up at him in surprise and relief.

"Heladra, I'm afraid," he said, squeezing her tight.

8

THE TIPPING SCALES

GALADRATH LAY IN BED, bare chested. He had thrown the silk sheets aside, allowing the cool breeze of the evening to flow over his skin. The heat and the events of the day clung to him, and he wished they would be carried off into the salty air.

"Heladra," he whispered.

He rolled onto his side to face her. She was peacefully asleep, the thin nightgown and sheet covering her figure.

"Heladra, are you awake?" he asked.

She was still, her face showing the tranquility of unconsciousness. He thought for a moment about how he could wake her. The events of the day were crushing him, like a massive weight on his chest. She would be able to set his mind at peace, but it meant he would have to disturb her slumber. It would be unfair of him to rouse her for such selfish reasons, but he was still jealous that she could sleep, knowing that tomorrow might bring ruin to them all.

Galadrath rolled out of bed and wrapped his chains as silently as he could around his waist. Then he dressed himself in loose black pants that hung like deflated balloons around his ankles, paired with a matching black silk shirt. Dark fog surrounded him, the dwelling dread amplified by the blackstone, and he moved silently to the floor below.

"You're up early, Galadrath," Raatel said, unfazed by his sudden presence.

The lanky butler sat in the darkness, barely illuminated by a streak of moonlight that washed into the covered windows. Galadrath was surprised to see him sitting at the long dinner table.

"What are you doing up in the middle of the night?" Galadrath asked.

"I made tea," the servant said.

Galdrath pulled up a chair, sitting across from the man. Raatel poured a cup of steaming liquid and pushed it toward his employer.

Galadrath had always been surprised at the unexplainable cunning of the old man. He had trained Raatel in the ways of the Many for years, but even before the butler had touched the divine metal, he had eyes in the back of his head. He could sense things before they happened; he could smell danger; and with a brief look, he could assess the intentions of a person before they ever made a move.

Galadrath lit the candles on the dining room table.

"Thanks, Raatel. A little tea might put me back to sleep."

"The court sent a messenger late in the night. You've been summoned. Early this morning, they have called you for a private meeting. I was going to wake you before, but I didn't want to burden you with the news," Raatel said.

"I appreciate all you've done for me and my family. Soon you may have to find a new employer," Galadrath replied.

"Even the City of Light is drenched in darkness during the night, but the Sisters rise every morning," Raatel said.

"Yes, they do. Back in Dradofir, they call the Sisters something else. Remind me, what was it?" Galadrath asked.

"Your people, Thainegom, love to make the gods something they can relate to. Sisters, brothers, mothers. Friends. We call them what they are—something far beyond what people can comprehend. They are very different. We call them the titans, the sentinels of the skies."

"Do you think they judge us for what we've done?" Galadrath asked.

"Undoubtedly," Raatel answered.

"Then how different can they be? We who love to judge, in turn, are judged by those... titans."

They sat in silence for a moment, sipping at their tea.

"Remember the day you saved my life? I was a simple man, a cartwright, and I had taken up my tools as weapons, in defense of my homeland. The Keepers of the Peace stormed in, with you leading them. I was ready to die, and you gave me a command—as if there were no war, as if the killer in my heart and the soldiers who threatened my life did not exist," Raatel said.

"'We have carts that need fixing,'" Galadrath repeated what he had said that day.

They laughed together at the absurdity that had unfolded so long ago.

"I will never forget their faces, those poor soldiers, as I walked past them with my tools in hand. I've been working for you ever since, and I'll never work for anyone else. No matter who judges us," Raatel chuckled.

Galadrath finished his tea and held the cup out toward Raatel. The old man grabbed the kettle and filled the cup once more.

"Do you think the titans will account for the lives you've saved, along with those you've taken?" Raatel asked.

"The scales always tip in favor of the dead," Galadrath grumbled.

"But without the living, the scales measure nothing," the old man said.

Galadrath drained his cup of tea, nodding toward his servant. He walked quietly up the stairs, the chains around his waist clinking softly, muffled under the fabric of his clothing. When he reached his bedroom, he undressed again, letting the chains clatter onto the floor.

Heladra shook awake at the noise.

"Galadrath! What's going on?" she said.

"Heladra, you're awake."

"I am now, you oaf," she said sleepily.

He slid into bed next to her and began to whisper in her ear. She giggled and rolled over to face him, curling into his chest. He drifted into a peaceful sleep, and the night melted away like morning dew.

Galadrath was jolted from his slumber by a sharp rap on the door to the bedroom.

"I'm awake—I'm up," Galadrath managed.

He fell out of bed with a heavy thump on the floor. The door opened just a sliver, and Raatel peaked inside.

"Breakfast is ready," Raatel said.

Galadrath dressed, selecting the newest replacements of his uniform, and headed down to enjoy the morning meal.

"The suns are barely up, Raatel," Galadrath said.

"The titans wait for no one, just like the court won't wait for you," the servant replied.

Galdrath grumbled incoherently, stuffing his face with buttered toast and slices of cheese. As he wedged the last piece of bread into his mouth, he vanished in a fog.

"Galadrath, the Court's Accuser. You've been expected," the Herald said.

The cold greeting struck him.

"On this twenty-sixth day of the second month, year seven thousand ninety-two, I call forth High Honor Galadrath Yaralok," she announced loudly into the room.

He turned toward the throne, where only half the lords were assembled, and the king was absent. The great circular room was mostly empty. There was a full complement of guards, and a collection of Emissaries gathered about the room. Teratos sat glumly behind Lord Ostiphan.

"High Honor Galadrath, we appreciate your attendance at this meeting. In the light of recent events, we ask that you cede your symbols, as an act of submission, as a fortification of your oaths you've made to Thainegom. You understand that this is merely a formality of the court," Lord Sigrol Braf said.

Galadrath stood for a moment, hesitant to shed his divine metal. He stared at Teratos where he sat behind the lords. His oldest friend nodded in agreement with the order of the court, and Galadrath took off his chains, the symbols of his honor.

The divine metals clattered to the ground unceremoniously.

"I serve the court, on the honor of my oaths. I pledge my heart and my body, in servitude to Thainegom," he said.

The court pages quickly descended on him, grabbing the heavy chains and carrying them before the court.

"We are pleased to see you uphold your vows, Accuser. Let the court show that, in light of the previous day's events, Galadrath Yaralok, High Honor, the Court's Accuser, has shown us that his fealty still lies with the crown," Lord Sigrol said.

Galadrath sighed heavily. The fear that had clouded his mind dissolved completely. Teratos had cleared his name—and his own. This pageantry that the court required would soon be over, and everything would be back to normal.

Lord Ostiphan stood from his seat and waved toward one of the court's guards. A group of people, led by an Emissary, entered the throne room.

"Larl Rihhi, Emissary, High Honor of the court, let it be henceforth known that you are now the Court's Accuser," Lord Ostiphan said.

The page holding Galadrath's chains, draped them over the shoulders of the Emissary, like a stole. Larl bowed deeply before the court, the ends of the long chains clinking against the ground. There was no ceremony of the flame, and the events unfolding were hasty and unofficial, leaving Galadrath uneasy.

"Galadrath, we have witnesses to your attempt on the life of Administrant Callidron. An inquisition will be formed to unearth any other acts of treason that you may have already conducted against the court. You're hereby stripped of any titles you hold," Ostiphan continued.

Galadrath stood by in shock. They had disarmed him and preyed on his loyalty. He made out the faces of the rest of the group that had entered with the Emissary. The librarian and the guards that he had seen in the library stood by.

"I was acting on orders given to me by the court. Teratos... Administrant Callidron can provide the letter—" Galadrath said.

He realized the situation he was now in. He could not prove his innocence without providing evidence of another crime. Either he was guilty of trying to assassinate Teratos, or he was guilty of actively defying his orders.

"We've heard the appeal of the Administrant, but in light of your shared past, we can not rely on his testimony. This document you speak of does not exist," Ostiphan finished.

Galadrath had left the letter with Teratos. His mind reeled with questions, unable to understand what was unfolding before him. Why had Teratos not given them the letter? Surely, disobeying the court order was better than being accused of treason. Why had they sent him to accuse Sebbatin, a man loyal to the king? Why wasn't the king present? Surely, he could appeal to the majority of the court.

"High Honor Rihhi, please begin the trial," Lord Ostiphan said.

"Galadrath Yaralok, hereby accused of murder, abuse of authority, and acts of covert insurrection, chronicled by Lord Ostiphan. The trial is to be carried out by the court of King Thestus, 48th of his name. The accused, if found guilty, is sentenced to death," Larl Rihhi stated.

"Teratos! Say something!" Galadrath yelled.

He watched as his oldest friend looked at him in alarmed silence.

"You've betrayed me! You've betrayed your vows!" Galadrath spat, the rage rising in him.

He felt the air begin resisting him. He could feel as the influence of the Emissaries in the room closed in around him. The energy in the air became thick and palatable. The swords that hung at his sides would be useless, and the only other weapon he had was the black, divine metal ring, the Stepping Stone. He drew on the emblems to protect himself, but the energy he could hold was throttled by the capacity of the ring.

He felt the blast of wind growing ahead of him and threw himself sideways, launching out of the way of the scythe of air. It barely missed, slicing through a portion of the cloak trailing behind him. Emissary Rihhi followed up quickly with an assault of fireballs, conjuring globes of flames and hurling them toward Galadrath. He responded with a wall of water, the moisture forming around himself. He had no influence, no island of safety to protect himself with, only the energy in the emblems he still carried on his person.

The fireballs collided against the water, cutting holes in his defense, the last of the flames scorching his clothing. He forced more water out of his veins, his vision fading to black as he reached the capacity of the ring. The water quenched the flames and formed a wave hurling toward the Emissary. He could see the surprise in his eyes. They expected him to be defenseless; they had expected his resistance to be minimal. He exhaled deeply, and breathed in again. There was no room in his body or mind for anything else.

The wave of water collided with the Emissary, and there was a loud crash, as the rush of water solidified into ice. For an instant, his opponent was encased in a cold prison, but the element of surprise was expended. Galadrath could feel the energy in the room rise as the other Emissaries prepared their own attacks, and he knew he would be met with an overwhelming force. His own power was limited. The wall of water had taken his full concentration, and even then, it lacked the effect he had hoped for. He was hopelessly outmatched.

He blinked, and he stood in front of his house. He could sense the fusilade of fire and air behind him. The surrounding black fog carried the echo of the chaos of where he once stood. It was as if he had Stepped through an open door and shut it just before an explosion was set off behind it. He instinctively pushed outwards, claiming a tiny influence over the street around him.

He took a moment to collect himself, the pinpricks of pain in his chest flowing into his mind, a reminder where the flames had singed him briefly. He looked around quickly, the street empty of people, except the beggar that had become somewhat of an ornament under the shaded awning of a receded doorway. Galadrath stilled his mind, the energy of the emblems still flowing through him. He knew he would only have a short while, before the court would send their Emissaries to kill him.

The filthy old man looked up at him and nodded slowly toward Galadrath. There was a certain look of expectation in the man's eyes. The Accuser knew he could not waste precious moments paying the beggar, so he turned to open the door.

Stone spines shot out from the ground around him. One pierced through the flesh of his calf, and he drove himself forward through the doorway, diving out of the way of the spiky protrusions that reached out against the air he controlled. The heavy wooden door shattered and pulled loose from its hinges, as he flung himself forward, propelled with the inhuman speed and strength of the emblems. He rolled onto his back and saw the old man get up from where he sat, readying to attack again.

Galadrath looked up at the startled face of Raatel, where the sinewy man stood in the entrance to the kitchen.

"I've been accused!" Galadrath roared.

He felt the spines of stone form again, shooting instantly from the roof and walls of his home, like his dining room had come alive, an iron maiden set on impaling him from every angle.

He blinked again.

He still laid on his back, the bright sunlight shining down on him. The sky was a spotless blue, and the birds chirped calmly in their familiar voices. He looked up at the looming statue above him, as if Myriad was looking over where he lay and checking to see if he was okay, her one outstretched arm urging him to stand.

He glanced around the Park of Marrette. The epicenter of his trial with Sebbatin was once again clean. Most of the rubble and traces of destruction had been rectified in the prior weeks. Only the scorched remains of the plants and trees still showed the aftermath, and a few of the massive statues were still being painstakingly restored.

He saw two men at the end of the open courtyard. He could tell by their uniforms that one was an Architect and the other an Emissary. The Emissary was watching, idly making conversation, as the Architect molded the stone of a partially destroyed statue.

Galadrath's mind was swimming in pain, but he slowly began to understand what was happening. The beggar outside his house was an agent of the court. They had become acquaintances over the course of weeks, sharing a few brief formalities each day. The man was a spy, placed at his doorstep. The emissary here at the park, surely placed as some contingent should he escape his trial.

Galadrath Yaralok, hereby accused... The words rang in his mind.

He had not committed treason. Teratos had betrayed him—plotted against him for months, setting the pieces of his grand scheme into action.

"Galadrath, you've become predictable," he whispered to himself. "You became soft. Your friend played you like a fiddle—your masters puppeteered you like a fool. Every ounce of your honor was used against you, forming you into an instrument of compliant ignorance."

"Let your plans be dark and impenetrable as night, and when you move, fall like a thunderbolt."

He recalled a quote from the great tactical text that had been written by the Ashmaker, so many years ago. The work of strategy that had allowed the Few to defeat the relentless evil of the last war.

The Emissaries would hunt him; the Pillars of the Lowest House that served as ambassadors would surely stalk him, root him out wher-ever he hid; but he knew where they would look for him. Afterall, he was trained the same way, and he had trained many of them.

There was one place they would look for him that he could not avoid. There was one last thing he had to do, before he could evade them—before he could vanish into the night.

Just as the Emissary finally noticed where he was bleeding on the ground, he blinked.

9

THE ONLY CHILD

HE LAY UNDERNEATH A bed, the dusty floor beside him illuminated by crisp sunlight, casting shadows from a collection of potted plants, cages, and small vivariums containing exotic or deadly species of flora and fauna.

"Friends for dinner, friends for dinner!" squawked a large bird from somewhere in the room.

Galadrath shuffled as quietly as he could from under the low base of the bed. With his head and partial shoulder exposed from the hiding place, he was able to crane his neck upwards toward the bird, twisting one hand free and placing an index finger against his mouth.

"Shhhhhhh!" he said, unintentionally disturbing the heavy layer of dust and debris on the floor.

The large black bird twisted its head upside down on its perch, staring at him from an impossible angle with one penetrating eye. Galadrath watched the large wings unfurl, stretching slowly to their wingspan. The sunlight caught the wings, and the feathers shimmered, iridescent in the light, like it was caught in an oil slick. It slowly retracted its wings, shifted its footing a few times, and cocked its head toward the sky.

"Friends fooooor dinnnnerrrrr!" the bird screeched loudly.

The door to the room was ajar, and Galadrath heard the shuffling of feet. He retreated back under the bed, trying to stifle a sneeze.

"Ah, yes, Brixby! Good man, good man. Thanks for reminding me," an old man's voice shrilled from beyond the door.

Galadrath recognized the voice of his father.

"Sirs, you better leave me. I'm expecting guests, and I still have much to prepare! Brixby, come!" his father said again.

Galadrath heard the fluttering of wings, the clacking of talons and a heavy beak against the hard surface of the wooden threshold, as the shadow of the opening door extended across the floor.

There were a few awkward exclamations as the bird left the room he was in and invaded the adjacent space.

"You're sure your son hasn't made any form of contact?" a strange voice said.

"I may be old; I may be senile! But I'm not old and senile!" the old voice rasped and screeched.

"Galadrath has been accused of treason against Thainegom. The court believes he is trying to break the alliance between Barkrill and the crown. These are very serious accusations, and we believe he will attempt to contact you. He has escaped custody," the unknown voice said sternly.

"When was he accused?" his father's voice rasped.

"Just this morning."

"And you've already come knocking at my door? An ocean away, here in the heart of Barkrill?"

"He Stepped away. Time is of the essence, the Emissaries and the ambassadors of the Lowest House have been dispatched to find him. He could be anywhere."

Galadrath could not understand how the message had reached the remote island so quickly. He had fled mere minutes ago, yet these men were very aware of the situation. This was obviously an elaborate plan and cleverly executed. No one in Thainegom could get a message here so quickly.

"An enemy of the crown and an enemy of Barkrill is no son of mine, but you're a fool if you think he's stupid enough to come here. A traitor he is, but he's also clever," Galadrath's father said.

Galadrath smiled to himself where he lay, accidentally breathing in some dust. His father was lying about believing this agent of the court, but he could not pass up complimenting Galadrath's intelligence.

"I think it would be best for me to stay, just in case he decides to show up—uninvited," the unknown man said.

"You will do no such thing! You have overstayed your welcome already, and though I've been a good host to you, I now have to host some old colleagues of mine. This is my house! I am still a citizen in good standing—*of Barkrill*. You Emissaries show up unannounced, and unless you intend to occupy the house of an old man *illegally*, I suggest you leave," the old voice screeched.

Galadrath could hear Brixby beating his wings and squawking along with the old man, feeding off the emotions of the situation.

"We'd be no trouble—just let us stay a while longer. You'd hardly notice us," the Emissary said.

"I'll not suffer your indulgences for a moment longer! Stay, if you dare! I'll call the full force of the Archons down upon you! You are trespassers, and I'll treat you as such. Threaten me and you threaten the sanctity of the alliance! I am Vostranis Yaralok, and I'll bring war if you don't give me a moment of peace!" the old voice rose to a level that made Galadrath shudder where he hid.

The bird kneaded his talons along the back of the chair, shifting his weight from one foot to the other, his heavy beak banging at intervals against the surface of the table, scattering silverware. The Galadrath felt someone's influence envelop him. Dread filled him. If the influence belonged to the Emissaries, he would regret coming here. They would sense him, and no matter the outcome, his family would suffer for it.

"Last chance, trespassers," Vostranis grated.

Galadrath realized the magnificence of the maneuver. The influence was that of his old man. The Emissaries would not be able to extend their own without contesting it. Galadrath was covered in the shelter of his father's influence. The argument was a clever ploy to hide him from prying eyes, to remove the men from the house that had come to kill him.

Just like when he was a child, he was once again safe in his family's house.

He heard the footsteps retreat, the grumbling half apologies of the men excusing themselves from the house. A few moments passed, and then there was silence.

"Come on, Galadrath, get out from under that bed before you sneeze your way into prison," the screeching old voice said.

He pulled himself out from under the bed, standing painfully on one leg, the loss of blood leaving him light headed. The door swung open slowly as his father pressed against it. He spent a foggy headed moment inspecting his old bedroom. The menagerie of strange creatures and plants had spread like an unchecked jungle across the room. The bed he had been hiding under was still the one he knew as a child. The pattern on sheets was his own, stale and unchanged.

He had spent many nights in this home when he was a child, and even when he was grown, he had visited. His parents had always insisted that he stay in his old room, not in the more appropriate guest chambers. He had fallen asleep to the soft clinking of spider legs on glass, alongside plants growing so quickly that the stretching of their fibers could be heard. He remembered waking in the middle of the night to the peppery sweet bloom of a flower that was indigenous a thousand miles away.

"Oh, my dear, let me help you. We must fetch your mother; we don't have much time," his father said.

The old man pulled up next to him, the frail form hefting Galadrath completely off his feet. Galadrath sighed loudly, and allowed his father to carry him like a baby, into the living room.

He plopped down painfully into a seat.

"Julera! Come here—we have many things to do before our guests arrive!" the old man screeched.

Brixby cawed, hopping onto the table, scattering the place settings.

"Friends for dinner!" he said.

An old woman came hobbling up the stairs.

"Those oafs left mud all over my floors. You better help me, old man," the woman said.

"Your son is making a mess, as well," his father said.

She entered the room and saw the battered frame of Galadrath sitting at the table.

"Galadrath! I didn't realize!" she exclaimed.

"Keep your voice down, my sweet flower," the old man urged her. "He's bleeding from his leg. Fetch the dressings—we'll need whatever you can muster."

She scurried over to a cabinet and began to rummage through it.

"Oh, my dear child. How could you commit treason, and we have to find out from those oafs?!" she said, jars scattering across the floor as she searched inside the furniture.

"I didn't commit treason, Mother," Galadrath said.

"Of course you didn't, Gally. But to find out from those oafs that you did! The embarrassment!" she continued.

"Julera, my periwinkle, maybe staunch his wound before you scold him," the old man said.

"Oh, my baby boy, what have you done?" she said, tearing off the blood soaked pant leg.

"I've been working for charlatans and thieves, mother, I did nothing wrong," Galadrath said.

"Nothing is a strong word. You must have done something," Julera said.

"Teratos betrayed me. He fed me to those dogs. Thainegom, the court, and maybe even the king—all think I'm an enemy," he continued.

"Oh! How is Teratos? And his lovely wife? We haven't seen them in so long! I wish they would come and visit. We don't get many visitors," she said excitedly.

"Mother. I just said he had me accused," Galadrath grumbled.

"But he was such a good boy! He was always my favorite. So kind! Always had such nice things to say!" Julera said.

"Yes, he has a way with words. It would seem that's why I am in this predicament," the Accuser continued.

"But I asked how he was! Is he doing well? Such a nice man," she continued.

"Julera, my magnificent peony, let me get a word in. Gally, my boy, it would seem you have more than just the court of Thainegom after you. They've sent Pillars, and my fellow Archons have sent messages. It would seem the whole dominion of the world is after you," Vostranis said.

"Please don't call me Gally—I'm the Court's Accuser, not a boy anymore," Galadrath said.

"Accuser! Court's Accuser! Hah! You aren't that anymore. They've come and told me. But you are my boy. Hah!" Vostranis said.

"Our only boy! Our only child! We'll always be older than you, Gally!" Julera chimed in.

She splashed some cold water on the wound, washing away the caked blood. Galadrath grunted in pain.

"I'm still a powerful man," he said through clenched teeth.

"You're a powerful man with a hole in your leg. Tell me how that happens to powerful men?" his father muttered.

"Fetch him something to eat, Vos. He'll need his strength. Some cured sausages from the pantry and a glass of something strong. I'll have to put in some stitches," she said.

"They took my symbols. They stripped me of my titles. They sentenced me to death," Galadrath said.

Julera sniffled for a moment, the words descending on her like blows from a hammer.

"A powerful man—and they *took* your symbols. Yield to none, we say. Yield to none," Vostranis said.

"Yield to none," Galadrath echoed.

"Shut up, you two. I've got to put in these stitches, and you're making me emotional," Julera murmured.

She began to pack the wound with a mixture of herbs and creams. She held up a large straight needle, and in between frail fingers and bulging arthritic knuckles, she bent it into a half loop.

"Dearest, could you do the honors?" she asked.

Galadrath instinctively began to draw on the emblems—and his mind was swimming uncontrollably. His father caught him as he lost consciousness. When he came to, a moment later, the room was stifling hot.

"Not you, little Gally. If your late father was paying attention he would know better!" Julera shouted.

"I'm not dead yet, and as much as you think, you should know I can't control this boy of ours!" Vostranis yelled.

The room began to cool, the temperature teetering on the edge of chilly.

Galadrath watched as a fuelless flame appeared around the needle, the shiny metal transitioning to a red hot. He reached to his side where a goblet of strong spirit had been placed and took several loud gulps. He did not feel the needle puncture his skin, but he smelled the burning and heard the sizzling.

"They'll be getting suspicious soon," Vostranis said.

Galadrath could still feel the influence of his father in the house. The shroud of control could stop the Emissaries from knowing exactly what was going on, but the influence being sustained was a sign in itself.

"Where will you go?" Julera asked.

"I have an idea. I don't think it's wise to tell you," Galadrath said.

"I didn't ask you to tell me! As long as you know," she replied.

Galadrath leaned back and rolled his eyes. His parents were both intensely trained on applying a cure to the sewn up wound, and then began to wrap a bandage around it.

"Your wound is tended to, but these clothes of yours are in terrible shape. Let me get you something else to wear. I think there are some of your father's work clothes that will fit," his mother said.

She stood from where she had been inspecting his leg, patting him softly on the shoulder.

"I'm quite fond of my uniform," Galadrath mumbled.

"It's your skin I'm worried about," Julera said, leaving the room.

She returned quickly, tossing some baggy canvas workwear on the table, along with a big straw hat.

"Come on! Up and out of those rags and into these," she urged him.

Galadrath hobbled back into the room with its collection of growing curiosities, the bundle of stinking clothes under his arm. He dressed as quickly as he could, bracing himself on the bed as he tried not to aggravate his accruing old and new wounds. He carefully placed the ring into his breast pocket, before he transferred the money and the emblems he carried into the baggy carpenter's pants.

He emerged from the room, no longer wearing the torn and burned field of regal flowers. He looked like a farmer.

"Eat, eat, my boy. You'll need your strength," she said.

Galadrath glared at her for a moment as if he was still a child, unwilling to finish what was on his plate. Eventually, he stuffed in another mouthful of sausage and drowned it with some more of the spirits.

"Don't drink too much of that—you still have some travels ahead of you," she said, watching him eat.

"You know I'm the Court's Accuser, right?" Galadrath slurred.

His face was gaunt and colorless. He felt faint, but the drink was fighting the pain and the mixture of discomfort and numbness that had emboldened him.

"Yes, my dear. Yes, I know," Julera said softly, her voice beginning to crack.

"You're not, you know," Vostranis added.

Julera shot him a foul look, on the verge of tears.

"You're not a bad man, Gally. You know that, right? You've always done the right thing," he said.

"Father, I know... I know," Galadrath said.

"You'll be careful, won't you? You're okay to get where you're going?" Julera asked.

"I'm fine, mother. I'll be safe."

The parents stared at their son for a moment, as he stood and made to leave.

"You'll be alright, too? You won't get in trouble?" Galadrath asked.

"We'll be fine—you just need to get out of here before they get suspicious, if they aren't already," Vostranis said.

"Yea, I'm going, I'm going. Love you, I'll miss you."

He vanished in a cloud of smoke rolling onto the floor.

"We love you too, our dearest boy," Julera sniffled.

10

THE FARMER IN THE STRANGE LITTLE TOWN

THE SUN WAS STILL high in the sky as the acrid smoke drifted off Galadrath, standing before the Thumblethin Inn and Alehouse.

He pushed hard with his stronger arm against the door, and it flew open on rusty hinges. He swayed slightly, trying to compose himself. His mind was still in disarray, but he recalled his own words.

Be unpredictable.

That was why he was here, after all. He had come to a den of thieves, a house of crime, because the last place the Emissaries would look for him was among the honorless.

Galadrath placed his weight on his newly bandaged leg, letting the pangs of pain grow through his numbed body, and he hobbled slowly toward the bar. When he reached it, he slammed down three gold coins. He had planned to place them down neatly, but in his state, they slid and clattered across the bar top.

"A drink for anyone that wants it. I'm here to make some friends, and I'm in need of a job," Galadrath mumbled from beneath his straw hat.

"Seems you don't need a job with coin like that," the bartender said.

"Pour the drinks," Galadrath growled.

He had forgotten how wealthy he was, what a gold coin meant to a man. His mind wandered to the beggar—the spy who had tried to kill him in his own home. He had given the man a small fortune in gold over the time that he was posted in front of his door. It meant nothing to him. Even now he cared nothing for the gold he had, only where the next few coins would take him.

The only thing pounding against his skull was the love of his family, from whom he had been driven away from.

"Drinks are paid for! Gather round!" the bartender yelled.

Galadrath pulled on the power of the ring buried in his pocket and pushed his influence outward. The air, the ground, and the boards of the rickety building all greeted him with joy. He expected another of the Many, even another Emissary, but no one reacted to him.

"The harvest isn't in yet, farmer. What are you doing spoiling your kin's inheritance?" a man said.

"All I do is reap," Galadrath replied.

He grabbed a filled cup from the bar in front of him and emptied it.

The bar swelled as the men and women sitting at tables came and grabbed their drinks. As the bodies pushed against Galadrath, he became irritated.

He snatched up another cup and raised it high, as far as his arm could stretch. Most of the contents splashed against the ceiling, and rained down onto the people behind him.

"Honor and Glory!" he yelled.

He stood and turned as the drink-soaked folks stepped back. The crowd around him paused for a moment. No one returned the cry.

Galadrath heard a knife blade plant into the countertop.

"None of that to be found here," a familiar red-bearded man said.

A silence poured over the crowd.

"The drinks are paid for, my friends, and I'd bet his purse might hold another month of rounds for us!" the man urged the rest of the denizens.

"The only thing I've ever seen you do with that knife is dig shallow holes in this wood, Emmett," Galadrath replied.

He tipped the heavy straw hat backwards and glared at the man.

"I remember you. Do you remember me?" Galadrath said gravely.

Emmett squinted and took a step back, plucking the knife from the countertop and waving it around menacingly.

"I think I'd remember some farmer with a purse full of coin," he said.

"I'm looking for Dietrich Bledfett," Galadrath stated.

Galadrath watched as his voice rang clearly in the ears of the man. He watched as the red haired oaf tried to place his voice, unable to reconcile this homely farmer look with that of an Accuser.

"Dietrich is dead, he was accused," Emmett said.

"That's a shame. What about Farrah, Farrah something?" Galadrath mumbled.

The red haired man reflexively turned around, searching the room.

"Emmett, don't. Don't you see? He's the Accuser," a young man said.

Galadrath turned to the young man. The three men looked back and forth at each other.

"Scar breathes, Justus. *Again*? Speak up sooner next time," Emmett said through gritted teeth.

"Don't worry Emmett. I'm no longer in the employ of the court. I haven't come here in any official capacity," Galadrath slurred.

He regretted the statement; the drink had coaxed the truth from him.

"Hah! I'm supposed to believe that? The Court's Accuser, the Grim Wreath, retired?" Emmett laughed.

Galadrath replayed the events of the day in his head. The truth was an absurdity that even he did not want to accept. He considered lying to create a more believable story, but he knew that the truth—as unbelievable as it was—was his only chance to get what he needed.

"I've been accused of treason. I'm a fugitive on the run, from the court. I am being hunted as we speak. I've been stripped of my titles. I'm looking for Farrah. I have some bad news for her. Maybe we can help each other," he said bluntly.

Emmett smiled a wide smile. He looked back at Justus, and then to the others crowded around the bar. He began to laugh wildly, the others soon joining in. Emmett banged the edge of the knife blade against the bar top with a muffled pang, before he pointed it menacingly at Galadrath.

"If all that is true, then I'm sure there is a hefty reward in turning you in. What's to stop me from cutting you up and selling your pieces back to the crown?" Emmett grinned.

Galadrath pulled on the fire emblem in his pocket and poured the energy into the blade. The metal began to glow red hot, and the wrapped handle began to sizzle in Emmett's hand. The bearded man cried in pain, the knife clattering onto the bar. The heavy wood countertop blackened around the intense heat of the metal, before it spontaneously caught fire. The blade lost its shape, liquid steel pooling in the flames. The crowd jumped back, stumbling over each other and yelling at the sight.

The flames vanished, and the pool of steel solidified and cracked, squealing as the heat was replaced by a thin layer of frost.

Galadrath breathed out, the suddenly frigid air leaving a trail of condensation.

"Because I'm still armed, Emmett. Are you?" he said.

The man stared at him with wild eyes, unable to form a response. Galadrath reached out slowly, grabbed one of the many wooden mugs brimming with drink, and put it down in front of Emmett—on top of the remains of the knife.

"Drink with me."

Emmett hesitated, and then carefully grabbed the drink.

"I really liked that knife," he muttered.

"I'll get you a new one," Galadrath replied.

"That one had sentimental value," Emmett said sheepishly.

"What? You killed some people with it?"

"Well, yea. It was good for threatening too."

"Not that good," Galadrath slurred, picking up another mug and draining it. Then to the bartender, he said, "Sorry about the bar."

"As long as that is the last thing of mine you break, all is forgiven," the man said, snatching up the coins.

Galadrath could feel a figure approach him from behind. The drinks were fogging his mind, but the energy in his veins was like a sheathed weapon.

"If you two are done roostering about, I'd like to introduce myself," a feminine voice said.

Galadrath turned in his seat to face its source. The crowd parted slightly. A woman with heavily tanned skin and an aquiline nose studied him. Her clothes were plain but well-tailored, and she wore a sword at her waist.

"I'm Farrah Kane. Please understand, this is a somewhat unconventional way of introducing yourself. Truthfully, I'm not sure what to make of this situation. You killed my friend, Dietrich. Now, you've come here saying you're a fugitive and asking for me by name. You're looking to make friends while threatening us. What is your purpose, and why here, of all places?" she said.

Galadrath sighed loudly. "It's already been a long day. Please, sit," he said.

He waved her over and listlessly sipped at another mug. She sat next to him and waved off the rest of the crowd. Some of them stopped to grab a fresh drink, but all of them complied with her command.

"It's all true," Galadrath slumped in his seat. "I've been accused of treason, and I need to know why. I have few allies, and I'm unsure who to trust. I'm being hunted by the most dangerous people on the northern continent, and as far as I know, so are you. An Administrant mentioned your name, and you are to be accused. I'd been sent to root out these treasonous persons, to accuse the enemies of the court. Now, I'm afraid they were innocent. Dietrich..."

"Dietrich was guilty, but so are we all. Not a soul here is loyal to the crown. Though, I shouldn't admit that to you. How am I supposed to trust you? How do I know you're not a spy?" she demanded.

"Don't trust me. Just put me to work. I've already been accused. There is nothing I hate more than taking credit for something I haven't done. If I'm branded as a traitor, then it is a title I'll have to earn. That, or I'll have to clear my name. I need resources. I can't do it alone," he said.

She smiled and laughed. She took her mug and banged into his where it rested on the counter, and took a drink.

"Unbelievable. The Grim Wreath, reduced to rags, sitting in the finest establishment of thieves and cutthroats, offering his services to me. You looked so majestic, so poised, that day you had walked in here. Now you're just another stinking drunk," she shook her head, smirking.

"I didn't realize you were there that day," he said.

"Why? Because I'm a woman?"

"Hah. No. Because you weren't a threat," he said, narrowing his eyes at her comment. "You're one to talk. I'm a stinking drunk because I dress like one? Because I've had a few drinks?"

"Maybe we shouldn't underestimate each other," she said.

"It seems that is a mistake I've made often, recently," he said sullenly.

Galadrath glanced up from his mug and saw his own sadness reflected in her eyes.

"We've all been betrayed. I understand your pain," she replied.

"Not like this. I've lost everything. I've lost my family," he choked, voice cracking.

"Do not underestimate us." She put a hand on his shoulder, stood, and grabbed another mug. "Be ready in three days, and meet me here in the morning, before the first Sister rises. We have a job to do."

He looked up at her in surprise.

"You'll take me, then?" he asked.

"It would be unwise to turn down such a powerful ally, Grim Wreath."

"Please, just call me Galadrath."

"You might want to consider a different name, Galadrath."

He thought for a moment.

"Vyhn. Call me Vyhn," he said.

She burst into laughter. "Even at your lowest, you can't escape your hubris. So be it, Vyhn Annya, god of exiles and hermits."

"You know the name?"

"Don't underestimate me," she repeated, turning to walk away.

He shook his head slowly and pulled a few more gold coins from his pocket, placing them on the counter.

"I'll need a room, if you have one. Make sure everyone here is well taken care of," Galadrath said to the bartender.

The man reached into his pocket and produced a bundle of keys, picking through them slowly. He took one from the pile in his hand and slid it toward Galadrath.

"Upstairs, third door on the left. The locks are a bit... rusty," the bartender said, glancing around the room.

"Thank you," Galadrath said.

He stood, swaying slightly from the drink and the dulled pain in his injured leg. His joints were stiff, but he tried his hardest not to let his weakness show. He walked out the door into the sunlight. His eyes were slow to adjust to the brightness of the day, his mind foggy from the drinks. He pulled the wide brimmed straw hat low over his eyes and meandered around the rutted dirt streets of the small town.

He walked past a small facade of three adjoined buildings. The smell of fresh bread wafted out of one, which bore no sign or name on its exterior. The wonderful aroma was enough of an advertisement. The next building was slim, as if it had been crushed between the two larger ones. A dilapidated plaque next to the warped wooden door read, "Threshook Kurzwaren."

Galadrath looked down at his own clothes. The haggard workwear could be as old as he was and came with the unwelcome flavor of someone else's sweat. He walked softly into the building, heaving slightly at the door as it scraped across the floor.

A young man looked up at him from a rocking chair in the corner. His clothes were those of an artisan, simple, functional, and clean. Over the outfit, he wore a small leather apron, wide and short, too small to serve much of a purpose. Across from him sat an old woman in another rocking chair, dressed lavishly in thick colorful layers of spun wool. It was an old traditional Thainegom dress, an artifact of fashion from long ago.

The young man stood slowly, rolling forward onto his feet. Galadrath waited for him to come completely upright, but the young man remained bent over, his back curved at a strange angle. He reached down where a small monocle dangled from a chain. The eyepiece was a peculiar sight in the tiny workspace. Such pieces of jewelry were expensive, painstakingly carved from the purest crystals or conjured by one of the Many.

The man placed the small eye glass on the gaunt features of his face, and hobbled forward.

"Welcome, welcome. How may I assist you?" he said.

"I'm in need of some new clothing; I'm sure I've found the right place," Galadrath said.

"Indeed, you have. I'm Randolph Kent, a humble tailor at your service. I've just received a delivery from one of our finest purveyors of wooden toggles and buttons, fleece and burlap. Even some handkerchiefs, if you're looking to impress. All very affordable," Randolph said.

The man was overtly pleasant, but Galadrath could tell Randolph had already taken his dimensions with a keen eye—and also the weight of his purse.

"I'd like to commission a wardrobe. I have a very specific piece in mind that I would like to have completed before I leave—and others to follow. You have three days. I'm willing to pay," Galadrath said.

He knew his words would need to be fortified, to be convincing. He reached into his pockets and produced gold coins, a few at a time, placing them on the counter. He kept the silver, knowing his funds were not limitless. Randolph watched as the coins began to pile up.

"I didn't mean any slight at your expense, sir. It isn't often we get such taste here, so far from the nobility. I'd be happy to take your request," the crooked young man said, adjusting his monocle.

"I'm led to believe that you're proficient in many of the old styles of wear," Galadrath said, pointing to the sleeping woman.

"I have traveled at great lengths to collect designs from every inch of the world. You see, my father was Richard Kent, of Kent Mercantile," Randolph said loftily.

He hobbled to the counter behind him, straining to reach a large leatherbound book, dusting the cover of the tome carefully, before he plopped it on the counter between them. He leafed through the pages.

"Sister's blessings, it is fate that we meet. Can you mimic the Arbiter's of Tirv, the modern nobles of Thainegom, the dancers of Sijis, and the heavy elegance of Irah?" Galadrath began to spout off, looming over the book as the pages turned to pictures of varying designs.

"That... that is possible," Randolph said hesitantly.

"It needs to be light, to breathe, not too bulky to move in. And black—black as a moonless night," Galadrath continued.

"This is a request like no other, good sir. The color, however, will pose a problem. Give me a moment."

The young man disappeared into a room behind the counter and rummaged for a moment. He reappeared with a small swatch of dark fabric, placing it on the counter.

"Please, hold it in the light," Randolph said.

Galadrath grabbed it and held the fabric to a candle on the counter.

"Outside, please," Randolph urged.

Galadrath stepped outside, and in the bright light, the cloth shimmered a deep blue. It reminded him of Brixby's iridescent feathers, and his heart sank as he was reminded of his family.

"This will do perfectly," he said, bringing the cloth back to the counter.

"I'll work tirelessly, but I'm afraid there will be little time for alteration. We must talk about design," Randolph said, a spark of fire and excitement in his voice.

"I trust your judgment. Make it so," Galadrath said.

A wide smile crept across the face of the tailor, and he began to sketch immediately with a piece of shaped charcoal. As quickly as he began, he stopped, and looked up.

"Your name, sir?" he asked.

"Vyhn, and I'm no sir. Three days, I'll be back before first light,"

Galadrath said.

The young man nodded deeply, his form already poised in a permanent bow. He shuffled toward the old lady and carefully roused her from her slumber. He spoke through his nose, as if his mouth was filled with marbles, in a language Galadrath recognized but could not understand.

"You're from the islands?" Galadrath asked.

"My mother was, and my grandmother," Randolph nodded toward the old lady.

"Strange little town, this place," Galadrath grumbled, walking out the door.

He walked back to the cramped room he had rented from the bartender. There was hardly enough space for a small bed, a few short shelves, and a small nightstand, which held a bowl, a carafe of water, and a thin candle.

Galadrath locked the door, testing its sturdiness, and began to draw on the power of his ring. A spontaneous flame lit the candle, and the bowl filled with steaming water from an invisible source. He barred the door with stone wedges and pillars. The floor creaked slightly, straining to bear the weight as the stone fortifications formed across the door.

He stripped off the old clothes and washed them slowly in the bowl, cleaning away the events of the day. Each item left the warm water brown and murky. He dried them quickly with the help of the emblems, until the clean clothing was steaming and warm. He dressed himself again.

He snuffed out the candle with two fingers, letting the little flame flicker around the pads of his forefinger and thumb for a moment before pinching it out.

He lay on the small bed in the darkness, hoping he would dream of his family—to be able to hold them again.

11

THE EVIL ONE

GALADRATH WOKE TO THROBBING pain in his leg. Even after three days had passed, his wound was still painful, and now the stitches had begun to itch. His scars ached on his arms and his chest from the cool morning air wafting through the small, barred wooden window.

He pressed the ring onto his finger and felt the cold dread of the blackstone fill his veins. The nightmares in the back of his mind came alive, and he concentrated on keeping them locked away.

"*Le Malin, être parti, mal,*" the old woman in the tailor's shop said.

She was sitting in the same chair, a robe of frilly white silk covering her frail form.

The black fog rolled off Galadrath, where he Stepped in front of the counter.

Randolph came crashing through the door from the back room, holding a dagger in his hand. He looked up from his hunched pose, his eyes wild. He saw Galadrath's figure and breathed out heavily.

"Vyhn, I didn't hear you come in—my apologies," he said.

"I didn't," Galadrath said, the black fog pouring from his nostrils.

Randolph stared at him. His eyes were puffy, his gaunt form showing a lack of sleep. He seemed unperturbed to the telltale signs of Stepping. Galadrath made note of it. Not only had the tailor seen it before, but he also entertained the obvious lie that was Galadrath's new persona.

"Did you finish what I asked for?" Galadrath asked.

"We worked tirelessly, Vyhn. Let me show you."

Randolph hobbled into the back room, before he appeared again, his arms laden with the dull black vestiges. He placed them carefully on the countertop, as though offering a body to be sacrificed to a god on an altar, his own crooked form prostrated to the higher powers.

Galadrath looked at the collection of shimmering, almost-black material.

"Do you have some privacy, so I can change?" Galadrath asked.

"Please, follow me," Randolph said.

Galadrath rounded the counter, grabbing the clothing, and followed the tailor into a small back room. He quickly threw off his old garments, collecting them in a pile on the floor. He pulled on the loose fitting pants and the accompanying flowing shirt, fashioned in the styles of the Sijisian royals. The stitching was fine, almost invisible, and the large buttons of the shirt were made of mother-of-pearl, contrasting the vast darkness of the material. Epaulets of furs draped over his shoulders, a nod to the powerful war hounds of Thainegom. He wrapped the belt around his waist, over and over, forming a cummerbund of hammered metal scraps—a homage to the iron armies of Irah. He tugged two simple wraps over his forearms, adorned with tiny silver chains—an acknowledgement of Barkrill, the symbol of his homeland.

He stepped out from the small room, the flowing folds of the baggy pants following behind him like a rippling shadow.

"Magnificent, I dare say," Randolph smiled.

"You dare, and justly so. Truly, you are a craftsman who could stand before kings. You've created a masterpiece," Galadrath said. He pointed to his forearms, to the silver chains. It was an old traditional symbol of the servants of Barkrill. "I never mentioned Barkrill, when we discussed the design."

"You are the Grim Wreath, are you not?" Randolf asked. "The chains seemed fitting. My grandmother insisted when she did the stitching. She may not be able to see well, but she recognized you."

"Gods, dead and alive—why does that stupid name haunt me? Is it so apparent? Does everyone know me, even here, in this town of outcasts?" Galadrath scoffed.

"Great men cast long shadows," Randolph shrugged.

Galadrath mulled the statement over in his mind, and he slowly began to chuckle.

"A poet and a tailor. We'll see each other again soon. Thank you," he said.

Galadrath walked out into the darkness of the early morning. He shook out his stiff arms and legs carefully. The constant ache of his mending puncture wound was an ever-present reminder of his current situation.

He drew slightly on the power of the emblems that he had carefully arranged in the pockets of his new clothes. The fire and air mixed in his veins like a minty cocktail and lent him the strength to ignore his pains. He walked toward the door of the inn, unencumbered. The divine power acted as an invisible crutch.

He slowly pushed the door open and saw only a handful of faces gathered around a table with a single candle. On the other side of the room, the bartender stood in the previous day's clothes, obviously tired from working late and getting up early. He looked up from wiping a wooden mug, first toward Galadrath, then toward the stairs. Shaking his head, he set down the mug, poured a helping of dark liquid into it, and slid it across the char mark on the counter.

"We've been waiting for you. Vyhn," Farrah said, crossing the distance to the counter.

Galadrath drank from the mug. The liquid was room temperature, tasting heavily of grain and barley. It was a common table beer, like liquid bread, lightly fermented to bring just a touch of alcohol to the mixture. It was the staple drink of the hard working, calloused hands of the countryside.

He drank deeply, draining the mug while he looked up and down the faces of the five individuals sitting at the table. Farrah, Emmett, and Justus he recognized. The other two he could identify from the previous encounter, but he had not yet learned their names. He could see Farrah impatiently expecting a reply to fill the silent void.

"You've got some new clothes. Seems to me you have a knack for fashion—or maybe you just do your best killing while well-dressed?" she said.

He met her gaze, ignoring her goading question.

She continued, trying to draw a response from him, "It's a little darker than I would expect from you—almost like Mirrora decided to walk through our humble doors."

"Don't say her name." His voice cut through the air, his teeth on edge. He could hear the cackling come from deep within the prisons of his mind.

Farrah looked back and forth between her table mates and him. She was surprised at his response, but he could see she was happy she had provoked him.

"What? Are you scared of the tales of old maids? Ghost stories made up to terrify misbehaving children? Have you been misbehaving, Vyhn?" she added, laughing.

"Just don't say her name," he warned. "You said you're waiting for me. Let's get to work."

He approached the table but stopped behind an empty stool, refusing to sit.

"Up and at 'em then, I guess. I'm sure I don't need to remind you, but you're working for me—you'll be taking direction from *me*," she said.

"Clearly."

"Good. Come then, we're late. Hester, go on ahead. We'll meet you on the Flat," Farrah ordered.

They walked outside, and the younger woman that Farrah had addressed disappeared behind the building. Galadrath heard a horse whinny, and heavy hoof beats hammered into the road, Hester almost standing in the stirrups.

They traveled long enough for the suns to rise. During which, Farrah explained the plan in detail.

"We'll be working a caravan headed toward the bay. We're not sure exactly how many wagons will be in the train. Many will be carrying foodstuffs—basic provisions and other sundries for the port—and likely for the ships making ready to set sail. We're really only after one of these wagons in particular, which should contain a large shipment of salt. That's what we're after," she said.

"You're planning on stealing a cart full of *salt?*" Galadrath asked.

"Yes. Gold can buy swords and men, but salt can be bartered and traded. Anyone in the countryside has a use for it. It raises little suspicion and can negotiate goodwill with ease. We are fugitives, after all. Being caught with a bag of salt is much less deadly than being caught with a bag of gold."

Galadrath pondered her logic for a moment. He was used to rich spices and exotic flavors, ferried in from the edges of the continents. Salt is as commonplace for him as water, or at least it was.

"Thainegom is a large exporter of salt. These barrels will be headed across the ocean to Sijis. If the shipment isn't made, we weaken the bonds of diplomacy. We diminish the image of the king here in his own lands—and abroad," she explained. "Trading is a public thing. If we were to rob a weapons caisson or a treasury, the Lords would likely replenish it from their own stocks and coffers to hide their weakness. Not to mention, a chest of gold or a load of weapons will be much more heavily guarded. We do not have the resources to fight a war... not yet."

"What about godstuff? I'm sure they still import the divine metals," Galadrath asked.

He looked down at the small silver chains. The mundane metals were a meager icon in the place of the powerful symbols he used to carry.

"We're farmers, tradesmen, and beggars—not mercenaries or warlords. Even if we could somehow manage to find some, we wouldn't know what to do with it. I don't know any Dusters, do you? A fist full of divine metal, ore or even a forged piece, would be worth less than its weight in salt to us," she rebuked him.

"It is worth its weight in gold—a thousand times! In my hands, it is priceless. With enough, I could conjure gold itself. I could dream up more salt than you could ever steal," Galadrath replied with exasperation.

Silence passed between him and the group, his words lingering in the air.

"Yes. That does change things," Farrah agreed solemnly, voice heavy with understanding. "We're almost to the Flathorn Pass. We'll set up there, gather our supplies, and wait for Hester."

The open terrain was quickly changing before them. Open fields of wild grasses, pockmarked by a few lonely trees, soon rolled into broken hills and light patches of forests. They made their way to the top of one of the hills, which was densely packed with large oaks. Farrah sat against the trunk of a tree, enjoying the shade.

"We'll wait here. Tibel, Justus, Emmett—go and fetch our things," she waved the three men off.

They walked slowly from view, slightly down the far side of the hill. Farrah lazily dug in one of her pockets and produced some dried meat. She tossed a piece to Galadrath and stuck another in her mouth. He failed to catch the piece she threw, and it landed in the dirt in front of him. He quickly grabbed it, dusted it off, and looked drably at it.

"I thought you're supposed to have eyes in the back of your head, ready for anything," she chuckled.

"I'm never ready to have meat tossed at me—to be fed like a dog," he mumbled.

"You should be honored to be treated like a dog. The war hounds eat better than we do," she smiled.

"I've never had an affinity for the Sturms, or any animal really. Except maybe birds," Galadrath struggled to make conversation, as he fought to soften the tough meat with his teeth and tongue.

"And flowers?" she asked.

"Yes, flowers. Plants create, and thrive under the sun; animals only consume, and pant in the heat," he replied vapidly.

She nodded, chewing softly.

The three men returned, arms heavily laden with weapons and bags. Galadrath had been wondering how they were to fight, armed with only a few long knives between them. Now, it began to make sense. They had traveled overland during the day, and anyone they might have passed would be curious by a surplus of weapons. This wasn't a half-hatched plan; this had been prepared for at length, for weeks. Suddenly, he felt uneasy, unprepared for what lay ahead. His arrogance had clouded his judgment. His fall into treason had happened such a short while ago, and his pride had already allowed him to forget his new station.

"What do you need me to do?" he asked Farrah.

"Hester will have scouted the caravan. She will create a distraction and mark the appropriate cart. While the guards are dealing with her, Justus and I will dispatch the cart driver and any passengers. Then we'll commandeer it and drive it south off the Flat, through the valley at best speed. Emmett will ambush any followers on foot that attempt to pursue. Tibel will remain on a hill close by, making sure we don't get shot. You... I expect you will be able to lend a hand managing anyone or anything that stops any of us from doing our jobs," she laid out the plan.

"Dispatch? You'll be killing the carter? And the guards?" Galadrath asked with alarm.

"We'll kill anyone who stands in our way," she answered.

"I'm not about to spill innocent blood."

"Then make sure no one stands in our way. The path into the valley is uneven and will be slow to traverse with the heavy cargo. If they continue to chase us into the woods, we'll have no choice but to fight. I'd rather not kill good people, so if you value their lives—and most importantly ours—slow them down by whatever means necessary," she finished.

Emmett handed him a saber. The blade was plain and somewhat dull, but in size and function, it was similar to what he was used to wielding.

"Do you have another of these? I'd like to have two," Galadrath said, studying the blade.

"No. And you still owe me one. So now, you owe me two," Emmett snipped.

Emmett turned his back to Galadrath and passed out a few other swords and daggers between them. Tibel stood, propping up a heavy barreled rifle as tall as he was. He started by cleaning and preparing the firing mechanism, and then he measured out powder and ball, ensuring his ammunition was dry and easily accessible. When he finished, he moved onto the next of the three long guns propped up next to him.

Hester slowly approached on foot, leading her horse by hand.

"Farrah, we've got a bit of a problem. The train is much larger than we thought. Seven wagons, eighteen guards, and at least twenty more followers—a third of which could fight. There are three salt wagons loaded to the brim. It seems Bartron and his crew have been working hard, and the merchants are trying to backfill their shipments to make up for the losses. The carts are third, fourth, and sixth in the procession. I think we may have to let this one slip by."

"Bartron?" Galadrath interjected.

"He's another one of us. You didn't really think we were the only five traitors in the kingdom?" Farrah replied.

She didn't wait for an answer, turning back toward Hester.

"Nothing is going to slip by. We have Galadrath—I mean Vyhn—here to pad our numbers. We'll take the first cart, mark it and try to draw the guards to the rear. Do they have rifles?" she said.

"Yes. Keepers of the Peace, six of them," Hester said.

Farrah sighed.

"Draw as many as you can to the back, into the followers. They may not be as willing to shoot into a group of women and children. Tibel will silence any strays. Hester, are you okay with this?" she said.

Galadrath knew the rifles were slow to load, but a cool headed marksman would only need one shot. Even on horseback, Hester would make an easy target.

"I can help with that—I'll take care of the rifles. I'll need to get close, though that's not a problem. Hester, stick to one side of the caravan and make them cross over to your side to find their mark. I'll do the rest," Galadrath said.

"Then we all know what we have to do," Farrah said.

The men grunted, almost in unison. Hester wore a worried expression. Each of them dispersed, taking up their positions.

Galadrath lay next to Tibel on the top of the rocky incline, the three long barrels of the rifles nestled neatly in a row among the long grass. It was not long before they heard the slow hoofbeats on the seamless, smooth slab of the stone road. Shortly after, they could see the beginnings of the procession. A few of the wagons were covered, the goods inside kept out of the sun and the sight of prying eyes. Others were open, barrels and crates stacked neatly in piles and rows.

"Try not to kill anyone that doesn't need killing," Galadrath said softly.

"They all need killing," Tibel replied.

"These people are just making a living, same as you."

"At who's expense? My dead father's? My starving sister's?" the young man growled.

"Stealing from thieves is just stealing. We're not here to take their lives," Galadrath replied calmly.

"They've taken so much more than just a life from me," Tibel said smoothly.

The heavy clatter of a galloping horse interrupted them. Hester had started her approach. She sat so low in the saddle that she was almost invisible behind the charging head of the horse. Her screams echoed over the heavy hooves.

"The cents are coming! Patchwork! Patches on the road!" her voice carried distress.

Galadrath had underestimated her ability for theatrics—and of riding. The horse was quickly bearing down on one side of the column of wagons and their guards. He could see them spreading out, stepping off of the road, getting clear of the wild rider approaching with ominous news. Even a hushed mention of the Patchwork would set the fiercest of men on edge. The shambling, slick black horrors of knitted flesh were a reality. Manifested nightmares from an all-too-recent history.

The first wagon stopped in its tracks, the driver unwilling to test the warning. Hester passed by the second wagon that was already slowing down. As she came alongside the third, she reached her hand out and threw a fist sized bag out to the side. The bag collided with the cart and burst in a small puff of red chalk. The horse began to veer slightly side to side, as if she was losing control, and the guards scattered even more.

"That's our mark," Tibel said.

Galadrath pulled on the emblems, the blackstone, the air, and the earth. His body felt cold and heavy, tingling at his toes and fingertips. He drew in as much as he could—as much as the ring would allow him.

"Then I better get going," Galadrath muttered.

He did not wait for any response, and whatever Tibel said, if anything, was wasted on the puff of black fog flowing in between the grass and weeds.

Galadrath appeared next to the first of the Keepers of the Peace, still resting prone on his belly. He grabbed the man by the ankle with one hand and pulled him off his feet. The soldier dropped his rifle as he braced himself for the fall. Galadrath rolled forward onto his knees, snatched up the weapon, and struck the stock against the man's head. He squeezed the gun hard along the barrel, collapsing the metal in his fist, and tossed it aside.

"We're under attack!" someone began raising the alarm.

Galadrath turned to his left and saw another guard, standing ten feet away, struggling to unsheathe a sword. In a burst of speed he launched himself toward the man, drawing his sword and raising the blade high over his head. He banged the pommel of the sword into the temple of his target, rendering him unconscious. As the body fell limp, so did a cloud of the acrid black smoke.

The second rifleman had looked in the direction of the shout, and Galadrath appeared next to him. He ripped the rifle from the grasp of the man and hammered it into the hard stone surface of the road. The barrel bent, and the wooden stock and firing mechanism shattered against the ground.

"Stand down, soldier," Galadrath said, meeting the startled eyes of the armored man.

Another man rushed from behind, sword drawn. Galadrath turned and met the outstretched weapon with his own, swinging with all the strength in his veins. He heard a pop in the wrist of his attacker, as the power of the swing wrenched the sword from his hand. Galadrath's own saber broke clean in half from the impact, leaving him with a blunted and unbalanced knife. The man grabbed at his injury, backing away slowly.

"Over here!" the man yelled in pain.

"Patches on the road!" Hester yelled from the back of the column.

Most of the guards were now looking in the direction of Galadrath. He could make out the alarm on their faces, their hesitance to approach him. He could assume none of them had ever seen a Patch. They were scarce, and deadly. It was rare to encounter one, and those who did find themselves face to face with one would be lucky to survive.

Maybe they thought he was one of the demonic monsters; maybe the cries of Hester were enough to convince them. He saw the last rifleman on this side, in the distance. A woman holding the long gun was caught between the unfolding combat, the screams and disarray of the working class citizens panicking, and Hester's massive horse rearing and snorting.

Another rifleman stepped out from between the carts ahead of him, between him and Hester. She failed to notice him, as she drew her own sword and clubbed the riflewoman over the head with it. A shot rang out as the woman collapsed, her weapon discharging into the air with a large plume of smoke. The man ahead of Galadrath shouldered his stock and aimed at Hester.

Galadrath instantly felt fear. He was moving too slow. Sparing lives might cost Hester her own. He Stepped toward the aiming man, crossing the distance in an instant. Just as he appeared next to the shining breastplate of the soldier, Galadrath heard a distant crack. The rifleman's face ruptured, much to Galadrath's surprise, and the cart he was standing next to was covered with flecks of splattered blood and viscera. He fell forward against the cart, bounced off lifelessly to the ground. On the adjacent hill, Galadrath saw a plume of smoke rising from where Tibal hid.

Galadrath burst into a run, heading between the carts toward the other side of the train. A man in light leather armor and a sword appeared ahead of him. Galadrath sent a blast of air from one side, knocking the man into the back of one of the barrel-laden wagons—then another blast, throwing the man in between two panicking beasts of burden, out of the way of his charge.

When he reached the other side, Galadrath looked around briefly.

If only I had some influence, I could move more quickly.

Half a platoon of guards were beginning to move across the line of wagons, heading toward the commotion. He identified the last two of the rifles, as well as a few more targets of interest, closer to the front of the convoy where Farrah and Justus would already be headed. Galadrath vanished.

He struck the first of the two remaining Keepers of the Peace with a fist behind her ear. Then he picked up the rifle and threw it away into the brush. He vanished again.

The second Keeper of the Peace, Galadrath caught in a full run and slammed an elbow into her sternum, knocking the running woman completely off her feet. The shining breastplate crumpled under the blow, and for a moment, Galadrath was uncertain if the woman was still alive.

He felt a pang of regret. His upbringing had deeply instilled in him how dishonorable it was to strike a woman. She lay at his feet and gasped painfully for breath, and he felt a little better.

Soldiers, they are all just soldiers.

He vanished. He struck his next target. He vanished.

With each Step, it felt as if his veins were crystalizing into ice. Each time, the cackling madness in the back of his mind rattled against its cage. Louder and louder.

He struck. He vanished.

He felt a clawed hand scratch against his neck. He struck, and vanished.

The instants in which he appeared in the sunlight along the road seemed to grow shorter. The moments in which he moved through the ethereal fog grew longer. In those moments, he could see his next target, the ghostly forms of the scene around him distorted as he moved through the space. The cackling grew louder, as his nightmares creeped along the edges of the dreary fog.

He banged a clenched fist into the spine of the guard, and disappeared.

He stood at the center of a horde of ghostly Patches. He knew it was only a memory—a memory that was not his. He knew he was merely standing in the center of his own mind, caught between the real spaces. The horrors reached for him, tugging at his clothing, stroking him with chilling care. The dread in his mind held a sliver of love, a twisted semblance of comfort, as if the creatures sought to console him. Then came the maniacal, screeching laughter, ringing against his skull as though it was trying to break free.

He appeared again, after what seemed to be hours, standing next to the wagon they were supposed to commandeer. He looked back at the moaning, writhing, and slumped bodies of his enemies. He watched the clouds of black fog roll to the ground next to each of them, blowing away slowly in the mild breeze of the day. He had moved between the fighting men and women in an instant, taking only a few seconds to inflict his punishment. The deep cold of the blackstone still lingered in his body and sent a shiver down his spine.

A yelp came from above where he was standing. He turned in time to watch Farrah toss the driver of the wagon unceremoniously from his seat to the ground. He landed at Galadrath's feet, gawking up at the menacing form covered in furs and metal and dripping with black smoke.

"Run," Galadrath calmly stated.

The man scampered to his hands and knees, crawling to a run, terror on his face. Farrah grabbed the reins of the team of oxen and looked over her shoulder. The scattered collection of injured soldiers caused her to raise her eyebrows.

"Not leaving much for Emmett, I see," she said, cracking the reins and pulling the animals to one side.

Justus stood on the seat next to her, surveying the scene from the vantage point, a broad smile on his face. The smile disappeared, though, as he pointed toward the back of the convoy. Galadrath followed the line of the young man's arm. Hester had rounded the back of the wagons and spurred her horse into a gallop. A small group of armored guards were chasing her, followed by tradesmen and women brandishing cleavers, knives, and walking sticks.

Galadrath broke out into a jog, heading toward them. He was afraid to Step, not knowing what would haunt him if he did. He waved at Hester, urging her to pass him and escape the mob. She sat low, and the animal roared passed with flared nostrils.

The mob slowed as their target broke away, and they began assessing the situation. Galadrath, the black clad man, clothing shimmering a deep blue in the sunlight, ran toward them, the distance between them littered with the injured.

Galadrath tossed his broken sword aside. Just as he shed the weapon, he let the unexpended power of the earth flow back into the emblem. As the power drained from him, he replaced it with fire, drawing on another power source. He spread his arms wide as he came to a stop. He conjured two gouts of flame and let them wick around his hands and open palms.

The crowd ahead of him stopped, some gasping and murmuring at the sight.

"We've taken what we need. I don't think it would be wise to risk your lives any longer," Galadrath boomed.

He watched their reactions. A young man wearing a shoddy coat of studded leather, with a long sword in hand, seemed to be trying to muster up his nerve to charge at Galadrath. He was rocking back and forth on his feet, surely waiting for someone else to spur them into motion. Galadrath could see a bit of himself in the young man, back when he was filled with emotion and the pursuit of glory. The foolish idea of becoming a hero and making a name for oneself shrouded the judgment of many young men who would inevitably find themselves dead or broken.

So he made the choice for the young lad and squashed any other ideas of vengeance or justice floating around in the group. He threw his hands toward the nearest wagon, one of the remaining two that were carrying salt. The flames formed into jets, their length and intensity growing instantly to lap and wick around the wooden frame of the vehicle and its cargo. The crowd watched helplessly as the wood blackened and began to burn on its own.

Galadrath quenched the flames on his own hands, satisfied that they would prioritize saving the cargo before pursuing him and his cohorts. They would try, in vain, and it would buy Farrah plenty of time to disappear down the precarious pass and into the valley.

He turned away as the thick cloud of smoke billowed from the burning wagon.

"What's your name? Who do we say attacked us?" the young man asked.

"Vyhn. Vyhn Annya, one of the Many," Galadrath said.

As he started to leave, Galadrath heard the commotion spur behind him as the people dispersed, unhitching the animals still tied to the burning wagon and attempting to combat the flames.

"Oh, I almost forgot," Galadrath mused. "I'll need a few swords."

He pointed at a few of the nearby guards.

"I'll take that one, and that one, that one," he said, eyeing the ones in their hands. "Ah, and this one will do." He reached down and undid the sword belt from an unconscious man on the ground, rolling him over to pull it off. The guards he had gestured to froze and stared at him with confusion.

"Come on, swords and belts. I have a few debts to repay," he said, pointing at the three men whose weapons he had selected.

They each looked stunned, but then they quickly unbuckled the belts, tossing the weapons and their sheathes toward Galadrath. They hesitantly returned to their work, watching as he idly retrieved the weapons and slung them over his shoulder.

Walking away, an old marching tune came to mind. Galadrath began to whistle as well as he could, and when his lips were dry he began to hum, mumbling the words he remembered.

Hammers strike, hammers strike.
What is it the king would like?
Hammers up, hammers down.
Swords and spears to please the crown.
Hoes and plows we do not need.
Foreign lands to take, decreed.
Anvils sing, anvils sing.
The men are armed, and death they bring.
Anvils sing, anvils sing.
Honor and glory, for the king.

12

THE BEAST OF BURDEN

GALADRATH WANDERED DOWN THE rocky trail, enjoying the lively chirping of birds, each singing its tune as he whistled his own. The valley was lush with tall grasses and bushes thriving in the sunshine that managed to filter through the dense canopy of the old oak trees. He was happy, at peace in the uncontested nature. It cleared his head, and the spotty rays of sunshine reaching through the illuminated green leaves above him were enough to push the strange dark memories back into their cages.

Only now did he realize how heavily his recent demotion had weighed on him. A fire still burned in his belly for Teratos and his betrayal, but he refused to let it dampen his current mood. He would kindle that fire soon enough, though, and let the rage overflow when he exacted his vengeance. Until then, he would have to find happiness in the days ahead. He thought of his family, hopefully still in the safety and comfort of their home. The small victory with Farrah had lifted his spirits and given him hope.

He pulled the small emblem of blackstone from his pocket, rolling the tiny shard of stark, lightless power between his fingertips. It had shrunk in size; he could feel it. Blackstone was the strangest of the emblems, and though there were still many of its secrets that were yet to be discovered, Galadrath knew it was finite. The other emblems were

125

also finite, but they could be easily replenished. Even as he walked he could absorb the stones around him, drink in the air and add to the stock he carried in his pockets. It was painstaking work, but he could even convert them from one type to the other, if he wished to expend the time and effort. Blackstone, however, was not so easy to gather and was impossible to convert. Every time he Stepped, he expended a tiny portion of his reserve.

As he fiddled with the blackstone, his mind circled back to his family. He could visit them. He could see if they had also been subjected to the defamation that he suffered from. He could find out if they were held guilty by association. Hopefully, the court still held onto some shred of honor, and his family would be left alone. Thankfully, his father had managed to chase away the Emissaries with a few strong words. Surely Heladra, with her viper-like grace, would not let just anyone into their home without threatening to sink her fangs into them.

The bushes near him rustled, branches cracked, and Galadrath was disrupted from his thoughts.

"Gala—Vyhn!" Emmett said in a strained whisper.

He fell forward through the bushes, tripping on a root. He wrestled his way out of the passive strangle of leafy branches and brought himself back onto his feet.

"Is that how you ambush people?" Galadrath asked.

"No, I usually—You know what, I don't have to explain myself to you! I could hear your whistling—Are you being followed? Are you trying to get us caught?" Emmett fumbled with his words.

"If I'm being followed, then they are much sneakier than you are. Here—I brought you something, payment in full," Galadrath said.

He pulled on two of the swordbelts draped over his shoulder, still adorned with their weapons, and handed them to Emmet with a broad smile, the brigand's comical entrance fortifying his happy mood.

"Two for you, two for me," he chuckled.

Emmett took the weapons, unsheathing the metal partially to inspect the blades. He paused for a moment, then hurried to catch up to the still-walking figure of Galadrath.

"I guess these'll do. Not a knife—nothing close to the one you destroyed—but good enough," he said begrudgingly.

"If I ever stumble onto a likeness of that warped pig sticker, I'll make sure to pick it up for you as a gift," Galadrath chortled.

Emmett scoffed in his direction, "I'm glad to hear they didn't give chase, but I'm a little sad I missed all the fun. It must have been quite the ruckus. I wasn't sure how it would go with such a large caravan. I guess Farrah was right... She's always right. Did Hester make it out alright? I was—" Emmett stopped himself.

"Worried? She's half your age and has twice your skill. I'd keep your worries for yourself—and keep any stray thoughts away from her, too," Galadrath said.

"No, no. It's not like that. She's my half sister," Emmett said, almost embarrassed.

"Oh. Sorry, I didn't know. I don't really see the resemblance. No slight intended then, at either of your expense," Galadrath said, his manners kicking in instinctively.

"Yeah, she got lucky and didn't inherit my father's good looks, like I did," Emmett smiled broadly.

Galadrath nodded, afraid that if he said anything more, he would insult the man who had just opened up to him.

"She made it out just fine. She rode circles around them," Galadrath said.

He left out the part where she was almost shot. Near misses in combat are countless, stacking up to nothing. There is only the victor and the victim, the living and the dead.

"Good, good. One of the only good things my father ever did for her was to teach her how to ride," Emmett smiled.

They continued down the rocky path, winding in between the trees. It was a few hours before the mild downhill evened out into level ground. The trees gave way to a clearing, where shallow marshland filled with long reeds and the buzzing of insects greeted them. The wagon stood in plain sight, off to one side of the open area. Justus leaned on it from behind, covered in mud.

Galadrath could make out where the wagon had slipped and sank into the wet ground. The terrain was deceiving. The grass and mosses that covered the ground hid the silty mud, blurring the edge between where the proper marsh ended and the packed dry dirt began.

"Hyah!" Farrah yelled.

Galadrath heard the reins crack as she urged the two oxen forward. The wagon lurched a bit as Justus pushed and lost his footing. He fell back into the mud. The ground at his feet was churned into paste, and the thin banded wheels of the wagon were slowly sinking further with every attempt to break free.

"Well, that wasn't part of the plan," Emmett grumbled. "She gets angry when things don't go accordingly." He sprinted ahead, lifting his knees high with each stride, trying to keep his feet aloft as long as possible to avoid the mud's pull and maintain some of his speed.

Galadrath looked down at his own boots. The shiny black leather and high laces were both functional and fashionable. He sighed before following loosely behind Emmett, tracing a wide arc around where he thought the mud would dirty his footwear. When he came abreast of the wagon, still safely on dry ground, he spotted Farrah's sweaty, exasperated face.

"Are you stuck?" he asked loudly.

She simply shot a glare in his direction, unwilling to answer the snide question.

"Hyaaaaaa!" she screamed the guttural cry.

The panicked oxen lurched forward, faltering in their steps as their hooves dug into the mud, straining against their yokes.

"You know the divine metal that you had stated was so worthless? If I had a bit of that, I could fix this whole mess in less time than it takes to swallow one of those wooden pieces of trail meat," he said, enjoying himself immensely.

"You get your pompous, trussed-up ass down here and push, or else the next thing you'll be swallowing is your own manhood!" she screamed back at him.

"Well, now I know what she looks like when she's angry," Galadrath chuckled under his breath. Then he said loud enough so Farrah could hear over her own frustration, "Unhitch the animals. Give them a rest. I don't want them getting in my way."

He crouched, sitting on the soft grass, and began to unlace his boots.

"I said get over here! If this wagon doesn't move, I'll sell you to the crown myself!" she snarled.

He began to unbutton his shirt with one hand, while he collected the emblems from various pockets. He looked up, and saw Justus panting, folded over with his hands on his knees, exhausted from struggling in the mud.

"Farrah... just... give him... a chance," the young man said in between breaths.

She dropped her head between her legs, shaking it slowly, before she released the reins and splashed into the mud as she dismounted the wagon. She stormed toward where Galadrath was sitting. She swept her long, black hair back, gathered it in her hands, tying it up and away from where sweat had begun to collect on her neck. She stared down her remarkable nose at him.

Galadrath stood up, his shirt now neatly draped over his boots, and began to unbuckle his belt. He saw her eyes trace his arms and his chest—not taking in his features, but instead only following the map of scars to see where they led. When he unbuttoned his pants, she turned her back to him.

"Are you planning on seducing the wagon out of the mud?" she asked.

"If that's what it takes," he replied.

As he removed his pants, he watched as Justus, covered head to toe in mud, led the oxen away with the help of Emmett. Galadrath snatched up the handful of emblems and played with the ring on his finger for a moment.

"I'm ready," he said.

Farrah glanced over her shoulder for a second. She looked relieved that he was not completely naked. Other than the long, baggy shorts shielding his dignity, the only other cloth covering him was wrapped around his injured leg. The bandage was dried brown and yellow. The wound had bled, and his dried blood mixed with the remainder of the cream his mother had treated him with.

Farrah's eyebrow nearly touched her hairline. "You did what you did today with that bad leg?" she asked.

She turned back toward him, still inspecting the scars intermittently, her eyes flicking between his body and his face.

"Luckily, I don't have to rely on my legs alone," he said.

He opened his palm and shook the emblems together. Fire, a jagged blood-red quartz, sharp at the edges; Earth, a dull glimmer of brown, rough like impure ore. Air, smooth and translucent, shimmering like opal; and Water, a deep blue sapphire, its surface alive with waves catching the sunlight.

Farrah's anger dissipated, and her face was filled with greed and wonder. Galadrath knew that few people had ever set eyes on real emblems. They were closely guarded, items of immense power and worth, rarely displayed in the open.

He closed his fist again, pulling Farrah out of her short-lived trance. He quickly swat at his own bare shoulder, crushing a small insect that had landed there. She flinched, frowning at him.

"Gah. Bugs. I'll make this quick," he muttered.

He gingerly stepped into the soft mud, letting it squish in between his toes. The coolness was pleasant, and he allowed himself to enjoy it for a moment. When he reached the wagon, the buzzing of insects and chirping of birds were the only noises surrounding him. The posse of thieves stood together and watched him silently.

He positioned himself at the front of the cart and tested his footing. With his chains, he could have turned mud to dirt to stone. He also could have exerted his influence outwards and willed the wagon up onto the air—or shifted the ground under it into a ramp. The ring he carried, however, was insignificant in comparison. It was great for controlling blackstone, especially for Stepping, but it had diminished power over the fibers from which reality was woven.

He stuffed the emblems into his mouth, having nowhere else to put them, and drew upon the fire and earth emblems. The dense cocktail of energy flowed from his mouth into his veins. He felt heavy, as if he had gained a thousand pounds, his arms lethargic yet powerful. He conjured wide stones underneath his bare feet, the mud bubbling out of the way as the hard rock appeared in its space. He grabbed the pole that the oxen had been yoked to and began to pull ever so slightly. He was afraid of yanking too hard and breaking the shaft. If that happened, then they would be in a whole other predicament.

His feet pressed hard against the stones, causing them to sink. He gradually tugged harder, and the mud underneath the stones oozed outward. His arms and legs strained, veins bulging and muscles taut—emboldened by the energy they held. He leaned back, his heels and toes fighting to maintain their grip. He felt the wagon budge a little, and he increased his pressure, maintaining a fine balance between keeping his footing and adding momentum to the freight.

The wagon rocked forward in the muddy ruts, and Galadrath took a step back. As soon as his foot touched the mud, another stone appeared underneath it. He heaved slowly, as the wagon wheels were once again being resisted by fresh mud.

"Should we help?" Justus asked Farrah innocently.

The mud on his face and arms had dried, and he resembled the rough bark of a tree trunk. His bright blue eyes blinked through the cracked mud, and his light, effeminate tone betrayed his strange appearance. Farrah never answered him. Instead, she reached into a pouch on her waist and popped a piece of dried meat into her mouth.

Galadrath overheard the question in the relative quiet of the day and understood the lack of response. The stones beneath his feet grew and encased them completely up to the ankle. He stamped one after the other, hammering the stone anchors into the mud, and heaved with all his might. He heard one of the hitch pins bend and screech against its housing, and the wagon lurched forward. Step after step, each footfall of the immense weights sent a splatter of mud in every direction. The wagon slowly came loose, like a whale being dragged onto shore by a skinny fisherman.

Once on dry land again, the bulk of the freight seemed light in comparison. The energy still pulsed heavily in his muscles, as he led the wagon slowly in a wide arc, ensuring it would not roll back down the slight incline, and eventually dropped the post. He spit the emblems into his hand and poured the energy back into them, while simultaneously drawing in water. The cool crisp feeling was a relief from the heavy heat, and he began to wash off the splattered mud from his legs.

Justus ran over to where he stood.

"That was… unconventional," he said, tittering lightly.

"Have you never seen a man in his underwear pull a wagon from a cesspool with his bare hands before?" Galadrath joked.

"I…this would be a first for me. I've also never seen a man wash himself with water, coming from… seemingly nowhere," Justus said carefully.

Galadrath continued to rub away the mud, sweat, and grime. Water formed from his palms as if they had hidden faucets in them. He stopped for a moment and looked up at Justus.

"I'm not washing you," he said gravely.

"I didn't… I mean… I wasn't asking," the young man stammered.

"The mud will probably keep the bugs off you," Galadrath mumbled.

"Yeah, which would be a relief if I wasn't already so itchy," Justus said. He picked at the dried mud listlessly, flaking it off in small chunks.

"Fine. Strip," Galadrath sighed.

"*Strip? Really?*" Justus said, stunned.

"Or don't—that honestly suits me better," Galadrath said, as he finished washing his feet.

Justus urgently began tugging at his clothes and his boots, all caked in dried mud.

"By the Scar and everything that is unholy, what is going on there?" Emmett yelled.

The group broke out into laughter at Emmett's curse and question.

"I was beginning to wonder myself," Hester's voice rang out from among the trees.

They turned to watch her emerge from among some bushes, leading her horse on foot. Tibel followed closely behind.

"Looks like you found yourself a stray," Farrah greeted them.

Hester gave a short bow and waved Tibel past her.

"And so did I. Along with a whole bounty of mushrooms," Tibel said.

He pointed at a small deer carcass laying across the back of the horse, also taking a short bow.

Galadrath watched as the group made their reunion, before he turned his attention back to Justus. The young man was standing barefoot, wearing only pants.

"Pants, too. We'll wash you first, then your clothes."

"I don't have anything under this," Justus croaked.

"Gods living and dead. Who doesn't wear... Just cover your shame. Let's get this over with," Galadrath grumbled in frustration.

"But... the women..."

"Justus, I assure you it's nothing they haven't seen before," Galadrath said through gritted teeth, his frustration mounting.

"Even Hester?" Justus squeaked.

Galadrath glared with intensity at him, and then his look softened.

"I can't believe this is the most difficult thing I'll have to do today. Emmett, get over here! Bring a bed roll or a blanket or something," he yelled.

"Yes, my liege. Tibel, can you dress that deer? Seems I'm still missing a knife," Emmett said.

He retrieved a tattered blanket from one of the saddle bags and brought it over to Justus and Galadrath. He spread the ends in his hands, creating a meager partition, and the young man stripped off his pants.

Galadrath pushed the water from his hand, drenching the muddy brown curls. Justus began scrubbing vigorously, flecks of debris spattering onto Galadrath and the blanket. Emmett chuckled, and the others, all watching, joined in.

"The water must be cold, Justus!" Emmett teased.

The others roared with laughter, and Farrah walked over, standing next to Emmett just on the other side of the blanket from Justus. She and Emmett exchanged banter, snickering heartily at the scene. Farrah feigned peeking over the blanket, at which Justus recoiled. He hurried as quickly as he could, and even Galadrath chuckled at the absurdity of it all.

"Justus, I think this may be the last time you ask me for a shower," Galadrath smiled.

"I'll never clean myself again. I'd rather be an itching, stinking, stained mess than suffer this embarrassment. You'll all come to regret it," Justus sputtered.

They laughed again.

"I'll go next," Farrah said.

They all abruptly stopped, stunned at the honest statement. An image of her bare, olive skin and wet black hair crept into Galadrath's mind. He shook his head violently.

"No, no. No, no, no," Galadrath muttered.

She let the suspense grow for a moment, and then broke out in laughter. She winked at Emmett, walking away. Galadrath stared into the back of her head, still unsure if she was serious.

When Justus had finished, Galadrath quickly helped him clean his clothes, drying them with his fire emblem. Steam rose off the fresh garments, and both men dressed themselves.

Tibel had cleaned the deer and dug a hole, with a fire already lit inside. They all gathered close around the fire, using the smoke to deter the insects from preying on them. They traded details of the day's adventure, each recalling their own version of the events.

"We couldn't have done it without you, Vyhn," Farrah said earnestly. "You turned something that could have been treacherous into something quite easy. That was before you pulled the wagon out with your bare hands."

"Tibel, it was a good shot. A clean kill," Galadrath nodded at the man.

Tibel nodded back, and the two men were in silent agreement, their conversation on the hill now concluded.

"You all did very well," Farrah added.

"I didn't do *anything*!" Emmett said, annoyed.

"You're pretty good at holding up blankets," Hester grinned.

He glared at her.

"Maybe you should squire for Vyhn. You could fetch his boots and carry his things for him," she pressed.

They burst out laughing.

"Only if one of those things to carry is a knife," he muttered.

"You really haven't let that go, yet? You poor thing," Hester mocked him.

"Hester," Galadrath said, changing the tone of the conversation. "During your distraction, you'd mentioned the Patches. The guards definitely took it as a real threat. Are they this far south?"

"This far *North* you mean. The Serenity mountains, these hills surrounding us right now, are often the spawning ground for the Patchwork. The town of Silt, to the east, almost always has a garrison stationed there for protection. It's another reason why we hit the caravans at the pass—it's a good distance from any of the surrounding towns, except for Threshook. However, I'm sure they'll bring the Keepers into our sleepy little town, soon enough," Hester said.

"Do you think we can find some Patches? Where are we headed next?" Galadrath asked.

"You want to willingly go find a nest of Patches?" Tibel interjected.

Galadrath sighed and pulled the tiny blackstone from his pocket.

"I have a bit of a problem. Blackstone—this emblem right here—is the fuel source that allows me to Step. But it's not unending. If we keep this up, I'll soon run out. Patches are a known source of blackstone. If I can find them, then I can harvest it from them. If I'm lucky, I might even stumble upon some divine metal. Even unrefined, that would improve my worth considerably," he said.

"Dead or alive?" Farrah said.

"Dead is fine, preferred even," Galadrath stated.

"Have you fought Patches before?" Emmett asked. "You want us to go out and act like a bunch of Rat Catchers?"

"Yes, I have hunted Patches before. Sometimes there is a freak outbreak, and the Accusers are the fastest to respond. They send us out in teams of two or more, depending on how bad the infestation is," Galadrath answered.

"*Hunting* Patches. Madness. Two or more Accusers? We have one, and he's limping," Tibel turned to Farrah.

"I don't like that. I don't like that at all," Hester shook her head.

"Scar on your backside!" Emmett yelled. "I agree. We're not Many, not even Dusters. We're salt thieves!"

Farrah crossed her arms as she spoke firmly to the group, "And we want to be more than just salt thieves. We're heading up into the mountains in the morning, on our way to Bracken Village. We'll drop our freight there and put an ear to the ground. Maybe the local folk will know something. Surely, rooting out any Patches will serve them well. We may even earn some good favor, make a few friends for our cause. Those people don't live in these mountains because it is comfortable. They already share our disdain for the Crown."

She was met with sighs and grumbles, but no one argued any further with Farrah. She had made up her mind, and Galadrath could see she was a woman not easily swayed.

For the rest of the evening, the conversations were dampened, the mood somber. Even the flavorful mushrooms and the well-salted, roasted venison seemed dull.

Eventually, they each turned in, laying close to the dying embers of the fire as they slept.

13

THE WANDERER

THE MORNING HOURS MOVED slowly as they ushered the large wagon up the precarious, winding paths. The nights grew cooler with each passing day the higher they climbed into the rocky, sparsely vegetated mountains. The pine trees were large and old, untouched by wars and fires, axes, and hungry men.

The mood among them had lightened. The clouds were idle, offering only shade from the suns that danced around them. They had a few troubles navigating their freight through gullies and some other narrow gaps, but for the majority of their trip, it was peaceful. Nature surrounded them on every side, and between long intervals of silence, someone would speak up just to hear a voice again.

"I've never been to Bracken Village," Hester said.

"Not much to see, really—well out of the way. It's a little place where people don't want to be noticed," Emmett said.

"The old Bracken Fort is up there—what's left of it," Justus chimed in. "It has quite the historical significance, believed to be built sometime around the 5200's, a few hundred years before the first awakening. A lot of that history was lost, but it was said that the fort was used by refugees during the wars. It's been harboring lost souls for almost two thousand years—remarkable."

"Just old rubble and ghosts," Tibel murmured.

Justus continued, "Not *just*. They say that the Votary was to be buried at the fort. Or more accurately, they would have put up a marker in her honor, since she never returned from beyond the first Tread. She was the only one of the Few who did not have a tomb. Sad really, that such a hero was not remembered. Now people have turned her into a villain, saying her restless soul walks the earth, wreaking havoc on those who have forgotten her."

"More ghost stories. Bah! Mirrora—" Tibel grumbled.

"Don't say her name," Galadrath interrupted.

Tibel chuckled menacingly. "Just ghost stories. Why are you so afraid of her?" he said.

"The divine metals are a conduit for the emblems. When an emblem is created, it stores memories—sometimes messages. Make them large enough and they can even store personalities. I've touched emblems a thousand years old, and some much more recent. I've experienced memories you wouldn't believe. She's not a ghost—she's real, and she's done terrible things," Galadrath said.

"And you think I'll somehow summon her by mentioning her name?" Tibel laughed.

"Maybe it's not something you should test," Hester said softly.

Farrah demanded, "Leave it alone, all of you. We'll be there soon."

They crept up the hill, the oxen straining against their harnesses. A few simple structures came into view. Low, mortared walls of unhewn stone, covered in thatched roofs, were strewn about. Each building was nestled into the rocky terrain, some spewing trails of smoke out of squat chimneys. The rugged street was empty.

There was a popping noise, and something shattered.

"Scar be damned!" a woman's voice came from behind a building. "Let the gods know I curse them for putting me here in this heap! What was I thinking! Ruined! They'll all be ruined! Stupid pots! Scrape together a little clay and a little wood. Try and make a living. Blast! Blast it all! Slave away in the middle of nowhere and what do I get? Scrap! Not even scraps I can eat."

"Sounds like you, Farrah," Emmett said.

She glared at him. "Only when I have to deal with your idiocy."

Farrah brought the wagon to a stop, and they disembarked, heading toward the screams and profanity. On the far side of the building stood a woman in a large leather apron, inspecting a kiln. The heat coming off the bricks made the air into a shimmer, and the woman was attempting to open the kiln's door with a set of large, crude iron tongs, fruitlessly pulling with all her weight.

Galadrath watched her struggle, and after she had all but given up, she turned to them, pointing at no one in particular.

"Get over here and help me with this confounded thing! Watch out, it's hot," the woman said, straining.

Galadrath moved to the edge of the kiln and drew on the power of the ring. The waves of heat rippled from inside. He grabbed the handle on the door and pulled it outwards.

"It's hot, you fool!" the woman screamed.

She watched as nothing happened to Galadrath. His skin did not burn, and he showed no pain. He shifted the heavy door with one hand, and then it cracked—one side breaking off and falling to the ground. She jumped back, letting go of the tongs as the door dropped and shattered.

"That's not helping!" she scolded him.

Another pop came from inside the open kiln. The hot inside exposed to the cool air, and fragments of ceramic exploded outwards, showering them all in tiny pieces. Farrah and the group ducked out of the way of any more potential shrapnel.

"Clay was probably still too wet," Justus said.

"Don't you think I know that?" the woman said. "Now I'll just have to wait for this mess to cool off. Nothing left to salvage. What a waste." She threw her hands in the air, paced around in exasperation, and eventually came to a standstill, placing her hands on her hips.

"I can cool it down for you," Galadrath said hesitantly.

"No. Whatever you were doing, stop it," she glared.

They all stood around, not sure what to do.

"We're here to make some friends," Farrah said, shooting a glance at

Galadrath.

"I'm sorry, I was trying to help," he shrugged.

"Is that how you help? Break people's things?" she lashed out.

Still pacing back and forth around the broken items, the woman glanced into the opening of the kiln for a moment.

"No use. This project was doomed. I'm afraid I don't have the knack for it. Metal. Metal speaks to me. It can be hard, flexible, soft, and malleable. It sparkles when it's too hot, it hardens when it's cooled. It lives and speaks. Clay? Bah. For fools!" she yelled, speaking mostly to herself.

"You're a metal worker?" Emmett asked.

"Are you dull? Yes, that's what I just said. I am a metalworker. Well, I was. Now I'm stuck in this heap," she answered.

"Where is everyone else? We've got a shipment of salt to unload," Farrah said.

"Unload it yourself. We don't get shipments. Hardly anyone ever comes up here," the woman replied.

"Where is everyone else?" Farrah pushed.

"Putting up a new fence. Something passed through, scared a few of our cattle and they broke through, got loose all over the place."

Galadrath took a moment to look over the woman. She was short with bare arms, sinewy with strength.

"Something? Do you know what kind of something? Patches?" Hester asked.

The woman gave her a strange look.

"Not likely. A bear probably. Patches usually don't leave much alive. Besides, they usually head east, downhill toward Silt. Always east," she said.

"Toward the City of Light," Galadrath said absentmindedly.

"Sure. Or toward something they can eat. Listen, I don't really care what you're doing here, but I should get back to work," the woman said.

"And so should we," Farrah said, ushering them back toward the wagon.

"Why would the Patches be heading to the City of Light?" Hester asked Galadrath.

"Because they are partly made of the energy that makes up blackstone. Energy that holds memories. It is the last memory they have, the last order that was given to them that makes sense. To destroy the city and everything in it," he said.

"Who gave the order?" she asked.

"The Votary did. Which is why Thainegom never gave her a resting place, destroyed every statue of her, and erased her image from history. She was a traitor. Her last acts were to wage war and end the lives of hundreds of thousands of innocent people," he said.

"I didn't... know any of that," Justus said sullenly.

Farrah interrupted, "We've got a lot of freight to unload. Vyhn, would you mind using those muscles of yours?"

"I've got something more important to do," he replied flatly.

They looked at him with incredulity. He walked to the wide base of a large pine and sat there. He closed his eyes, feeling the power of the ring. He drew on the blackstone emblem and found himself in the dark fog of the surreal.

"Scar on my backside! Unbelievable that man..." Emmett's voice faded.

Galadrath could feel his body sitting under the cool shade of the pine, but his mind was Wandering. He searched through the distorted landscape, trying to bring his surroundings into view. It was painstaking work, imagining something that existed that he had never seen. It was like fumbling around a room in the dark, knowing it was filled with furniture, bumping into objects along the way, and then trying to guess what color they were in the complete blackness.

He found where the townsfolk were building the fence, the ghostly mirages of men and women struggling to dig holes and sink posts into the ground. He found clarity along the path his fellow travelers walked while escorting the cart. He could make out distant pieces of land and forest with certainty–places he had seen from between the trees, places his mind had stored in his subconscious.

Between those islands of clear memory lay vast uncharted layers of fog. He began to wander through it, attempting to suss out the reality with his mind. He traveled east, floating down rocky hillsides, far from where his body still sat underneath the tree. He bumped into a family of deer, and as he focused on them they appeared from the fog. One of the deer looked up, as if their natural senses could somehow perceive his touch.

He felt a cold chill, as if something was watching him as well. The deer scattered, and he turned to see what was there. Even in the dark fog and misshapen surroundings, he could feel the clouds of sinister energy moving toward him. The connection between the energy inside him and the energy they held made them clearer, requiring less concentration and proximity to make out.

The shambling shapes of the Patches walked past him. A few fumbled slowly forward, another lunged with more agility. His spine crawled as they moved close by, and he reflexively held his breath, unable to tell if they could sense his ghostly wandering. He followed loosely behind and watched as they corralled one of the deer against a small cliffside. The animal was trapped, afraid, with no clear avenue of escape. It broke out into a run, trying to skirt by the horrible shapes. The Patches exploded with a burst of unexpected speed, their deformed shapes and seemingly broken appendages acting suddenly with unnatural grace.

As the deer tried to pass, a slippery mass of broken bones and flesh latched onto it. The animal struggled to escape, pulling wildly at where the malformed arm had grabbed it, but the tentacle-like, black mass wrapped around its neck. Another one of the Patches lunged, gripping at the hind legs of the deer with several hand-like protrusions. A third Patch rammed into the deer, and Galadrath heard the animal scream as the monsters broke its bones, ripping it into pieces.

He opened his eyes and waited for them to adjust to the bright sunshine. The echoing scream of the dying animal still rang softly in his ears. He looked toward the wagon and saw the others still struggling with the immensely heavy barrels of salt. The wagon was still mostly full.

He stood and walked over.

"Fine time for you to nap, Vyhn," Tibel spat.

"I found them," Galdrath said.

"Found who?" Justus asked.

"The Patches."

"You were just sitting there. How'd you find them?" Justus asked with genuine interest. He was in the process of attempting to shimmy one of the unloaded barrels across the rocky road, toward the edge of a building. He seemed to forget what he was doing, paying no more attention to the barrel, and focused on his own question instead.

"I went for a walk. How long has this been going on?" Galadrath replied cryptically.

"About an hour. How long... how long was it for you?" Justus asked.

Galadrath could see the young man's mind open, trying to grasp ideas that were completely new to him. He watched the puzzled look, as if Justus was studying him like he would a book.

"Days, weeks, seconds. Time doesn't really pass. Like a dream or a memory, we remember people and places and events, but they don't pass–they don't move on," Galadrath answered.

"Truly profound. But you can't see... backwards in time?" Justus said, still deep in thought.

"What is a memory? Maybe you should ask what time is instead?" Galadrath asked rhetorically.

Galadrath took off his vest and hung it haphazardly over the edge of the wagon. He watched as Emmett grunted, holding a set of ropes tied around the waist of a barrel. They were slowly lowering the vessels, one by one, onto the ground. Tibel and Farrah were attempting to control the barrel's descent, but the diameter was too great to hold easily, and the small wooden lips were not thick enough to painfully support the weight on fingertips. Hester stood nearby, clutching her head in both hands, anxiously anticipating disaster.

Having removed any clothing that might get ruined by the strenuous physical labor, Galadrath drew on the emblems and wrapped his arms around the girth of the barrel. The ropes went slack, and Tibel and Farrah's straining faces showed signs of relief.

"I'll get this one," Galadrath said softly.

He walked to the edge of the nearest building, cradling the barrel in his arms. Adjusted his grip, he set it down softly and neatly against the wall.

"You can get them all. It's my turn to nap in the shade," Emmett said.

He brushed off his forearms, where the ropes wrapped around his arms had chafed him in the struggle. He placed his hands on his hips, surveying the scene, taking in the ease of which Galadrath had moved the freight. He shook his head and hopped down off the back edge of the wagon.

"I wouldn't mind some of that," Farrah said.

The others turned to her, not sure of what she meant.

"You know, the strength of ten men," she said flippantly.

Tibel chuckled.

"I'm sure you've had the strength of more than ten men, Farrah," he said.

The others snickered while Tibel laughed at his own joke.

"If only you were man enough, maybe you would know," Farrah said, looking coyly over her shoulder at him.

They all burst out laughing.

Galadrath hopped into the rear of the wagon, and began moving barrels closer to the edge where he could reach them from the ground.

"When I'm done here, we'll go hunting. We still have plenty of sunlight, and the Patches won't stay where I found them for long. We'll need spears. Whatever you can find—the longer the better, strong and stout. Boar spears are preferred, pikes and halberds. Barbed javelins and rope. Swords will not do much good, neither will rifles," Galadrath gave instructions while he worked.

"I've killed many men with a rifle. A spear can't do what powder and ball can," Tibel argued.

"How many hearts does a man have? How many heads? If you cut off his arm does he keep fighting? Patchwork... Patchwork haunts. Their names say everything. They are a woven mess of beasts. I've seen them made of Sturms, livestock, men, women, and children—Vermin, trees, insects. They stitch the flesh of the dead into themselves with slick black ichor. I've seen a Patchwork made out of swarms of rats. It had a hundred tiny biting heads, thousands of latticed bones and muscles making up arms and legs. Little rat hearts, each one smaller than a finger tip, all beating as one. Which head will your rifle aim for? Which heart will you pierce to kill such a horror? That one we had to burn to death. Almost nothing was left before the monster stopped moving, before it gave up on trying to kill us," Galadrath recalled.

"They're afraid of fire?" Justus wondered.

"They're afraid of nothing," Galadrath said flatly.

Galadrath hopped down from the wagon and hugged another barrel, carrying it toward the building. He heard the others murmur to themselves as they went to find the weapons he had requested. He knew what they were thinking. He knew the madness of what he had described and what they were about to set out to accomplish. Inside he glowed with pride, impressed that even after his speech, they would follow him.

His mind wandered as he worked. The death throes of the deer were replaced by the screams of fierce warriors. Fighting men crushed in their armor, torn asunder by the relentless writhing masses of Patches. The sounds of cannon shells exploding, ripping apart the ichor covered flesh. Then his mind shifted, and he thought of the banter of his current companions, how well they worked together. He thought of the conversations they had shared on the road. How he had gotten to know all of them a little. Then he felt a pang of fear, knowing that one misstep could get any one of them killed.

14

THE BAIT

"I GUESS SHE NEEDED some salt, after all. I told you, Vyhn, people can't eat gold," Farrah said.

The wagon was unloaded and pulled aside into a small space between a few trees, and the oxen unhitched and allowed to graze. Galadrath was helping load Hester's horse with the supplies they had scrounged up on such short notice. The wooden shafts of several spears stuck out from a makeshift bag attached to the back of the saddle. He could tell the points on them had most likely been tools, shoddily reforged into weapons long ago. Though they were crude, they would function as intended.

"Apparently they like eating more than they like fighting. Some of these weapons haven't seen use for some time," he replied.

"Most people do," she said.

"That's true—most people do. But not us, right gang?" he asked.

He was trying to get a feeling for the atmosphere between them. They were thieves, not hardened warriors.

"Hear, hear!" Emmett yelled in affirmation.

Galadrath laughed. It seemed to him that the man was always ready to kill something.

They headed out. Galadrath led them down a small animal trail winding down the precarious embankment. They had far to go and would undoubtedly venture into rarely traveled terrain.

Moving slowly, Galadrath took the opportunity to explain what they could expect. He made sure to emphasize the lack of compassion they would receive from their enemy. There were no mind games to be played. Even a wild animal could, at least, be scared away, intimidated by gestures, or corralled by groups. He laid out a simple plan that would keep most of them farther from harm but leverage their skills.

"Keep your distance. If they come for you, stay away. They can jump and lunge farther than you can expect, so always be ready. Never turn your back. Keep a spear leveled at all times—if they come for you, plant the base in the ground and find a mark with the tip. Leave the weapon if you have to; we have plenty. They are immensely strong, and if you're caught in their grip, you will die. Let the shaft of the weapon take the brunt of the force. We'll try to harpoon them with the javelins and tie them off. I can't guarantee the ropes will hold, or even that the strongest of these weapons won't snap clean off. So stay away. I can't stress that enough," Galadrath said as they walked.

"What will you do?" Farrah asked.

"We'll set up close by, weapons at the ready. I'll try and bait them in one at a time, hopefully weakening them before they get close," he replied.

"The Grim Bait! Hah!" Emmett roared.

Galadrath could see the look on his face—and saw the same on Farrah's and Tibel's. They had fought before; they were emboldened by the thought of victory. Maybe he had underestimated them. Hester and Justus looked more timid, uncertain of what they were heading toward. He looked up at the sky, trying to find the suns through the cover of the trees. They had wasted more time preparing than he had hoped, and the travel through the terrain was worse than he had thought. He did not want to fight in the dark, and he most certainly did not want to spend the night in the woods so near their prey.

"Quiet now. We're close," Galadrath said.

He gestured for them to follow the winding switchbacks around outcroppings of brush covered rocks. Using the emblems, he made a more direct descent down the hillside, bounding down the treacherous incline with grace and precision. He ensured that they would not be ambushed. Soon, Galadrath reached the place he had seen in his mind. He waited while the others caught up to where he stood. Blood splatter painted the rough trees. Bushes were churned up by heavy feet and claws. What was left of the deer was scattered in every direction. Bloody tufts of fur, bone, and viscera clung to the otherwise uninterrupted nature. The aftermath of the single act of violence tainted the natural beauty of the landscape.

"You're going to be the *bait*?" Hester said, gawking at the scene.

"It would have taken them some time to consume it. They can't be too far ahead," Galadrath muttered.

"What was *it?*" Hester asked.

"A deer," Galadrath replied.

"They ate it?" she asked, her voice quivering.

"They took it in—they made it part of them. We eat. What we devour becomes part of us, in a way. For them, they skip a few steps. They do not build muscles—they steal them and stitch them in. They'll be stronger than when I spotted them," Galadrath said.

"Perfect. That's just what we need," Farrah said sarcastically.

Galadrath sighed. "We have ground to cover. Time is the only thing we have to fight right now," he uttered.

"Then, we go," Farrah stated.

She was invested, and the chase had put her on edge. Galadrath could see the anticipation of victory and the idea of what they would actually fight were separate motivations.

"I'll be here, and I'll find them. Move northeast, down the pass. We'll head them off as soon as I know where they are," Galadrath said.

"What if they catch us before we catch them?" Justus asked.

"I'll be there, trust me," Galadrath said, closing his eyes as they left unwillingly.

He flew down the embankment, his mind racing to find his prey. He crashed into the fog of the surreal world, as if there were no terrors to be found. He catapulted himself down the foggy landscape, searching.

He felt the sky move underneath him; he felt the grip of the earth swelling above him; he felt the pull of the Earth Mother, beckoning him down, but his own will overreached hers as he plummeted through the forest. His mind was like a hammer, propelled by the gods living and dead, ready to strike against the evil that encompassed the dread landscape of his mind.

He saw the Patches slowly making their way down the hills. Their botched shapes, cruelly moving toward their next kill, were easy to spot. Galadrath stumbled through his own mental fog, trying to make out the shapes of the objects with which he collided. He dropped off the side of a cliff, his spirit hurtling through the unknown haze and onto the new, unforeseen ground. He splashed into a pool of fog that materialized as a horse. He immediately made out Hester's steed. The group had moved with speed down the hill, and they were aptly positioned for the ambush. He knew the slowly shambling horde of Patches were not far behind.

He opened his eyes, the black mist dripping from him in the real world.

"Here! Quickly, tie off the harpoons! Unload the weapons!" he urged, his orders coming in a hushed breath.

The black fog rolled off his tongue, and the others, already on edge, reeled at the sight of him appearing from nowhere.

They made ready, following the orders in a silence, interrupted only by the jostling of spear shafts and clanging of poorly formed iron. He pointed briefly at the natural downward slant between the rock faces.

"I'll put the first one there. You have very little time before they arrive," he said.

His words had barely reached their ears before he disappeared in a fog.

Galadrath appeared on a rocky outcropping above the monsters. The ring's power was already in use, and he filled his veins deeply with the elements. The most limber of the Patches was his first target.

He blasted gouts of fire downward off the hillside, instantly conflagrating the terror in a heap of pure fire. It turned vaguely, showing a head of a woman posed on four claws and just as many hooves, and shot up the steep cliff toward him.

Galadrath pushed with the earth in his veins against the rock wall. Precariously placed boulders, put there by untold years of erosion, answered his call. As the beast leapt up at him, a rockslide came crashing down on it. The monster was pinned under the rocks, limbs flailing wildly.

He jumped from where he was standing. As he fell he drew his swords, the bright steel shining in the light of the suns. The earth energy inside him made him feel like a thousand pounds, and he willed it downwards. He carved into the remaining heads sticking out from beneath the boulders. With both blades lashing out, Galadrath severed the screaming faces of inhuman flesh, scoring the earth deeply as he cut with every power-filled fiber of his body.

The cries of pain, the human voices of the monster, finally subsided. He looked up quickly, and the others converged on him with unfeeling, graceless movements.

Three more. I thought I only saw three. They must have spawned another one.

He jumped down from the rubble and carnage and ran toward the incline between the cliffs. The Patchworks followed, and he could feel the hate radiating behind him.

Galadrath knew he had given up the high ground, and they were now chasing him down hill. High ground was a defensible position; it was also a very offensive position. Charging downhill was much easier than having to fight elevation upwards. However, there was a bit of information in his mind that was rarely shared: those rules only applied to beings who followed the natural laws. For an Accuser, these tactics meant nothing.

Spikes of stone blasted from the ground and impaled the first of his demonic victims. The thrashing hands, made up of bones and muscles, skewered on the defenses, wrapped their tendrils around the multitude of spikes and ripped at them. Still squirming, it snapped off the igneous spears.

Galadrath vanished, before appearing behind the thing. He blasted a razor of air in the direction of the beast as it freed itself. Two of its arms, still clutched around the crystalline growths, were severed at what could be called a shoulder. There was a melancholy scream from the mass of flesh and black ichor.

"Gyaaaaaa!" Emmett roared.

He lanced the already injured horror with the long iron speartip. As soon as the blow landed, the man planted the end of the shaft into the ground and backed away. The creature screeched and threw itself against the remaining spikes, the spear propping it up against its own will.

There was a boom, and the impact of a bullet against the thrashing monster. Galadrath looked back and saw Tibel standing with the long, smoking barrel of the just-fired rifle.

Idiot. Guns are no good. I told you that.

Then came the other Patchworks. The first fell like a drunk over the top of the hillside, not caring what it landed on. It stood on twisted limbs, each shape indistinguishable, using them interchangeably as arms or legs. The bulk of the monster was three times the size of a person, and Galadrath could tell that it had consumed the lion's share of the deer. The dead head of the animal, adorned with a small rack of antlers, poked out from the center of the monster. It looked like some long-deceased, disembodied king, wearing a crown of the damned. The second was leaner and longer, like a panther hastily painted on a canvas of corpses, which launched itself onto the trunk of a tree, clearing a twenty-foot gap through the air. They were beginning to maneuver, to corner their prey, more clever than Galadrath remembered.

The impaled Patch squirmed, slowly breaking free from the impediments that had skewered it. Hester launched a makeshift harpoon into its side, the barbed points hooking deeply into the soft, half-rotten flesh. Galadrath was surprised at her strength. Her lithe, petite figure—fueled by fear and adrenaline—was very capable with the weapons. His eyes followed a thick rope attached to the harpoon, its end fastened around a large tree to restrain the Patch. More ropes lay ready, also tied to sturdy trunks, neatly arranged with additional harpoons to reinforce the trap. Without hesitation, she ran back to another coil and grabbed the harpoon laying on top.

Galadrath ran away from Hester towards the precarious hillside, ignoring the impaled Patch to protect their flank. The form of the panther Patch slowly descending through the branches, loomed above him. Black goo dripped along the pine needles and onto him, as the creature began to move more quickly, heading down toward him. He willed the ground under the tree to boil and churn, the large trunk beginning to sway as the roots came loose, and pressed his shoulder into the bulk of the tree, and it began to topple slowly. The moving tree caused the monster to shift, and would soon be hanging precariously over another cliff edge.

The crowned Patch was now headed in her direction. It swerved in a serpentine pattern. Galadrath could not discern if the movement was intentional, but it was effectively unpredictable. Hester's second harpoon sailed through the air at the gaunt human head of the creature and bounced off the jawbone, the barbs stripping the flesh from the dead face. She turned and ran, and Farrah stepped up, a spear in each hand.

Farrah planted the spears into the ground and pointed the tips at the approaching target. It leapt forward at her, and she braced herself. She flinched at its unexpected speed, and the first spear point dipped, catching the beast in the midsection. It flailed wildly, massive arms of bone and grisly flesh wrapping around the spear shaft. It swatted away the second point, and the spear was flung aside, wrenched from Far-rah's white-knuckled grip. It pushed forward, and the metal crossbar of the spear buckled, scraping against large bones in the monster.

The spear shaft snapped under the weight, and Farrah collapsed as it broke, her only weapon folding under the onslaught of the beast. A huge makeshift claw grabbed at her torso, and she screamed in fear.

Galadrath Stepped passed her, placing himself right beside the monster. He heard her bones begin to pop, her chest giving way to the iron grasp of the Patchwork. He swung both swords in a wide downward cleave, severing the arm of the monster at the middle joint. His swords, now both drenched in black ichor, sprayed an arc onto the rocks nearby. He spun around, carrying the momentum of the weapons and adding to their speed. A half-circle carried the blades back into the center of the target, an elegant pirouette placed the steel deep in the core of the beast.

"Get out!" he yelled at Farrah, laying at his feet.

She was unresponsive, but he heard the guttural, high-pitched war-cry of Justus. The young man leapt at the monster, planting a spear in its back. Galadrath watched as the man refused to let go, and the beast turned to face him. Justus whipped around, still clinging to the spear like a toothpick jammed into an hors d'oeuvre, his body flailing at the end of the shaft like a precariously placed garnish.

It bought Galadrath a precious second to do something he had not done in years. He reached down and grabbed Farrah, and he Stepped with her. He had moved objects countless times—his clothes and weapons could all be brought under his influence and Stepped willingly with him. He had even moved bodies, dead flesh. The complexities of plants and animals did not matter if they came willingly, but moving a mind—a soul—through the fog between worlds was not an easy task. An untrained mind might wander into the darkness, never to return.

He met her eyes as the black fog billowed around them. Her mind was wrapped in the chaos of the blackstone. She opened her mouth to scream, but her voice never came. The reverberating agony of a thousand dying men rang in his ears, and he watched in horror as a set of ichor covered fingers began to claw their way out of her mouth.

In an instant the hands were gone. The fog dispersed, and the warmth of the day played on their skin again. Farrah gasped for breath, her face covered in agony. He could see the fear in her eyes, but it was overshadowed by the pain she felt with every breath. He nodded at her softly, a silent reassurance that she was once again safe. Hester's horse snorted and bounced on its hooves, unsettled by the sudden appearance of the two people and the deadly monsters still fighting the rest of the group a short distance away.

He looked up and saw Justus thrown from his grip on the beast's back, landing heavily in a dense shrub.

"Leave him be! You demon!" Hester screamed.

She hurled another harpoon into the belly of the twisting monster. She grabbed the rope attached to the weapon, now firmly lodged in the writhing mass of flesh, and in a vain attempt, she tried to keep it from pursuing Justus. Hester was immediately pulled off her feet and dragged behind the shambling heap of meat, heading toward her friend.

Galadrath sighed heavily, the black smoke pouring from his mouth. Moving Farrah had tapped heavily into his concentration, physically draining him. But the selfless heroics of the young Hester, throwing herself at a superior enemy, had given him a second wind.

I am not done. I can not be done.

He Stepped in front the lurching mound of rot, shielding Justus where he lay. He poured every ounce of power he could from his fingertips, and a lance of glowing molten rock blasted forth, cleaving the creature completely in two. He felt the energy burn his fingertips, the power carving small, fractal patterns into his own flesh. The ring was not enough to channel the amount of power he was trying to control, and his body would pay the price.

The stench of burning meat filled his nostrils, and the creature collapsed unceremoniously. He quickly turned and surveyed the scene. Emmett was in a reckless fury, launching anything at hand into the struggling Patch, still partially impaled and grievously wounded. He threw spears and javelins, then makeshift harpoons, and finally, stones. He even tore his own purse off his belt and launched it at the body of the horror. Tibel had abandoned his rifle and was fueling the rage of Emmett, passing him any weapon he could find. The monster was failing, each stab of a spear or bludgeon of a rock weakened it. When Emmett ran out of ammunition at hand, he yelled the foulest of insults; yet the monster still lived.

Galadrath turned again, looking at the partially toppled tree he had left only moments ago. The Patch that had mounted the bulky trunk had made its way off its perch, and no longer dangled above the over-hang. It was heading toward the duo of fighting men, moments away from tearing them to pieces.

"Run! Emmett! Tibel! Run!" Galadrath yelled, pointing at their new assailant.

They turned and saw the fresh wreck of decaying flesh bearing down on them. A harpoon shot from beyond his periphery. Hester had wrenched it loose from the smoldering corpse and, once again, landed a blow with perfect aim. The tip sunk in deep on the moving target, and the rope uncoiled, immediately growing taut. The events of the struggle now had the rope winding at odd angles between the thick tree trunks, and as the creature yanked hard against the restraint, the rope snapped up as it pulled tight and batted Hester to the side.

The momentum of the creature met the unyielding rope, and it was violently tugged from its trajectory, straining against the harpoon. Galadrath was out of energy. His hands burned painfully, and it took all his strength to toss his swords the distance between him and Tibel and Emmett.

"Kill it! Kill it now!" he yelled hoarsely.

They glanced quickly between him, the filthy steel blades, and the Patch barely held back by its leash. Emmett snatched up the sword that landed closest to him. Holding the cutting edge in both hands, he hammered the pommel into the monster.

Galadrath's vision faded slightly, the image of the red haired man becoming blurry. He rallied back into consciousness, the sounds of bludgeoning wet meat stirring him from his exhaustion. He looked up from where he had collapsed. The two men wildly hammered away at the collapsed Patch. Emmett's hands were blood red. His skin flayed and peeled open around his palms, as he stuck over and over at the lifeless corpse of the shambling horror, the blade of the sword cutting into his hands with every strike. Tibel had the other sword by the handle, sucking air deeply and quickly, completely out of breath as he paced side to side around the monster, looking for heads, organs, and anything moving. He whacked the steel edge into the pile of stitched flesh and bone listlessly.

"It's done. Stop, brother," Hester said.

She limped toward the last act of violence and carefully placed a hand on Emmett's back as he continued swinging the improvised hammer, as though he were mindlessly chopping wood. His eyes were wild with hate.

"Stop, you're hurting," she said softly, hiding her own pain.

He drew in a heavy breath and dropped the sword to the ground. Blood dripped from his half-curled hands, and they finally relaxed, as if the fight in him was draining away with his own lifeforce. Galadrath stood, uneasy on his feet, and approached them.

"That's not how I expected that would go," he said, slurring slightly.

"We almost died. You almost had my sister killed!" Emmett's temper flared again.

"Tibel, can you make the rounds?" Galadrath asked.

The man was mostly uninjured, though his pride showed the worst wear. He was still gasping for air, and Galadrath could tell that the man, accustomed to sitting on a hill with a rifle, was not prepared for the exhaustion that came with killing up close.

"Farrah is just down the hill by the horse. Justus needs some tending to, as well. I think he struck his head when he was thrown—please," Galadrath said.

"Gods living and dead! I'll take care of Farrah—you go and see to the boy," Emmett spat.

He had no concern for his own injuries, and anger fueled his decisions. Galadrath could see the care in his eyes, even behind the mindless rage. Tibel nodded and went to tend to Justus, while Emmett took off in a half jog, heading down the hill, still dripping blood from the deep cuts on his hands.

"Are you alright?" Galadrath asked Hester.

She looked down at her right calf where the rope had struck her and massaged it lightly with one hand.

"I'll be fine. The others need me," she replied, and hobbled away.

Galadrath sighed heavily again.

They'll live, I think.

His head felt like it had been slowly crushed in a vice. He had no energy left, but he knew what they had come for, and his work was not done yet. He pulled on the power of the ring and began to consume the ichor covered flesh of the Patchwork, dissolving it into nothingness. He could feel the cold dread of the blackstone filling his veins and the haunting murmurs that accompanied the energy. He slowly poured it into his own emblem, the mass of the stone increasing in size.

As the energy poured into him, he felt the sliver of memory tug at his mind. It was familiar, not ancient like some, but relatively new. There was hardly enough energy to convey a complete thought—or the focus to impart a message. It was simply a latent sense of sorrow, a final hopeless act of sadness punctuated by a notion of peace. The feeling was eerily familiar. It was the last memory of the Votary, before she died—before the gods were shattered.

When he was finally done consuming and processing the corpses of the nightmarish beasts, his mind was a blank slate. He listlessly collapsed near the others. He did not have the energy to speak.

Galadrath heard the short, painful breaths of Farrah. She was laying on her back, trying to steady her broken ribs. He looked at her gaunt face, beads of sweat trickling on either side of her proud nose. Her lips were gathered close, forcing shallow bits of air between them. He rummaged in a pouch at his belt and produced a collection of brittle purple flowers.

"For the pain," he said.

Farrah glanced over at him quickly and focused her eyes on the leaves suspended between his fingertips. She reached out slowly, gingerly trying to grasp them without upsetting the rest of her body.

"One at a time," he added, extending his hand toward her.

She took one of the petals and tucked it behind her lip, contorting her face momentarily at the fresh pain caused by moving too abruptly.

"The Patches are merely innocent children, playthings. The true terror lies in that place—that dark and cold place that exists behind... everything," she mumbled through the flower.

"They are far from innocent. They are the horrible creations of a twisted mind. Don't dwell on the feelings. They are not yours—they are someone else's," Galadrath replied.

"Whose are they? You looked different. In that moment, you were an older man, with kind brown eyes. You *loved* me," Farrah professed.

"Those are just old memories, and they are not yours. Leave it be," he murmured.

"But you... loved me, so much. And I loved you. And we were torn apart. It felt... like years," Farrah said, painfully speaking each breath.

"You lived a moment that isn't yours. You saw the mind of the Votary, you saw her love," he forced out the words.

"For who?"

He sighed softly.

"The Ashmaker. The first Prince of Death."

15

THE LIVING AND THE DEAD

THE SUNS WERE ALREADY sitting low on the horizon. Seli and Sari had shone their rays on the motley group of travelers, and with the help of the treasonous Accuser, they had snatched victory from amongst the corpses of the Patches.

They had convened just a short distance from where the fight had taken place. The hillside below the craggy cliff sides that was now covered with vivid signs of a daring fight: abandoned weapons, broken branches, trampled vegetation, and blood and ichor.

Farrah was deep asleep, her lips stained purple from the Nightbloom flower, after she fed herself petal upon petal in an attempt to abate the pain of her injuries. Emmett had wrapped his hands in shreds of clothing, the fabric already soaked through with his blood. Tibel had taken it upon himself to make a fire and was sulking in the nearby dusk as he collected firewood.

"We need to stitch those wounds, Emmett," Hester said. "And Justus, please, drink some water. You've hardly said a word."

Emmett grunted, and the young man looked vapidly at Hester.

"The first... the first Prince of Death," Justus said.

Galadrath stuffed a piece of jerky into his mouth. He chewed vigorously at the hunk of salted meat and nodded. He had rallied from the complete drain of his energy, but it came with a fierce hunger. He was dead tired, but he could not sleep until his belly was full. He stood, wobbling slightly, and crossed in front Justus, looming over Emmett where he sat.

"We need to stitch those hands. You're still bleeding, and the way you keep fidgeting with those bandages, the blood will never set," Galadrath said.

Emmett growled, before he offered up his hands. Hester looked at Galadrath in thanks and began to unwrap the myriad of cuts on the calloused hands of her brother. She delicately unwrapped a small bundle of supplies, unpacking the variety of cures and tools. She collected a small needle, painstakingly whittled from the bone of a bird beak, the natural curve of the bill forming the instrument. She threaded the eye with a sturdy but lean silk thread.

"It's gonna hurt. Want something for the pain?" she asked sweetly.

Emmett grunted and held his lacerated palms up toward her. She offered the needle up to Galadrath for a moment, and his drained mind took a moment to catch her meaning. He conjured a small flame and ran it along the length of the needle, burning off anything that may have collected on it during their travels.

"You'll have to clean his hands, too," she said.

Galadrath drank in the seriousness displayed on her fine features. Hot water poured from his own hands and he began to wash them vigorously. The water was hot enough to steam in the cooling evening, and cascaded from between his joints, pattering softly onto the ground below as he rubbed the flecks of dirt and sweat from them. He turned back to Emmett, and the water flowing in his veins became icy. He spread the cool water carefully along the flayed skin and muscle of the bulky hands, hoping the frigid water would numb as much as it could. He brushed the flecks of congealed blood from the cuts and watched as the irrigated wounds poured forth more fresh blood. Some of the injuries were lighter and had already begun to maintain themselves. Others were grievous cuts, deep into the flesh, and he scrubbed at them.

Emmett's eyes did not waiver. The hatred that had filled them earlier was still present, and the firelight danced in them like the devil in his heart did. It was rare for Galadrath to see such unrelenting perseverance in a person, but he could see the wild in the man. The Sons of Dradofir, the wild men, were somewhere in his bloodline.

Hester stitched carefully, sewing the cuts with as much grace as she could muster. She knotted each one carefully as Emmett clenched and unclenched his hands, making sure that his own bonded skin would not inhibit his ability. She worked in between his fingertips, placing the fine bone needle on either sides of the joints, working with dexterity and calm as she put him back together. Galadrath watched closely, both admiring her work and care and trying to make his own uneducated assessment of the damage. Emmett had meaty, tough hands, and even the deepest cuts had not touched tendon or bone. His firm grip on the blade had made sure of that.

"We all agreed to this, in more ways than one. We didn't know what was expected of us, but we all followed. Thanks for what you did," Emmett said, his words pockmarked with pain.

"Thank your sister. She wrangled those things like they were stubborn cattle. That arm of hers can pull up the skirts of the Scar with one hand," Galadrath uttered.

Emmett gave a brief chuckle, between the sharp pricks of the needle. "I saw what you did for Farrah. You pulled her from the clutches of that hell. She overreached and put herself in danger. You said it yourself—if we got too close it would be over," he said.

"I put her there, so I had to pull her out. She did her best, willing to give everything," Galadrath mumbled.

"The Ashmaker. The first Prince of Death," Justus chimed up.

"Even a blow to the head won't stop that big head of yours from churning," Emmett said, annoyed.

"Glad to see you're doing well," Galadrath said.

The young man scratched his head precariously. Dried blood matted his hair, and he tried to alleviate an itch without dislodging the clot.

"What did Farrah see? She said you loved her," he asked, a dull tone in his voice that was seldom heard.

"Boy, that's a tail filled with nails. It's not one you want to chase," Emmett laughed.

"Stay your words, Emmett," Justus said.

Emmett glanced back and forth between Hester and Galadrath, not sure how to take the statement. It was rare Justus found any of his curiosities important enough to interrupt someone, and never important enough to silence them. But Justus forgot what he had said as soon as he said it, and only his question was left, hanging in the air.

"The first Prince? You mean to tell me that the Ashmaker, the first of his name, over a thousand years old, dead and gone, killed by the Few, still has his memories floating around?" Justus said coherently.

"This world is overrun with them," Galadrath said. "The Few, the second Ashmaker, and all those that came and went—their fibers touch everything on the two continents. Memories of the Shattering rained despair across the world. Each act is captured, each stone has its own secrets. It doesn't matter, though. None of it matters. All you need to know is that Farrah has seen a piece of the past, and she'll have to return to the present," Galadrath said.

"But, you can uncover those secrets?" Justus said.

Galadrath could see the young man's mind reeling, once again probing the fabric that separated the known from the unknown. Justus had an insatiable curiosity, but this was not a topic a bright youth should delve into. Galadrath wished he did not know as much as he did and hoped to shield anyone else from it. He could hear the silent screams probing at the back of his head; he could feel the fresh horror of the monsters he had consumed.

"Some stones are best left unturned," he replied gravely.

Justus moved his mouth, but the words did not come out. Galadrath watched as the young scholar mulled over the bits of information he was given, then turned his attention to the sewing work of Hester. As she finished, Galadrath poured more water from his fingertips, washing the stains from her brother's hands with care.

The group settled, each nursing their own wounds, and kept to themselves. They had a cumbersome night, sleeping in shifts, each one waking early from a well-deserved slumber to stare into the night, watching for anything nefarious in the darkness.

And they were all haunted by the words of Galadrath.

Farrah woke with a gasp. Pain settled on her face with sweat clinging to her like morning dew. In the darkness, before the suns had begun to cross the sky, she only heard her own breathing.

"Sleep, sleep if you can, or be still," Galadrath said softly.

His figure was dark, cloaked in the faintly shimmering blackness of his new uniform.

"Walter. Save me, Walter," her voice was hushed, crying between broken ribs.

Galadrath was afraid this would happen.

"He's gone, Farrah. But you're here, you're here with me. Try and remember who you are. Forget him," Galadrath said.

"Where did my love go?" she murmured.

"He's not your love. He's been dead for a thousand years. Farrah, remember when you were sitting on top of the wagon? Stuck in the mud? Do you remember my name?" he asked.

"Vyhn. Galadrath, the Accuser who killed Deitrich," she strained.

He paused for a moment. He had expected the worst from her condition, traveling between worlds. He had not expected the painful truth.

Galadrath could see she was still not herself. He could make out the fear in her eyes, possessed by memories that were not her own.

"Farrah," he said.

She looked up at him with hate and jealousy. Her eyes glowed with subtle elegance in the twilight. He could see the vengeance boiling up in her, the slumbering surreality could not be allowed to grow.

He walked over to where she lay, reached over her, and kissed her. She did not expect it, and the hate and jealousy behind her eyes faded.

As if some spell had been broken, as if the action had loosed the bonds that had wrapped themselves around her mind, he saw her come back to herself, truly awakened.

She looked at him, her face turning from a longing want to a jaded skepticism. Her brow furrowed and met the edge of her nose, creating a deafening glare of resentment.

"I can still feel him, and her, but they feel farther away," she shivered.

She tried to sit up but only managed to prop herself up on her elbows.

"Why did you kiss me?" she asked, each breath painful.

He spun on his heel to face her where she was laying.

"I did it for you. I have a wife, a family. I have oaths that I've taken," he growled.

He could see her veins chill, her posture changing as she saw the reflection of his regret. Whatever she had felt—whatever love she still had in the fiber of her being—was crushed under the booted feet and harsh tone of the Accuser.

"I've only made two promises in my life. When I was a boy, I swore to uphold the sixteen swords of Barkrill, as a Pillar. The second I made to my wife. I do not break promises," he said.

"You haven't," Farrah said, stunned by his words. "You saved my life. Twice."

He turned toward her, and his gaze softened.

"Understood. I am a man of honor—it is all I have," he said.

"I felt like I was trapped in a fog, like I was in her body—my mind caged, looking out through the windows of her eyes. How did you know it would work, the kiss?" she asked softly.

"People are simple. Humans are tied to emotion, enthralled by the moment. We love many things, but by far, we love connection. The other memories, we learn to forget. *She* wanted to be kissed by the man she loved, but he was long gone. So she kissed the man who had taken his place. Her last act was one of love, and she didn't want to die alone. The memory you were trapped in ends with that kiss, because they both died in that moment," Galadrath mumbled.

"Now I feel ashamed, like I'm an imposter to the beauty they shared. How do you do it? Carry so many lifetimes? Is it always like this? Do you live your whole life in the shadows of other people's memories?" she asked.

"It's not always like this. You were lucky to find such a... pleasant memory in the fog. It could have been much worse. I do my best to make sure they live in my own shadow, not the other way around. It's a skill I was taught long ago, not to let them take control," he said.

He turned to leave into the darkness of the morning.

"Where are you going?" she asked.

"There are still a few things I have to collect," he answered.

Galadrath retraced the steps of the fight. Each moment rang in his mind like a bell, a claxon of doom. In the darkness, he recalled every thrust, every feint, every killing blow. He made his way to where each of the Patches had fallen, to collect the ore amongst their deathbeds. He had consumed their ichor coated flesh and filled his own blackstone with their power. But divine metal could not be absorbed—could not be soaked into the flesh of even the most powerful of the Many. He bent over at the final resting place of each monster and rummaged through the dirt and loose rocks, rooting around for the tiny, raw pieces of the Shattered Children.

He spent the quiet moments letting his fingers do the work while his mind wandered. He was worried about Farrah and what she had seen, how it would change her. Just like any experience changes a person—sometimes only the tiniest bit—inherited experiences were just as impactful. He had not lied to her; it could have been much worse. He began to recall his own first trip into the fog, when he was just a young boy, deep underneath the caverns and tunnels of the Lowest House.

When he had opened his mind, the blackstone in his body had covered him, like he was plunged into a pool of ice water. The edges of his vision were a foggy mirage of darkness. A woman emerged. He could sense her maternal instinct, her genuine care. She walked slowly toward him, in a long black dress, and she reached out a satin-gloved hand. He had looked at her skeptically, like the lost child he was, and she was a stranger who was willing to help him find where he belonged.

He had squinted at her face, trying to make out her features, but it was as if her face mimicked his own ideas—as if he looked at her through a warped mirror, and every time she changed her expression, her face shifted between familiar and that of a complete stranger. He had taken her hand, and they had walked for a long time together, wandering through blurs of violence and loss and unending fields of grief and pain. When she delivered him from the fog, she never spoke. She only smiled and laughed, as if she had a secret that he could not understand—as if she had seen his fate. That laughter, that feeling of not knowing, still haunted him.

Galadrath ran his fingers listlessly through the dirt, sifting for the tiny specks of the divine ore, as he tried, years after that day, to picture her face once more—to finally place her smiling features with the name that haunted him.

"Vyhn," Tibel broke his thoughts.

Galadrath looked up, pocketing the last of the ore.

"The others are awake. I've cobbled together some breakfast. We should eat and get back up the hill," Tibel added.

"You're right. It'll be slow going," Galadrath replied.

He stood and walked back to the others alongside Tibel. It was a short breakfast, and between bites, they talked some and even laughed sparingly. Their spirits had begun to pick up, and the victory, even in their current condition, was beginning to sink in. Other than Farrah, the others were able to work while dealing with their injuries. They bundled up the salvageable weapons and ropes, along with their own supplies. When they were about ready to leave, Galadrath turned his attention to Farrah.

"You're going to have to move. We can help you up onto the horse, that way you won't have to walk," he said.

Hester had been riding most of the morning, using the reins to guide the animal slowly through the littered mess, her feet dangling out of the stirrups. Her one pant leg was rolled up to the knee, showing a swelling horizontal bruise wrapping around her calf. When Galadrath first saw the shades of red, purple, and black covering most of her leg, he was surprised the bone had not broken. She wandered on horseback alongside the men, while they collected the weapons and arranged them along the horses bags and pack.

If Farrah took the horse, Hester would have to walk, and he felt bad even suggesting it, but they had to move, and Farrah was by far off in the worst condition. He had heard her bones break and hoped that was the extent of her injuries. Hester had helped Farrah bind the injuries as best they could after breakfast. Galadrath could not help but look from a distance, while Hester carefully wound a makeshift bandage around the shirtless torso of Farrah. Her chest and stomach were a spider web of broken blood vessels and bruises, wrapping all the way around onto her back. He could make out where the fingerlike tendrils of the massive hand had applied the almost lethal pressure. He dared not imagine what she would have looked like if he had hesitated another second. A cloud of regret settled on him, thinking of how much better her condition would be, had he acted even a moment sooner.

"I can... walk," Farrah said through short, pained breaths.

"You've got an incredible resolve. I've seen the fiercest warriors die, doing what you did—fully armored soldiers crushed like grapes," Galadrath said. He paused for a moment before asking rhetorically, "That's not helping is it?"

She parted her lips to speak, but stopped. Instead, a small smile crept across her face, and she gave a curt nod.

"Let me help you up. Maybe I'll call you 'grape' from now on," he said.

He carefully supported her weight as she stood, and she briefly chuckled, followed by a groan.

"Good point. No more jokes," he grunted.

She stood precariously on her own, her arms stiff while her legs did all the work of trying to keep her balance.

"I can carry you," he said.

"No," she replied softly.

She took a few careful steps and looked up the incline between the cliff sides. He read her face and reiterated his offer.

"If you change your mind, let me know," he said.

As she nodded, Galadrath called on the collection of tiny pebbles of ore. He filled his body with air from the emblems, drawing in as much as he could. If he could hold enough and control it, he could float, fly, and dance on the whipping wind. He could feel that it would be insufficient to carry himself—and impossible to carry her with him. If he had more power, he could whisk her up the rocky terrain and turn hours of slow travel into a few short minutes. He considered Stepping with her for a moment, but the idea was insanity. She had already borne so much physical, emotional, and mental strain, he would not dare.

The travel was slow and treacherous up the steep, meandering trails. Justus and Tibel stayed within arms length of Farrah, offering help at intervals. Sometimes she took their aid, but she mostly waved them off with a stiff hand, her fingers straight and tense, like she was wielding a knife to keep them at bay. Emmett walked alongside Hester, and they filled the air with idle conversations and some laughter. Her brother was back to his jovial self, waving his bandaged hands around, retelling the events they had all taken part in. He praised Hester over and over, and she laughed at his embellishment of her acts of valor.

Galadrath smiled to himself.

They'll live; I'm sure of it.

16

THE EXILE

By the time they got back to the town, the Sister suns centered the sky. Though the mountain air was still cool, the stones under their feet baked with the heat of the day. The sky was an immaculate blue, interrupted only by the band of debris that made up the Shattered Children. Galadrath scanned the celestial expanse, shading his eyes from the bright light, and found the last moon, Led. The large white orb hanging serenely over the far horizon warmed his heart.

He remembered the last time he saw his family. It seemed like an eternity ago. He had thought of them every day, every spare moment that his attention was not needed, and he missed them fiercely. Paired with his melancholy was always a boiling hate for Teratos. His brother in arms, his best friend, who had robbed him of his beloved.

"God's living and dead, let me see them again," he mumbled.

"What was that, Vyhn?" Justus asked.

"Nothing. No matter," Galadrath replied.

"Tibel, Emmett. See if you can... go make some friends," Farrah wheezed.

She had fought her way through their travel back up the hill, gaunt and sweaty. Her hair was tied up into a messy bun, threatening to come undone. She moved to sit by the tree that Galadrath had meditated under, and Hester helped her relax.

"What do you need me to do?" Galadrath asked.

"Mind your own business," she managed in one uninterrupted breath.

Tibel and Emmett were already walking toward a tiny building with a door propped open. There was no sign or name painted anywhere that Galadrath could see, but they seemed to know where they were going, so he decided to follow.

As they entered through the crooked doorway, Galadrath was met with a mixture of smells. The musty and natural smell of freshly tanned hides, the welcome aroma of cracked barley, and the stink of sweaty people—all came together into a comforting and humble amalgamation. Other than the three of them, there was one gruff-looking, incredibly overweight man standing behind a sales counter. He had strong features in his face, and his dark skin made his eyes bright, almost glowing in the dim space. The slab of wood in front of him was barely wide enough for a single person to occupy, and the man that hung over it made it look even smaller. He wore a tattered shirt that, by Galadrath's calculations, had been washed just recently enough that it was still able to show individual stains. The armpits were sweaty and permanently browned, the sleeves tattered to the point of nonexistence. The front showed two blotchy vertical streaks from where the man chronically wiped his greasy hands, which was what he was currently doing. After a few wipes, he extended a hand out to Emmett.

"Pleased to meet you, stranger. The name's Green," the man said.

Emmett grabbed the meaty bulk of the man's hand and shook it vigorously. He stepped aside and let Tibel move into the confined space in front of the counter. Tibel also grabbed the hand and pumped it up and down a few times.

"And who's this?" Green said.

"Vyhn's his name. He can be trusted," Tibel said.

Galadrath realized there had been a bit of pageantry, some deception, in the introductions. These men all knew each other. Farrah had lied: They were not here for the first time, nor were they here to make friends and win over strangers for the cause. *This* was the cause.

"Pleased to meet you," Galadrath said.

Tibel was still standing in front of the counter, and there was no way for Galadrath to get close enough to shake the man's hand, even if it had been offered to him. Green simply nodded.

Galadrath surveyed the small space around him. The room was actually fairly large, but the horde of goods and supplies of every kind seemed to shrink it. The building itself was much larger than the tiny facade, nestled among other entryways, suggested. Tiny aisles, barely big enough to fit between, wound between stacked barrels and crates. A plethora of farming tools lined the walls in heaps. Herbs and dried goods hung from the ceiling, encroaching on him at every angle. A few pieces of finer furniture stood in one corner, covered in iron pots, tin carafes, and a variety of earthenware jugs and bowls. There were enough items here to start a small town—or to supply a decent militia.

As he absentmindedly perused the goods, Galadrath contemplated the lies. Farrah had withheld a lot of information from him, under-standably. But he was now replaying every conversation, every piece of every story they had told. Even Justus, in his seeming innocence, had talked about Fort Bracken like he had only read about it. They had all conspired to keep him in the dark. Galadrath was unsettled by his own naivety. He had only shared the truth with them, and they had told him only lies. Tibel's last statement may be the only true words Galadrath had heard from the group.

But at least they trust me now.

"You've brought in quite the haul. Color me surprised," Green chuckled.

"Farrah will want to lighten the load, as light as possible," Tibel said.

"That's a tall order," Green grumbled.

"She's the one who gives them," Tibel said sternly.

Galadrath stepped forward, squeezing by Emmett, and placed a small, soft cloth pouch on the counter.

"I'm not exactly sure what your dealings are, but it's only fair that this is considered part of it," he said.

Green scooped up the bag, glancing at Tibel. He pulled gingerly at the draw string with his colossal fingers, opening the bag as carefully as possible, and shook the contents into his hand. He dropped the bag on the counter and began pushing the small pieces of ore around his vast palm with the stubbed nail of his forefinger.

"This is…" he said, half a statement, half a question.

"Divine ore. We salvaged it just this morning," Galadrath stated.

Green looked up at Tibel in surprise. He picked up the bag again and painstakingly placed the pebbles back into their container. He neatly tightened the strings and handed it back to Galadrath, his bulk completely consuming the countertop as he reached forward past Tibel.

"I've no use for this," Green stated flatly.

Galadrath was relieved, taking back the tiny treasure.

"Where is Farrah? I'll need to speak with her. Gods living and dead, divine metal? What's she got planned?" Green continued.

"She's outside, resting—worse for wear I'm sad to say," Tibel answered.

Green grunted and shuffled through a door to the side, disappearing into the back of the cavernous building. Tibel pointed toward the front door, signaling their own departure.

"Who doesn't want divine metal?" Galadrath muttered, mostly to himself.

"People who don't want attention. Stuffs pretty much useless, anyway," Emmett stated.

Galadrath chuckled at the absurdity of the statement.

"It's amazing to me that what I've done—what you've seen me do—is 'pretty much useless.' The gods could drop a miracle at your feet, supply one to you by your own hands, and you'd wave it away in ignorance. Is this why the temples stand crumbling?" Galadrath asked.

"Did the temples crumble before their gods died—or after?" Emmett grumbled.

"I doubt the depth of that statement was intentional, Emmett, but I think you're onto something," Galadrath replied.

Green emerged from the side of the building, taking long strides, effortlessly moving his hulking form. He carried a large leather bag in one hand, and when he had crossed the rocky street and reached the tree where Farrah was reclining, he dropped the bag at her feet. Galadrath heard the clink of tightly packed coin jostling as the bag hit the ground.

So much for the 'salt is more useful than gold' speech.

"This is all I have. It'll cover most of it. I don't appreciate your boy here tapping me on the shoulder for it though, and Bartron isn't going to like it either," Green said, staring down at her.

"Bartron can take it up with me if he has the stones—if he can stand and isn't crawling out of a cup of ale," Farrah said.

Galadrath could see her concentrate on her words, not allowing her condition to depreciate her intention.

"And you bring this" —Green pointed at Galadrath— "this raven-looking pretty boy, touting godstuff? Scar swallow me—what's possessed you, Farrah?" he finished, struggling openly to find the correct insults.

"Figured you might want a peek," she said, sweating through the words.

Galadrath had not told anyone about the ore he had gathered. It was likely that they did not even know where it came from. The inner workings of the Patches were a mystery to all, and the little that was known was shared with few. She was improvising—and did so perfectly.

"No, no—keep it to yourself. Or better, get rid of it," Green replied. "What happened to you? What got you all bent up like this? I've never seen you worse."

"Ran down some Patches yesterday. Gave better than we got," Farrah huffed.

"*Ran down*? You've gone mad, woman!" he exclaimed.

"Then you've been a lunatic as long as I've known you," she said.

A smile crept across her face, and Galadrath could feel the tension between them dissipate. Green began to chuckle, then laugh, and finally roared, his whole body shaking as he grabbed his round belly.

"Rumor has it Green killed a Patch himself—attacked his family years ago. He was the only one left alive," Tibel said softly to Galadrath.

Galadrath nodded in thanks, appreciating the explanation. Emmett overheard and leaned in, as well.

"Not just one, they said he killed three of them—crushed them with a siege maul, tore the last to pieces with his bare hands," Emmett said.

"And that's why it's a rumor, you fog-headed idiot," Tibel replied.

As Green's rowdy laughter died down, his face became stern again. "*Hah!* Farrah, ever the sly fox, I'm going to tell Bartron and the others. Our business is finished for today, but this isn't over," he said.

He pulled down his bottom eyelids with two of his fingers and stared at her, as some sort of omen, an ancient curse. Galadrath could tell the man originated from the far off land of Sijis, but he was not familiar enough with their customs to decipher the meaning behind the act.

"Don't you worry, Green. We're sticking around for a while. If they come through, I'll tell them myself," Farrah said.

"Scar have you instead," Green said.

He turned and walked away, his hands fluttering by his sides restlessly.

"How long will we be here?" Galadrath asked.

Farrah pointed at her ribs, staring up at him incredulously.

"Sorry. Foolish question," he said.

"We almost died, you know," Justus said.

"And have nothing to show for it, no less," Tibel added.

"Except a few new scars," Emmett finished.

Galadrath looked at each of them in turn, struggling to keep his face blank as he took them in. He had used them for his own selfish gain. As their words cooled in his ears, he regretted putting them in danger. He knew that if he had to do it again, he would, and he regretted the thought even more.

"I'll be back soon," Galadrath said.

"Where are you going?" Hester asked innocently.

"Tomb," he said.

"Why? What's there?" she asked.

"Someone I accused."

"But I thought you ki—" Hester's voice faded into black fog.

Galadrath appeared in an old, dilapidated courtyard of a kingdom away from where he had vanished. Flowerbeds and statues all showed the slow crumble of age. The heavy stones he stood on were worn at the edges, broken by the hundreds of seasons they had weathered since they were cut. The landscape was bleak, the only greenery around was a few ancient trees and a few hardened weeds creeping from between cracks. The brilliant blue sky was gone, the suns drowned out by the heavy mist. The air was cool and wet, smelling of mold.

An assortment of small structures surrounded the courtyard, but they looked out of place. Most of them appeared on the verge of collapsing, as if a faint breeze could make them crumble under their own weight. Made of rubble and reclaimed timber, each one of them was a unique abomination. Even the courtyard looked delicate and well-maintained compared to the crudeness of the newer constructions.

He walked down from the courtyard, weaving between the dilapidated structures. The incline stretched before him, and he continued along the remnants of the paved path. Eventually, the trail morphed into gravel and loose stones, and the incline grew steeper, more jagged as rocks and craggy sheets of stone jutted from the earth. As he reached his destination, he climbed up one of the larger boulders and looked out over the vast expanse before him.

He stood on the edge of the Scar. His eyes traced its edge as far as he could before it disappeared into the heavy mist. He looked down into the depths of the massive fissure in the land. There was only darkness and fog, and far beyond his sight lay its bottom. Over the gap, he could not see the other side. There was no horizon and no telling where the cliff faces ended. It seemed endless in every direction.

He had grown up around the unfathomable expanse. In Barkrill, it ran through the center of the island, where it had cracked open—a gash through the land and ocean that nearly destroyed their entire civilization over a thousand years ago. Here, it seemed to run deeper, wider—even more sinister—a gaping wound left unclosed. It was a testament to the gods, living and dead, a vivid proof of their power. He tried to imagine, like he had so many times before, what it would have been like when it formed, when their planet quaked and cracked.

With his chains, as one of the Many, he had held immense power. Here, he felt small and insignificant in comparison to the Few, the chosen champions of the gods. It was inconceivable for a single person to hold such power, yet even they were mortal.

A long while later, when the magnitude of the Scar no longer unsettled him, he climbed back the way he came. He headed back to where the fractured earth was mostly level again, where the pockmark of buildings lay in every direction. Retreating from the vast edge of the bottomless depth had reminded him of the lullaby he had heard in the Lowest House, as if it had wafted into the misty windows from the darkness below. He began to hum the melancholy tune, listening as it floated away into the unknown while the words only played in his mind.

Do you sing a song
Does it grasp at your neck,
It drowns you in myrth,
Or in blood.
It sings you to sleep,
But you wake.
Do you sing or do you drown?

He did not know where to look or what he was searching for, but he would recognize it when he saw it. He passed many of the small buildings, disregarding them entirely. The larger structures he inspected briefly, though he never bothered to knock on any doors. A few figures emerged in the mist, but they paid him no mind—each one dirty and haggard, worn down from a life in exile.

Do you sing or do you drown?
Death will find you,
Like it finds us all.
It will feel like a bed of roses,
Or a bed of needles.

You may scream, A cry, a plea.
A prayer or song, A warcry if not wrong.
Do you sing or do you drown?

Then something strange caught his eye—a large dome standing twenty feet high and a hundred feet in diameter. The outside was dark brown, spotted with hues of red. A large mortared stone chimney protruded from its roof. The dome and the chimney were stark contrasts to each other. There was a little smoke rising from the chimney, but judging by the size of the stack, whatever fire was glowing inside was insignificant.

This is it, no doubt.

His thought ended the tune murmuring in his throat. He walked the circumference of the dome, running his fingers across its rough surface at intervals. Flecks of the red and brown came off and stuck to his fingertips. He rubbed his fingers together and sniffed them.

Rust. Solid iron.

He continued to walk slowly around the strange construction, until he found an interruption in the design. It looked as if a portion of the dome had been cut off and formed into a flat wall. The wall had a door and two large grated vents on either side. Flakes of red chipped off at the corners of the door, showing the bare metal.

He pushed out his influence. It was pitiful compared to before he was stripped of his rank, but the ore allowed him more than he had been accustomed to in the past days. It was a comfort to him, as the door and the surrounding metal answered his call. The ground underneath his feet praised him, the air mixed with flecks of moisture whispered happily in his ears. He pressed himself against the door and felt what was beyond it. The dome extended below the ground, though he could not hold much of it under his control, he was under the impression that the structure could be an entire ball. More importantly, it was hollow. The walls were a few inches thick, the door was much thinner. He let go of his influence, stepped back, and knocked politely.

He waited and waited—and knocked again, more loudly. There was still no answer. He drew in on the earth emblem, striking the door once. A hollow thrum echoed as the entire building reverberated like a muted bell.

"That should get her attention," Galadrath mumbled to himself.

He waited a minute. No answer. Irritated, he Stepped past the door. The interior was vast, cluttered, and well-lit. He was surprised at the brightness of the candles, until he realized they were not candles at all. Small globes of glass sat on top of finely crafted golden stalks, all attached to a bulbous golden base. He had seen such devices before, but they were extremely rare. Mechanisms like these were directly copied from the designs originally created by the Draughtsman. Machines, powered by emblems. Galadrath had never trusted such creations. An emblem should be controlled by a mind, nothing else.

The floorplan inside the dome was open, each section separated from the others only by the utility it provided. He could make out bookcases in one corner and tables strewn with vegetables close to the large furnace-looking fireplace. Other tables were covered with fine glassware of swirling pipes and alchemical supplies. Nearest to him, stacked haphazardly around the doorway were crates, chests, burlap bags, and earthenware vases that stood as tall as his shoulders. From the ceiling hung neatly crafted models of bizarre inventions he was incapable of naming. In another corner laid a bulky suit of armor made for a man of immense proportion.

Galadrath walked idly around the room, surveying the collection of oddities, tools, and unfinished projects. His own footsteps on the hollow floor, along with the crackling flames of the tiny fire, were the only sounds in the room—until he heard thumping coming from the far side.

A stout woman in a neat, plain brown dress rose from a staircase he had not yet discovered. She raised a short, six-barreled rifle to her shoulder, taking aim at him.

"Get out! Get out, you mongrel! You thief!" she screamed at him.

"Taroosa Pix?" Galadrath asked.

"What? I said get out! Move it or I'll put a few extra holes in you!" she yelled.

"Taroo—" he began.

"How'd you even get in here? Get out!" her voice grew hoarse.

"Taroosa Pix?" Galadrath said, his voice slightly raised.

"Who's asking?"

Galadrath had not considered how his introduction would go before now. With an intimidating weapon leveled at his chest, his best option would not be the truth, but a lie would not get him anywhere either.

"I'm an exile, a traitor to the crown. My name is Galadrath Yaralok. You might remember me—we met long ago," he stated loudly.

He expected the muzzles of the rifle to flare, and his veins were already fueled with a mixture of energy, his senses poised to dodge whatever came next.

"Galadrath! How could I forget! Exiled? Scar swallow you for your lies! Come to finish the job? Couldn't just let me live in this forgotten waste in solitude? Why shouldn't I cut you in half with this here piece?" she replied shrilly.

"Because I need your help. I need your help to destroy those who've wronged me—redeem myself, my name, and my title," he stated, his voice wavering slightly.

"And who might these people be? The ones who wronged the great Galadrath Yaralok?" she said, spitting at his name.

"The Court of King Dartan, for starters," Galadrath replied.

"Hah!" she laughed, paused, and laughed again with the same abruptness.

"You mean to kill the king? You mean to take on the whole of Thainegom in all her glory?" she asked.

"I mean to kill anyone who stands in the way of my absolution. If the king is among them, so be it," he said.

"The enemy of my enemy... is a pretentious, donkey faced lout!" she screeched.

"I don't mean to—" he started.

"Shut it! I've had a moment to think it over. I'll help you."

Galadrath's mouth hung slightly open before eventually closing. He looked at her, puzzled.

"Spit it out! What do you need help with?" she asked.

He pulled the small cloth bag from his pocket and handed it to her. She weighed the bag in her hand, then opened it slightly. She held it up to her nose, sniffing it loudly.

"*Mmmm.* This is fresh, not too fresh though. It's got the stink of Patches on it. Where'd you get it?" she said, still mulling the bag of ore like a fine wine.

"You can tell what it is, all that, just by sniffing it?" Galadrath asked incredulously.

"Idiot. You remember what I was before you accused me? Do you need a reminder?" she said.

She did not wait for an answer and turned quickly, crossing the room to a table scattered with various metal vessels.

"You were a Jeweler. You were incredibly bright and showed lots of potential. You also had incredibly sticky fingers. You could have been the Court's Jeweler, you know."

"Court's Jeweler! Bah! And end up here like you? The same fate decades later? I simply borrowed a few things to further my studies. I might be a thief, but it's all for good reason."

Galadrath shrugged off the insult.

"You stole forbidden artifacts from the Reliquary of Light, then you experimented with them. You activated them—had contact with the Tyrant, who is and always will be one of the greatest enemies of the state. You were a menace Taroosa, and they still let you live," he said, pleading his case.

"All those so-called artifacts are mere toys compared to the greatness we can achieve. A machine without a mind is useful, practical, but combined we could see things and accomplish what we can't even dream. The Tyrant was the key, the machine with a soul, a masterwork of sciences," she said feverishly.

She began to work, pouring the tiny nuggets of divine ore into a mortar, furiously banging at it with a pestle.

"It seems you're not done with him yet. Is that one from the Meyer incident?" Galadrath said, pointing to the suit of armor.

"No. Merely a facsimile, a partial reconstruction. No core, no emblem, no soul to connect to," she mumbled.

"Where did you get all of these things? I left you with nothing," he said.

"You left a trained mind—one of the Many—alone and unchecked with idle hands. I scraped and scavenged, much like you're doing, bringing me this meager sampling. Then, I built this forge with my own hands. Once the impurities are removed, the metal is a much clearer conduit. Divine metal does not melt, nor can it be broken or penetrated. It only responds to commands; it can only be changed and formed by its own power," she said.

She took the mortar bowl and began straining the contents carefully.

"So you crafted your own trinket?" he asked.

"Obviously. Once I had something to work with, I built this place. There are many peering eyes among the scavengers and exiles of Tomb. Many hungry people, many hungry men," she said softly.

Galadrath reflected on the statement. Exile in itself is a cruel punishment, but he had not considered what else must be endured along with it. She was roughly his age, and they had both been young when their paths had first crossed.

"I'm sorry," he said.

"No matter. Anyway, once I was established I simply continued my research. I got the attention of the Tirvian traders, and they've supplied me well with all kinds of things that are beyond my reach. We have an amicable relationship," Taroosa said.

"You trade with Tirv? There are Tirvians on Thainegom soil? That could be considered an act of war," Galadrath said.

"After the Shattering, when the alliances of Dradofir, Thainegom, and Irah disseminated, Tirv made a plight to Irah. The Timeless Mother, the Queen of Irah, saw they were suffering the same fate her people once had. They had been abandoned, left suffering and waiting to die. She offered them vassalage, and in return for their loyalty, she hefted them from squalor. She sent fleets of airships with supplies and workers, cultivated their land, and built them cities overnight."

"I know all that, but Tirvians on—" Galadrath began.

"They hardly set foot here. The mighty walls of Tirv are a stone's throw away from here. The weather has been rather terrible, but usually you can see the city from across the Scar. It's beautiful, lights dancing in every window. The whole city glows. Pinnacle of innovation. Machines that cut wood and fire their own bricks, and wagons with iron wheels that move without beasts pulling them. I wish I could see it. But no, they send over a small flying skiff with supplies, and I provide them with emblems and some of the finer creations their own artisans are incapable of producing—along with some Jeweler related services, as necessary," she explained.

"Why don't you just join them? Become a citi—" he tried.

"Peering eyes! Peering eyes I said, you buffoon! Being an exile has its distinct advantages. I've been ignored and forgotten, and that suits me. Why would I give up my own peace to once again become a servant to another master?"

"I'm starting to understand—"

"Shut it! I'm trying to concentrate!" she yelled.

Galadrath watched as she collected the partially refined ore in one hand and produced a broach from a pocket in the dress. The brooch was shaped like a butterfly, the shining silver of divine metal finely crafted into swirls and flourishes. Tiny emblems of every color were embedded into the curls, each placed perfectly and surrounded by exquisite detail. She closed her eyes, holding the two objects in separate hands.

"Do you have a preference on the form?" she asked softly.

Galadrath paused.

"Maybe another ring? I hadn't given it much—" he said.

"Shhhhhhh!"

The energy in the air changed, the strange feeling of another Many bringing power under their control. There was a tingle on his skin and in his heart, almost like the beginning of a sunburn.

Her thumb and forefinger stood erect, pinched around nothing.

Then he saw the metal begin to flow from her hand—some collecting like water droplets, liquid ore running up from her fingers. Other pieces sprouted like tiny creeping weeds out of the closed fist, searching for space to bloom.

The ring began to form around the last digit of her thumb, her forefinger holding the band in place. The divine metal shimmered and stretched, the band swelling and thickening, and tiny flowers began to form along its surface. They began as buds, as if the natural growth of the plant had to be taken into account in the manipulation of the metal.

"A lily, please," he said softly.

She did not reply, her eyes still closed, but he saw the flower at the center of the ring bloom and wilt, shriveling back into the band. In its place a new bud grew and bloomed, and Galadrath could make out the long flowing petals and stamen of a lily flower. The movement began to slow before coming to a stop. The magical image unfolding before him became frozen in time.

She opened her eyes, looking down at the newly formed ring—then to him.

"I always knew you liked flowers. It seemed only fitting to make you a grim wreath. Who is the lily for?" she said pensively.

"My wife," he said.

"I'm sorry for your loss," she said softly.

The statement rang in his ears, a reminder of his wife's uncertain fate.

"No, she's alive. She loves lilies. The flowers are a symbol of purity," he replied.

"And a symbol of grief. Who do you grieve for?" she added.

"I grieve for the wrongly accused, for those I've killed who did not deserve to die, and for the innocent who've suffered by my hand," he said.

"But you'll kill again," she stated.

"The *wrongly* accused," he emphasized. "Those who stand in my way will receive no mercy. I will destroy them all, with peace in my heart. I will leave only blood and rubble."

"And you are to be their judge?" she asked.

"No, I'm to be their Accuser."

17

THE DEBT COLLECTOR

GALADRATH AND TAROOSA SPENT a while in each other's company. They talked and drank tea, sharing stories about their lives and the outside world. He could see she was very tired after forming the ring, but she was propped up by her loneliness. He could imagine she had no friends and few acquaintances. She was happy to share her ideas and aspirations with him, and her fatigue was eventually drowned out by her own excitement.

"Where will your journey lead you next?" she asked.

"Home. I have to see my family—I have to know that they are alright. If anything has happened to them because of me and my situation, I could never forgive myself," he answered.

"I understand. When will you repay your debt to me?"

"Debt?" he asked.

"You asked for help, but my help isn't free."

Galadrath sighed and placed his head in his hands.

"What are your terms?" he mumbled through his palms.

"Make them pay for what they did to me—make them suffer," she spat.

"And if they're innocent? I don't recall who signed the order. Was it Ostiphan?" he said.

"Lords Braf, Freid, Drumm, and yes, Ostiphan," she recited.

"I'll do my best."

"You'll pay your debt, by your honor, Accuser," she said sternly.

"On my honor then," he sighed.

"I know it isn't what you had in mind, but I can sweeten my end of the deal," she said slyly.

He picked up his head and looked her in the eyes.

"Before you accused me and dragged me out to this horrible place, I hid a few things—a few of my favorite trinkets and other sundries. It may not be of much use to you, per se, but among those sundries is the Eye of the Marksman," she said with a smile.

Galadrath looked at her with wild eyes and threw his hands up in the air.

"So you absolutely did rob the Reliquary of Light! You stole the weapon of the Marksman! Gods living and dead!" he shouted.

"Of course I did! That's probably the only reason they kept me alive, so that one day they might be able to extract its location from me. But you're not listening! I hid them—trinkets intended for Emissaries. They'll be invaluable to you, and you have the ability to retrieve them," she said.

He glared at her, still beside himself with disbelief.

"Seems my only friends these days are thieves," he grumbled.

"Then you keep good company," she smiled.

Galadrath let out a single guffaw.

"Maybe you're right. At least I can expect betrayal at every turn," he said.

"Thieves have a code just like you do. The good ones at least. Nothing worse than a thief that isn't good at thieving," she said.

He thought about Farrah and the others. He remembered how Tibel had vouched for him. Slowly, he nodded.

"So where did you hide—" he asked.

"Well, I couldn't just bury them in the ground. Any self respecting Many can sniff out such an item. During my studies as a Jeweler, we spent some time on the practice of melding machines with the power of the emblems, hence my love for the mechanical. We started small, like these lamps you see, each powered by a small fire emblem, capable of producing light for several centuries. I had plenty of time to study all kinds, and more importantly, we were given access to the spires," she said.

"The towers driven by air emblems that pushed the mists away?" he asked.

"Obviously. They are no longer in use, but they are still maintained and well-stocked with emblems. I've hidden the trinkets inside the constructs. One in the spire south of Silt, one in Springletter, and the best of all is in the coastal tower east of the city," she said.

"It's very clever, really. Hiding a source of power next to a power source. Like staring at the sun and not being able to—" Galadrath pondered.

"Shut it! Stop explaining things to me that I've just explained to you. Obviously I'm clever! Look around you," she screeched.

Galadrath looked at her with annoyance.

"You have a bad habit of interrupting—" he began.

"Shush! I only interrupt people when they're being stupid, which is constantly!" she exclaimed.

He sat in silence, staring at her.

"The Eye of the Marksman is hidden in the Hercolid," she said.

"Oh, so I'm supposed to break into an impenetrable fortress—" he stopped himself.

"Good, you're a fast learner. Yes, the Hercolid was gifted half a dozen heavy guns by the Tyrant after the war, while they were still working together. The Eye is in the internal workings of the northernmost gun."

"Heavy guns? Cannons?" he asked.

"Heavier than any cannon. Lances. Dreadnought class desolator lances," she said.

"That doesn't mean anythi—" he said.

"Then shut it!" she squealed.

His eyes hung half-mast, and he smirked at her.

"They are immense weapons capable of incredible destruction that are well beyond our own understanding. It doesn't matter. Retrieve the items or don't. Just don't fail me," she said.

Galadrath marked the end of the conversation, having grown tired of being interrupted, and decided it was a good time to leave.

"I won't fail. I appreciate your kindness, the tea, the information, and your immense help." He looked down shamefully and played with the new ring seated on his finger. "I'm sorry for our past. Hopefully, this will set things right between us. I'm glad you didn't shoot me," he said.

"I'm sure I'll have the opportunity to draw my trusty gun on you again. Water under the bridge. You did your job, and in a way, you gave me the opportunity to pursue my life's work without the constant bureaucracy of the Emissaries. It's good to have a friend again, Galadrath. I trust you'll visit often," she said.

"If everyone I've accused was as forgiving as you, I'd have an army of the dead at my back," he said.

"No, no. Resurrection isn't feasible. Death is inevitable, and there is no way back. Not even for the Timeless Mother, not even for the Few," she stated.

"I didn't mean it litera—" he said.

"Shut it! Yes, I know what you meant. Just be careful. There is no way back," she replied.

"I should go," he sighed.

They looked at each other for a moment, emotions speaking silently on their behalf.

"Good hunting, Accuser," she finally said.

He stood from his seat, offering her a hand to shake. She stepped forward and wrapped her arms around his waist in an embrace. She was much shorter than he was, and her head rested against his chest. He could once again feel her loneliness. It had taken a toll on her, and she held him for too long.

"Till we meet again," he said.

He vanished from her grip, leaving her awkwardly holding a cloud of dissipating black fog.

The faint smell of sea air greeted him in a light breeze. The coast was far south, but the salty winds carried themselves effortlessly over the sea and over the plains. The suns had long set, and he was jarred by the darkness of the night. The well-lit interior of Taroosa's dome had not given any indication of the passing of time. The waning moon, Led, fortunately sat large in the sky, illuminating the landscape with eerie white light. The shapes and colors of the landscape were washed out, but he knew exactly where he was. He turned toward the direction of a small hilltop several hundred yards away, confirming his bearings, and made out the looming tower perched on it in the moonlight.

Galadrath knew the spires of Thainegom were well-known around the world. They were icons of progress, bastions against the great mists that had swallowed everything. They were ever-present reminders of the Few and their accomplishments. He also knew they were of strategic significance, and even though they were no longer in use, they were very well guarded.

He could make out the light of fires and torches at the base of the tower. Small guard houses, barracks, and watchtowers were dwarfed by the height of the magnificent spire. Even though the day had been mostly physically relaxing, his mind was tired. He wanted a comfortable bed; he wanted to rest without the constant paranoia of being an outlaw, but it was not yet time for that.

He walked toward the spire, staying out in the open. He kept an eye out for bushes and small trees that were scattered loosely along the plains, places where he could hide when the time came. Mostly, he concentrated his attention on the watchtowers, looking for any movement from the guards that would be posted there. He expected them not to notice him until he was much closer, but he did need to keep an eye on them. Hopefully, they were not asleep or, otherwise, distracted from their duties.

"You there! Halt!" A voice came over the distance.

Good. They are vigilant.

He continued to walk slowly, changing his course slightly toward a rather large bush.

"Halt and identify yourself! Halt or you'll be fired upon!" the voice came again.

He did not stop, nor did he plan to. He tucked himself in behind the bush nonchalantly, roughly fifty yards from the palisade and the guard tower beyond it. He vanished, appearing farther away, behind a small tree, and walked out from behind it, moving in a different direction, once again heading toward the fortifications.

"Halt whoever you are! I demand you stop!" the voice rang out.

He continued his stride and ended up behind another bush. He did this over and over, Stepping behind a previously unused piece of cover and ending behind another. He could only imagine what the guards were thinking as they continued to shout commands and threats in his direction.

Do they think I'm a Patch? A ghost? An army of ghosts? Hopefully their imaginations run wild.

A gong sounded from within the watchtower, alerting the entire camp to the threat. From where he stood, he could hear the distant shouts of men brought to attention and action. He saw torchlight from behind the palisade, the flames dancing off the shiny armor of the soldiers wielding them. They were preparing for conflict against an unknown enemy.

"Identify yourselves! This is your final warning!" the voice shouted.

Good. I have become more than one.

A shot rang out, and he heard the bullet snap through the twigs and leaves of a bush not far from where he stood. Rifles were a threat, even to an Accuser. Predictable fire could be avoided, but if they began firing randomly, it would be problematic. He thought back to the trial of Sebbatin, when the Dead Hand had filled the sky with a field of meteors. *If an enemy is hidden, take every place he has to hide, fill every space he could stand with a threat.*

But this is not the place I plan on standing.

He Stepped from his concealment and hung from the side of the spire, the ground far beneath him. The black mist dissipated quickly in the cool breeze. He did not have the influence to feel the area around him, to be able to accurately Step to where he needed to be, but this vantage point would work to the same effect. He could see the tiny shapes moving below, their torches illuminating the ground around the spire in spots, and he knew no one would take the time to look up.

An armored bulb formed the base of the spire. Much like the mechanical lights that he had seen at Taroosa's, the spire's intricate machinery was held there. He could see the formations of troops begin taking positions with rifles and spears below him, all facing out in an array toward where he had placed his misdirections. The other watchtowers would still be manned, covering their own sections of the plains beyond their fortifications.

He made his second-to-last Step, landing at the door to the spire. In an instant, he pushed out his influence to feel beyond the door. The pull of the emblems stored inside was impressive and jockeyed for his concentration. He could feel the shape of a man on the other side of the wall, the outline of a soul that would not yield to his power. He drew his swords and Stepped beyond the door, appearing behind the man.

"If you open your mouth, you'll be dead before you make a sound. If you move a muscle, I will cut it from you," Galadrath whispered.

He shifted slightly to the side and caught the edge of the man's left eye. The guard had been standing at attention, but his body was now awkwardly stiff. Only his eye moved, trying to make out his attacker without turning his head.

"Good," Galadrath said.

He laid the blade of one of the swords on the armored shoulder of the man, the point touching him on the cheek, just below the wildly searching eye. Still he did not flinch, but Galadrath could feel the uneasy breaths caused by fear.

"Good. Slowly tuck your thumbs into the back of your belt and place your forehead on the wall here. If you move from the position, or make a sound, it will be your last," Galadrath said.

The man complied, his hands shaking as the thumbs fumbled their way into the belt. Galadrath turned to face the machine. There was a dizzying amount of exposed pieces. Finely crafted metal gears and rods intertwined with stone bases that seemed to melt around structural points. Tubes of glass held collections of air emblems. They caused his senses to tickle as he searched for the trinket that was hidden here.

It was not obvious at first, as he tried to make out the elaborate designs of each piece of the incomprehensible machine. He was searching for minutes—what felt like hours—trying to locate which of the sources of power felt different.

The guard whimpered slightly. The strain of holding himself upright against the wall using only his head was taking a toll on him.

"I'm almost done here," Galadrath said, trying to calm the guard.

He focused his efforts to where he felt the strongest pull, and at the base of one of the glass canisters, he could make out the almost imperceptible difference in color between the large chrome tube that extended from the vessel—and something else.

He reached into the machine and pulled at the object, sliding it down on the tube to where it began to constrict. He removed the semicircular band that clinged against the other metal.

The touch of the divine metal bangle filled him with ecstasy, and combined with the fearful whimpers of the guard, he began chuckling softly to himself. The muted laughter bounced off the hard metal walls of the tiny interior. His echoes sounded like a chorus, and he began to laugh louder. Just like so many of his own nightmares, which always ended with cackles of an unseen host, he left the guard standing alone in the fleeting shadows of his own laughter.

He appeared next to a well on the outskirts of the quaint town of Springletter. The moonlight was still present, and its source had shifted backwards in the sky slightly. He was moving west and would continue to do so until the night was over and the trinkets were safely in his possession. He would relive the same hour over and over as he travelled.

He placed his hand lightly on the rough stones of the boarded-up water source. He had brought his family here for a holiday away from the city. They had used the well as a table top for a picnic. He had lifted his daughter onto the edge, so she could help herself to the collection of fruits and cheeses they had set out on the wooden lid. She had been too small to reach them otherwise. It had been a wonderful day, playing and eating and lazing about in the shadow of the massive spire that stood on the outskirts of town. He had even taken them into it. His station as the Court's Accuser had granted passage with ease, and the garrison commander had been zealous to please.

Now, the memory was faded. The well and the spire also stood in moonlit darkness. It had been a few years since, but he expected not much had changed.

He held up and inspected the bangle of divine metal. It was larger than most trinkets he had seen. The Temple of Light had specifications to which each one was made. The designs could take any form, but the mass of divine metal used in each one was the same. Each one was identical in weight; each inscription followed the same format. The bangle was plain on the outside, which had made it so easy to conceal around the pipe. There was an inscription on the inside.

We do not choose the end or the beginning.

He did not expect such philosophical words from Taroosa. Maybe she was less absolute in her youth, still reeling with the potential of an unlived life. The statement was simple, but what it did not say was more important. One does not choose to be born or when to die, but one does choose what to do with the life in between.

He Stepped into the small room inside the spire, finding it unguarded. Through the metal wall, he could hear the bombastic voices outside engaged in story telling and revelry. The nightwatch here was lax and undisciplined.

I wonder what the garrison commander would say if he knew what his men were doing now.

Locating the next trinket did not take long, and without fanfare, he departed again, appearing in the town of Silt. The town and the spire were heavily guarded, with the constant threat of Patches. With the help of his two new trinkets, his power and influence had grown exponentially. He felt closer to his old self, slowly becoming whole after he had been stripped of his chains.

Recovering the trinket was more problematic than before. He used the same distraction as with the first towers, Stepping from cover to cover, but was met with a fusillade of cannonfire. With no real plan, he was forced to burn down several buildings and set fire to an ammunition store, the explosion of which could probably be heard in the City of Light, or even the Hercolid. In the confusion and destruction, he was able to slip into the spire, and after beating a few guards senseless, he left with his treasure.

He was beyond tired. The day had been long and filled with countless uses of the emblems. He did not have the energy or the desire to attempt sneaking into the impenetrable fortress. The last of Taroosa's artifacts would have to remain in its hiding place.

He Stepped one last time into the front room of Green's store. The inside was pitch black, the door locked and bolted. The counter was empty of the large man. Careful not to make noise, he unfolded a few of the blankets he had previously spotted in the collection of goods and made a makeshift bed in a corner under one of the larger desks. He crawled into it, hoping no one would find him and disturb his sleep.

18

THE DEADBEAT

HE WOKE FROM THE midst of a dream to the sound of Green scraping open the bolt and lock of the door, and dragging it open against the misshapen floorboards. He lay there for a while, waiting for the large man to become busy enough that he could sneak from his sleeping place without being noticed. He took the time to inspect the other trinkets more closely.

He lay on his back, holding the first find close in front of his face, constricted by the height of the table he was under. It was a roughly-made pendant, resembling a caterpillar hanging from a branch in the process of encasing itself in a cocoon. The ridges of the body were rough and uneven, and the details were vague and poorly conceived. He wondered, for a moment, if the butterfly broach Taroosa used as her own trinket had started out as a caterpillar. Like how the metal flower bloomed, wilted, and died, he imagined her bringing the insect through all its stages of life, only halting the process when the butterfly was fully matured.

He tucked it away and produced the next one. It was a set of earrings connected with a long, thin chain. He recognized the style, even if it was not commonly worn. The chain wraps around the back of the wearer's neck, creating a dangling loop in front for a pendant to be attached to, then back around to the other ear. When the wearer turned their head, the chain would shift and cause the pendants to sway and jingle, drawing attention to it. The style was something that had fallen out of fashion, considered uncomfortable and garish. The earrings themselves were larger than the first digit of his thumb, one shaped like a cocoon already broken open and the other a butterfly with wrinkled wings. It was clear that the pieces were intended to be used together, although the bangle was of a simpler design.

He assumed she had managed to create and steal these pieces at different points while learning to become a Jeweler, since the quality of craftsmanship varied so much. She had been right: The pieces would be invaluable to him. However, he also knew that his new identity was now linked to a string of grievous crimes. The salt theft had taken place more than a week ago, his sentencing and escape only a few days prior. In that time, much could have happened, and he still had no idea of his family's fate.

Galadrath placed the trinkets safely in his pockets and slid silently from underneath the table. He straightened his garments and tousled his hair before emerging from the packed aisles and into plain view. Green's eyes glanced up from where he was weighing out measurements of herbs.

"Vyhn, I didn't see you come in. Are you just wasting my time or are you here to buy something?" Green said.

"Morning Green. A pleasure to see you too," Galadrath said flatly.

"Rough night? You look like twice cooked catfish," Green said.

The large man rubbed his own chin and pointed at Galadrath.

"Yeah, it's been a while. I'm assuming you have a razor I could use?" Galadrath replied.

"I have one you can buy," Green replied.

"Can you take it off Farrah's credit?"

"Certainly."

"Maybe you have a bar of soap?" Galadrath nudged.

"Anything else, my liege?" Green simpered.

Galadrath shook his head with exasperation.

"What is it with you people? Basic cleanliness isn't something reserved for royalty. Everyone washes—everyone *should* wash. It keeps the fleas away, boils and diseases, too. Didn't your mother teach you these things? If you'd ever met the king, you'd know he poops and bathes just like the rest of us. And he doesn't shave—he has a beard," Galadrath said angrily.

"I never knew my mother," Green replied.

"Then maybe your wife?" Galadrath spat back.

Green just stared at him. Galadrath carefully retrieved the razor and the soap from the counter, well aware he was within the man's reach. He was still tired from the night before, and he had allowed his irritation to show. He made an effort to regain his poise, finding calm and control once again.

"Thank you," Galadrath said.

He walked outside quickly, leaving Green standing at the counter still glaring at him. He trekked up the hill on the opposite side of the town, avoiding any roads or paths until he was sufficiently alone. He stripped down among the bushes and began the process of scrubbing away days of filth. He found a few flecks of the black ichor that had splashed onto him. As he washed away the sticky substance, he saw the red and irritated skin underneath. He scrubbed vigorously at the marks, and the first few layers of his skin began to peel back.

Once he was content with his level of cleanliness, he grabbed the razor and shaved. The water he had conjured to clean himself was not draining well in the rocky landscape, and he made use of the forming puddle, stilling its surface to a mirror like state. As he shaved, he inspected his own face. His skin was darker, having tanned in the long days spent outside. His eyes were puffy from the uncomfortable nights. When he finished shaving, he cooled the water and splashed his face.

He cleaned and dried his clothing with care and then dressed. He moved back down the hill, feeling much better and ready for what he had to do. He passed several of the denizens of the small town. Each looked at him strangely, but they all gave a polite nod, some even dispensing the formalities of a greeting. Galadrath returned every kindness and every greeting, doing his best to be as pleasant as possible.

When he reached the main thoroughfare of the town, he saw Hester sitting high on her horse, talking to some of the others from their group. As he approached them, they paused their conversation and turned to him.

"Did you have a good day, babyface? Did you go to Tomb just for a shower and a shave?" Emmett joked.

Galadrath took in the statement. It felt like the day before had been so long ago—that he had not seen them in weeks. The constant Stepping, the endless night moving across the kingdom in darkness, and the lack of sunlight during the long hours he had spent in Taroosa's home—they had all taken their toll on his mind.

"I reconnected with a… friend. A woman I exiled to Tomb a long time ago, one of the Many. She's made quite a life for herself in that barren waste, trading with the airships of Tirv and creating machines unlike I've ever seen. I also visited a few of the spires and collected a few things she'd left behind. I'm afraid I may have stirred the hornet's nest. I destroyed a large ammunition battery in Silt, so I'm sure they will be looking for me," Galadrath recalled the events of the previous day.

"Gods broken! I heard the rolling thunder come from clear skies. I got out of bed to make sure doom wasn't descending upon us," Emmett exclaimed.

"So now you wage a one-man war against the kingdom? You'll bring them down on our heads," Tibel replied.

"Not a war. I was just running a few errands," Galadrath said.

He pulled the trinkets he had salvaged from his pockets and offered them on an open palm.

Hester reached out and picked up the earrings, held them up to her ears, the chain dangling down over her shirt. She smiled.

"How do I look?" she said coyly.

"As beautiful as ever," Justus said.

Emmett shot a glare toward him.

"You blew up an armory to recover a few pieces of jewelry?" Tibel asked, unbelieving.

"These are trinkets made of pure divine metal. They are conduits capable of channeling great power. It's best if you keep that information to yourselves. I probably shouldn't be telling you about them at all," Galadrath answered.

Hester reluctantly placed the earrings back in his open hand.

"You moved across the whole country twice, all within a span of a few hours?" Justus asked.

"You've seen what I can do. It's not so unbelievable, is it?" Galadrath asked.

"Not unbelievable, just incredible," Justus replied softly.

"How is Farrah?" Galadrath replied.

"She's getting better. She's settling, eating well. She's been in Green's stash of spirits, so she's still hurting. It'll take some time for her to mend," Tibel said.

"I wish I could do more for her," Galadrath said.

"You can make sure we're left alone," Emmett sternly replied.

Galadrath nodded gravely.

Hester looked back and forth between them, her face growing nervous.

"We're headed up to the Fort. Want to join us?" she said with artificial cheer in her voice. "Green said some of the others are coming back soon. We're setting up some shelters and planning for a bit of a festival."

"Thank you for the invitation, but I need to go home. The City of Light will be abuzz as soon as the messages from the spires reach it. I have to move quickly," Galadrath said.

Emmett crossed his arms and rolled his eyes.

"It's convenient how you're never around for the heavy lifting," he said.

"You said it yourself, I need to make sure you're left alone," Galadrath replied.

Emmett sighed loudly.

"I need to go," Galadrath said.

"Good luck, Vyhn," Hester said.

He nodded and smiled. The energy of the emblems poured into his veins, and the chill of the blackstone crawled down his spine. He drew his swords, and they took a step back, as the fog rolled over him.

He appeared in the doorway across from his own home. The suns still sat low in the morning sky, and the familiar smells of the awakening city greeted him. He had suspected his home would be guarded, and he was right. The influence of another shot out immediately around him, and he met it with both blades. The beggar spy's eyes were wide with alarm. The black smoke had hardly revealed Galadrath's form before the two swords plunged through his neck. The influence flickered and faded as the injuries broke the man's concentration.

"You attacked me in my own home. You spoiled what is sacred to me. You put my family in danger," Galadrath growled.

The beggar simply gurgled as blood poured from beneath the blades piercing his throat. He reached up slowly and grasped a blade in each hand, his mouth forming words that his voice refused to produce. Galadrath could not read his lips, but he could make out the intentions. It was the look of fear, the call for mercy that he had seen in the eyes of so many of those that he had accused.

The arrogance of the man angered him. There would be no mercy for this man, or any other who acted so dishonorably. He felt the resistance in the blades as they were held in place by the flesh and bone they impaled. He pulled them slowly apart. The power in his veins and the strength of the steel were no match for the beggar's neck. He crudely severed the head of the man from his body, blood pouring heavily from the rough stump of the corpse. He wiped the swords on the already-bloodied rags of the spy, a vain attempt to clean them before they were resheathed. He exerted his own influence and felt for the symbols and emblems that the dead man carried. Galadrath tore open the bloody rags, exposing a dirtied uniform underneath. He quickly gathered the emblems and a large chain adorned with the symbols of the court.

He shifted his concentration to the influence he felt around him, reaching out through the buildings and the street. He felt the forms of his household, held the air that surrounded each one of his family, embracing them from a distance. He choked and sputtered as his heart leapt. Tears began to well in his eyes, and he smiled to himself.

They are safe.

He unlocked the door with his power and stepped quietly inside.

"Raatel?" he asked.

"Galadrath!" the familiar voice rang out.

The lanky shape of the butler appeared from around the corner to the kitchen. His long graying hair was neatly pulled up into a bun, and the wrinkles on his face accentuated the wide grin he wore.

Raatel ran over and wrapped his lean, spider-like arms around his employer. He held him tight for a moment, and then pushed him out to the end of his long reach.

"I see much has changed, including your sense of fashion!" Raatel said.

"So much has changed," Galadrath said, wiping away a rogue tear on his face.

Raatel's smile softened, and he nodded.

"Let me fetch the lady!" he said.

"Let me," Galadrath replied.

Raatel nodded deeply.

"Would you like something to eat?" the old man asked.

"No army could keep me from your cooking. Please, I'm starving," Galadrath replied graciously.

The wide grin returned to Raatel's face, and he paused for a moment, inspecting Galadrath once again before scurrying into the kitchen. As he left, Galadrath headed for the stairs, climbing them quickly and heading for his own bedroom. He opened the door softly and saw Heladra still sleeping. He walked to the edge of the bed and took a moment to admire her peaceful face.

He reached out his hand and lightly ran his fingers across her shoulder. Her breathing changed. The heavy breaths of a deep slumber vanished, and she mumbled his name.

"I'm here, my sweet lily," he choked out between tears.

Her eyes opened slowly, searching her surroundings from where her head still rested on the pillow. They closed for a moment and then opened wide, her bright irises constricting, locking on his face. She shot up in bed, and her eyes filled with shock and wonder. The silk slip she was wearing draped down over her arm, and as he sat down on the edge of the bed, he ran his hand up her arm, pushing the material back onto her shoulder.

"It's you!" Heladra cried out.

She lurched forward and grabbed him, pulling him in close. He fell forward at the sudden tug, and they fell back into the bed. She laughed and shifted her hands into his short hair, drawing his lips to hers. He instinctively ran his hands along the slim nightgown and kissed her. Time seemed to stop as they held each other, passionately sharing their lips and their love for the first time in what seemed to be an eternity. After a while, he reluctantly pulled himself up to look at her, and she drug him back down by the bulk of his clothing, laughing as she did.

"I thought I lost you," she whispered in his ear, his head resting under her chin.

Words died in his throat, and his body tensed as the emotion hit him like a tidal wave.

"I can't imagine what you've been through," she whispered softly.

"And I, you," he managed to sputter.

"They came to the house. A whole army of Emissaries. I've never seen so many, except at court. They told me you were a murderer, a traitor, that you had stood trial. They made it sound like you were dead. They turned over every spoon, every stone, every sheet, looking for something—looking for you. It was the only relief I had. I knew if they were looking for you, you were still alive. Teratos finally came, and he told me what had happened. He doesn't understand what happened," she said.

Galadrath reeled up against her grip, staring into her eyes.

"Teratos! He was here? Gods living and dead, I'll kill him. That treacherous worm, crawling around my own home!" he growled.

"What do you mean? He's been so kind; he's done everything he can to help us. They were going to throw us in prison, to torture us for information of your whereabouts. He was the one who talked them out of it. He's been the only thing protecting us," she said.

Galadrath was overcome by another wave of emotion. He could not even protect his own family. He had run, hidden like a coward to save his own skin, and left them to fend for themselves. Now, his sworn enemy, the man who had betrayed him and spurred all of these events into motion, was the only one saving his family from pain and destruction. He could not quell the tempest of feelings inside him, the two opposites were irreconcilable in his mind. Teratos had handed him a letter containing his own name, to be sentenced to death. Had he relied on Galadrath to fail?

What if I had killed him there in the library? He can not be working alone. He didn't recognize the letter. Was he lying? Am I so naive that I can't tell when my oldest friend lies to me?

"The letter he gave me had his own name in it. When I refused to kill him, the court said I had attempted to murder him. They accused me of all kinds of false claims. Why would he condemn me to this fate if he knows I'm innocent?" Galadrath said.

"Maybe that's a question you should ask him," she said.

"I expect I'd hear nothing but lies. He's a snake, and he threw me to the dogs without so much as a warning," Galadrath said angrily.

"I'm not sure what's happening here, my sweet husband, but I urge you not to be blinded by your own assumptions. There may be more to this than we know or understand. I know you have a strict code, but you can't expect to see the bottom of a lake through murky water. You have to dive in and dig around for what you intend to find. You can't expect to see through the clear lens of honor and duty, when others don't maintain the same principles," she said.

"I'd boil it dry," he mumbled.

She sighed.

He had heard her words and absorbed her wisdom. She had always been able to make him see what he was unwilling to admit. His heart held hate and vengeance, and it clouded his judgment.

"I understand, my beautiful flower. I'll keep your words close," he said softly.

"Good. Let me go wake the children. They'll want to see you," she nodded.

"Yes. It feels like I haven't seen them in so long. I probably don't have much time... I left a dead man lying headless in the street," he said.

She turned around abruptly to face him. Her eyes were wild, and she threw her hands up in the air.

"Is this kind of behavior going to become commonplace? You leaving corpses on our doorstep like some feral cat? When I married you, I never thought that would be a discussion we'd have to have. Clean it up! The children will be leaving for school. I'd expect you to know better!" she replied incredulously.

She waved him along, ushering him into action.

He chuckled at her response. The first day he met her, she had almost ended him with a shovel; now she would bury his crimes with it. He stood and followed her out of the bedroom, heading back outside to dispose of the body. By the time he had removed every trace of the dead Emissary, dissolving and consuming him entirely and depositing the energy inside his emblems, he heard the children making a racket in the house. He walked back through the front door, thankful that the street was always quiet in the early morning.

"Papa!" Radralia called out.

His little girl ran to him and wrapped her arms around his legs. He reached down and returned the embrace.

"Come here, Marcanus, I want a hug from you too," Galadrath smiled.

The boy hesitated, swaying back and forth slightly, unsure of what he should do.

"The Emissaries said you are a bad man," Marcanus said.

"Marcanus, he's done nothing wrong. Go to your father," Heladra said softly.

"But you always told us we shouldn't talk to bad people. We should be honorable," the boy said.

"I am honorable, Marcanus. I have done nothing wrong. There are people who have made me out to be something that I am not. *They* are the ones who are acting without honor," Galadrath explained.

"But they work for the king!" Marcanus replied.

"The king's men, even the king himself, can be dishonorable. They are just people, people just like us, just with more power. Sometimes that power can change a person. They start to believe that they are above us—they begin to believe that they are more than just people. Trust me, my son, I will make this right," Galadrath said.

He waved one arm at Marcanus, while holding his daughter in the other. The boy hesitantly walked over and gave a half-hearted hug to Galadrath.

"I did miss you," Marcanus said.

"I missed you as well, terribly. I'm so sorry I've been gone. I have so many exciting stories I want to tell you, but I don't have much time, and you still have to get ready for school," Galadrath said.

"Do we have to go to school? Can't you stay a little longer?" Radralia asked, her tiny voice pleading.

"I'm not supposed to be here, my little rose. I don't want to make trouble for you, or put you in any danger. It's important that you act like I was never here. Come, let's have some breakfast before I have to go," he replied.

They all collected around the table, taking their seats as Raatel produced plates steaming with small fish filets, asparagus, and potatoes. Galadrath was not accustomed to such common faire, but everything was well-spiced and delicious. Halfway through the meal, as they shared the events of the past week, he looked toward Heladra and pointed to his plate with a fork.

"I haven't eaten this in so long. What made you decide to try it again?" he asked as innocently as possible.

"I've been going with Raatel to the market. It seems things have gotten more expensive since you left," Heladra replied.

The message was clear. The Court had been paying him an extravagant salary, and their lifestyle had matched his income. Without the influx of money they had grown to expect, changes had to be made. He knew they had plenty of money tucked away in the house, but Heladra had already taken steps to make sure it would last as long as it could.

He nodded silently and continued to eat.

There was a sharp knock at the door. The impacts on the outside rang loudly and with impatience. Galadrath knew it was a kind of knock that did not wait for a door to be opened.

"Raatel! Fill my seat!" Galadrath said, pointing to his half-eaten breakfast.

He stood and made room for the butler to take his place.

"I love you all. I'll be back soon. Stay safe," Galadrath quickly said in a strained whisper.

He could not wait to receive a reply, vanishing in a cloud of black smoke.

19

THE SHELTER

"Accuser! An Accuser is here!" screamed a young woman.

The smoke rolled down onto the ground around Galadrath. He spoke softly, the last of the dark vapor spilling from his mouth like a corrupted breath.

"It's just me, Vyhn. Nothing to worry about," he said.

He was standing back in Bracken village, and for the first time since he had set foot here, it was the only time he had encountered a complete stranger.

Green barged out of the side door of his tilted warehouse, before coming to an abrupt halt.

"Not to worry Elenn, he's one of ours," Green said.

"An *Accuser*?" the woman replied.

"One of Farrah's," Green added.

"Farrah has Accusers working for her? Why doesn't anyone tell me anything? God's dead, what is this world coming to?" Elenn yelled in outrage.

"Sorry to startle you," Galadrath said.

"By the Scar and everything unholy, does Bartron know about this? We're trying to run a wholesome criminal enterprise here, and you've got Accusers popping up out of the ground! He'll have your head, Green! You don't even have the decency to warn a gal that one of

209

these court spooks could be showing up at a moment's notice!" she continued.

"Stay that tongue of yours, or I'll nail it down for you," Green said gruffly.

She huffed at the threat, crossing her arms.

"Glad to know where I stand. Unbelievable!" she said, turning to leave.

"Farrah never said anything about an Accuser," Green said to Galadrath. "Neither did the others. They said we could trust you—maybe I should have asked if I could trust them. I should've known as soon as you handed me those rocks."

"They did nothing wrong. It's for your protection," Galadrath said.

He watched as the woman hastily disappeared into the distance.

"Everyone's protection—all of you," he added.

"That's something else I refuse to believe," Green replied.

"Suit yourself," Galadrath said.

He began to walk up the hill, toward the fort, hoping to find the others there.

"Who are you really?" Green asked.

"That's something else you'd refuse to believe," Galadrath replied over his shoulder.

He did not look back at Green to see his response, but the silence that followed indicated that he swallowed his own words—words Galadrath had thrown back at him.

He quickly grew tired of walking up the small path leading up toward the fort. He realized that the young woman and Green would undoubtedly share their discovery of his past, so any further attempt at hiding it from the other locals was pointless. He drew in the energy of the air emblem and launched himself upwards on a gust of wind.

As he gained altitude, he looked around. The mountains came into view, the trees shrinking away on their sides. He could see all the way to Delia's Flat, the wide uninterrupted road that ran from the City of Light—the one they had ambushed the caravan on. To the south, he could make out a few ships slowly making their way to the east.

This is a beautiful place, really. It's unfortunate it has been wracked by so much strife.

He made out the broken outline of the old fort below him and began his descent into the center opening, where the roof had collapsed centuries ago. The wind whipped around him, kicking up dust as he landed softly amongst startled townsfolk.

"Settle down! We know him," Emmett yelled, hushing the crowd.

"Probably not the most discreet entrance you could have made," Tibel said.

The people stood and stared, expecting something else to happen—to explain why one of the Many had landed in the midst of their preparations—never suspecting that he was actually a former Accuser.

"You're just in time to help us sink a few posts," Tibel continued.

Galadrath looked around. Large, elaborate tents had been temporarily erected within the fort walls. Some had been fastened to the brittle walls themselves, while others were suspended on large poles, their canvas stretched tight by ropes and stakes. He saw a few men working in teams, trying to break up the hard dirt and rock underneath as they dug holes to plant the wooden beams in. Around them, crates and woven baskets stood filled with food, brimming with cups and cutlery.

"I can help, though I think I should lay low for a while. I just killed an Emissary in the City of Light. Between that and the attacks on the spires, they'll probably be looking for me," Galadrath stated.

"Hah! This just keeps getting better," Emmett laughed.

"I thought you were supposed to be keeping them away from here?" Tibel said with unbelief.

"Well, I could be anywhere. The Emissaries and the ambassadors of the Lowest House all know that. They'll be clever enough to know not to look for me, but instead try and gain some insight to where I'll go next. They'll spread out to anywhere they think I might turn up," Galadrath said.

He walked over to the large piece of lumber, drew in on the emblems, and lifted it easily onto his shoulder. He walked over to where the men stood digging, the others following him.

"And where will you turn up?" Tibel asked.

"I'll be here," Galadrath said, smiling at them.

The end of the post swung around as he turned to grin at them, and the men around the growing hole scattered, avoiding being clubbed by the hefty pole.

"We haven't finished digging yet! It'll fall right over!" one of them yelled.

Galadrath plopped the end of the post into the hole, and the post sank further than what was dug as he liquefied the ground beneath it. He tilted it completely upright, and when he judged it was deep enough, the ground solidified around it. He let go and meandered away, leaving the digging men completely baffled.

"See, I figure they'll expect me to turn up somewhere soon. They're not prepared, and they know they've underestimated me. I can't believe that they haven't drawn the parallel between a hunted Accuser and a man clad in black destroying their things and killing their men. They'll expect me to strike again soon, to use my advantage. So I won't. You said you're having some sort of picnic out here? May I join?" Galadrath said.

Emmett and Tibel attempted to process his strategy, their mouths hanging open. They mirrored the dumbfounded men holding picks and shovels.

"Of course you're invited! We'd love to have you Vyhn!" Hester said, a little too much excitement in her voice.

"If you have an advantage, shouldn't you use it?" Tibel scratched his head.

"Is an advantage an advantage if your opponent knows you have it?" Galadrath asked.

His voice was chipper and upbeat. The combination of seeing his family and knowing that they were safe had lifted his spirits. The power of his newly acquired trinkets, and the awe with which he had been received, all coalesced into euphoria he had not felt for quite a while.

"Yes?" Emmett answered.

Tibel shook his head in Emmett's direction.

"No?" the red haired man answered again.

"Which is it, big brother?" Hester chuckled.

"I still think it's yes. If you see someone lift a cow with one arm, you know he's strong. If he comes to clobber you, then knowing he's strong doesn't stop him from being able to clobber you," Emmett explained.

They all laughed at the imagery he had created.

"Am I wrong? Tell me I'm wrong," Emmett said, placing his hands on his hips expectantly.

"Mister..." a coarse voice said from behind.

Galadrath turned toward a gruff-looking man.

"Call me Vyhn," he replied.

"Vyhn, could you help us with another?" the man said, pointing to a post.

"I'll do them all—just point me in the right direction," Galadrath said.

He lifted another post, his body still holding the energy of the emblems. The work went quickly, becoming some sort of sport, and a crowd of people gathered to watch the Accuser work. Each time he let go of another sunk post, they would cheer and laugh. He introduced some pageantry to the mundane work, swinging the heavy beams around his head or tossing them from one hand to the other. Each act would be met by gasps and cheers.

Barrels of ale were brought up the hill, a cow and a few pigs led to the outside of the fort and slaughtered. A large cooking fire had been built in the center of the open area, and Green carefully tended it, poking at the burning logs and churning up hot coals. The preparations continued throughout the day, and with the help of the Accuser, the revelry started early.

As the suns set and the denizens of the town had all gathered, enjoying the festivities and abundance of food and ale, Galadrath found himself sitting next to Farrah.

"You've made quite the impression. I've never seen them all so invigorated, so happy. I've never seen you smile so much either," she said.

"I went home. I had the chance to see my family, to hold my children. I got to share a meal with them. They're safe. It's strange how so much can change. We've all lost loved ones—it happens all the time, all over, to everyone. But even though it is an ever-present reality, we don't appreciate the moments we have with them until we lose them," he replied.

"That's the truth. It's one that's been repeated countless times. What do you think it will take for people to appreciate each other before they lose them?" she asked.

"There is nothing we can do. We can not live every day like it is our last. We can only live our last day once. We do not choose the end or the beginning. We must simply be present in every moment, even in the mundane. Even that is impossible. I'm not sure there is an answer to your question. I don't think humans have ever understood the reason for their own existence and, therefore, will never be able to appreciate what they have," he replied.

"Then what is it that we should do?" she asked.

"Simply, our best. Whatever that may be." He shrugged and held up his cup toward her.

Farrah extended her own mug slowly, careful not to aggravate her injuries, and bumped it against his.

"This is nice," Galadrath breathed out heavily.

"It is," she replied.

They sat with silence between them, enjoying the makeshift music and enthusiastic dancing. At the edges of the crowd, other onlookers sat as well. Some concentrated on their drinks, while others arm wrestled or played games of dice.

Few people noticed a group of men walking up the hill, beyond the reach of the firelight. Galadrath's easy posture tightened, and he pushed his influence outwards. More than twenty men were coming up the hill, and he could feel the weapons on them. He sensed their heavy footfalls as they disturbed the earth beneath them. He felt their idle breaths leaving their bodies, and the air calmly being sucked back into their lungs. He did not sense the presence of Many, and their nonchalance put him at ease.

"Your friends are here," Galadrath whispered to Farrah.

He pointed into the darkness, and as he did, the first man emerged into the flickering light of the central bonfire. Galadrath began to make out his features. Piercing eyes sat under a heavy brow, his face covered in a thick red beard, with wild hair to match. The man's bare forearms swung rigidly from broad shoulders; his barrel chest was covered in a heavy leather tunic reinforced with large metal plates. He kicked at the edge of a table as he drew near, chipping the wood with the heavy spikes that protruded from his metal-toed boots.

"I see you decided to start without us. Not a single sentry posted," the man spoke loudly.

Galadrath watched as the group sitting at the table removed themselves from it with haste. The man's voice matched the rest of him, dense and ruthless. The crowd grew quiet as they turned their attention to the disturbance. The man slowly rummaged through the mugs on the table, idly picking up each one and inspecting its contents, before setting it back down. He settled on a large earthenware carafe, scooping it up in a gauntleted hand. He raised it to his mouth and began draining it, the fluid streaming down the sides of his mouth into his beard.

The crowd was restless, murmuring amongst themselves. Galadrath was still fixated on the man. He was not intimidated, but he paused in admiration of the giant. He recognized the lineage immediately, a perfect specimen of Dradofir. He could have been one of the Six Sons, or a direct descendant of those lords.

"Bartron, good to see you," Green bellowed back. "Preparations went quickly with the help of Farrah's Accuser, so we decided to begin early."

Green was the only person in the crowd who could match the size and sound of Bartron.

"By the gods living and dead, Green. So much for peaceful introductions," Farrah mumbled to herself, just loud enough for Galadrath to hear.

Bartron began to scan the crowd from where he stood next to the bonfire. Galadrath saw the firelight reflected in his eyes, matching the intensity of the brutish man's gaze. His head turned slowly, pausing briefly on Farrah, before stopping on Galadrath.

"Accuser," Bartron growled.

"Vyhn Annya, at your service," Galadrath replied without hesitation.

Bartron scowled deeply, his stern face hiding his confusion. He lumbered toward their table, his heavy steps sending vibrations through the glasses of ale. His immense calves flexed and relaxed with each step as his big metal boots crunched against the dirt and gravel. He stopped just short of where Galadrath sat, the spikes on his feet grazing the fronts of the Accuser's own footwear. Bartron loomed over him, still scowling deeply. Galadrath could not stand without getting his head stuck in the man's beard, or falling gracelessly forward into a hug. Bartron had pinned him to the table without laying a finger on him.

"How did you come to work for Farrah, Accuser?" Bartron said in a low rumble.

"Probably the same way you did. She picked up a stray," Galadrath replied coolly.

Bartron's face slowly turned red. Veins emerged from the bulk of his neck and from under the wild hair covering his forehead. His ears moved slightly as his jaw muscles clenched, and he bared his teeth angrily.

"I don't work for Farrah. She works for me."

Bartron spit the words out like a bitter poison had been resting on his tongue. Farrah shifted her weight uneasily, throwing a glare at Galadrath. Everyone else was silently looking on. Only a few of Bartron's men were disinterested enough in the confrontation to continue foraging for food and drink at the tables. The rage-filled eyes continued to stare wildly at the nonplussed Galadrath, who was now leaning back on the table with his elbows, trying to get away from the wine-soaked breath of his aggressor.

Galadrath could not help but recall the old stories as Bartron stared him down. Not so long ago, when men still fought men—before the Few and the tides of Patches—the armies of Dradofir walked into Thainegom with a hundred thousand of the fiercest men and women the continent had seen. Their leader had been destroyed by her pride, and Galadrath suspected this man would ultimately suffer the same fate.

"Bartron, that's hardly a... fair... statement. We're more like equals, partners," Farrah said.

It was the first time Galadrath had heard her choose her words slowly, the only time he had ever seen her cling to caution so tightly. Without moving his head, Bartron's eyes flicked over to Farrah, still holding his looming posture over Galadrath. He rested his meaty hands on the heads of two of the many axes draped around his belt. Each one of the hatchets were oversized, with long, bearded heads—the length of each cutting edge half as long as their handles. These were not axes made for cutting wood or limbing trees.

Galadrath slowly pulled one arm forward and reached his open hand out to the man.

"It is a pleasure to finally meet you," he said.

"Put that paw back where it came from before I take it as a trophy," Bartron said through gritted teeth.

"Look, I'm not here for trouble. I'm here to help. I've been branded a traitor, and Farrah was kind enough to take me in and put me to—" Galadrath tried to explain.

"You're the one they're looking for. Emissaries are scouring the countryside looking for the man in black who burned down a whole caravan."

"A whole caravan? I only set one of the carts on fire," Galadrath replied incredulously.

A snort and a stifled chuckle betrayed Bartron's face. He straightened up, tossing his head backwards to look up at the night sky, trying to regain his composure without anyone noticing. He looked back down, his face once again stern, and slapped Galadrath heartily on the shoulder with a rough hand.

"I don't trust you, and I want you to make yourself scarce," Bartron said.

"I work for Farrah—she's made that abundantly clear. I'm not here to serve your wants, and I don't believe you have the power to make me," Galadrath stated.

Bartron's face transitioned to a darker red, bordering on purple. He turned his gaze toward Farrah, picking an easier target.

"I'm not done with you yet," Bartron threatened her through gritted teeth.

He turned toward the crowd of onlookers and nodded toward his own men in turn. He raised his armored hands high above his head and yelled.

"Who said to stop the music? Drink! Eat! Be merry you fools!" his booming voice commanded.

The crowd sprang into action and cheered. The musicians and their motley assortment of instruments began playing, each their own song in their own time, and eventually the chorus of chaos became one jaunty tune.

The party went well into the night, and Galadrath retired early after almost falling asleep where he sat. The drinks and excitement had allowed him to forget his pain for a moment, but when he stood to go, the dull pang in his arm and leg reminded him of his current condition. Farrah had arranged a room for him, and he praised the stiff uneven mattress of the bed as he lay down, happy not to sleep on the floor, or out in the elements.

20

THE WARDEN

THE NIGHT WAS PEACEFUL, and he slept like he was dead. The cool mountain air woke him in the morning. Rolling over, the cool sheets around him came as a shock. He had been perfectly cocooned under the heavy blankets, and his movements disturbed the warmth, allowing the crisp air to creep in under the coverings.

He grunted and tossed the covers open wildly, letting the cold embrace him quickly. He sat up in the bed, only wearing black silk shorts. He flexed his toes against the rough floorboards and tested his appendages, shaking the stiffness from them. He rummaged around under the blankets, retrieving his clothing from where they had been resting under his feet. It was an old soldier's trick he had learned long ago, to sleep next to your clothing in cold weather. A warm shirt and pants worked wonders for the spirit.

He quickly fell into a routine. The weeks passed slowly as he established himself in the community. His daily activities kept him busy, but they were tedious and mundane in comparison to the work of an Accuser. He often thought of his family, carrying conversations with them in his mind. He asked them about their days, imagining what their responses would be. He missed them fiercely, but the time away from them built him up. His wounds were healed, and the freshly knitted skin was no longer stiff.

Bartron and his crew had left a few days after the festival had ended, and the spirits in the community lightened. The people had respect for the bulky warlord, but there was also a latent fear of him. Only Green and Farrah were daring enough to stand up to him and his horde. Others had come and gone in the time that had passed. Smaller bands of thieves drifted through often. Larger, more organized groups strode in with bags of loot of all kinds of goods and weapons. Galadrath was surprised that such a small town in the middle of nowhere had so much traffic. Thainegom had a festering sore of traitors that it was unaware of—or simply ignored.

It was unsettling. He had never seen this portion of the kingdom. He was unaware that things were going so terribly on the outskirts of society. The old stories of a kingdom of peace and prosperity were no longer valid. The times when the Keepers of the Peace wandered the fields with nothing to do—and people could live their lives unmolested—were long gone.

Galadrath spent his time helping where he could, bartering his services for goods to maintain himself. He dabbled often in creating things, specifically building things. He sunk wells, repaired structures, mended fences, and cleared and plowed fields. The townsfolk had begun to rely on him. Something that would take them weeks of backbreaking work, he could complete in a few hours without so much as a drop of sweat. He built his own little one room home on the outskirts. A simple structure with a few furnishings. Every morning he would be met at his door by a collection of people who required his help. Each of them would present an offering of whatever they could afford. Sometimes he would rebuild a collapsed wall for a loaf of bread or wrangle stray livestock for a handful of eggs.

It felt good to be of service, to be useful without destroying. Some days he forgot he was a fugitive—the most wanted man in the kingdom—but the feeling always snuck up on him at dusk. He could feel the prying eyes, the relentless search that would eventually root him out from his safe haven. He knew that his mind was not the only one that Wandered. The Accusers would eventually find him, and out of the darkness, they would come and kill him.

As time went on, the work began to dwindle. The tasks became smaller and smaller and got to the point that even the laziest of the townspeople had nothing for him to do. The more idle he became, the more the future in front of him loomed like a thunderhead.

"I think it's time for me to get back to work," Galadrath said.

He sat across from Farrah at a tiny wooden table in a crowded corner of Green's shop, sipping at a large mug of weak beer. She had recovered nicely from her brush with death. Sometimes, he could see her frown when moving, as if her limbs and torso were inhibited—muscles pulling in strange ways, ribs knitting back together at imperfect angles.

"I thought you said you were running out of things to do around here?" she answered.

"I am. I have to go back to *work*," he stressed.

"Oh, I understand. I've had my feelers out for a few new jobs. I'm getting a bit antsy sitting around here as well, and the boys are drinking up a lot of our stores. It's best if we get moving, as well. There is a juicy warehouse I think we could liberate—with your help—just north of the Valley of Heroes. No one here would dare touch it, but I've got coin. With you amongst the ranks, anyone would follow us," she said.

"I've done some looking around, as well. There's another group of Patches far to the south, across the mountains, heading toward the sea. I need more blackstone," Galadrath stated.

She looked at him with disbelief.

"No. Absolutely not," she said intensely.

She subconsciously rubbed her side with one arm.

"I understand. I'll go alone," he murmured.

"What about my warehouse?"

"You've already forgotten Farrah—I can do both," he smiled.

She nodded and returned the smile.

"I'll get you the details of where and when we'll set out. We probably won't leave for a few days," she said lethargically, the plans forming in her head taking priority over her speech.

"No need. I'll find you."

She blinked softly and half smiled.

He stood and clinked his mug against hers, draining it.

"Next round is on me. I'll see you soon. Gods be with you, Farrah."

Her face held a pensive look. She looked healthy. Her olive skin had regained its light sheen, and the look she gave him said many things. The heavy bridge of her regal nose separated her dark brown eyes as if they kept secrets from each other.

"Good hunting, Galadrath."

He nodded and vanished.

Tracking down the Patches took little time. He had Wandered in meditations and found their dark pull, like a beacon of void. Even in the dark fog, they stood out—each of them a black silhouette on a dark gray background.

There was something unsettling Galadrath, though. These patches did not march the distinctive path toward the City of Light. Each day he stayed close to them, hesitating to strike. He was overcome with curiosity, mentally plotting their path as they headed for the great ocean. At first, he wondered if this was just a detour they were taking to more easily cover ground, or maybe they had learned to circumvent Silt and the garrison there.

Could they be learning? Or am I simply seeing what I want to see?

Galadrath discarded his speculations and applied logic to fact. Their unwavering course was into the ocean, heading south east toward the islands—or slightly farther to the east, to the first Treadfögz.

Could they be headed to that hellish portal? The gate that summoned the armies of darkness a thousand years ago?

He himself had considered going to the first Tread to harvest the blackstone at its richest source. Even the idea of it had stood his hair on end. The desecrated ground and the unyielding chaos that surrounded the massive portal that crossed the Scar was accompanied by distant cackles buried deep within his mind.

He shook the images from his head. He could follow the Patches into the shallow waters and accompany them to their destination, wherever it may be. It could take days, weeks, or months for the shambling shapes to cross along the ocean floor, emerging from the water with bits of fish and crustaceans assimilated into their forms. Fighting underwater was just as easy as fighting on land or in the air. But if they were heading for the Tread, and that was where he fought them, it made him uneasy. Even if that dark entrance gate had lain mostly inert for an eternity, the lack of understanding bred superstition in all men—even the Pillars of the Lowest House.

Eventually, he made up his mind: He would follow the Patches to the edge of the water, and that was as far as he would allow his curiosity to dictate his actions.

It took a few more days. Each morning he woke, ate a cold breakfast, and Stepped toward the beasts. He followed them on foot, keeping their quick pace with the help of the emblems. When they reached the ocean, it was noon, and they began to lumber across the rocky beaches. Washed up driftwood—full trees deposited up by the strong tide—covered in barnacles and seaweed littered the pristine white sand. The stink of mild decay and sea air filled his nostrils, and the cool breeze mixed delightfully with the heat of the suns beating down on his black clothing.

He took to the air, jumping into flight, the wind whipping around him. He pushed his influence outwards, and a million grains of sand sang his praise—a hundred stones joining them in a low chorus with the water beyond the beach humming along. His collection of divine metal made the work easy. Massive spikes of stone blasted out of the white sand, throwing branches and debris high into the air. Each spine jutted through the core of the broken monsters, and at his command, they peeled back into quarters, like the petals of a lily in bloom. The shale spikes pinned the horrors to the ground, tearing them apart gruesomely as the petals spread.

It took a few minutes for Galadrath to destroy the final one. The severed pieces of the monster attempted to crawl away as he landed next to them. He made out the mangled face of a bearded man, the thick hair matted and slick with black ooze. Along with the face, a few beavers had been caught up in the mess. He smashed each head in turn, launching first-sized stones into them with speed and precision. Eventually, the shapes all lay inert.

He began the bone-chilling process of consuming them, drawing the bodies into himself and watching them evaporate into their black-stone essence and nestling their ancient memories into his veins. The feeling was primordial, with no words or ideas conveyed, only a singular hate for hubris. A need to destroy a feeble opposition. The feeling was old and raw, and the nature of it was unsettling to him. He tried to suss out the mind that had felt it, each unique entity leaving a trace of itself on the feeling it imparted to the matter it had held. He had felt the countless memories of the Many, even those of the Few still trapped for so long. This was different, and he shuddered as the emotion licked at his brain like the raspy tongue of a feline. He feared he had touched the pure emotion of a god—and it was hate. A hate that had driven these creatures into the ocean toward an unknown target that was meant to be destroyed countless years ago.

Then, he felt another's influence butt up against his own. His concentration immediately shifted, and he spun on his heels to face the threat. Standing on a large rock jutting out into the beach, he saw the loose pants and a tight brown vest with a single red flower embroidered on the edge. He squinted to make out the face of the figure, to be sure. The woman wore her hair up in a braided bun, and he could make out a latent fear in her features.

"Living and dead, why *her*? Why now?" Galadrath whispered to himself.

"Vyhn! If that is your name. Stand down!" Her voice carried on the breeze between them.

"Accuser Diatara. I will not," he growled.

He watched as she set her jaw, and he could feel her heart sink.

"So it is you, Galadrath," she said softly.

The words crossed between them, the fields of influence handing them to each other like a passed note.

"Yes. You've come to accuse me? They sent you? Alone?" he asked.

He could feel the power radiating from her, and her threat still lingered in the air between them. He was armed, and so was she.

"I don't want to kill you, Diatara, but if you stand in my way I will not hesitate," he added.

"No. I'm not an Accuser anymore, just like you. Though they might reinstate me if I bring you in," she said.

"Have you been stripped of your titles as well?" Galadrath boomed.

His voice rang like an explosion, the emblems projecting it with power. The surface of the water splashed as the small waves were hammered by the sound, and the wet sand around his feet splattered outward as the shockwave propagated around him.

"Nothing like that. They've demoted me to a Rat Catcher. That's why I'm here."

The rage in him subsided, and he looked confused for a moment. He paced a few steps in one direction and then back toward the half-absorbed pile of goo laying around the flowery spikes.

"Just come down here so we can talk," he mumbled, waving her over.

She floated on a gust toward him, the soft sparkle between the contesting spheres of influence dissipating as each of the Pillars retracted them.

"Rat Catcher? You're an Accuser with three symbols to your name. Explain yourself," he said.

"You first, Galadrath. You've brought dishonor on the Lowest House—you're a murderer and a traitor. Explain yourself," her voice broke.

He opened his mouth to speak, and closed it, clenching his teeth tightly.

"I'm no such thing. On my honor, on my oaths, I merely did what I was told. Teratos framed me. *He* betrayed us. He fed me to them. I was sent to put him to trial, and I refused. He delivered the letter to me himself. He gave me his own name to accuse," Galadrath said, pacing back and forth. "Then, he betrayed me. He held me liable for my failure—he sentenced me to death for sparing his life," he spat.

"I wouldn't have believed you if you'd told me this a few weeks ago, but now I have no doubt," she said softly, tears in her eyes.

Galadrath spun to face her again, his eyes wild. He saw her pain and softened his face.

"So, you don't intend to kill me?" he asked carefully.

"I told you—I'm just a humble Rat Catcher."

"But *how?*"

"After we heard of your treason, the court suspended the use of the Accusers. Some were demoted, some disappeared. I'm not sure if they fled, were imprisoned, or otherwise. They found Accuser Elenn Tinistar with a knife in her back, slumped over a bar table. She was my friend during our lessons at the Temple of Light. She wasn't the kind to be helpless or to frequent drinking establishments. They're getting rid of us, Galadrath. I don't know why. I was taken before the court and resworn. They made me a Rat Catcher as some form of penance. They said the ambassadors had to re-earn their trust since the foundations of the alliance between Barkrill and Thainegom had been shaken by your actions," she explained.

"An Accuser sent to clean up this filth. I can't believe it. Has any word come from the Archons? Or has Barkrill made any statements?" Galadrath grumbled, pointed at the remains of the Patch.

"Archon Kammul sent a single message: 'Yield to none,'" she replied.

"That's not very useful," he mumbled.

"Why are they doing this?" Diatara asked.

"I'm not sure, but I intend to find out. I'll make them pay for this. Teratos and his lackeys will suffer."

"You really think the Administrant has something to do with this? Why would he turn his back on us? On Barkrill and the Lowest House?" she asked again.

"Power. It's always about power. Maybe the court has blurred his vision; maybe they've convinced him they hold more power than the Lowest House."

She laughed abruptly. He frowned at her, unsure of her sudden outburst.

"That would be utter stupidity! Since when has Thainegom had even a fraction of Barkrillen power?" she shouted.

"Not since the first Few died."

"Exactly!" she yelled in outrage.

"I don't know, Diatara, I just don't know. I'll have to ask him, right before I drive a blade through his heart," Galadrath grumbled.

"Galadrath! He's like a brother to you. Don't you think you should show some mercy?"

He listened to her words, but they did not match her emotion. She was defending Teratos and damning the court. She had been demoted and was doing the bidding of the court by chasing Patches, but she openly implied the assassinations of other Accusers. The past weeks had changed his mind, and his naive nature had been replaced with a latent distrust of everyone.

"He betrayed me. You know, as well as I do, there is no mercy to be given to a betrayer. Lest you wish to be betrayed again."

She sighed at his words.

"You're giving them exactly what they want. This rogue Accuser persona, Vyhn, has the capital buzzing. They've tried to make the connection to you, but they lack any evidence that isn't just speculation. They know it's you; they just can't prove it. But to the public, they're using the man clad in black—the terrorist who is schooled in Stepping to fortify their arguments. They're turning everyone against Barkrill. They're bringing up the old stories of the king's assassin. The alliance is crumbling, and they are fueling its destruction," she said.

"Barkrill has done nothing but help since the second war. If Thainegom wishes to throw that away, they will be weaker for it," he grumbled.

"What if they've learned to Step?" she asked with worry in her voice.

"It's the most guarded secret of the Lowest House. If someone has betrayed it, they've betrayed us all, and they will be destroyed by my hand or by the will of the Archons. We can handle our own," he said sternly.

"And what will you do with me?" she asked.

He shot a puzzled look at her once more. She was not herself. She was hiding something.

"Nothing? You've got your job to do, and I have mine. Looks like I've already taken care of these creatures for you, so you can be on your way. I'm sorry we met like this Diatara. I bear no ill will against you. We're both just pawns in a game. It was a pleasure seeing you again, and I do appreciate your kindness and your insight you've shared with me," Galadrath said, his tone formal and clean.

"I still have my honor Galadrath. Like you said, we handle our own. I can't just let you leave," she said softly, another tear forming at the corner of her eye.

He felt her influence extend around him. The breath he tried to pull into his lungs resisted him as the air calmed and galvanized itself against him.

"You mean to kill me?" he choked out.

"No, but I'm afraid you'll have to kill me," she sputtered.

He grunted and drew on the emblems. He could see the fear dancing in her eyes as she felt the power surge inside him. She did the same, drawing on her own energy.

"Goodbye, Diatara," Galadrath said in a steely tone.

As she braced for his attacks, he Stepped away.

The darkness and mist surrounded him, and the cold chill of despair replaced the glowing warmth of the suns. He moved with his mind, the hours and days passed as he found his way back to a hillside he had camped at two nights ago. As he moved through the blackness, passing the ghostly forms of trees and rocks, he felt something behind him. He turned and obscured by the darkness, he saw a figure. A woman was following him.

He always felt alone in this place, but not completely alone. As if he had walked into a room that someone else had just left, not sharing the same space, but aware that their spirit had lingered there for a moment. He feared Mirrora had finally come for him.

Out of the shadows, the woman stepped. Diatara's face was like stone in the surreal dimness, the tears flowing from her eyes were the only thing that made her look alive. She had followed him as he

Stepped, something only another Pillar had the skill to do. She was not Mirrora, though. He sighed in relief. He should have expected it for he had taught Diatara himself.

"I can't let you go," Diatara said.

Her voice was calm and pure.

But there was another voice behind it. An echo of his mind, his past, that came from beyond the walls of fog surrounding him.

I can't let you go.

I can't let you go.

I can't let you go.

There was a trickle of laughter from all around him. He locked his eyes on the ex-Accuser in front of him, and hers flitted around, searching the darkness.

"You can hear her, too?" he asked.

"Who is that? What is that?" Diatara asked.

"Don't follow me. This place holds a fate worse than death. I'll kill you if I must, but not here," Galadrath pleaded.

The laughter grew from the faint far off sound. It became louder, growing closer.

"Diatara! Leave! Now!" he screamed.

She ignored him, turning to face the darkness from which the cackling was coming from. From the fog emerged two gaunt hands as big as buildings, fingernails sharpened and glistening black. They reached high above them, each as wide as a ship's sails and each finger as thick as a mast, and fell downwards toward Diatara.

He ran toward her and grabbed her from behind, wrapping his arms around her. He closed his eyes tightly, expecting the claws to crush them, but felt nothing but warmth. He peeked through one eyelid, still vividly aware that he was holding onto Diatara. Sunlight beamed down on them from between the tops of the tall pines.

Galadrath had pulled them back to reality. He released his grip from her and spun her around to face him.

"Are you alright?" he asked softly.

"I am," she said slowly, in shock.

She blinked a few times, moving a hand to wipe the remainder of the tears from her cheeks. With a deep breath, she regained her composure.

"I've seen a lot of things while Stepping, but nothing like—" she said, stopping herself.

She looked at the ground around them. Giant furrows had been plowed through the rocky ground. Four on either side of them. He saw the realization dawn on her face, as she stared at the claw marks running down the hillside where they were standing.

"Don't follow me," he said.

21

THE STORM

HE SWIFTLY FOUND FARRAH and her cohorts. He appeared in the field where they all had gathered, and the thick black mist that rolled off of him unsettled them greatly. Bartron and his men were there, and Galadrath recognized a few of the others he had met at the festival. All together, he counted forty-three men and women.

"We've been waiting for you," Farrah said casually.

"Sorry I'm late. I had a few unintended encounters," Galadrath replied.

"Anything we should be worried about?"

"No. Leave the worrying to me," he replied briskly.

She stared at him in annoyance.

"Accuser! You took your time showing up. I was beginning to think you'd turned tail and ran," Bartron said.

Farrah shifted her glare from Galadrath to the bulky fighter.

"Not this again. Let's get down to business. The warehouse sits on top of that small ridge to the north. It's surrounded by some other structures, barracks, kitchens, officers quarters, and armories—all military. No civilians, so we're in for a fight, but at least we don't have to worry about innocent people getting in the way. Bartron and his boys have done some scouting. We're looking at a full garrison of hundred and thirty or so and a full complement of artillery. We don't have much

231

cover from any side, as we'll be moving across the open fields," Farrah laid out the plan.

"Are there Many? Emissaries?" Galadrath asked.

"None that we could tell," Bartron said quickly.

Galadrath was skeptical of this statement. There was not an abundance of Emissaries at the crown's disposal, but a strategic asset like this one would be well-guarded.

"I'll disarm the cannons before anyone makes their approach. Once the storm starts rolling in, that will be your signal to start the assault," Galadrath said.

Bartron and Farrah both looked up at the cloudless sky in confusion.

"I think you're mistaken, Accuser," Barton said flatly.

"I'm not mistaken. I am the storm," Galadrath replied.

Tibal, standing with the others, was close enough to hear and laughed.

"This is going to be fun," he said.

Bartron frowned in his direction, as if a joke he did not understand had been made at his expense.

"Is everyone ready? Might as well get started," Galadrath said.

"Shouldn't we wait for the cover of night?" Bartron asked.

"They'll be distracted, and you'll be able to close the distance without cover."

Galadrath nodded at Farrah and the others in turn, holding Tibel's gaze for a moment, where the man stood, resting on his rifle.

"Take prisoners if you can," Galadrath finished as he lifted into the air.

He floated high above the scene, propelling himself quickly on a gust to where the air was thin and cold. He loved flying, even though it was a tricky thing to master. The Many could manipulate matter as they saw fit, pouring matter and energy into the world at a whim, but the forces of nature were absolute. Gravity had to be overcome with force; inertia had to be generated and dispersed. The time it took to master flying was worth it—to float in the sky on the whipping wind was a form of freedom that could not be measured.

He looked down at the small fortress of buildings, the faint outline of the wooden palisades that made a crude ring around the assortment of brown roofs. He looked south for a moment, making out the tall, elegant spire that stood in the distance. To the north, he took in the craggy plains between the rolling hills, the place known as the Valley of Heroes.

It was hardly a valley, merely a field of grass skirted by a few shallow hills. From the ground, it was unremarkable. Someone making their way through the valley would stumble into the rifts and ridges left behind by the battle that had unfolded there. From the air, Galadrath could make out the root-like formations where the earth had caved into fiery pits that had swallowed men and monsters alike. The lattice of shallow trenches surrounded a single, untouched plateau—the place where the Ashmaker and the Votary had fought. The vast landscape of mud and blood, once littered with the unburied dead, was now peaceful and blanketed in long-waving grass.

He turned his attention back to the warehouse and the tiny covered bunkers at the outskirts where the cannons would be. He mentally cemented the positions of each one that could fire in the direction of the fighters on the ground. Then he began executing his strategy.

He vanished from high up in the air in a puff of telltale smoke and appeared at the entrance of the first bunker. He crumpled the surprised guard with a heavy blow to the stomach. The noise alerted the crew just beyond the doorless entryway. He sent a blast of air from one side to the other, knocking the cannoneer into the heavy barrel of his weapon, propelling the other two off their feet into the wall to his left. He drew his swords as they staggered from the gust and pummeled them into unconsciousness. Galadrath pushed out his influence slightly, bringing the elements of the bunker under his control. He was still not sure if an Emissary was present and did not want to alert them to his presence.

He felt the loaded cannon under his control, the metal eagerly answering his call, the powder and the ball inside greeting him happily. Then, he felt something he did not expect. The core of the cannon shell was hollow, filled with more explosives, and at its center was a delicate mechanism encasing an emblem.

Loaded with Bursts.

Shells like these were relics from the first great war. Each one could turn a normal cannon into a weapon of great destruction. The charge and the mechanism was enough to destabilize the emblem, releasing its energy all at once with devastating effect.

He soaked the powder inside the barrel with water and left the emblem behind, unwilling to take the time to retrieve it without disturbing the mechanism.

He closed his eyes and searched his memory for the next cannon's location. It was not an exact calculation, without extending his influence to cover the area, but it was a skill he had practiced to perfection. He vanished and appeared four more times, quickly dispatching each crew and disarming each heavy gun without raising any alarm.

The chill of the blackstone left him as he replaced its energy with that of the other emblems. His body tingled and grew heavy, his veins filled with fire and ice. He drew in the power until he was filled to the brim, and it threatened to burn its way out of his skin. It was time to create the distraction.

He thought of Heladra for a moment. How she would drag him onto their balcony when the clouds pushed in over the City of Light from the sea. When those torrential winds would bring the rain in sideways, she would laugh and dance. Every attempt he would make to keep himself dry and warm, she would scold him for. She would drag him to the edge and hold him against the railing and laugh as the rain battered against his back, soaking him. Sometimes, she would begin to cry. Not out of pain or sadness or even happiness, she seemed simply to be swept up in the moment, sympathetic to the clouds, also desiring to nourish the ground with moisture and wash away the stagnant grime of life. She wanted to cry how they cry and give how they give from themselves.

His mind tugged him in a different direction. He remembered Diatara standing in the fog—the tears rolling down her cheeks before the monstrous hands reached out to destroy her. He did not understand why she cried, nor why the horrible manifestation of Mirrora had come to kill Diatara. He had not seen Mirrora since he was a boy, and that was so long ago he could hardly say his memories of her were real. Regardless of this, he knew she was real. After all, she had left her hungry claw marks in the dirt under the two suns. She had manifested herself, ready to drag them back to Tor Zuer, the realm that she called home. It was the surreal space the Pillars merely borrowed from her when they Stepped.

Why do these thoughts plague me now?

He shook his head and returned to the task at hand.

Instantly, he expanded his influence to cover the entire complex. In that moment, he felt the hollow spaces of each of the living men and women that filled the fortification. Only a second later, he felt the reply of seven of those shapes, as the Many that had been enveloped by his influence became aware of his presence.

He had expected one or maybe two Emissaries, not seven. He did not have much time.

He pumped the energy inside him out into the air above him, and the beautiful day answered his command, the sky darkening with black roiling clouds. The wind howled outside the wooden walls of the bunker, the tempest he had summoned growing from nothing.

Cries of urgency and distress filled the whipping gusts of air. He could feel their bodies move through the space he controlled, as they ran outside to assess the abrupt change in the calm.

"This one's for you, Sebbatin," Galadrath said under his breath.

Fist-sized hail formed in the clouds above him. Like nature's bombardiers, they released their payloads silently into the unsuspecting fray below them. When the first of ice impacted, the cries of alarm were drowned out by the deafening blows. Roofs were hammered as the large ice balls shattered against them. Sharp clangs of armor and helmets receiving their beatings, and the muffled thuds of the heavy skyfall striking unarmored foes filled the air. Screams of pain and panic replaced the calls to arms.

Then, he felt his influence begin to crumble. Pockets ripped out from under his concentration. He struggled to sustain the storm while the Emissaries across the camp launched their counter-assault.

One Emissary moved into the doorway of the small enclosure. A tall man with white-blonde hair—young and handsome stood there—an air of nonchalance around him. He wore the customary white and silver robes of the Emissaries. Galadrath's attention moved to the silver chain holding a pendant, a token crafted in the shape of a family crest, openly displayed for all to see.

Pride.

"You must be Vyhn. Thorn of the crown," the man spoke in a gruff voice.

"I am, and so much more," Galadrath replied.

"You haven't asked me my name. Shouldn't you be curious to know who will kill you?" the man said, his words difficult to hear over the hail.

The air grew hard and cold as Galadrath focused his energy. He added just a touch of blackstone in the place of the energy he had expended conjuring the storm.

A blast of air cut through the space between them and sliced the cloud of black fog where Galadrath had been standing in two.

Galadrath stood behind him, conjuring a large wave of water and sent it hurdling around the man. The wave crystalized, icicles shooting out in large glistening spikes at odd angles all around him. As the water became solid and its momentum ceased, Galadrath pulled it back in around its target. The pillar of ice surrounding the Emissary shattered as the spikes drove their way back into the solid block.

It is unwise to work against an opponent without holding your own influence. This isn't theater, this is warfare.

The icicles and the ruptured block melted away into a muddy puddle as quickly as they had formed, leaving the broken and bloody form of the prideful man. Galadrath stepped closer and plucked the necklace from the corpse. The emissary's head had been punctured and crushed, flopping loosely as the light jewelry chain strained against his neck—until the metal gave way and broke.

A gout of flame shot out at Galadrath, and he pushed it aside with hardened air, the flames barely missing him. He looked up quickly and saw two more Emissaries standing on opposite sides of him. Their tiny bubbles of influence shimmered and sparked against his, as the air wicked between them, changing allegiance from one mind to another.

He gripped the trinket in the shape of the coat of arms tightly in his fist, and it lent its power to him. Two more blasts of fire shot toward him and collided with each other where he had been standing. Smoke dripped from his form, and then tiny spikes of metal shot through the ghostly fog. He had Stepped again and again, each time the Emissaries launched a new attack at the black formless mist where he had appeared and disappeared from.

He could feel the assaults, the power penetrating into his influence as they focused their own energy. The man and woman were not as prideful as the first Emissary, and he could feel their control and their fear. The faint cackling seemed to whisper their inner thoughts to him, the chill in his veins did not stiffen his muscles or crawl into his mind; instead, it empowered his reflexes.

Then, he felt the man draw in energy off the emblems, much more than he had before. Galadrath saw his opening: The killing blow that was meant for him had consumed the Emissary's concentration, leaving him defenseless. Galadrath pulled on the earth inside of him and focused it all into a spear-like spike of iron. The spear thrust from the ground underneath the man and impaled him, running at an angle through one of his feet and appearing from underneath his collar bone.

The Emissary screamed, and he lost control before he was able to launch his attack. Galadrath watched as the energy began to burn its way out. The skin along the impaled man's arms and chest ruptured in a bright light, his clothes instantly catching fire. His scream—the perpetual scream of agony—transitioned to a gurgling rasp as his throat burned away. Galadrath saw the look of terror on the woman's face, and she launched herself backwards into the air, knowing what would happen next. The Accuser knew he could distance himself from the blast, but she would not be so lucky. He imprinted her face in his mind and Stepped away.

He appeared in front of the group of bandits who were lightly jogging toward the outskirts of the battle, still outside the walls.

"Take cover!" he yelled.

They looked at him in alarm, his booming voice dissipating the black fog around him instantly. They dropped to the ground—not understanding, but obeying with haste.

Light shot upwards from inside the walls of the encampment, mirroring the brightness of the suns above them, a star born for an instant, followed by the explosion.

The palisade, the bunker, and a nearby watchtower were instantly turned to shrapnel as the ground heaved upwards, the sky filled with lightning arcing wildly—and a deafening boom roared outwards. Dirt, debris, splinters, and timber exploded outwards from where the impaled Emissary had stood, leaving only a chaotic charred crater at the epicenter.

Farrah and Bartron, along with their fighters, hugged the ground and covered their ears and heads as the cascade of rubble showered down all around them. He heard the faint whistling of the cannon barrel tracking far overhead. The weapon was now its own projectile that would land far behind them. Galadrath was pleased that they were in relative safety—that they had not crossed the open ground more quickly. The Bursts loaded into the cannons would have had a similar effect, but he had forgotten that each Emissary could prove to be just as destructive.

"There's an opening for you now," he said, loudly with nonchalance.

They did not seem to hear him, their ears likely still ringing from the incredible release of energy.

He returned his concentration to his influence, and the storm that had dwindled as his attention shifted. He Stepped back into the smoldering fray, where the hail hissed and continued to fall on the burned ground. There was nothing left of either of the Emissaries, even their trinkets had been scattered. The unbridled power had consumed them both. He felt the other four shapes holding power, making their way through his influence amid the disarray of the regular soldiers. There were fewer now. Two smaller buildings had been swept away, along with their inhabitants who were seeking shelter from the storm. The bunker and the unconscious crew he had left there were just a memory now.

One of the Emissaries took flight. He felt them struggle against his influence, the air resisting their advances as they swam upwards into the low-hanging cloud. He saw the silvery-white form rise behind the buildings, robes flapping wildly.

My next target. Galadrath smiled to himself.

Then the other three Emissaries he felt rushed toward him, and he traced their path between the buildings and up over them, onto a nearby roof. At the same time, a large group of soldiers appeared from around a corner, shields of wood and metal held above their heads, the banging of hail sounding their approach.

"Vyhn! Stand down! You are outnumbered! Give yourself up!"

Galadrath did not recognize the voice, but he could make out the stern face and bushy beard. It was one of the Emissaries who had attacked him in the court. He pulled the hood of his cloak low over his eyes to hide his face, but it was too late.

"Galadrath, it's over. We're taking you in, dead or alive," the man stated.

"I've already killed three of you," Galadrath said coolly.

"Neophytes—eager to please and overzealous, if you ask me. They don't train them like they used to. The court gives trinkets for anything these days. Not like the old ways—when crushing rebellions, starting and finishing wars, and dealing with horrors earned respect and honor. Those trinkets were earned by blood and valor, not by bureaucracy, not by mercy," the man said.

More pride.

The other two younger Emissaries exchange glances. They both wore three symbols each, half as many as the bearded man. Galadrath guessed they had not earned their titles in combat, based on the fear they wore on their faces.

"I agree. The Temple teaches a great many useful things, but you cannot train to fight without fighting," Galadrath replied.

The Emissaries were stalling, and the soldiers were slowly closing the distance between themselves and Galadrath. He was stalling, too. He was outmatched—again. Even inexperienced Emissaries knew how to wield their power, and though the soldiers would serve as nothing more than a distraction, they would still divide his concentration.

Galadrath hatched a plan. Slowly, he pushed water into the ground beneath the soldiers feet, and as they took bated steps toward him, they began to sink, each footfall swallowed further by the ground.

"If you come willingly, I can see to it that your family sees you one last time. To my knowledge they are still alive, even if they are rotting in a dungeon," the man added.

Galadrath felt a pain in his heart. He had thought of his wife and children often over the long weeks past, but always with joy, knowing that they were safe. He assumed that if the court had left them alone before, they would not have a reason to harm them now.

Have my actions jeopardized them again? Or is this man simply goading me into a rage?

His thoughts spun around, the possibilities were endless, and he had no idea what the truth was. He could not bear the thought of his family in chains or worse—tortured. His blood boiled with emotion and energy.

True or not, rage is what I have to offer.

As if to answer him, his storm clouds caught fire. He could feel the writhing flames jet out in every direction, burning away the moisture and the hail. But it was not his doing. The Emissary he had spotted earlier rising into the air had waited for his concentration to fail, and in this moment, had found his weakness and exploited it.

The hail stopped abruptly, and the soldiers launched themselves forward, shields down in front of them. The slick and watery mud caused them to falter, their boots sucked against the embrace of the wet earth beneath them. The Emissaries began their attack, as well. The earth beneath him came alive, rocking upwards and parting beneath him. Razors of wind lashed out, and serpents of flame coursed through the air, burning their way toward him—all of which carved into his influence.

Galadrath knew he would not be able to fend off a sustained assault from the Emissaries. Their power was too great compared to his own. The words of the bearded man had stung him, and all he could do was think of his family.

Time for a little interrogation. Break the ranks up.

He gave it all up. Like the man who had exploded in brilliance, Galadrath filled himself to the brim, brought all his power under a single focus, and let his guard down. His influence vanished, and his rage took its place.

He Stepped in front of the bearded man, the concentration of attacks cacophonously converging behind him. His hands snapped around the neck of the man, and for an instant, their eyes met. Violence, hate, and the thrill of battle were mirrored between them. Galadrath drew his concentration to a point and Stepped again, holding onto the man in his hands and his mind.

The chill of Tor Zuer and the blackstone in his veins was no match for the relentless anger he felt. He did not know where he was going, and he left no room in his mind to find a place. He glared with hatred at the Emissary, and the silent darkness surrounding them gave way to chaos of where Galadrath's subconscious had chosen for them.

The sky was dark with black and purple clouds. Icy wind whipped around them as perpetual thunder rumbled and lightning flashed across their faces. The sea boiled and swirled far below the crude pillar of stone they stood on. Hatred vanished from the man's eyes, replaced by dread, as if Galadrath had siphoned his emotions away while they transitioned from one reality to another. This dark nightmare they found themselves in was not some alternate realm—this was the real world.

"Where did they take my family?" Galadrath screamed over the chaos.

"Evelyn, I'm sorry, Evelyn," the man choked out.

"What's your name?"

"It's me, William. I've failed you, Evelyn. I'm so glad you are safe. I'm sorry. I'm sorry. Your friends, your family, they all lie at the bottom. I'm sorry," the man wept.

The Emissary pointed with one shaking hand toward something behind Galadrath. Still gripping the man by the neck with both hands, he swung his head over his shoulder. Realization struck him as he understood where they had gone.

Behind him loomed the Tread—the immense tubelike portal of black obsidian—the vast Scar that it stretched across, and the ceaseless chaos of energy unleashed during its destruction. They stood on ground forged by the Ashmaker, and the mind of the Emissary had witnessed the events that had unfolded here.

"Where is my family?!" Galadrath spat again.

"The bottom—the bottom of the ocean," the man sobbed.

Galadrath knew there was no point. The memory was too strong, and he did not have time to nurse the Emissary's mind back together. The lightning around them grew more intense, sizzling in the water as the bolts struck closer and closer to their pillar of stone. The flashing light and menacing clouds seemed to search for him, to be drawn to his power.

Farrah will be running into her own death at the hands of those Emissaries. No time.

He squeezed the man's neck, collapsing it with his hands. He felt the cartilage and bone pop and crumble under his knuckles, the flesh yielding completely. He ripped the trinkets from the Emissary and drew in the blackstone once again. He had not yet Stepped, when the cackling drifted to him on the torrent of wind. It came like a whisper that should not have been heard over the din surrounding him. Unsettled, and still holding the corpse by the neck, he Stepped.

The darkness and the chaos of the Tread became a distant memory as the fog surrounded him. The surreal calm was welcome, and the silence was only interrupted by the ringing in his ears. He moved with his mind back toward the warehouse and the fight that awaited him. The days and months that seemed to pass as he moved tempered his feelings, but a thought crawled back up his neck, plucking softly at the hairs along his spine.

He was tired. The calm gloom of the ethereal space tugged heavily on his eyelids. The battle of influences, the expenditure of so much energy, and the single act of Stepping with another living body had drained him.

The pleas of the Ashmaker rang in his ears, projected by the Emissary. The words played over and over in Galadrath's head.

Evelyn, I'm sorry, Evelyn.

The memory was strange. Evelyn was the name of the Timeless Mother. Galadrath rarely heard her name—or felt the memories of the Ashmaker. Mostly, they came from battlefields where his wrath clung to every stone. But this memory was raw despair, overwhelming failure. Galadrath could feel the crushing pressure as though physically sinking into an abyss, a heavy weight pressing down on his chest, driving him into a coffin.

Evelyn, I'm sorry, Evelyn.

"Evelyn, I'm sorry, Evelyn."

The voice speaking the words in his mind had changed. It was no longer the gruff, sobbing words of a man about to die. It was *her* voice. He looked down at his hand clutching the neck. He felt the soft skin his thumb pressed into. Long, black hair ran over his fingers cradling the back of her head. The body of the Emissary was not there. Instead, Galadrath's hand was wrapped around the neck of a beautiful woman. Her jaw was strong, her eyes intense, and her features were light and frail—her shoulders wide and powerful. Her body was clad in a flowing black dress. She raised an open palm with slender fingers to his hand and softly caressed it.

"Evelyn, I'm sorry, Evelyn," her voice came from beneath his fingers.

He flinched at the sight, reflexively squeezing tighter around the feminine neck. The woman smiled, and he saw slick, black fingernails where her teeth would be.

"Don't let me go," she croaked.

He appeared between the two remaining Emissaries and dropped the body as if it was on fire or covered with disease. The woman he had held was gone, and the lifeless bearded face had returned—the flowing black dress once again the silver and white robes.

The experience left Galadrath both shaken and completely exhausted. He found himself standing between two people ready to kill him, and it took everything he had to maintain his composure.

"Surrender or die," he bluffed.

The Emissaries hesitated, the energy still flowing through them, and looked at each other. They glanced at the corpse of their leader.

A shot rang out. They all turned toward the group of encumbered soldiers and the collection of brigands who had mounted the small hill inside the scorched opening. A puff of smoke obscured Tibel. His shot was not at them, but instead it flashed high above them, where the third Emissary was descending from the dispersed cloud. The bullet fragmented against the hardened air, the friction breaking it apart and liquifying the metal as it met resistance.

Galadrath watched the tiny burns form in the pristine clothing of the flying man. The molten chunks would be painful but not lethal. He summoned the last of his strength and channeled it into an unwavering voice.

"Last chance," he said.

"I surrender," one of the Emissaries resigned.

The soldiers followed suit quickly, watching the stalemate unravel. They abandoned their weapons and shields, expending their effort to free themselves and each other from the thick mud.

Galadrath took the surrender unanimously. He glared at the Emissary who had not yet stated her submission.

"I'll take your trinkets," he added.

His glare was answered wordlessly, as he felt the energy subside within her. She pulled the beautiful bangles from her arms, tossing them to the ground at Galadrath's feet. The Emissary still flying in the air retreated upwards, picking up incredible speed, and fled at the sight of the defeat.

Galadrath sighed with relief.

Everyone had seen the exchange, and the tensions subsided. Fighters on either side transitioned into their appropriate roles of captive and warden. Farrah walked to the side of the building where Galadrath and the two Many stood. She beckoned for him, a look of worry on her face.

He dropped down and followed her into a small building where they could be alone. The smell of ozone and burning wood wafted into the small space, mixing with the musty and comforting smell of stored grains. The faint rustling of harvested wheat greeted him as he sat on a large sack, resting his fatigued form.

"I don't really know what I was expecting here, but this was not it," she said.

"What do you mean? We've secured an arsenal, cannons, Bursts, food, and supplies—without so much as a scratch. This was an overwhelming victory for the cause," he replied.

Her face twisted between worried seriousness and the intensity of greed and joy.

"Galadrath! Those are Emissaries out there. Any one of them could have wiped out our entire attack. Bursts! They weren't merely guarding this place—they were ready. They were waiting for you," she protested.

"Yes, I know. They were expecting me. After weeks of nothing, hiding without a single contact with the outside world, they send seven Emissaries to meet me. This was no coincidence."

"Bartron, he hung back with his men. I've never seen him miss leading a charge," she whispered.

"You think he sold me out?"

"It only makes sense. He's not fond of you, and he is a great tactician. If he gave you up and you were killed or captured here, I suspect he would have collected a great reward. If you succeeded, like you did, the spoils would be ours. He knew he couldn't play a losing hand here," she speculated.

"I'm putting everything you've worked for in danger," he replied solemnly.

"Great risk, and great reward," she nodded.

The way they spoke to each other was akin to a married couple, or well trained soldiers. The simple words were merely a placeholder for the ideas that flowed between them.

"As much as I'd like to remove his eyes from their sockets, Bartron is acting in the best interest of what you are working for. My goals don't wholly align with yours, and I'm sure he's picked up on that. We should part ways," he said.

"That would be best. I have to set the affairs of my house in order."

"And mine, too. One of the Emissaries said they've imprisoned my family. He recognized me, and I think he was just trying to weaken my resolve, but I can't be sure. It's been weeks. I have to see them—to make sure my wife and children are safe," he stated.

"God's living and dead, be good to you, Galadrath," she said softly. Then she added, "And thanks. You've done so much for us in so little time. If I can repay the favor, you'll know how to find me."

He nodded, stood slowly on his tired limbs, and left the small building.

It was going to take a long time for the capture and organization of the prisoners and supplies. While the camp was bustling with affairs, Galadrath slipped out mostly unnoticed. He weakly pushed out his influence at intervals, searching listlessly for the trinkets of the two disintegrated Emissaries. When he finally found the last one, he picked it up from among the tall grasses, brushed a bit of charring from it, and looked at the untouched divine metal. The faces the trinkets belonged to were added to the vast congregation of those who had met their fate at his hands, and their symbols were taken into the fold of his arsenal.

22

THE MASTER OF FORMS

THE COMFORT OF THE tiny home Galadrath had built in Bracken gave him a complete night's rest. His resolve was steeled and ready. The previous weeks of absentminded choring and idleness had awoken his long buried passion for his work. It was time to set things straight, to go home for good. He collected the mismatched assortment of trinkets in his hands, feeling their power. He read each inscription as he put them on.

The words of the Ashmaker returned to him.

"I'm sorry, Evelyn," he repeated curiously.

As he made his final preparations, the grief and sorrow of the statement washed over him, and he was overcome.

"I'm sorry, Heladra," he croaked.

He yearned to say the words to her, to hold her again.

He drew in the cool dread of the blackstone and Stepped into the dining room of his home in the City of Light. He stood there for a moment, the almost imperceptible hissing of the black smoke escaping from his clothing was the only sound. There was no laughter of children, no clinking of pots or plates in the kitchen. There were no smells of breakfast, no hint of Heladra's exotic perfumes—only the stale bittersweet of old Nightbloom.

Fear began to grow in his heart. He walked quickly and quietly through each room, searching for a sign. Nothing. He proceeded upstairs, finding everything in its place, everything but his family. Then he felt it, the grip of influence that was not his. The fear inside him grew into a reality, the multitude of nightmarish possibilities.

He strained as he walked up the last flight of stairs, onto the rooftop garden. He drew on his emblems and prepared for the worst.

"Ah, Galadrath. You've finally returned, as I suspected."

Galadrath immediately recognized the voice and the face of the man reclined idly in Heladra's favorite spot.

"Larl Rihhi," he said.

"Court's Accuser, High Honor Larl Rihhi," the man said.

He stood from where he was laying. He was not tall, nor was he of large build. Clean-shaven cheeks and dull brown eyes made up a handsome face. There was a faint and familiar clinking from underneath his cloak, and he threw one side open over his shoulder. Galadrath made out the chains instantly, draped like a long metal stole around the neck of Larl. He could recite every inscription—could remember how they felt wrapped around his own arms.

"You've inherited more than just my title, I see," Galadrath growled.

"Keen of you to notice. The most impressive of which is this remarkable view. I can see the palace, the docks, even into the distance across the plains. Beautiful. I've been quite pleased stepping into the skin of your former life, and I've had time to make it my own. Not that I've had to change much—you have good taste for comforts. If only I could have stepped into the skin of your wife," Larl said nonchalantly.

His voice was captivating, his words flowing out like warm honey—smooth and sweet—but they landed on Galadrath's ears like acid.

"Where is my family?" Galadrath hissed.

"Why would I tell you?"

There was a pause between them. Galadrath felt Larl's influence extended outward. Though he took very little under his control, the energy coursing through him was immense. The air around him grew dense, and Galadrath watched as frost began to form—delicate fractal patterns spreading across the floor, ice crystallizing on Larl's shimmering white and silver robes. He expected to see Larl's breath fog in the air, but he knew better; the man held enough air in his veins to breathe without breathing for a lifetime. He recognized the traditional teachings of the Temple—the combat form that Larl had already moved into.

"Your family is being tortured for information."

"Where? Why?"

"Where? I won't tell you. Why? You already know why." Larl's soft voice was accompanied by a smile. "How many fingers do you think they have left? How many eyes? If only we knew where to send the pieces, we would have been able to slowly get your family back to you."

The pain seared in Galadrath's head. Rage, anguish, dread and fear all threatened to pour out of him. The energy he held felt insignificant compared to the wave of emotions.

"I'll tear this whole kingdom down to find them. I'll destroy anyone who stands in my way," Galadrath spat through gritted teeth.

"Then you'll find their bodies among the rubble."

Galadrath glared with the intensity of the Sisters. Every muscle in his face tensed and strained, cheeks reddening. The veins beneath his skin stood out, as if they, too, would break free—lashing out at Larl, willing to spill their own blood and destroy their own host just to strangle the enemy to death. His mind raced so quickly that it reached an empty place–it reached Calm.

Galadrath emptied his mind and let the energy flow back into the emblems. He closed his eyes slowly; when he opened them, they were devoid of emotion. His face was blank, and his posture relaxed. He drank in the emblems again, centering the energy within. Then he pushed out his influence as lightly as Larl had. Their bubbles remained small, just shy of touching across the small distance between them.

I can not let him unbalance me. I can not change the fate of my family at this moment. First, I must deal with this—in this moment.

"I'm ready," Galadrath said.

"I'm impressed. I'm humbled, even, to have underestimated you. I should have known better—expected more from a Pillar, an Accuser.

There is honor in you yet, something they will never be able to take from you."

Galadrath felt the situation evolve, the strategies change. He remembered the sparring matches he watched at the Temple, the trainees moving slowly through the forms they were taught. Now this looked very similar, as if he was about to compete against another student, to test their mettle and skill.

"Thank you, High Honor. Honor is among the few things I have. Delay no longer," he said softly.

"Everything else of yours will be mine," Larl replied.

The entire rooftop was instantly covered in flames. The air itself seemed to crack and pop as it caught fire. Only the two tiny spaces where the men stood were safe from the writhing heat and intense torrent of fire. Galadrath could feel the heat press against him, wicking into his influence. The walls charred and the furniture burned wildly. His flowers growing along the railing wilted into ash. The vivid colors of the curtains and window coverings blackened and shriveled into dancing cinders.

Galadrath launched his first attack. An array of metal spikes appeared at his feet, growing from the floor instantly, surging into the fire and across the small space between them. They squealed as they moved between the heat of the room and the frigid sphere Larl had encased himself in. The air resisted them, dulling their points and slowing them before they could reach their target.

He uses the traditional forms. With the power of my chains, he will be impossible to reach.

In return, Larl ripped down the surrounding roof and walls. Each burning timber and plastered brick became a projectile heading for Galadrath. They fragmented and slowed against his own defenses, but Larl's power was immense. One of the beams dropped heavily through the fortified air and came down hard on Galadrath's shoulder. He Stepped too late. His ligaments popped, sending a sharp pain coursing into his neck and head.

He appeared in the fire at the edge of the roof. The flames immediately caught his clothing on fire, and he pushed out with water in a wide arc around him. Fine beads of moisture sprayed in every direction. The flames hissed and retreated, water evaporating into a cloud of steam. He continued to rain outward from his body. He pushed harder, each water droplet turning to ice, and accelerating toward Larl.

"I see you've opted for the Grey Armor. I prefer the Light, a less sporadic, omnidirectional defense," Larl said over the chaos.

The flames sizzled away, and ice pelted against what was left of the structure, bouncing harmlessly against the cocoon of power Larl had created for himself.

He's quoting Forms to me, in the middle of combat.

"You're destroying my home!" Galadrath roared.

"When I'm done, there won't even be a memory left of you," Larl chimed.

Galadrath felt his influence fail, as Larl ripped it away from him. Instantly, a stone struck him in between the shoulder blades from behind. He fell forward, his vision fading slightly as the agony of the blow spread to every nerve in his body.

Larl reached forward and snapped off two of the iron spikes still protruding from the floor—as if they were brittle twigs—and sauntered toward Galadrath. The mirage of impenetrable air followed him like an aura.

Galadrath looked up, his vision returning just in time to see the first dulled spike come down with incredible force. Larl drove the blunt metal in between the bones of Galadrath's left arm. The impact shattered the charred wet tile beneath it.

Galadrath cried in pain.

The second spike began to glow white hot at the end, the air around it a crackling wave of heat.

"I expected a little more from you," Larl said.

He stabbed the white hot rod of iron at Galadrath's head.

I'm sorry, Heladra.

Galadrath jerked his head to the side, but the molten spear caught him in the eye and burned a hole through his temple. He screamed a guttural scream as he heard his own flesh boil and burn.

I'm sorry, Heladra.

"I forgive you, Galadrath," a soft feminine voice came.

Galadrath felt as though his pain had been granted a voice. As if his anguish had taken a physical form. It took control of his mind, and in a moment of clarity, he vanished.

The pain throbbed with each heartbeat. With every hollow thump in his chest, a new nightmare greeted him. His whole body was a prison of agony, his senses overwhelmed and unable to make out his surroundings. He opened his remaining eye, and there was only darkness. A scratchy hum from a shrill voice wafted around him. He could smell only burned meat.

"It looks like you've failed me, friend," Taroosa stated.

He opened his mouth to speak, his dry lips clinging together for a moment before they separated.

"Shush!" she said.

He felt the edge of a cup, then cool water poured slowly between his teeth and over his tongue. He sputtered and choked as he tried to swallow.

"Now don't go drowning—that wouldn't be appropriate."

He gulped down a few sips, trying but failing to relieve an unpleasant film inside his mouth. His mind grew numb, and the throbbing of his pulse faded to a far away rhythm.

He woke from his slumber, his whole body unresponsive. He could not feel or move anything. As he opened his uninjured eye, the only sign of his existence was the light scraping sound as his eyelashes moved against coarse cloth.

"Are you awake? Let's see what's going on here. Of course, you won't be able to answer me. I've given you a very potent anesthetic. Your muscles will be nice and relaxed," Taroosa's voice greeted him, her footsteps growing nearer. "I should really consider giving this stuff to more people. It's much easier to carry a conversation with someone when they can't speak. Hah!" she said.

Galadrath's vision returned as the cloth on his face was pulled away.

The bright light of the room bled into his unadjusted vision. He laid on his back, looking upwards at the curve of the large dome that made up the home of Taroosa. She loomed over him, her downward gaze quickly studying every part of him, her eyes shifting as they examined him. She began to speak again, her bent posture causing her chins to wrinkle and expand.

"You won't regain full motor function from your extremities for a few hours, but I've tied you down. It's best if you don't move for now. I'm not sure how you're alive. When I dragged you onto this table, your body sounded like a bag of marbles. There are quite a few loose bits in there that shouldn't be loose. I'm no physician, but if I were, I think you'd be better off dead," she blabbered.

She held up the earrings and the pendant he had liberated from the spires, and he watched as she mock wore them, holding them to her ear and chest, swaying back and forth slightly.

"I see you found some of my things! I see they haven't served you very well. No fault of their own, a tool is only as good as its wielder," she trailed off.

He tried to speak, but the best he could manage was a flare of his nostrils.

"Yes, yes, I want to hear all about it. First, I think I'm going to have to do something about your bones, before this sedative wears off."

She rolled him onto his side, and he looked idly into the room. The strange shapes hanging from the ceiling cast warped shadows on the walls. He could not see what she was doing, nor feel anything but pressure—the push and pull of her struggle as she carved into him. She produced tools and devices from beyond his field of vision, not asking or telling what she was doing. Anything was acceptable, he supposed, as long as it would allow him to find his family.

He heard the clinking of metal and the smell of fresh blood. He heard cutting and banging, cursing and small noises of epiphany coming from behind him where Taroosa worked.

"I think that will do," she finally said.

She rolled him onto his stomach, his limbs flopping carelessly around him.

"You won't be able to lay on your back for a while... well, ever again," she chortled. She then stuffed flower petals one by one under his gums. "Something for the pain."

The bittersweet of the intoxicating flower reminded him of home, and a single tear dripped from his eye onto the table where he lay staring at it.

Eventually, his fingers and his toes began to respond to his commands, and he wiggled them furiously in an attempt to accelerate the process.

"I... have to go—" he slurred.

"You're not going anywhere."

"—Back," he finished.

"Back? Your back is broken. Like I said, you're not going anywhere," she chastised him.

They were silent for a long time. Galadrath eventually pulled himself to a sitting position, swaying precariously over the edge of the table. He sturdied himself by gracelessly flopping his arms to each side, trying to get his fingers to grip the edge of the table. He smacked his parched lips together. Taroosa approached with a cup of water, never too far to rush over if he were to collapse.

He drank deeply and slowly, allowing the water to flow into his mouth and fill it, before swallowing with intention.

"How long... have I been here?" he mumbled.

"Only a few days. You appeared over there while I was having tea," She pointed to her disorganized desk. "You fell out of the air, smoldering, onto my research. You're in terrible condition."

His head flopped over to one side, and without righting it, he turned slightly at the torso to face a tall standing mirror. His back was stiff as he turned. He shuddered when he glanced at his own appearance. One gaunt, bloodshot eye leered back at him. Where the other one would be was a charred hole. His cheek was badly burned and his nose blistered. His eyebrow was completely gone, showing a hint of bone underneath. His hair was burned away on one side, and his ear was missing at the end. The burns were weeping a clear yellow ooze, as if the missing eye was crying for the last time.

While he studied himself, Taroosa looked on with sadness.

"There's nothing I can do for the eye. Honestly, all I've done is highly... experimental," she said softly.

His gaze wandered down from his own face. His torso was bare, and bruising ran around his whole body. The hole in his arm was the least of his concern. He grabbed a nearby polished silver tray, fumbling its contents onto the ground, and pointed its face towards the standing mirror so he could see the source of his stiffness. His back was a mess of dried blood and roughly sutured skin. From the base of his neck to the back of his pelvis ran long shiny fins of metal. Each one curved upwards and had a series of rods and joints tethering them together. He looked like a spiny, silver-scaled fish was growing out of him.

"It supports your weight but will inhibit your movement. Your spine was crushed partially. I'm surprised it worked—you shouldn't be able to move your legs. When the Ancients fought during the war, they wore great suits of armor made of stone and metal. Trouble was, they were old, with brittle bones and stiff joints, so the Draughtsman and his acolytes devised a few solutions to try and aid their movement. Most of those were never used; they were considered too barbaric. Like I said, highly experimental," she said.

He flopped his head forward and watched his toes wiggle. He mumbled something, his chin resting on his chest. She leaned forward and helped pull his head upright.

"I need... more power," he blubbered.

He dragged his hand across the table, raising it slightly, pointing a hooked finger toward the massive suit of armor in the corner.

She looked at the suit and back toward him.

"No, the armor can't be powered, not like the hollow soldiers. You'll have to use your emblems," she answered the statement as best she could.

"Hercolid," he added.

"The Eye of the Marksman?" she asked.

He shook his head side to side slowly.

"Look, Galadrath, this is a stimulating conversation, as ever, but I have some things to do, and you need to lay down. We can continue this when you're a little more articulate," she chastised.

He did lay down. While she toiled at seemingly meaningless tasks, he sat and brought his body back under his own will. The pain began to return—the slow overwhelming throb that dulled his vision and sat in his mind like a burning fog. He stuffed more of the Nightbloom flowers into his mouth, chewing and swallowing them slowly.

Hours passed as he thought of the events that had transpired: his battle with Larl Rihhi, his stripped chains, his own lack of power, his family who was most likely imprisoned, and his failure. His thoughts were calm in between his slow heartbeats, but each throb brought pain and hate that wracked his entire body.

He wished he could tear Larl into a thousand pieces; he wished he could burn the man who had stolen his home—to turn him into dust and scatter the ashes under the feet of the masses, to be trampled and forgotten. A portion of his mind wished for the serenity of a beatless heart. There was a Form of combat that Larl had not studied. It was the one that purchased victory, no matter the cost.

"You said the Hercolid... has weapons of incredible destruction. How far can... the guns fire?" he asked.

Taroosa looked up from her busywork, giving him a surprised look. He had become no more than a fixture sitting on a table, and she looked bewildered at his words.

"The lances? They can touch the horizon; they can destroy anything they can see," she said.

"How far? How far can they see?"

"The Hercolid sits on a large butte—the walls are even higher. The fortress officials have bragged that they can see well into Dradofir, on a clear day, and spot ships on the sea to the south," she stated.

He had seen the fortress from afar, even passed by the high bluff. He had seen the impressive walls adorned with the flags of Thainegom, a testament to the power of the court.

"The City of Light?" he asked.

Her eyes widened.

"Yes, I believe so," she said softly.

"I have a plan," he growled.

23

THE LUNATIC

HE HELD HIS BODY immobile to allow his wounds to heal. During the days of stillness, his mind had plenty of time to churn his wandering ideas into concrete strategies.

He explained the plan to Taroosa while she changed his bandages, and she tore it down with impunity. To him, it was poorly formed vengeance, but in her eyes, he could see her mind working. She would feed him bites of food between the iterations of ideas. This was a thought experiment to her, a problem to solve, a puzzle to piece together. When he had the strength to move without injuring himself, his plan had also become more robust. From the inside of the dome more days and nights passed without notice, as his singleminded focus was interrupted only by restless sleep.

They argued and theorized. Taroosa sketched rough ideas, threw papers aside, and pulled schematics from small nooks and crannies among her littered workspace. She yelled and whispered, paced and paused pensively. He mimicked her, not understanding the papers she pointed at as she cursed. He shuffled his feet slowly, hobbling behind her as she moved about the room.

"Can you work the guns if—" He started.

"Shut it!"

She glared around the room.

"We'll need help," she said. "*Capable* help."

"I'll see what I can drum up," he said.

He began to dress. His shiny black clothes were in tatters, but he wore them anyway. The burned and bloodied rags came together loosely. The fins of steel holding him upright protruded from the ripped shirt, and his posture made him look feral, primal and dangerous. He glanced at himself in the mirror, and for a moment, he saw a Patch in his blurred vision. He shuddered again, before he tore a long strip of the shiny black material from the dirty cloak. He bound it around his head, covering the gruesome hole where his eye and the side of his face had been.

"I'll be back shortly. Get me that airship we talked about," he said flatly.

She nodded and stood looking at a dissipating cloud of black fog.

It did not take him long to find Farrah. He stumbled into the dimly lit room and met the eyes of Green, where the bulk of the man once again rested on the greasy countertop.

"Galadrath! Gods living and dead! You look like... What happened?" she exclaimed.

He saw the horror on her face, her mind unable to reconcile who he had been when they had last seen each other versus the tortured creature who stood before her now.

"Doesn't matter. I need a favor. I don't ask this lightly, but I'm planning on breaking into the Hercolid," he said sharply.

Her mouth opened and closed slowly. Her eyes danced back and forth, as her face cycled through every emotion. Green looked at her blankly for a response. Galadrath waited impatiently, giving only enough time for her mind to shift from his grotesque appearance to his unthinkable request.

"I'm serious," Galadrath added.

"Tagger," Green said.

"No! No. I'm not—" Farrah exasperated.

"Tagger could do it. He's a professional," Green affirmed.

"Who's Tagger?" Galadrath asked.

"He's a lunatic," Farrah sighed.

"Perfect. I'm going to commandeer a giant cannon inside the most heavily guarded fortress on the continent. Anyone coming would have to be a lunatic," Galadrath said.

"You're serious?" Farrah's eyes searched his face.

Galadrath pulled down the makeshift patch over his missing eye and frowned as best he could.

"Look into my eye and tell me I'm not serious," he growled.

"Scar breathes," Farrah gasped.

"What's sticking out of your back?" Green asked.

"Desperation. Absolution. Vindication," Galadrath murmured.

"I don't know about all that, man. You look like a thrice cooked catfish," Green replied.

"Thanks, Green. Come on, where's this Tagger fellow?" Galadrath said.

Farrah darted her eyes from Green to Galadrath.

"Whitespur," she mumbled.

"Let's go. You'll introduce me," Galadrath said.

He reached forward and grabbed her by the arm.

"Right now? That's weeks away!" she protested.

"We're going my way."

"No, no, no, no, noooo," she mumbled, before her face twisted into a snarl and she wrenched her arm free. She screamed, "I'm not going back into that mind bending fog again!"

"It's part of the plan Farrah—you've already done it once and you're... fine. You'll get used to it," Galadrath beckoned.

She stared at him with wild, exasperated eyes.

"You're scaring me, Galadrath," she said. Her tone was filled more with sadness than fear.

"Farrah. Please. I'm going to war against the kingdom. I'm going to end this. I need your help."

She stared for a while, holding her hand over her mouth, her nostrils flaring against her fingers. He had not chosen those words. They had come from his heart, and he watched as they worked their way into her mind. He could only imagine what she thought of him, a madman—a wounded animal lashing out against the trap that would kill it. She closed her eyes and pressed her fingers into them with a deep scowl.

"Let me get my coat," she said.

She gave Green some basic instructions, a few messages to pass onto the others, and threw a satchel over the heavy fur coat she had pulled on.

"Now what?" she asked.

"Hold this and tell me what you feel," Galadrath said.

He placed a tiny blackstone emblem in her palm, closed her hand around it and held her fist in his hands. She closed her eyes, and he could feel her squeeze the tiny stone tightly. A moment later she opened one eye and looked at him.

"It's you. I feel you. I feel a beach, sand under my feet, and a sea breeze. I feel victory. How can I feel this?" she said.

"Each emblem holds the memory of the person who created it in the moment of its creation. The bigger the emblem, the more vivid the memories contained. During trials, we use these memories as a message, a ledger to record information about who was tried. Keep this one, get used to the feeling, and speak with the emblem. Clear your mind, but don't let the memories take over," Galadrath explained.

She frowned and smiled coyly.

"Why do I need this?" she asked.

"It's part of the plan. Also, it will help control the 'mind bending fog,' or whatever you had called Tor Zuer."

She nodded, a seriousness returning to her face.

"We're leaving, Green. Farrah, clear your mind. Remember, Calm."

Galadrath grabbed her hand softly. She nodded at him, and they vanished in a cloud of black smoke.

The wind was blowing heavily, snow blustering through the air. The suns were bright smudges peering through thick, shapeless clouds. The rocky outcroppings of the landscape were disguised by collecting snow, and the pockmark of buildings stretched around them through the peaked hills. Galadrath looked into the wind, toward the high, far-off peaks of the great mountain range.

"Welcome to Whitespur," he mumbled.

"It's not my first time, but thanks. This way," Farrah snipped.

"How was the trip?" Galadrath asked.

"Much better than last time. No haunting emotions from long-dead demigods," she sighed.

"Long-dead," he scoffed.

She frowned at him. "I've gotten a taste of what you've experienced, and I cannot imagine what else is in that mind of yours."

"It's deep and dark as the Scar, filled with as many horrors," he grumbled.

"You scare me into the very fiber of my being, you know that?" she said.

"And you're my friend. Imagine how my enemies feel," he smiled, his face twisting horribly against the burned skin on his cheek.

She wrapped the coat around her tightly and pulled the furred hood up over her head, and they set off.

The furs on Galadrath's clothes had been burned off during Larl's intense onslaught, leaving only the charred skins behind, but the chill was no match for the burning hate in his veins, and even the snow was afraid of him.

Approaching a large building, Farrah swung open a heavy door leading into a spacious tavern with a high vaulted ceiling. Music and smoke wafted in the air as the two travelers entered, the cold at their heels replaced with a cozy and jovial atmosphere. At least three dozen men and women sat around chatting loudly.

There was an angry yell, and two men jumped up out of their seats, knocking over chairs and pointing fingers at each other. Galadrath studied them quickly. One was stocky, covered in heavy leathers and furs, with wild red hair. The other was lean, a dirty loose shirt hanging open in the front, with a cleanly shaved head showing bumps, scars, and a few recent cuts and bruises.

Patrons from tables around the disturbance turned to watch the two men. The scrawny, poorly-dressed man was being accused of cheating at a game, and he defended himself only by cackling madly at his accuser. The red haired man began to come around the table, ready to swing at the skinny one, when a deep, caring voice interrupted.

"Fingers, come sit."

The words were soft, but they seemed to land heavily on the ears of everyone in the room. The man who had spoken to them was sitting at a far table in the corner, a set of small spectacles sat in front of his calculating eyes. He was looking out over a tiny book, dwarfed by his bulk. Galadrath was surprised to see someone reading, with spectacles no less, in such a far corner of the world, where the tables were covered in stale, spilled beer. He was even more surprised at the youth of the man. Everything about him seemed to be a contradiction.

"Is that Tagger?" Galadrath asked.

"That's Lucky. Don't bother talking to him. The skinny one is Fingers—don't bother talking to him either," Farrah said.

Lucky had returned his attention to his book, turned a page with a hairy hand attached to a massive arm. His head was small compared to his body, his neck buttressed by massive muscles that extended into broad powerful shoulders. It seemed he could turn over the table with the same ease he turned the page. His face, however, was clean shaven, and his short brown hair in good order. His deep rumbling voice carried the tone of a caring father calming a child.

"But you can talk to me," a sensual voice whispered.

Galadrath turned around to meet the face of a beautiful blonde woman. She was standing directly behind him, and now, they were only a few inches apart. She placed her hand on his chest and began to run her fingers up toward his neck.

"You can do whatever you want to me," she whispered.

She leaned closer to him, her breasts pushing against him from under a finely crafted woolen dress. She looked down at her cleavage and back up at him.

"Oops. It must be cold in here. I guess I'm just looking for warmth," she smiled coyly.

Galadrath looked at Farrah in alarm.

"Nice to see you too, Stars. Shove off will you? He's married," Farrah said coolly.

"I'm married too. Doesn't mean much," Stars said with raised eyebrows.

She walked off, her hand tracing the heavy metal belt of Galadrath as she left. When she reached the bar top after an idle stroll, she looked back over her shoulder at him.

"That's... Stars. Don't believe anything she says, and don't talk to her," Farrah sighed.

"So who am I supposed to talk to?" Galadrath asked childishly.

"Him. That's Tagger," Farrah said, pointing to a man behind the bar.

Two men stood behind the bar, one was a well-dressed, handsome blonde man, and the other was a portly balding man in an apron. The balding man was annoyed about something, and the blonde man was reassuring him with spectacular hand gestures.

"Tagger!" Farrah yelled, walking over to them.

Galadrath followed her to the bar, where Stars leaned against it with her back, legs apart, allowing the dress to fold neatly between her thighs and over her knees. She beckoned Galadrath with a finger, even though he was already headed in that direction, which made him uneasy.

"Get out from behind my bar, you lout," the bald man said.

The blonde man, Tagger, retreated from where he stood with a bow and a wide smile.

"Farrah! So good to see you! What brings you to our lovely home?!" Tagger said jovially.

"She brought me something good to eat," Stars said with a sultry look.

Tagger glanced at Stars, then at Galadrath, and smiled even wider.

"I can see that! Who is this vibrant young man?" Tagger said.

"Vyhn—" Farrah began.

"Galadrath Yaralok. Ex-Accuser of Thainegom. Pleased to meet you," Galadrath said.

"Ah. Seems you've seen better days! I've heard of you. Better yet, I know all about you. Just because we stand on the Dradofir side of the fence doesn't mean we live under a rock. You must have come a long way. Please, come sit and have a drink," Tagger said cheerily.

He waved them toward the table where Lucky and Fingers were now sitting. Stars followed, leaning over and perching her arms on Lucky's shoulder. The large man flitted his eyes upwards to see what the annoyance was, only to continue reading when he saw who had interrupted him.

"These are my associates! Pleased to introduce Lucky and Fingers. You've already met Stars, and there's Jack." Tagger waved an open hand at each member in turn.

A clean, slightly overweight man had appeared from somewhere behind Galadrath. He gave a sheepish, gap-toothed smile.

"Pleased to meet you," Jack said.

Fingers only stared at Galadrath in response to the introduction, playing restlessly with a small, dull knife. Lucky refused to look up from his book, turning the pages at slow intervals.

"Nice to meet you all," Galadrath said with hesitation.

They seemed to live in a reality he was not a part of. They treated him as an old friend, completely ignoring his grotesque appearance.

"Please! Eat! Drink! An occasion to make a new friend is one worth celebrating!" Tagger belted.

"I have a job I'd like to discuss. Farrah says you're more than capable, professional," Galadrath started.

"Stealing something?" Fingers squeaked.

"Not quite. I'm not sure how to say this..." Galadrath sighed.

"Just put that pretty mouth of yours to work—one handsome letter at a time," Stars said, twirling a lock of Lucky's hair.

Galadrath shifted uneasily in his seat. "I need to break into the Hercolid. I need to use one of their guns, a lance."

He paused for a moment, waiting for them to react to the absurdity of the statement. None of them moved, except for Tagger, his eyes flicking for a moment to Jack, who returned an almost imperceptible nod.

"Do you understand?" Galadrath asked.

"Yes, please continue," Tagger said.

Galadrath sighed again and laid bare the absurd plan he had concocted with Taroosa. It took hours to divulge the details, each individual interrupting, questioning, collaborating, and affirming facets of the endeavor. Stars hummed softly, as if she was enjoying an exotic delicacy. Fingers broke into animated shouting at intervals. Jack spoke kindly, raising his own considerations. Only Lucky never spoke, never looking up from his book.

"Seems like a straight forward job. Before we accept, we should discuss payment," Tagger said.

Galadrath was surprised. What he had described was nothing short of a fantastic fever dream, and none of them had even raised an eyebrow at him.

"I think Farrah... brought some gold?" Galadrath said.

He looked at the satchel she had over her shoulder, hoping she had brought something with her. He had not even considered that they would expect to be compensated.

"This? This is filled with jerky and spare clothes," Farrah answered.

"We aren't worried about gold. You're an Accuser, one of the Many. Three favors from the Accuser—three wishes from a man who can bend the physical to his will—should suffice as payment," Tagger smiled.

Galadrath looked at Farrah, whose face had grown serious.

"What are the terms of these favors?" he asked.

Tagger flashed a wide smile.

"Those are the terms, my dear friend. Non-negotiable, I'm afraid," Tagger said.

"That's too vague and ominous," Galadrath replied.

"Correct on both counts! Vague, ominous, and—I'd like to reiterate—non-negotiable," Tagger smiled again.

"Done," Galadrath sighed.

"Then when do we begin?" Tagger asked.

"I'll come by again, hopefully in a few days, with another friend."

Tagger simply nodded and smiled widely. Galadrath made to leave, but sat back down.

"I'm curious. What part does he play in this?" Galadrath said, pointing to Lucky.

"He's a contingent of sorts, a glue. He keeps us together and out of trouble," Tagger smiled.

"Is that why they call you Lucky?" Galadrath joked.

The room grew quiet. Galadrath instantly became aware that their whole discussion had been heard in the open of the tavern—that the other people in the room had eavesdropped throughout.

The broad shouldered man looked up for a moment over the rim of his glasses, set his jaw, and looked back down.

"Time to go!" Farrah said with fake enthusiasm, her voice strained.

She pulled him up from his seat, gave a nod in the direction of the group, and hauled him toward the exit.

"Thanks again, Tagger! See you soon!" she yelled over her shoulder.

"Did I say something wrong? They just all have strange nicknames, and Lucky hadn't spoken—" he asked.

"Remember how I said they're a bunch of lunatics?" Farrah hissed in a hushed tone. "Lucky used to be a land surveyor for the kingdom. One day, he comes home early and finds his wife in bed with the local farrier. Tale as old as time, right? Well, Lucky starts choking his wife and the farrier runs to go get help. When he gets back with the townsfolk, Lucky's wife is dead."

"That's not so strange. Like you said, tale as old as time. I still don't get the name though."

"I wasn't finished. So the townsfolk want to have him accused and executed, but he wasn't willing—"

"So he ran?" Galadrath interrupted.

Farrah stopped walking and sighed. "He beat sixteen men to death with a horseshoe."

Galadrath paused for a second, remembering the calm control framed by the man's spectacles.

"I guess horseshoes are like rabbit's feet, not that lucky for the rabbit," Galadrath chuckled.

"You're in a good mood," Farrah mumbled.

"I am. I'm excited. And I'm afraid the pain has made me go insane."

"Then Tagger and his crew will be good company," she answered lightly.

They continued walking through the snow, with no real direction in mind.

"Can we go now?" she asked.

"I guess I don't want to know where Fingers got his nickname," Galadrath smiled.

Farrah shot a glare in his direction.

"No. You really don't," she scowled.

"And Stars?"

"No one knows her story. Maybe Tagger, but I've never heard it. Even if he does know, it's probably a lie. Everything she says is a lie."

"So she wasn't really interested in me? You know you gave me a look like that once," he recalled.

"Where do you think I learned it?" she said in a mockingly sultry tone.

He laughed, and she exchanged her stern face for a smile.

"Ok, we can go. Ready? Like I showed you. Calm your mind; let go of all your thoughts. Let me lead you," Galadrath said softly.

He took her by the hand, and the black fog rolled peacefully onto the snow around where they had been standing.

Farrah screamed until her lungs were empty. She flailed her arms wildly where they had appeared in Taroosa's workshop, knocking over several instruments standing on the table next to her. Taroosa dropped a flask of questionable liquid as the sound and sudden appearance of the black fog instantiated next to her.

"Farrah! Come back to me!" Galadrath yelled with urgency.

Her eyes rolled back into her head, and she stood shuddering and incoherent.

"Farrah!"

Galadrath grabbed her by the shoulders and shook her, trying to wake her.

"Don't let me go," she croaked.

He stared at her for an instant, before he wrapped his arms around her and hugged her tight to his chest.

"*Pas jusqu'à ce que le monde s'effondre sous mes pieds,*" he whispered into her ear.

He felt her muscles soften and her body relax.

"I'm sorry. I'm here. I didn't clear my mind—I was thinking about Fingers," she said painfully.

"What was that you said?" Taroosa said, holding her nose with one hand. "Sounded like Sylan."

"I don't know what it means; I've just heard it said before," Galadrath replied.

"Oh, and don't breathe this stuff in. It'll knock you right out," Taroosa said.

She worked quickly to place the knocked over instruments upright with one hand, now holding a damp cloth over her nose and mouth, and carefully pushed away a wooden stand holding a collection of stoppered glass vials partially filled with liquid, stepping around the broken glass on the floor.

Galadrath fell forward, still holding onto Farrah, and the two of them collapsed onto the floor.

He woke to the light banter of the two women chatting, and saw them sitting leisurely, holding a set of fine porcelain teacups.

"Looks like he's up!" Taroosa chortled.

She shuffled out of her chair, squinted at a complicated device on the wall, and muttered to herself.

"I might have to adjust the formula a bit, although this was hardly an accurate testing environment. If only I had a few pigs... or maybe we should field test it..."

"You left me lying on the floor?" Galadrath slurred.

"You're heavy. I didn't feel like moving you after I broke your fall. I woke up with you still passed out on top of me." Farrah said, rubbing the back of her head.

"At least you can still feel. My whole side is still numb, which is actually a relief," he said.

He lay on his side, pulling his sleeve up to expose the ugly sewing Taroosa had subjected him to. Thick black twine held the hole in his arm closed, and for the second time since he had been punctured, the pain was gone.

"What is that stuff?" he asked.

"Same thing I used for anesthetic, with some minor changes—figured we could spray it as an aerosol and subdue anyone who gets in the way of our little adventure," Taroosa answered.

"Aerosol?" Galadrath asked.

"A fine mist. I apologize; I shouldn't use new English words in uneducated company," she scoffed, pleased with herself.

Farrah rolled her eyes and poured herself more tea.

"Did you get the airship?" Galadrath asked.

"It's hardly been six hours, Gally! Where do you expect me to pull one from? My scar?" Taroosa screeched.

The nickname irked him, and her tone was not helping either. He realized how tired he was. Stepping with Farrah had drained him, and the effects of sedatives, along with the constant pain, had gnawed at his sanity.

"No, but you did say Tirv is right across *the* Scar. Can't you—"

"Shut it! What, you want me to fly over there and fetch one like I'm buying some ox cart!"

"Yes, do that," he grumbled.

He put his head back down on the floor and tried to roll onto his back. The metal fins pulled on his bones, and he was reminded that was not an option. So he flopped forward, his face and stomach feeling the cool floor, and closed his eyes.

24

THE COMPOSER

TAROOSA RETURNED AFTER WHAT felt like an eternity. There were no candles to burn down and indicate the passage of time. There was only artificial light inside the dome, never changing or flickering. The windowless structure lacked any sights to mark the night or day, only cool humid air. He and Farrah had sat around restlessly, conversing at first, then letting the silence settle in as they made themselves at home amongst the bizarre creations and experiments of the departed scientist. Galadrath eventually stepped outside, after having carefully inspected his wounds, and medicated himself to the point that the pain was only a very slight reminder that he was still injured.

He heard the low rumble of an engine and watched as the small craft appeared with a red-blue glow from the ever present fog. He marveled at the sight. It had a metal frame, like the hull of a ship, suspended by rigging and heavy chains to a massive oval balloon. A series of burners sat at the central deck of the aircraft, large red flames pouring into the cavernous openings at the bottom in the tightly stretched canvas bubble above them. Blue lights surrounded the bottom and rear of the craft at intervals, and as it got closer in its descent, he could make out the pure flames projecting the light. Most of the ship was painted black—some of which caught the light and gave off the shine of wetness.

273

As the airship made a wide circle, slowly dropping from the sky, the roaring grew louder until it set down near the dome, kicking up dust and scattering small rocks. The deafening rumble cut out, as the flames at all points sputtered out, and the ringing in his ears was punctuated by the panging of cooling metal straining against its joined pieces.

The noise had attracted Farrah as well, and he watched her reaction as she appeared from behind the heavy door of the dome.

"I've never seen anything like it," she said.

"Neither have I. Not in person," Galadrath replied.

"In the memories?"

"Yes, a few foggy images of the Tyrant and his angel," he murmured back.

"Who could have ever conceived of the idea of a metal ship flying like a bird?"

"Only the Few."

As the dust settled, Galadrath spotted the figure of Taroosa through the small glass section of a cabin dome at the bow of the airship. She rose from her seat, gave a hurried wave with a wide smile, and eventually appeared from a hatch jutting from the side of the hull.

"It's better than I could have imagined! The pinnacle of innovation! The speartip of science, thrusting us into the future!" Taroosa said giddily.

"I agree," Galadrath said.

"Quickly now, before she cools down, let's get the supplies!" she said.

They quickly hauled a few crates of various tools and goods into the metal hull. Taroosa intermittently fiddled with levers and valves, conjuring gouts of flame that ignited and sputtered, all the while mumbling excitedly to herself.

When they had finished, she closed the door on the dome, locked it, and patted it a few times. She sat in the finely upholstered leather seat at the center of the glass cabin, waving them closer.

"Hold onto something. This will be a sight to see," she said.

She pulled various levers again. A few heavy clunks came from around them and behind them. The rumble returned, and the metal skin of the craft began humming with vibrations. A heavy red glow came from small slits in a large metal burner behind them, the light filling the inside of the craft. It felt like they were sitting inside the head of a beast, its spirit flowing through the space with sinister intention.

Farrah balanced herself by grabbing some piping, but she gasped and yanked her hand away.

"It's hot," she said.

"Yeah, don't hold onto that," Taroosa replied.

"Then what am I supposed to hold onto?"

"Something else, just not that."

The ground fell away beneath them, and Galadrath watched as Farrah braced herself against the wall, her eyes growing wide at the scene.

"Never flown before?" he asked.

"As unpleasant as Stepping is, I think I prefer it to this," Farrah groaned.

"You'll change your mind once you get used to it. Flying is freedom. The relentless dread of Tor Zuer is much the opposite," he smiled.

The turbulence eventually smoothed, the drag of acceleration on their bodies releasing its grip. The landscape changed slowly before disappearing altogether as they entered the clouds.

"Do you know where you're going?" Galadrath asked.

"Of course. Whitespur," Taroosa stated.

"I mean, can you see—"

"Shut it! No, I have no idea. We could come out of this cloud and fly into the side of a mountain."

"I'll help," Galadrath said, sitting down and closing his eyes.

"Thanks," Taroosa said softly.

As they wandered through the cloudy sky, he wandered through the black fog of his mind.

"You're going to want to turn left a little bit," he mumbled.

"Incredible. Those are the most useless directions you could give. Port is left. Turn to port. And I need a bearing, or I need to know how far to turn. How many degrees? We're roughly heading north by northeast," Taroosa's irritation showed.

"Five? Turn five degrees," he said.

"Five degrees to port!" Taroosa screamed.

Farrah and Galadrath both flinched as the shout pierced the small space, and they felt the pull of inertia as the ship changed directions.

"That was too many degrees. Let's try two—two degrees to the right. What's the opposite of port?" he mumbled with his eyes closed.

The rest of the navigation went just as poorly, the airship veering from side to side high above the landscape they could not see. Eventually, they came close enough that Taroosa began to force the airship down, and they made several erratic circles through the mountains. Galadrath had never navigated a ship, but he could tell Taroosa had flown one before. She was by no means a deft pilot, but she would not allow them to see her shortcoming. Any stress or fear she hid deeply under her pride.

She sighed softly when the ship touched down roughly in a small opening just beyond the first buildings of the town. They stepped out of the hatch, and Galadrath could make out the faces of people poking their heads out of windows and doors. A crowd was beginning to gather outside to see what madness had descended on them. The snow around the ship's engines had melted quickly, exposing rocky mud.

"Saddle up boys and girls! Our ride is here," Tagger shouted.

There was a murmur of excitement.

Among the crowd was their crew, already assembling to embark on the strange airship. Stars was wearing a different dress, shimmering red and just as revealing as before, apparently immune to the frigid snowy winter of the north. Lucky was almost as bare, with just a satchel and a book, as he squeezed his way through the narrow door into the cabin. Jack took a moment to admire each piece of the flying machine independently, then sighed heavily with a sense of accomplishment. Fingers and Tagger boarded without ceremony, as if this was something they had grown accustomed to.

Taroosa nudged the ship into the air before they had all settled, and

Stars waved out to the crowd with elegance before pulling the hatch shut.

"This is a remarkable piece of machinery," Jack said. "I'd like a chance to study it."

"You'll have the rest of the day—we don't plan on being at the drop point until nightfall," Taroosa said.

"It's not as big as I'm used to, but that makes it all the more interesting," he replied.

Taroosa tilted her head at him.

"You've been in an airship before?" she asked, unbelieving.

"Often," he smiled.

"Who are you people?" she whispered.

"Just a group of like-minded individuals," he grinned.

It was a long trip taken in relative silence. Most of them sat to the rear of the hold. Lucky reclined against a wall, his bulk taking up a whole corner of the cargo area. While he was reading, Stars wormed her way in between his arm holding the book aloft and his chest, making him somewhat of a bed where she began to nap. Galadrath smiled in amusement, her sleek female form interrupting the man's muscly bulk at sections, like a cat perched inconveniently on its owner. He tried to make light conversation, but only Tagger was willing to entertain his questions. Farrah had better luck with her bag of jerky. As she munched on the dried meat, others showed interest, and she passed the pieces out. She even managed to extract a single polite word of thanks from the laconic hulk.

"You all don't seem to have any weapons, considering we're going to be entering a heavily guarded fortress," Galadrath noted.

"Do we intend to do much fighting?" Tagger asked.

"What we intend and what we do don't always have much in common," Galadrath replied.

"We're plenty armed. Taroosa has prepared crates of this wonderful little cocktail," Tagger pointed at a nearby crate filled with small vials. "Care to try one?" He held up the fragile glass to Fingers.

"No, I have enough here," Fingers grumbled.

The muscles on the dirty and bruised man went taught. He was so skinny that every action made his arms and legs tense, like he was always on the edge of erratic violence. He had fresh cuts on his arms and face, and none of them were tended to—some still bleeding as he moved. He held a large brown bottle, his only possession he brought on board, and drank from it at intervals.

Galadrath could smell Fingers from across the cabin. His ragged, loose clothes were sweaty and stained, and the contents of the bottle reeked of alcohol and tainted his stale breath. He looked like a beggar, and there was something in his eyes that Galadrath could not quite identify. The brooding blackness at the edges reminded him of something he had seen before, but unfortunately could not place.

Jack and Taroosa were the only two who really talked. They both shared an interest in the mechanics of the airship, and after a few sharp scoldings, Jack had quickly learned to ask only interesting questions. Soon, the two got along well, discussing each portion of the inner workings of the fine machine.

Time passed slowly, the murmurs of the two tinkerers in the cockpit blending with the low rumble of the engines, mingling with the ever-present stink of Fingers. Light streaming in from the front windows waned and vanished, as the night quickly descended on them.

"Almost time to get out," Taroosa announced.

"Who are you taking with you?" Galadrath asked.

"No one. I'll handle myself. You're in charge of the rest," she said sheepishly.

He grunted. The plan was to jump out of the ship high above the fortress. He had hoped Taroosa, being a capable one of the Many, would be willing to help him slow the fall of a portion of their group. Now, he knew he would be solely responsible for making sure none of them plummeted to their death.

He flung the hatch open, and cool, thin air greeted him, followed by a wild wind quickly sucking the putrid air from the hold. He quickly exerted his influence, bringing calm and warmth back to their surroundings. He looked out into the darkness, the pillowy gray of softly illuminated clouds below them, and the vibrant night sky alight with millions of stars above them.

"It's breathtaking, isn't it?" Stars said smoothly.

She had clung to him for support, even though during their travels she never faltered in a single movement. Even when the ship had shuddered and lurched, she merely swayed with grace as she stood inhumanly balanced. Now that they had stopped moving, she seemed unsteady. She peered out of the opening, looking up at the sky, and he felt her shiver.

"It is," he said.

"Shall we?" Tagger smiled.

"Everyone ready? Try and stay together," Galadrath said.

Lucky tucked the book back into his satchel along with his spectacles, and fidgeted with the toggle, making sure the bag was secure several times. The whole crew carefully climbed from the hatch, clinging to the railing and the hull on the outside of the ship.

"Lady," Lucky said, extending an arm to Stars.

As he did, Fingers latched onto the man's back, and Stars climbed into his arms. Lucky shot a glance at Galadrath and stepped off the edge of the ship into the open air.

"What? Go, go, go!" Galadrath yelled.

He pushed his influence outwards and dove after the large man. He felt the shapes of the others follow behind. Below, the shape of Lucky and his passengers disappeared into the starlit clouds. Galadrath wrestled to slow them and bring the others from behind into a rough formation as they fell.

In another moment, they broke through the bottom of the clouds, and the dark landscape beneath them stretched in every direction. There were pockmarks of light, fires and lanterns stretching fibers of illumination into the night below them. He made out the concentration of larger lights—the huge bonfires sitting atop the blocky turrets of the fortress. He had oriented himself with the Shattered Children to find north and south, making sure they would descend on target.

They slowed as Galadrath urged them upwards with a careful gust against the pull of gravity, and they swooped in low past one of the turrets, landing just inside the immense wall. All their feet touched down softly and silently, masked by the sound of the sudden whipping wind—except for Taroosa, who stumbled forward with a crate in her hands, under her own influence.

"Fingers, check to make sure no one on the walls saw us," Tagger whispered. "Stars, Jack, set a perimeter."

"What about us?" Galadrath asked.

"Find that gun."

Fingers popped the lid off the crate, grabbed a handful of vials, and nodded to Taroosa where she sat nursing her ankle. Stars bent down next to her, kissed the ankle softly, and winked while snatching up a few of the glass vials.

Galadrath turned to Farrah, shrugged, and set off in a direction.

"Shhh!" Taroosa hushed at them.

Galadrath saw her pointing at a large building along the perimeter, butted up against the bottom of one of the turreted towers. He grabbed Farrah by the arm and pulled her toward the entrance. The door was locked, and heavy mortared stone walls surrounded the iron-banded threshold. He pulled his trinkets back under his command and absorbed the entire locking mechanism. When finished, he pushed the door inwards.

The hinges groaned and creaked. Galadrath saw the wide eyes of a guard greet him, and he wasted no time knocking the man backwards into the wall. The expression faded as unconsciousness overtook him.

"This is it. Go grab some of those vials; make sure this gentleman doesn't wake up," Galadrath said.

As Farrah scurried from the room, he looked up at the metal construct sitting silently in front of him. Large metal plates came together at harsh angles, forming the octagonal body of the gun. There were a few panels that looked like they could open, and at the one side of the machine sat an array of instruments. Dials, levers, and a periscope that extended forward and out of view. He walked around the metal frame, past the controls, and looked out of the slanted opening that accommodated the front of the turret. The barrel was large-bore, almost tall enough for him to stand upright inside. It was surprisingly short, only sticking out of the armored body of the turret ten feet, barely twice as long as it was wide. From here, he could see the periscope tube widen into an intricate array of lenses and actuators.

A loud thud reverberated on the roof above him, and then Taroosa and Farrah ran into the room.

"Marvelous! Absolutely marvelous! Just as magnificent as I remembered," Taroosa said, running her hand along the metal of the gun.

Lucky ducked into the doorway, dragging a limp body behind him with one hand. Galadrath noticed the leather armor and insignia of a Keeper of the Peace. Letting go of the body, Lucky retrieved a small notebook from his satchel.

"Time for more light reading?" Galadrath asked incredulously.

Lucky stared at him briefly, then began leafing through the pages.

Fingers ran into the room, his bare feet making no noise, but his breath was ragged.

"That stuff works, but not as fast as I'd hoped. He fell backwards off the wall instead of forwards—it's not my fault," he said, panting.

"Fingers. Report," Lucky stated.

"Six bagged, plus this one. Two westerly point, thirty by thirty, counterclockwise dark. Eyes dim, two, south to southwest, sixty north point. Eyes bright, two, west to northwest, one hundred northwest point. Seven same, northwest wall, blind," Fingers recalled.

None of this meant anything to Galadrath. It seemed the man was babbling incoherently, but Lucky had understood and was scribbling in the book.

"Alright then, shall we get this fired up?" Galadrath asked.

"Wait," Lucky said. "Wait for Stars and Jack."

His voice was calm and assertive, but his eyes were intense, as if they were holding back viciousness.

Jack came huffing into the room, sweat visibly running from a receding hairline.

"The orphans are ready to wail. Six set to thirty. Best we be clear by then," he said.

"Full report, please," Lucky said.

Jack spewed off another set of words similar to the cadence and unintelligible nature as those of Fingers.

Tagger and Stars walked in, pulling the door shut behind them, and the bizarre exchange of information went on.

"Seems we're all set folks. Galadrath, you have twenty three minutes—best get to it," Tagger grinned.

"Jack, Taroosa, please do the honors," he continued.

"Ladies first," Jack bowed and smiled. Taroosa giggled and nodded back, turning to hoist herself with Jack's outstretched hand into the chair facing the controls of the gun.

"I'm going. Farrah, remember, clear your mind. You'll receive my signal when you least expect it, so be ready. Taroosa, find the blue flame," Galadrath commanded.

He watched as Taroosa and Jack coordinated, pulling levers and pushing foot pedals, mumbling excitedly to each other. The entire bulk of metal began to move. At first it sprang and lurched wildly, gears scraping against each other. The noise was loud inside the enclosed space.

"They're going to notice that," Tagger whined.

He turned to Stars and Fingers, pointing an open hand at each of them.

"Give me ten soft and ten hard. That leaves two minutes and then the orphans cry," he spouted.

They both nodded intensely, and Fingers held the door open for Stars. She began to sing as she left the room, and Galadrath recognized the tune—the surprising purity of her voice filled the space outside in the open air.

Fingers shook his head violently, spittle shooting in every direction, his tongue pushing forward out of his mouth as if to rid it of a bad taste.

"I hate that song. Why? Why that one?" he growled.

Then Galadrath recognized the look he had seen at the edge of the feral man's eyes: It was a look of a mind poisoned by blackstone. Afterall, the blackstone emblems were matter and energy, just like any other emblem. The black fog he shed as he Stepped—the ichor from the Patches that irritated his skin—were all a form of the same material. Prolonged exposure in high concentrations was deadly, or worse. It was an infection usually reserved for the oldest and busiest of Rat Catchers. A life surrounded by blackstone in its various forms, combined with poor hygiene, would ultimately end in the mind and flesh bent into patchwork horror.

"You've been poisoned by blackstone," Galadrath stated.

"Poisoned? No." Fingers replied.

"It will kill you, it will twist you into a monster."

"Will it? Or has it?" Fingers smiled, his eyes glistening with insanity.

Stars' voice became louder from outside.

She stood alone in the dark,
Where she lies now, we know not.
Never forgotten, she gave peace.
Never forgotten, she brought war.
He unleashed the suns,
And the devils cried.
All for naught,
All forgotten.
He could not break,
What the gods built.
Both lie in tombs,
Under the setting moons.

The ballad was written about the destruction of the Tread and recalled the moments in which the Brightcaller and the Votary had turned their powers on trying to end the first invasion. Their actions had crippled the portal, caused the Scar to split the world almost in half, and incited the sacrifice that trapped the Votary on the other side. A thousand years later the Votary, Ezidora, brought war—champion of the evil they had fought to destroy. The song was like most: abstract, embellished, and only a nugget of truth at its center. But Fingers' statement was irreconcilable in his mind.

A chill ran down Galadrath's spine, and he vanished.

He once again stood in the narrow street in front of his house. He looked upward, seeing that the fire and destruction from his previous visit had been deftfully repaired. The only difference left by the fight was the empty flower boxes that sat on the perimeter railing. With all the power of the Many, only one person had the ability to manipulate life. The flowers would have to be planted and grown, how nature intended it. He looked around at street level and found a rose bush creeping its way up the side of one of the other homes. He picked a flower quickly and made himself ready.

He floated his way to the roof, drawing heavily on his emblems for the coming event. He could not allow himself to be outplayed so easily this time.

Larl sat at a small table eating dinner and had undoubtedly felt the presence of Galadrath approaching. His influence was spread wide on the rooftop, and Galadrath had to push into it with resistance to plant his feet inside the railing.

"Back so soon? You're looking unwell," Larl said.

He carefully pushed a small bite of seared pork into his mouth, the honeyed sauce dripping slowly down the tines of his fork.

"I'm here to finish this. I'm not running this time," Galadrath said.

Larl let out a small noise of satisfaction as he chewed, emphasizing his enjoyment of both the meal and the statement, as he turned his gaze to Galadrath.

"I expected no less, obviously. A coward can run, but a conscience is more fleet of foot than even the most afraid man. However, you are not afraid. It would seem you've come to meet your end—maybe to redeem what's left of your honor," Larl said quizzically.

He sliced another piece of the pork loin and swirled it around on the plate before spearing a vegetable on the fork. He held up the utensil at eye level, glancing between it and Galadrath.

"Have you let your pride devour yourself?" he smiled.

He closed his eyes and placed the morsels of food skewered on the fork in his mouth, pulling them slowly in with his lips.

"I'll let you finish your meal. While you eat, could you please tell me the truth about my family?" Galadrath asked.

Larl chewed slowly, opening his eyes again and staring at Galadrath. He swallowed, picked up a golden goblet, and let it dangle precariously between his fingers before taking a sip.

"You won't run if I do?"

Galadrath lit a flame in the palm of his hand with a flourish. The intense blue flame burned purely. He waved it over the edge of the balcony, staring into it. The ritual of being granted a trinket, which the Many were subjected to, was sacred to them all and was something that Larl would recognize. Galadrath just hoped that miles away, Taroosa was paying attention as well.

"I swear on my power and my divine metal. I swear on my oaths—what's left of them. One of us will be dead before I leave," Galadrath grumbled.

"Good enough. I don't see the harm in telling you then," he mused, dabbing pork grease from the corner of his mouth with a napkin. "After we suspected you'd returned home and killed an agent of the crown, who still hasn't been found, they'd been taken into custody—that is true. They did spend a few nights in the dungeon—also true. Administrant Callidron had them moved, though, to his own home. They are under guard there. It seems he feels a mite responsible for them. I believe they are in good hands. Does that soothe the restless soul of a man about to die?"

Galadrath sighed heavily.

"It does. Thank you."

The idea of Teratos having taken his family in was like a jab into his heart. His betrayer was now harboring his kin, but even that pain was drowned out by the immense relief that they were safe and cared for.

"Would you like a seat? I can have a meal brought up for you? A glass of wine, maybe?"

Larl snapped his fingers loudly and a servant appeared a moment later in the doorway. The young woman was well-dressed and neat, her brown hair pulled up around pleasant features. Galadrath's haunting presence, illuminated ominously by the blue flame, did not seem to stir any emotion in her, and she awaited a command with a blank expression.

"Bring another bottle and a glass, please—I've company," Larl said sweetly.

"That won't be necessary," Galadrath stated.

"Suit yourself."

The woman nodded and left, and Galadrath felt a pang of regret for what he was about to do. She was one of many that would not survive this.

He pushed the blackstone out of his veins, into a new emblem. As he did, he held a few words in his mind.

Larl is on the rooftop. Fire in ten seconds.

The stone vanished as soon as he created it, and a tiny bubble of black fog drifted down through his fingertips, as he Stepped the emblem by itself into the hands of Farrah.

"I've brought you this," he said.

Eight.

He held out the rose he had plucked outside and placed it slowly on the table, counting down the seconds in his mind as he backed away.

"Poetic, I suppose," Larl said.

Three.

Galadrath stumbled intentionally as he stepped back, the railing catching the metal fins protruding from his spine, and he toppled over backwards falling from the rooftop.

One.

The sound was a deafening roar, matched in intensity by fire and light. The night sky was washed out by the bright beam of red glowing blaze, lightning, and fire. The rooftop vanished in the beam—the building that was once his home—exploding outward in the violent release of concentrated energy. The hillside opposite the street, densely covered in other domiciles, bore the brunt of the shot. The houses violently turned into a spray of molten rubble, and the concentration of fire hammered into the hill face, melting the stone and rupturing the earth.

Galadrath shielded himself, pouring his energy into the small influence he had conjured around himself at the street level. The rubble rained down all around him chaotically, and the buildings in the path of the beam were reduced to smoldering slag foundations. The beam cut out, the noise and light ceasing instantly. The dark of night returned, and the ground looked like a field of stars, tiny fragments of glowing rock littering the space of the once-peaceful street.

The hillside where the shot had terminated its path was a flowing river of lava, the two houses that had stood on it were gone. Small fires had sprouted like weeds from nowhere as the intense heat of the air ignited anything flammable.

He stood up, hesitating for a moment, waiting for the smoke and dust to be carried off in the shimmer of heat. Stepping over the rubble that surrounded his own untouched space, he walked into the littered remains of his home. He made out the bloodied arm of a servant that had been on the lower levels of the structure, crushed in the cascade of rubble.

The divine metal of his chains was the only thing that could survive. Larl had been caught directly in the blast and was completely annihilated.

"When I'm done, there won't even be a memory left of you," he mumbled at the rubble, quoting Larl's words.

Galadrath dug through the cinders and carnage of the building, feeling the pull of his trinkets that had been stripped from him. He gathered up the chains, still hot from the beam of energy, tugging at them from where they lay in the heap and wrapped them slowly around his arms. He called on the power of the chains and felt the intensity of the collection of divine metal.

"The Accuser has returned," he spat menacingly.

25

THE GRIM WREATH

He Stepped back into the small room holding the cannon. The giant metal machine was still whirring and clanking at intervals, and Taroosa sat fiddling with the dials.

"I'd love to take it with us," Jack said.

"That's not really an option," Tagger replied.

The heavy door swung open, and a guard stepped into the doorway, sword drawn and eyes wild. He looked to his right and saw Farrah, also startled, with her own weapon held ready in front of her.

Lucky snapped the book shut, held it tightly in his hand, and struck the man in the neck with the spine of it. The guard crumpled into a pile, the blow rendering him dead instantly. Lucky looked toward Tagger and shook his head.

"The schedule is shot. We're two minutes early. I'm going out to get Fingers—I need those ten loud minutes now. Taroosa, go get our ride. Accuser, I could use a distraction," Tagger said sternly.

Galadrath could see the serious worry on the man's face. Tagger's air of playful aloofness had vanished. His usual disposition was falling apart along with the plan.

"I don't know what to do!" Farrah chimed in.

She was startled and out of her element.

"Stay with Jack. He will show you where he needs to be when he

289

needs to be there. Then you'll meet us on the wall. Lucky, find Stars. *Now,*" Tagger spouted commands.

Lucky tucked the book into the satchel, adjusted his glasses on his face, and headed for the door. Tagger grabbed him by the arm stopping him before he exited.

"Is it time for the horseshoe?" Tagger asked as the large man loomed in the doorway.

"Not yet. We're still inside operational parameters," Lucky said in his low voice.

"Good," Tagger sighed.

Galadrath could see the relief wash over Tagger's face. He was also struck by the eloquently formed words of the large man, the calm and control with which he spoke. He remembered what Tagger had said in the tavern, about Lucky being the glue that held them all together, and then the story Farrah had told him.

Tagger followed Lucky out the door and the whirring of the cannon ceased, leaving the rest of them in the quiet. There were voices coming from outside the room, yelling and screaming as the garrison of the fort sounded the alarm.

"What did he mean by horseshoe?" Taroosa asked.

"If you see Lucky holding a horseshoe, we're done—and not in a good way," Jack said.

"Then I better get out there and make a distraction," Galadrath said.

He ducked out of the door, pushing his influence out into the night air. He felt the countless bodies of soldiers in action. Armories were emptied into the hands of roused infantry; formations of swords, shields, and spears gripped by fighting men and women, and the telltale presence of other influences.

Emissaries.

Among the forms he felt Stars, who was dangerously close to one of the Many. He Stepped closer, and as he appeared from the black fog, he watched her embrace the man.

"I'm glad I found you! Please, help me! I don't know what's going on!" Stars cried out.

Her arms were wrapped around the man in embrace, feigning fear and relief. The Emissary was startled by her approach, stunned as she pressed herself against him.

"I'm... Yes, I'll keep you safe," he said.

He placed his hands on her hips, lightly trying to pull her off of him. Galadrath watched as she slipped one arm down to the long slit on the side of her dress and pulled the material apart. High up on her bare thigh was a garter of sorts, and she quickly pulled a long, slender dagger from a sheathe. The Emissary's eyes locked with Galadrath, who stood to the side, watching from around the nearest corner. The man's startled expression from the stranger's embrace turned to fear and alarm, and as he tried to wrestle himself free of Stars' grip, she slid the point of the blade under his ribs and into his heart.

The man collapsed, and Stars gracefully let him fall, the muscles in her bare leg going taught, as she bore his weight and placed him on the ground. She pulled the dagger loose from the white robes, now pooling with crimson.

Galadrath ran forward to her, looking down at the Emissary as she crouched beside him.

"You just killed an Emissary," he said with disbelief.

"Not the first time. Won't be the last. It's amazing how easily men become distracted," she said.

She met his gaze and pulled the dress farther to the side, revealing even more of her form underneath. Galadrath was stunned by the sight, but managed to tear his eyes away after a glimpse. Just before he regained his composure, he noted a tattoo on the inside of her thigh, above the garter holding the sheath for the dagger. It was a simple figure of a woman with a skull instead of a head, clutching a sword between her breasts. The word "Widowmaker" curved around the side of the tattooed female form.

"Like what you see?" she said smoothly.

"I'm... I'm married," he choked out.

"That doesn't seem to stop you from looking," she laughed.

Galadrath had averted his eyes, now turning completely around.

"I didn't expect to see you half-naked in the middle of a fight for our lives."

"None of us expected it," she said sadly.

He turned to look at her, not sure why her tone had changed. She was decent again, the dagger out of sight, the dress covering her.

"Speaking of distractions, I need to go," he said.

Galadrath reached down to grab the trinkets from the body of the fallen Emissary, but as he did, Stars stopped his hand.

"I earned this one. It's mine to take, not yours."

"But I can use it," he protested.

"Not this one," she said.

She pulled the necklace carefully off of the body and draped it around her own neck.

"How do I look?" she whispered.

Her stare was unnerving, and he had to look away again.

"We're wasting time," he said.

"Maybe later we can waste some more time together."

The image of the inside of her thigh flashed through his mind, then the tattoo. There was a primal longing somewhere inside him, but not for her, and it was quickly replaced by a sense of danger.

"I'm going. Lucky is looking for you," he said.

As he floated up into the air, the neat rows of buildings came into view under him, and he could see the shapes of soldiers moving quickly through the narrow alleys between them. Continuing to rise, the courtyard at the center of the fort appeared, and with it came the wild image of forty men surrounding Fingers, holding him at bay with spear tips. The feral man had broken his brown glass bottle and was holding it by the neck, flailing the jagged glass wildly while lunging at the spears leveled at him, knocking them from side to side with the improvised weapon. Galadrath could hear his screeches and growls, as if he was a cornered animal. His dirty rags now soaked with alcohol and blood from head to toe.

Galadrath floated closer and turned the stone floor of the courtyard to mud underneath the soldiers. They sank in quickly up to their knees, then he once again solidified the ground into stone, trapping them where they stood.

Fingers pulled a few of the small vials out of a pocket and launched them deftly at two of the men closest to him. The glass shattered against their shining armor, and the contents sprayed over them. Seconds later, they slumped over on their spears, the points digging into the ground in front of Fingers. The tattered man ran up the shafts, batting at the weapons of the still-conscious guards. He jumped from the backs of the two slumped men, launching himself into the fray of soldiers, catching one in the face with the bottle and another in the chest with his bare feet. The men clamored to effectively use their weapons, but the long spears had to be discarded and swords drawn—Fingers was among them, moving like a blur.

From Galadrath's vantage point, it was hard to make out what was happening. The melee of carnage below him was a mess of screams, bodies, clanging metal, and general disarray. Fingers was diving between them, every part of his body a weapon—each movement he made was both an attack and a dodge. He struck his heel into the head of one man, elbowed another in the armpit, and threw his body forward and butted his head against the armored chest of another. He tumbled through one man's legs and struck him in the groin with a flailing fist. Laying on his back, he swept one leg in a wide arc knocking a man off balance and buckled his knee with a short kick. He was like a rubber ball bouncing between a cluster of wooden pegs, each soldier succumbing to a unique act of violence.

Finally, the motion came to rest. Fingers stood with fresh cuts, one of his eyes swollen shut and bruises already forming with a few other knots on his body. The men around him were motionless—dead or unconscious, limp at awkward angles, still propped up where their legs were rooted in the stone floor. The rest of the soldiers, who were out of reach of the feral menace, tried in vain to free themselves, screaming for help, barking orders, and turning at odd angles to train their weapons on their assailant.

Fingers took a short bow, before scampering into the night with a howl and cackle of laughter.

Insane. Every one of them is insane.

Galadrath shook his head in disbelief and looked for new targets amongst the buildings. Formations of soldiers were patrolling the alleys, and he began to corral them with fire. Each time they attempted to move toward the direction of the gun, he conjured a wall of flame. Some groups he herded with gouts of fire; others he simply trapped by raising solid stone walls from the ground, blocking the corridors. He felt powerful. With his chains, he felt whole again.

He had made himself a target, and he felt the Emissaries converging on him. One Emissary launched himself skyward, aiming to intercept where he floated high above the center of the fortress. A fusillade of ice shards shot toward him but harmlessly melted into a cascade of water droplets upon colliding with the hardened air around him. He saw the Emissary slow his ascent in hesitation, and Galadrath took the moment to rip the influence out from around him. He could feel the space around the Emissary come under his own control, and he pushed the air inward from all angles. The man's robes collapsed into his body, crushing him into a wad of cloth and viscera.

Eight more Emissaries came and fell. He impaled them, crushed them, tore them apart, and scorched them to cinders. They stood no chance. Galadrath and his sixty eight links of chain—with the other trinkets among them—was a demigod. The Emissaries were no more than playthings. The armored men, equipped with only conventional weapons, were even less than that—hardly more than nuisances.

As they died, their final screams—cut short by Galadrath's relentless assault—echoed with a familiar laughter, a cackling that threatened to break free from the back of his mind.

It's done.

He brought his sanity back to a place of calm, securing the terrors of his mind. He descended to ground level, picking the divine metal from the corpses of the fallen.

He heard a series of explosions, six heavy thumps on the far side of the fort. Farrah came running around a corner, stopping abruptly.

"The orphans..." she said, looking up.

The sky became bright with white light. Thunder roared as the succession of explosions ruptured the towers of the fortress.

The orphans are crying. Sunbursts rigged to explode, I should have known. It means we're out of time.

"We have to go..." Farrah said.

The ground shone as brilliantly as daylight, the balls of lightning and fire crackling overhead. He watched as Farrah surveyed the scene, shielding her eyes from the light. In the darkness, the aftermath of his fury against the Emissaries and their cohorts had been obscured. In the light, the landscape was a spattering of limbs and gore—a slaughtered spray of entrails and death surrounded him.

She stood in awe, captivated by the blood-covered shine of divine metal trophies hanging around his neck, along with the stained rings he had looted from the corpses. Pendants and chains, earrings and bangles, dripping with the remains of their previous owners, draped over his scorched armor, the sweeping fins protruding from his spine, the anger on his face of taught, ruined skin, and the fire burning in the pupil of his eye.

As he watched her, he began to understand what she saw. He had become more than a man; he had become the demon known by many names: Wrath, Vengeance, Fury, and Death—his trophies around his neck, a Grim Wreath.

He walked toward her, the rage melting from his face, and held out a hand. She recoiled from him, his fingers stained with killing.

"I thought you were against spilling innocent blood," she whispered.

"No one here is innocent," he said reflexively. The words did not feel like his own.

The light faded back into the darkness, the rumble of thunder replaced by the crashes of crumbling fortifications. In the distance, he could make out the low whine of airship engines.

"Weeeeeaaaaaaarrrrraaaaahhhhhaaaa!" Fingers came screaming around the corner.

He hopped up and down as he passed them, shuffling his feet as he ran. Galadrath noticed a spear was firmly lodged in the man's back, but it did not seem to hinder his movement or his enthusiasm.

"Time to run!" he said as he passed.

His whooping and howling continued as he faded into the distance.

"If none are innocent, then you're no longer an Accuser. You've become no more than an executioner," Farrah continued.

"So I have," Galadrath replied.

"Don't lose sight of who you are, Galadrath. Don't destroy yourself trying to save what you love."

"Look at me. What's left of me to destroy? Tell me I'm not willing to give everything to keep my family safe," he spat.

"But will they be safe with you, or will they have to be saved from you?"

He set his jaw, biting down on her words. He did not have a reply. He glared at her, knowing there was truth in her statement. He waved her forward and began walking.

Soon, they arrived at the wall where Taroosa had parked the airship alongside. They ran up the stairs, ushered over the crenellations in a hurry by Tagger. Once again, the group of lunatics all sat in the tiny hold of the ship, and the roar of the engines muted as the hatch shut.

"That went well," Tagger said, his pleasant smile returning.

"I wouldn't say that. If that's considered going well, I don't want to know what it looks like when things go poorly," Farrah mumbled.

"Fingers made it out alive. That's as good a sign as any," Jack said.

"Unfortunately," Fingers grumbled.

The man sat in soaked rags, smelling of alcohol and sweat. The spear had already been removed, and the floor beneath him was quickly pooling with blood.

"You'll die if you don't stop the bleeding," Farrah said in a hurry, surprised no one was helping already.

"I've survived worse," he said.

"And we didn't leave empty handed," Jack said, ignoring Fingers. He sat against the wall, polishing a strange device with a section of his untucked shirt. "Taroosa had us go on a bit of a detour, and we scooped up this little thing."

"The Eye of the Marksman. A weapon of legend," Galadrath stated.

"I'm sure someone will pay a pile of coin for it. Reminds me of the time we went to World's Edge. That didn't go as well as tonight did," Tagger laughed.

Galadrath looked at them in turn, bewildered.

"Wait. You've been to World's Edge?" he asked.

"Yea. That sword fetched a good price. I'm sure this will too," Jack said.

"Hold on. You stole the sword of World's Edge? You sold it? It's a priceless and holy artifact! It belongs in the impenetrable sanctum of its namesake. It belongs to the Archons of Barkrill! They've been looking for it for years!" Galadrath yelled.

"Technically not priceless. We got a price for it. Also, technically not the property of Barkrill. They stole it from the first Ashmaker. Also, now it's someone else's property. Also, people seem to throw that word around, *impenetrable*, the *impenetrable* Hercolid, the *impenetrable* World's Edge. It's too absolute, like never or always. It's just inaccurate," Jack mumbled.

"So you all make a habit of breaking into places that can't be broken into, and then you steal pieces of history to hawk at some street vendor!"

"Well, technically the Empress of..." Jack started.

"Too much Jack—you've already said too much," Tagger interrupted.

"Seems I've found myself in excellent company! What did I say about thieves, Gally!" Taroosa hollered from the cockpit.

Galadrath looked stunned.

"A widowmaker, a mute brute bookworm—Fingers is a moment away from death or turning into a Patch. I don't even know what secrets the rest of you have. Who are you people?" he asked.

"I've never been afraid of dying, not even before the Shattering," Fingers mumbled.

Galadrath's mouth hung open.

"You don't look more than thirty years old. How old are you, then?" he finally asked.

"All together, I'm seventy-four," Fingers grinned.

Galadrath held his head in his hands and slid down the wall he leaned against. His mind reeled with the information. Fairy tales, legends, and ancient artifacts—all spoken of as if they were mere paperweights, as if these magnificent events had taken place yesterday, as if they were commonplace. It made the incredible events of his life, especially the last few months, seem unremarkable. The jarring contradiction that was Fingers, and the few known scraps of his past, nagged at Galadrath. Reality itself felt as though it had been turned over, revealed something wholly different— and entirely true.

"I see you have some plunder of your own," Stars cooed.

Her voice was maternal and caring, the usual edge of seduction and danger gone. More than her words, it was her tone that spoke volumes— she knew he needed a distraction, a way to take his mind elsewhere.

Galadrath looked down at the collection of trinkets he had pilfered. The heavy chains wrapped around his arms were glinting from beneath the char marks, the thick smattering of jewelry now covered him. He began to tally the number of pieces in his head, matching each one to the face he had taken it from. They had been well-decorated—and now he was, too.

"One hundred and three symbols, including my own," he said.

"A one man army! That's enough to start your own country!" Tagger laughed.

"Or bring one to its knees," Galadrath replied.

Lucky grumbled in disagreement, clearing his throat and thumbing idly through the journal.

"That's a dangerous book you have there," Galadrath answered.

Lucky looked up at the Accuser and adjusted his glasses.

"Knowledge is power," Lucky's heavy voice filled the small space.

"Power is power. I've never seen knowledge break a man's neck,"

Galadrath argued.

"I have. I've seen dozens of men hanging from the gallows, strung up by their ideas. You'll wage your war with your trinkets—you'll accuse and you'll kill—but you won't win with them. To win with your ideas, you'll have to change minds, not destroy them," Lucky said.

Stars smiled and placed a hand on Lucky's shoulder.

"Well said, my darling, as always," she said.

Farrah nodded and looked up at Galadrath from where she sat. Her face brimmed with anticipation, and her eyes flicked back and forth over him with a hint of fear.

"Taroosa! Make sure Farrah gets home to her own folks!" Galadrath yelled loud enough so he was heard in the cockpit over the hum of the engines.

"I appreciate all your help. It's been... an enlightening experience," he said to the rest of them.

"Three wishes, Accuser. We'll come calling," Tagger said gravely.

"Understood."

"Where are you going?" Farrah asked carefully.

"It's time for me to sit down with an old friend," Galadrath spoke with a godless finality.

26

THE FRIEND

THE BLACK FOG HISSED slightly as it seeped from beneath Galadrath's eyepatch and the cracks in his armor, billowing out slowly from the folds of his clothing. The room was dimly lit, moonlight streaming in from a large skylight over a small atrium surrounded by sturdy pillars. The pale light illuminated the edge of large leafy vines crawling up around a small pond. The rest of the room was expansive and open. A dining room flowed into a sitting room, and velvet curtains surrounded a separate area for smoking. Only the kitchen, pushed to one side of the roomy interior, was enclosed with a wall.

The home of an Administrant was luxurious and intended to hold many guests. The grandiose nature of the floorplan, the indoor garden, and the lack of walls was all intended to create a feeling of calm and togetherness.

Galadrath surveyed the room slowly. He considered pushing his influence out but decided against it, unwilling to preemptively alert anyone who might feel it. A sweet, peppery smell was stale in the air, and it was a clear indicator of where he would find Teratos. He walked softly to the curtains and peeked through them.

The inside of the curtained dome was lined with pillows and furs, with the floor slightly sunken to create a shallow seating area around a raised stone circle, upon which a single hookah pipe rested. The coals on the pipe had all but gone out, and the melancholy glow of heat hardly reached through the pile of fine ashes. He heard the soft snore of Teratos. Galadrath pulled the curtains back, opening the inside of the sitting area to the moonlight.

His fat, traitorous friend sat reclined and sleeping with the hose of the pipe still cradled in his hand, his lips a faint blue. Galadrath sat down next to him, as comfortably as he could. The pain in his joints, his ribs, his back, and his face was returning, and the exhaustion of the night's events was beginning to weigh on him. He reached over to the small soft leather bag sitting next to the pipe, plucked a few dried petals from it, and crunched them between his teeth, softening them slightly before he swallowed them.

Then he proceeded to remove Teratos' symbols, stripping the rings off his chunky fingers, searching through pockets and pouches for the Stepping Stone—identical to his own—that all the Pillars of the Lowest House carried. Once the sleeping man was completely disarmed, Galadrath sat for a moment in silence, mulling through his own range of emotions. Had he caught Teratos awake, there would have been a blur of action and words—an exchange of feelings and thoughts, maybe even a battle.

Staring down at the sleeping man, Galadrath's own feelings were disarmed. Teratos was vulnerable and weak, and Galadrath's vengeance found no opposition. The wave that had built up inside of him had no rocks to crash against; the anger simply flowed out of him.

He began to toy with Teratos in his sleep, his annoyance that he could not exact his revenge turned into playful obstinance. Galadrath rubbed his hands against the beard and mustache of the man, teasing the finely tailored and oiled hairs into disarray. He pushed against the grain of the man's eyebrows, causing them to look wild and unkempt. He scooped up some of the warm ash from the pipe's bowl, smattered it onto the man's shirt and face, and then tied a thin silk sheet around his legs. He unbuttoned the regal vest that was tight around the bulk of Teratos' waist and rebuttoned it incorrectly.

As he committed each childish act, the bubbling rage dissipated into a sad recollection of memories. These were the things they had done to each other, deep in the heart of the Lowest House. The silly pranks they had played on each other, and the laughter they had shared because of it. He sat in silence, yearning for those trying times, when things were simple and tough.

He stood and loomed over Teratos, raised his hand high into the air, and let the weight of the chains drag his arm down. He struck Teratos across the face with a heavy slap, and the ash that covered him puffed upwards. His skin was bare and turning red where the blow had landed.

Teratos awoke with a shudder, his eyes wild and startled. His vision adjusted to the dim lighting, searching for his assailant.

"Who are you!" Teratos belted.

He recoiled, scrambling against the soft pillows, and tried to pull himself upright. He faltered, failing to catch himself on his bound legs, and fell over.

Galadrath laughed humorously. He lit the candles in the room, each wick on every table instantly springing to life.

"Don't you recognize me, old friend? You should see your handiwork—see what you've forced me to become."

"Galadrath, what happened to you?" Teratos shuddered.

"I suffered from the betrayal of my closest friend. I was chased from my home, my family. I fell in with the people I've spent my whole life persecuting; I killed many of those I devoted my life to protecting. I have traded honor for vengeance. The city I called my home burned me with her corruption, and now I've come to burn the corruption from her. She is already alight. You will join her."

The flames of the candles grew brighter as he unconsciously fed them with his words and his power.

"I've come to kill you, you traitorous vermin," he finished.

"I told you! I had nothing to do with this! I've taken care of your family—for love of the gods living and dead! I've done everything I can to restore your name, though your actions have smothered any of my attempts," Teratos argued.

Galadrath watched as Teratos absentmindedly wrung his fingers together where his jewelry had been. His abruptly awakened mind reeling to take inventory of his physical self, and assembled himself along with his train of thought.

"I can't take anything you say seriously," Galadrath scoffed. "Let me split that tongue of yours so you can talk from both sides of your mouth at once, you snake."

"The court! Something is happening; someone has been working inside the court. I didn't do this to you, Galadrath."

"You're just a propped up clown, Teratos. Everything you say is a lie, just foolish, slippery words to save your own skin."

"They've been breaking up the ambassadors, they're trying to shift power. They're asking Pillars to shed their oaths and swear fealty to the court."

"Empty words. What I can't understand is why you took in my family. Are they here? Are they asleep? Tell me why. Give me one shred of peace—one shred of truth—before I end you," Galadrath said.

"I'd never do anything to hurt you. I'm just trying to keep them safe in your absence. The court knew you'd return. After you killed their spy, they sent Larl to wait for you."

"Larl is dead," Galadrath said, pulling off the dark cloak he was wearing, showing the chains wrapped around his arms. He began to pace restlessly in the small space.

"They'll be looking for you."

"His death was somewhat... unconventional. It'll take time for them to understand that I was behind it. I'm assuming you didn't hear the explosion."

"Explosion?" Teratos said, rubbing his face.

He stared at his fingers in confusion, now covered in ash. Frowning, he reached down to adjust his vest that had become strangely uncomfortable, and when it would not release its grip on him, he grunted and tugged at it again to no avail. He shifted his attention to his other trappings, pulling the sheet wrapped around his legs loose.

"I'm not here to explain anything. I want to hear your confession, so

I can kill you," Galadrath spun on his heels to face Teratos.

"I didn't do anything! My oldest friend!"

"Stop lying! I'll remove your voice if you can't spin a truthful word with it!" Galadrath growled, rage boiling in his remaining eye.

Teratos reflexively tried to pull his own trinkets under his command. Galadrath watched as the surprise washed over the face of his betrayer, the flabby cheeks draining of color, matching the smeared ash.

"You've taken my things. You won't even let me defend myself."

"Defend yourself with words, with the truth. You've been accused, Teratos."

"I've told you the truth!"

"Then you've betrayed me for the last time. Death becomes you," Galadrath stated.

There was a gasp from the edge of the room. The intensity of the situation had distracted him. When he looked up, he saw Maxima standing at the edge of the room, her hair down in disarray around her shoulders, wearing a flowing purple gown.

"Galadrath! What's happened to you? You look terrible!" she gasped.

"Sorry to wake you Maxima. I've come to kill your husband," Galadrath replied.

His old habits returned, and his polite and amicable tone replaced the wild hate instantly. He realized the absurdity of it—his mangled form, covered in the dried blood of his victims, speaking of murder as if they were exchanging pleasantries at a dinner party. Her presence took the heat from the air, like a parent walking in on a child playing make-believe, the illusions of dragons dissipating, leaving only an embarrassing reality.

She crossed the room quickly and bent down to help her husband. She frowned at him, uncertain about his unexplainable disheveled look. She looked back at Galadrath, her sour face urging an explanation.

"That... that was me. I got tired of waiting for him to wake up," he tried to explain.

"What?" Teratos asked.

"Boys! Both of you! You've come to kill my husband? Why? Because he sheltered your family?" Maxima scolded them.

"He betrayed me. He ruined my life. He turned me into a traitor. Look at me, Maxima!"

Galadrath drew a sword, and in a swift flourish, the point rested against the chest of Teratos.

"Leave, or you'll watch him die," Galadrath said coldly.

She reached up slowly from where she crouched next to her husband and carefully wrapped her fingers around the blade.

"You'd really kill your oldest friend? You'll go through with it this time?" she pleaded.

Galadrath scowled, not understanding. He pushed the sword in slowly, feeling the resistance until the edge breached the vest and the steel sank shallowly into Teratos. He felt the pull of Maxima's hand holding the blade, trying to stop it, but she was not willing to flay her own flesh in order to save her husband's.

Teratos chirped in pain, trying to muffle his own scream. His eyes grew wild and flitted between Maxima and Galadrath. Like an animal led into a slaughterhouse, he could smell his own demise coming.

"Stop! He didn't betray you! I did!" Maxima yelled, desperation in her voice.

The two men froze in disbelief. Galadrath pulled back the sword, Maxima releasing her grip on it, the bloodied tip retreating from the shallow wound.

"What?" Galadrath asked.

"I exchanged the letters. I traded out the one Teratos intended to give you at dinner for another," she said, tears welling in her eyes.

"You... gave him my name?" Teratos asked, his breath hitching, unbelieving.

"I knew he wouldn't kill you."

"I mean, there was a chance..." Teratos mumbled.

Maxima glared at him, her eyes watery and bloodshot.

"Why would you send me to kill your husband?" Galadrath could hardly comprehend the absurdity of her words.

"Because I knew you wouldn't," she cocked her head to the side.

"But *why*? Why would you want me to fail? Why would you need to test me?" he said, his earlier rage leashed by confusion.

"Everything isn't about you, Galadrath. There are other things at play here. Your loyalty to the crown is unwavering. I simply needed you out of the way, and I couldn't find any other solution. I didn't expect the court to botch your execution so deftly," she said.

Galadrath exchanged incredulous looks with Teratos.

"This conniving shrew is at the center of all this? And I thought you were the one with the wicked tongue."

"Seriously Gally? She's my wife," Teratos interrupted.

"Who tried to have me killed! Look at me, Teratos!"

"In all fairness, she tried to have me killed too."

"Both of you! Quiet!" Maxima yelled.

They turned and glared at her. She understood quickly she was no longer in a position to exert any authority over them. Galadrath lunged at her, his instincts kicking in, his sword seeking her blood. Teratos wrapped his arms around Galadrath's knee, using his weight from where he sat to belay the attack.

"Please Galadrath! Give me a moment of calm!" Teratos pleaded.

Galadrath saw his own bewilderment in the man's eyes—a pendulum out of balance, swaying from surprise to fear, from reason to wrath.

"Wait, so you didn't lie to me? You didn't betray me," Galadrath mumbled at Teratos.

"How many times did I try to tell you!" Teratos spat.

"But at the trial they disarmed me, and you just sat there. They called me a traitor. They were going to have me killed. You did nothing after you had sworn to me you'd make it right. How is it that I am to believe that it was all a misunderstanding? You left me to die," Galadrath fumed.

"What would I have done? I spoke with them and expected no more than a formal admonishment, so that they could save face and wave away the misunderstanding. I didn't know they had planned the execution, and in that moment, I was just as stunned as you were. There was nothing I could do. I felt helpless, and there isn't a day that I don't wish that I could have found a way to stop those events from unfolding," Teratos said softly.

Teratos turned toward Maxima, his eyes tracing the floor upwards until they met hers. He placed his fingers against the wound in his chest, absentmindedly trying to stop the slow flow of blood soaking into his clothes.

"And you watched me suffer—you watched as the whole kingdom came bearing down on my friend. You watched me struggle and rue through my own thoughts, and you did nothing. Worse, you were the source of my pain," Teratos said to her.

The pained look in Maxima's eyes intensified, and the tears welled up all over again.

"You cry now, but I don't believe it is out of sadness or regret. You only cry for yourself," Teratos said through gritted teeth.

"If I had no love for you—if I was only selfish like you say—then I'd have let Galadrath drive that blade through your belly. Thousands of our countrymen will continue to suffer because I care more for you than I do for them—for the greater good," she sobbed.

Teratos' scowl intensified for a moment, then his face softened, but he did not have a chance to reply.

"What's going on here? The children are sleeping," a familiar voice came from the edge of the room.

Galadrath's heart sank and swelled at the same time. It was Heladra's voice. His whole body wanted to turn to her, to float on its own volition toward her. Every one of his emotions was drawn to her, as if she was an inescapable force, but he stood rigid. His shame was overbearing. He did not want her to see him like this. He was a broken monster, a shredded shadow tainted by blood and vengeance. He had abandoned her; he had left her to the whims of their captors; he had failed as her husband.

Gasping his name, she ran to him, and though he looked very different, he could see in her eyes that she only saw *him.* She only saw the man she had married, the one she loved. She wrapped her arms around him awkwardly, trying to embrace him, her hands fumbling with the metal fins holding his spine in place. Just as the moonlight mixed with the candlelight, their two starkly different forms could not be strained from each other.

"Galadrath! My love!" she exclaimed.

His sword clattered to the floor as he held her. She looked up at him with love and yearning, meeting his eye without a hint of disgust or fear.

"I missed you, my sweet," she cried softly.

"I missed you too, my rose," he mumbled into her hair.

Galadrath closed his eye and felt her warmth through the layers between them, as if her love could break through the impenetrable divine metal. His thoughts wandered, emotions overwhelming as they brewed inside him—yet calmed by her graceful presence.

He heard the light clinking of metal and opened his eye to see the point of his own sword leveled at the back of Heladra. Maxima held the weapon deftly, and her eyes were as sharp as the blade.

The rage returned to Galadrath. The fury he had cultivated for Teratos had not yet been unleashed, and now he had been given an answer—a new target. Maxima lunged forward with the sword, and Galadrath spun Heladra in his arms, shielding her from the thrust with his own back. The point found him, it met the resistance of his trappings and his power. It buckled, first bending and then breaking as he willed it into a fine collection of brittle pieces.

He carefully settled Heladra back on her feet and let her go, turning toward Maxima.

"You think you can end me?" he laughed, insanity seeping into his voice.

Maxima still held the hilt of the destroyed weapon. It vanished in a puff of black smoke, before appearing in the same fashion in Galadrath's hand. He pointed it at the ground where the pieces of broken metal lay. Just as he had willed the sword to come apart, he willed it back together. The metal turned to cool liquid, dripping upwards into the air onto his hand—collecting like rain water on a leaf, crawling back into place, and slowly reforming the keen edge.

"I am clad in the names of those who failed to kill me. I am covered in the scars of their best efforts. I wear the blood of their last acts, and I hold the screams of their failure in my mind. I stand among the hundreds of souls who have tested their mettle against me. Those who survived me did so because I gave them mercy—mercy that you will not be given, Maxima," he said through clenched teeth.

His voice carried into the room, and as it echoed off the walls, it doubled—a whisper of an ethereal, effeminate voice, barely audible, singing like a distant chorus. The air in the room cooled, an icy glaze forming around him, his last words taking a physical shape in the form of his visible breath.

"Now I come for you," he finished.

He stepped forward with the polished sheen of the newly formed weapon in hand, ready to cut down his true betrayer.

"Galadrath! Stop! My child!" Teratos cried.

"You cry for your child, but not for your wife?" Maxima chastised him.

"Woman, shut your venomous gob. You're my wife in formality only at this moment, and you stand inches from death. I'll wrap my own hands around your neck if I hear another word from you," Teratos said.

Galadrath looked toward Teratos, waiting for him to make his plea. The rotund man walked quickly to a nearby bookshelf, retrieving a large volume without looking at the words on the binding. He opened it and pulled out a dried flower from between the pages. He sighed heavily and turned to show Galadrath what he had found.

"This is the flower you gave me when you came to accuse me, before you spared my life. I'm asking you to extend that favor once more. I understand what you've set out to do, but please, for me—let her live. Let my child live," he pleaded.

"She betrayed us all, Teratos. She lied to us, manipulated us, and pitted us against each other. She drove the wedge of doubt and distrust between us, my friend. Tell me honestly what she deserves more than a swift death," Galadrath said.

"She's my wife, Gally," Teratos sighed in resignation.

"'Till death do you part.' You won't be bound by that vow for much longer."

"What would you do?" Teratos said, glancing at Heladra.

Galadrath turned toward her. She had not spoken a word, but there was a sadness in her eyes that told him everything he needed to know. The moment felt like an eternity. Only the flicker of candle light at the edge of his vision alerted him of the passing time. In her gaze, he found the strength to muster a sliver of forgiveness.

He took the pressed flower from Teratos' shaking hands carefully, and placed it in Maxima's still half open palm that had held the sword moments ago.

"You said it yourself, she's a wife in formality only. She doesn't stand by your side," Galadrath said.

"These things can be mended. Time and effort can fix what she has undone," Teratos replied.

"And my eye? Can you mend that with time? I'm in constant pain, Teratos. My head feels like it's still on fire. Every limb aches and pains. I can't lay down to sleep. When I do drift away for a brief moment of respite, I wake up covered in sweat and pus. The shreds of my sanity are only strong enough to hold one thought, and I choose vengeance."

Teratos glanced at the ground briefly, forming his words carefully.

"I don't believe you chose only vengeance. When I see how you look at your wife and your children, I see your love. Love is sacrifice, and I'm deeply sorry that you have had to sacrifice so much—and endure so much pain—for it. I'm filled with woe knowing that others have placed these trials at your feet, and that I was no help to you. I despise myself for becoming a pawn in their game to destroy you. So I hope you will punish me instead. That is a sacrifice I will gladly make—for my own love.

"I've spent a lifetime working to create a better place for us. We inherited an age of darkness and suffering, and the Few gave us hope, a light to follow. The road ahead is still long and perilous. Until I learned I was going to be a parent, those ideas of hope were just ideas. Now they are imperative. I will have a legacy, and that brings me great joy. But with that joy comes immense responsibility to give my best to ensure that the legacy is worth having.

"We live in a broken world, and I wish to give my legacy the best chance of making it a better place. My son or daughter will hopefully carry on my work, carry on my blood and memory, and bring the world to a brighter place for us all. But for any of that to happen, to matter, Maxima must live," Teratos pleaded.

Galadrath nodded slowly as the short speech ended, turning to Maxima.

"You'll live," Galadrath began.

"Thank you Gala—" Teratos interrupted.

"You'll live not because of my mercy! Not because of your own actions! You'll carry on because of the goodness of others" —he nodded to Teratos while not breaking eye contact with Maxima— "because there are bonds in this room that you cannot destroy! Try again, and I will come for you," Galadrath boomed.

Maxima shriveled away from him, and the others braced themselves against his anger. Even in the presence of his incredible power, his seldom-raised voice carried more weight. He began to pace aimlessly around the room, as the others stood stunned, watching like they had unexpectedly found themselves in the room with a hungry lion. They were unsure of what to do.

"Why? *Why*? Why did you do it?" he said eventually.

Maxima sighed. Galadrath watched her carefully as she stood, staring at the floor, collecting her thoughts.

"The Court of Lords wish to usurp the throne. Lord Tallus Ostiphan and a few others have been working to abolish the monarchy. King Dartan has been a puppet leader—a poor one at that. The Lords wish to oust him in order to establish a collective rule, to bring us out of this dark age that the king has allowed us to languish in," she said.

Galadrath fixed a murderous glare, and the awkward silence in the room compelled her to speak again.

"When Durium died—"

"*King* Durium," Galadrath spat back.

"When King Durium died, my grandfather established the Court of Lords. King Dartan was still young—too young to rule. Though he took the throne as a boy, my grandfather knew he would need help. So he recruited the governors of the cities and towns to form the Court. And it worked. It united Thainegom during that terrible time. But then the Shattering happened, and unrest followed. The people blamed my grandfather—for nothing he could control, for doing his best, for giving them hope and structure. They had him thrown out.

"My parents grew up in squalor, on the fringes of the very society my grandfather had held intact—all because of the mob of ungrateful masses that didn't know better. When my father died, I took a new name. I clawed my way out of that life and remade myself," Maxima explained.

She turned to Teratos, but could not bear his gaze, and began to cry again. She stood by the dimly lit table, and passed her finger slowly through the flame of one of the burned down candles. There was a light sizzle as her tears pattered into the molten wax. It seemed to Galadrath she was trying to dull the pain of the memory with the flame, to burn away the veil that hid the truth.

"You've said great things, and I admire you. I've strayed from your side—I've pushed you away because of some old grudge. I see the error in that now. Thus, I must come clean about one more thing: I have lied to you. My maiden name isn't what you think—it's Tavius," she said softly.

Teratos opened and shut his mouth a few times slowly.

"Your grandfather was Master Manibus Tavius," he whispered finally.

"Yes."

"The Warden of the Brightcaller. The only man who ever put one of the Few in chains. The man who single handedly crippled the forces who stood against evil, who likely caused the deaths of tens of thousands of his countrymen. That's the Tavius we're talking about?" Galadrath asked.

"That's not fair," Maxima protested. "He made the best choice he could and ended up on the wrong side of history. He made that choice because of the words of the King, and we all suffered for it."

"I don't understand. What does he have to do with you trying to get us all killed?" Teratos asked, still reeling from the cascade of truth laid at their feet.

"Dartan is weak! He's ruined this country! A new age has dawned, and he's clinging to the shreds of the past. My grandfather saw that, and he wanted something new—something better. If only he hadn't made that one mistake."

"It wasn't just a mistake—it was colossal," Teratos said.

Galadrath asked, "So you wanted me out of the way so you could stage a coup on the king?"

"I told you already, not everything is about you." She threw him a subtle glower. "That was simply a small portion of a larger plan. Although, when you fell into employ with Farrah, it was an unexpected boon. The raid on the warehouse was a great help."

"What! You know Farrah?" Galadrath jolted.

"Who's Farrah?" Heladra piped in for the first time.

"I don't know her personally, but I've had contact with her organization, and I've coordinated events with their help," Maxima interrupted.

"The Emissaries at the warehouse... you told someone I would be there."

"There were some of those faithful to our cause that were hoping to dispatch you more discreetly, yes."

"What else do you know?" he demanded. "Who else is loyal to the cause?"

"What else don't I know..." Teratos mumbled to himself, rubbing his head.

"I'm not sure. I might be involved in this thing, but I am not the one carrying the grand plan. I can't betray them before this revolution has a chance," Maxima continued.

"Your loyalties are still split, Maxima. You've made your choice to live. The price for that is not cheap. I need the names. I'm ending this," Galadrath stated.

She sighed and shook her head.

"Lords Ostiphan, Braf, Freid, and Tireod," she mumbled.

"Half the court? Unbelievable. Then there will be half as many—come noon tomorrow," Galadrath said.

THE LAST MERCY

WHEN THEY WERE ALONE, and the house was quiet once more, Heladra carefully undressed him. She inspected his wounds and cleaned them, sponging away the dirt, sweat, and blood from the prior chaotic days—soothing the weeks of yearning he had felt during his exile.

She bandaged his arm carefully after cleaning out the rough sutures Taroosa had put in place. Then she went to work on his back.

"Who did this to you?" she whispered.

"Larl Rihhi. The man they put in my place."

"And I thought the trial of Sebbatin would be your worst."

"Sebbatin was trained as a warlord, not an assassin or an executioner. Larl was much like myself."

"And he's dead?"

"Yes. We shot him with a cannon that we commandeered from the Hercolid."

"You are responsible for the attack on the city?" she asked without inflection.

If there was any judgment or fear, any emotion at all in her voice, he could not hear it. She was listening, caring, and collecting information, like a barber patiently sharpening a razor on leather. When she was done, he knew she would either carve into him with her words or shave him clean with them.

"The attack on the city, the attack on the armories, the attacks on the spires, and the attack on the fortress—it seems I've become a menace to this country," he grumbled.

"You always have taken your work quite seriously," she replied absentmindedly.

"This isn't my work. I'm doing this for you."

"That's sweet, Galadrath, but we both know you are doing this for *you*."

Her voice cooed softly as she focused on cleaning his wounds. Her words stung him more than the steaming water on his tender skin. She had stated a plain truth, nicking him with the edge of her words, the razor she had prepared now being put to use.

Heladra worked in silence for a moment. He waited for her to speak, but was afraid she had not realized his lack of response to her remark. He brooded on her words. The stinging pains were a welcome distraction from their conversation. She moved around the room, dousing dirty rags in water and wetting clean ones to drape over the grisly landscape that was his back. She carefully dabbed at the edges where metal wrapped around bone—where flesh met the hard edge of the fins.

"This is never going to heal in this state," she murmured. "I've never seen anything like it."

"That was Taroosa's doing. She said I cracked pieces of my spine. She wasn't trying to heal me; she just wanted to get me upright. She did her best—she's an engineer, not a doctor."

"I wasn't critiquing her work or her intentions. I just know this is an open wound, and it's beginning to turn. I can smell it. This will kill you, Galadrath, if you don't get better care. Who is Taroosa? Seems you've made many friends and had plenty of adventures."

"I've been from Bracken to Whitespur, and everything in between: Tomb, Threshook, Silt, the Hercolid, and even down to the beaches of Serenity. I've been employed by brigands, befriended someone I exiled—that was Taroosa. I met the people who stole the World's Edge, then helped them steal the Eye of the Marksman. Oh, and Brixby says 'hello'."

"You went to see your parents?" she realized.

"Of all the things I just mentioned, that's the one thing you want to know about?"

"We just haven't visited them in a while. It would be nice to see them."

"When this is all over, we'll take the children. We can tour the islands, relax, and maybe catch a fish or two. I can show them where I grew up."

"When this is over, you need to see a doctor. Immediately. Aren't you in incredible pain? How can you function like this? When will it be over?" she said, her tone swelling with emotion.

"Yes, I will. And yes, I am," he said. "Tomorrow, it will all be over tomorrow, one way or another."

"Then we better get our rest. Lay down so I can hold you."

He stuffed a few of the nightbloom petals into his mouth and then complied, shuffling stiffly onto his stomach so he could wrap his good arm around her.

"Larl said they tossed you in the dungeons. I'm sorry."

"'Tossed' is hardly the right word. Yes, once they found the man—or rather, found the lack of the man you killed in the street—they imprisoned me and the children. Considering we were behind bars, it was a pleasant stay. The guards were very polite and attentive. We were more like mandatory guests than prisoners. It seems even as a traitor they have some reverence for you. Teratos came down himself when he heard. He didn't even take the time to move through the proper channels. He simply waddled down there, red faced and threatening, and took us home with him."

"I'll have to thank him."

"The two of you have a lot to talk about," she sighed. Then her face scrunched with anger and disbelief. "Maxima of all people! The grandaughter of Tavius. Can you imagine?"

"I don't have to imagine—it just happened," he mumbled into a pillow.

"*They* have a lot to talk about," she said, snuggling against him. "You wouldn't keep secrets from me like that, right?"

"I tell you everything," he said listlessly.

In that moment, before he drifted off to sleep, he saw the face of Farrah frozen in terror, right before he kissed her.

"I *will* tell you everything," he mumbled, already half asleep.

Early the next morning, as the Sisters' light peeked through the drawn curtains, the laughter of children and the bustle of bodies filled the mansion. Galadrath woke from his slumber, keenly reintroduced to the throbbing pain. He wiped his hand over the linens on the bed, searching for the warm form of Heladra, but she had already gotten up.

He rolled onto his side, the sheets sticking to his face where the burns had wept during the night, and opened his eye slowly. He got up, eventually, and searched for something to wear. The scorched remnants of furs and metals of his fake persona lay in a disorganized pile in the corner of the guest room, and as he dug through them, he caught the stench they emitted. He left them laying on the floor and began to dig through the drawers of the dresser, wondering if Heladra had saved any of his clothing from the grasp of Larl.

He discovered a few of his things, a plain black silk shirt and a matching pair of loose pants. And as he rummaged further, he found his old torn vest and matching cloak—the shining white silk covered in a field of flowers dirty but not faded.

Heladra appeared in the door and remarked on the clothing he held in his hands.

"It seemed appropriate to keep. Although, I never thought I'd see you wearing it again," she said.

"I'll need another cloak, something big and inconspicuous," he replied.

"Teratos might have one. It'll be big, but I don't know about inconspicuous," she said.

Her eyes carried a sadness that her voice did not reflect.

"Will the children want to see me?" he asked.

"Of course, Galadrath, you're their father."

He dressed and headed down to breakfast. The air was filled with the smells of eggs and honeyed meats, the sounds of cutlery clinking lightly on plates, and the crunching of crisp fresh fruit. Whatever conversation that had been going on died as he entered the room. Even his children regarded him in silence. He stared eagerly at them, hoping they would show the blind compassion their mother had. The pleasant breakfast was a stark contrast to his unappealing appearance. He waited for a moment, anticipating a cry of disgust, but they took their cues from the others at the table, treating him as a formal guest.

"So, how is school?" Galadrath said, adding artificial cheer to his voice.

"Father, you're missing an eye. Do we really have to talk about school?" Marcanus said.

Teratos muffled a chuckle, choking slightly on his eggs.

"Straight to the point, as usual Marcanus," Galadrath replied.

"Where did it go, papa? Where's your eye?" Radralia asked.

"I traded it for some jewelry, my sweet lily," he answered.

"That doesn't seem like a very smart thing to do."

"I didn't have much choice in the matter, my dearest, but you're right, it's not a bargain I'm willing to take again."

He pulled Taroosa's pendant from his pocket, and handed it to his daughter.

"Maybe one day you can have this one," he said, smiling.

"It's so ugly! A big old fat worm. That's not worth an eye!"

"It's a caterpillar, but you're right again, it's not very pretty," he chuckled.

"Papa, you can keep it."

"Thanks my little daisy, let me know if you change your mind."

Maxima entered from the kitchen, her usual graceful aire veiled her transgressions admirably. At the sight of her, the knife Galadrath was holding split the plate beneath it, where he had been cutting his food into tiny bites. The sounds of the ceramic breaking stopped her in her tracks. Across from him, he heard Teratos whisper his name with a mixture of pleading and warning. His children gaped at the broken plate. It took everything he had to maintain his composure—to not turn back his agreement to let her live—and his glare melted the pleasant varnish from his betrayer's persona.

"So much to do!" she tittered, retreating back from where she had appeared.

He willed the plate back together and placed the knife neatly on the table, fearing the cutlery would catalyze his hate for her and become her undoing. He continued to eat with his fingers, carefully placing the small bites in his mouth to refrain from stretching the burned skin of his cheek.

His breakfast was brief, and none of them ate very much as they talked incessantly. The children interrupted each other asking about all his adventures, and he indulged them in all but the gory details. The rest of the adults listened, enraptured by Galadrath's friendly tone describing the depths of his treasonous acts and the horrors he glossed over. He made the mistake of looking up from Marcanus and Radralia, catching the stare of his wife. He could see she was not listening to the words he said, but instead she was filling in the spaces between them. Between each exclamation of victory and daring escape, there was the pause of death, the silence of defeat untold. There was blood and pain between every breath, and he could see the sympathy in her eyes for what had happened—and fear for what would come next.

"I best get going," Galadrath said. "The court waits for no one—I'm off to work. I expect you all to be on your best behavior."

"Aren't you still a traitor, father?" Marcanus asked.

Teratos chuckled at the frankness of the boy's comment.

"Not for long, son. My love to you all. See you soon," Galadrath replied. He smiled and looked around the table.

Leaning forward to peek into the kitchen, his eye landed on Maxima. "Except for you," he added sternly.

The coolness of his statement tempered the air of its joviality and set the tone for what they all knew came next.

He stood and walked around the table, placing a hand on each of his children in turn, then stopped behind Heladra, bending down to share a brief kiss.

"Careful, Galadrath," she whispered as he pulled away.

"There is nothing careful about what I am about to do. I'll see you shortly, my carnation."

He pulled the baggy black cloak over his other trappings, and as it swung around his shoulders, the veil of black fog surrounded him. He stood in the stark sunlight, along the flowerbeds in the Park of Marrette. He knew he could not walk into the throneroom empty handed. So he quickly plucked a bouquet and tucked it under the cloak, vanishing again. He appeared in Teratos' office, inside the cloister in which all the Administrants had their rooms and studies—where he knew he would be undiscovered.

Galadrath walked out of the Administrants' offices and down the long hallway to the throne room. He tightened the heavy cloak around his strange form, the back rising oddly as the material accommodated the fins on his spine. Only his heels showed from under the material, his face obscured by the hood draped low over his face. He strided quickly through the crowd that was gathering at the entrance, bumping into people at intervals and mumbling apologies from under the hood.

He moved at a speed that signaled some abnormal level of urgency and allowed him to pass by the folk trying to get to the same place—but not too quickly as to alarm the few Sentries monitoring the crowd. Luckily, many lords, ladies, and nobles of all sorts dressed in a similar fashion, attempting to obscure their titles from those who might seek to interrupt them if their identities were known.

It was busier than he had ever seen before. There were more people and guards, and he could feel the latent stress and fear of the unknown that followed his attack on the city. They were here for an explanation—to be put at ease.

He would give them the explanation, but there would be no ease.

He finally arrived at the nexus point where the long hall met the throne room walls, which opened into the circular expanse that formed the gallery of the court. The people pooled around the Herald to state their business and have their names recorded to be announced. After a brief pause, the herald turned toward the court, and Galadrath's heart sank, thinking he may have been spotted before he could make his entrance.

"On this fourteenth day of the fifth month, year seven thousand ninety-two, I call the court into session!" the Herald yelled, before turning back to those waiting to be admitted to the room.

Others skirted by, having no business and only required a seat in the gallery. Galadrath joined those in the thin procession, moving into the wide room.

He did not approach a seat. Instead, he simply walked down the central aisle of the room between the rows of chairs and ascended the shallow steps at the center, leading to the platform that held the sarcophagus of the Brightcaller. As he did, the Sentries, whose duty was to prevent such action, began to address him.

"Halt! This area is off limits. Find a seat!"

Galadrath ignored them, slowly climbing the stairs. They trailed closely on his heels, weapons at the ready. They grabbed him by the elbows and tried to pull him away from the sacred place, but they were met with unyielding resistance. The energy of the emblems already filled his veins, the command of the divine metal at attention, waiting for his orders.

He felt the court before him, already assembled in the thick rows of ornate seats flanking the king's throne. He felt the collection of Administrants seated behind the lords, and the smattering of scribes, prefects, court messengers, and the rest of the auxiliary that formed the bureaucratic army, clustering like barnacles to the hull of the throne.

"King Thestus!" Galadrath yelled from under the hood.

Silence fell upon the room. Few people had noticed him approaching the throne, and now, as he stood before it, everyone had turned to face the disturbance. Those chatting in their seats—the ones still waiting to be admitted—froze at his bold, direct address to the king.

"Who calls on me? Take him away!" King Dartan Thestus said, looking up from a large ledger.

"I yield to none," Galadrath answered.

The guards at his sides wrestled fruitlessly to yank him down from his perch, but his body was like stone—heavy and stubborn.

"I'll have you killed for your insolence. Get him down from there!" Dartan commanded.

The men struggled, and others joined at their sides, threatening Galadrath at spear point. Others pushed at him, but his immovable stature was both confusing and frustrating to the collection of armored guards.

"I'm here with dire news, my king. I'm here with news of treason, of a coup against your reign," Galadrath continued from underneath the hood of the cloak.

"And you'll wait your turn to do so in the dungeons if you refuse to obey!" Dartan responded.

"You'd imprison a faithful servant who comes to warn you, while your enemies coddle you at your sides?" Galadrath asked.

"Faithful servant! Bah! I'll have you reduced to ash by these Emissaries and swept into the cracks of the floor."

Despite his harsh words, the king's tone betrayed a hint of confusion, for a dozen men failed in their attempt to remove the cloaked figure. Galadrath knew that the king had expected to speak only once—to issue the command to have him removed—and that the interruption would vanish into the dungeons. Instead, he was locked in a dialogue with an immovable man.

"I have every right to be here, and I only wish to speak to you."

"Emissaries, assist in removing this madman from my sight," Dartan said.

Galadrath felt the fields of influence extend from twenty different points at the periphery of the room—and another twelve from around the throne.

"Send them to me if you wish, but let them know they face the Accuser."

A gust of air erupted from around Galadrath, scattering the initial sentries trying to arrest him. They were thrown from the raised podium at the center of the room, tumbling down the stairs unceremoniously in every direction. He stood alone. His heavy cloak incinerated flamelessly, the cloth turning to ash in fractal patterns of rippling orange, the mirage of heat carrying the tiny cinders high into the air.

He revealed the shining white cloak he had worn the last time he stood before the throne. It was still charred and torn, carrying the flecks of his own dried blood. The vest, in the same condition, completed his original ensemble. The sinister fins of metal protruded from fresh slits that had been cut through the back of the materials. The myriad of divine jewelry shone brightly in the focused light at the center of the room, casting their own reflected beams onto the far walls. In his arms, he held a large bouquet of roses, their rich red petals so dark that the bright light was barely enough to coax any color from them.

He threw the collection of flowers in a wide arc in front of him, and as they struck the ground, some of the ripe open blooms came apart, scattering the petals in small clouds on the sandstone floor.

There was a collection of murmurs, shrieks, and gasps as he revealed himself. The tension in the room was palatable, and soon turned to quiet expectation.

"My King, permit me to speak?" An old voice came from the far reaches of the raised platform that held the lords.

King Dartan shifted his eyes at the interruption, quickly recognizing the voice.

"Speak, Lord Ancient."

Galadrath turned his attention to the old yet venerable man sitting at the far end of the panel of lords. He wore simple, well-fitting clothing and did not carry the ostentatious, almost obligatory air of command that the other lords held. He wore no gold, but a single piece of jewelry hung from his neck. Galadrath could not make it out from the distance at which he stood, but he had seen it up close before. Engraved in the face of the round pendant was an oversized hammer, head pointing down, imposing on a mountainous landscape.

"I wish to excuse myself from court—and beg pardon for those in the gallery—so that we may all leave before you resume your business with Accuser Yaralok," the raspy voice said.

"And why would you choose to neglect your duties in overseeing this matter, Lord Ancient?"

"The first time I stepped into this room, I followed a man much like Galadrath into it. He carried the same look and similar power."

"I'm failing to see your point," Dartan said with annoyance.

"I knew that man by the name William Arbyd, but you may recall him as the Ashmaker. And what followed him can only be described as unprecedented violence."

"You fought alongside him that day?" Galadrath asked.

"I cowered in fear, much like I do now. I wish to live. Even at the end of this long life, I'd like to survive today. I think it would be a kindness if you would allow those of us who aren't a part of this madness to leave."

"And what madness is this you speak of? A rogue bringing news of a coup?" Dartan asked.

"Yes, King. He speaks the truth," Lord Ancient said.

"And I agree—we should clear the gallery before we speak further on the subject," Lord Ostiphan interjected.

"Yes. Guards, please clear the room. Galadrath, Lord Ancient may expect violence, but I impress upon you that I want answers. We will discuss any matters that come to light, and I will put anyone to trial that may have a part in these seditious acts."

"The trial started when I walked into this room, and it will end when I leave," Galadrath stated.

The room emptied slowly, and the audience was urged from their seats, funneling toward the large arch leading from the room. Galadrath glanced around the room as he waited impatiently, catching glimpses of their faces. Some wore looks of fear as they met his gaze; others carried looks of disappointment. He could not tell if they were disappointed that they had watched their hero fall, had heard the last accusations of a man twisted by vengeance, or if they were annoyed they were being forced to miss the most dramatic spectacle of the decade. He never could tell what went on in the heads of nobility, if anything.

The strange calm mingled with anticipation and the shuffling of feet. Galadrath was impatient. He had expected that his unannounced visit would be met with resistance and fear, but he wanted to hear the truth, to suss out the treachery, and to restore his own name and honor. As he stood waiting for the gallery to clear, he tried to recall and recite the facts that he knew in his head, to organize and rehearse the questions he needed to ask and the questions he would undoubtedly have to answer. All of these things taxed his concentration, and he could not allow his attention to waiver from the thirty-two men and women whose influence was butted up against his own. A platoon of the continent's deadliest Many stood poised to kill him in defense of their king. He could not allow his attention to be divided, not by them, not by his own thoughts. If the situation called for violence, he would not make their job easy for them.

There were slight crackling shimmers where the invisible borders of each influence traded tiny specks of dust and air. Whenever a rogue molecule traded its allegiance to one master for another, it was as if the friction between the two controlling minds was made visible in a tiny flash of light. The room was mostly empty, and behind the throne, he could clearly make out his aggressors. The flowing white robes, with the silver wolf's head embroidered onto them, marked the station of each of the Emissaries surrounding him and the throne. He made an effort to identify them, to recall their titles and the number of symbols they carried, to find their weaknesses. His combat strategy took his overt attention, and the shuffling of feet fading behind him signaled that the discussion would begin soon. His attention fractured—a sliver of which began to plan his own verbal defense of his actions.

Would I plead with the king? Reason with him? Can I convince him that I am not the treason he seeks to root out?

His eyes flicked between the Emissaries as he thought, making a point to look at each of the twenty-six who stood around him.

Twenty-six.

The number made him feel uneasy, that something had gone amiss. He had felt more, before the fields of influence had clashed. Some of the Many that waited to kill him were not visible from his position. He pushed his influence out farther and farther, until it extended around the orbs of those around him, until it reached beyond the walls of the throne room, and deep beneath the floors—that is where he found them. Six of the Many stood beneath the floor, encased in the solid limestone, and he could feel the energy they contained.

Ambush. They expected me. All of this is a ruse.

He sighed slightly, and the fraction of his mind that had been dedicated to his trial came back under the fold and into a singular focus. There would be no time to reason; there would be no plea. There would be no time to discover who is right, but only to find out who is left.

As the last of the stragglers were ushered from the gallery by the guards, Lord Jemat Ancient turned for a moment back toward the center of the room and nodded to Galadrath.

"Thanks for your mercy," he said, his raspy voice barely carrying across the distance.

"It is my last."

"We will not be so willing to overlook your neglecting—" Lord Ostiphan began in a nasally tone.

Ostiphan was a large man, his rotund nature carefully held at bay by the well-fastened buttons of his expensive clothes. Galadrath had always imagined the high-pitch whine of the man's voice had something to do with his bulk, as if his own flesh and fat weighed so heavily on his lungs that the air in them was constantly under immense pressure, squeaking out at intervals when allowed to escape.

A dull thump was the last noise the man made as Galadrath crushed him into a ball half of his original size. There was no gasp, or nasally squeak, nor the tearing of ligaments or breaking of bones. Just one collective change in air pressure as the lord was turned into a compressed ball of viscera. The pressure exerted by Galadrath was so extreme that even the blood refused to soak outward into the clothing that had covered the man. Not until he released his grasp a moment later—and the spherical corpse covered in the crumpled clothing dropped onto the chair and then onto the floor—did the bright clean fabric begin to form icicles of dark crimson.

28

THE DANCER IN THE SUN

THERE WAS NO TIME for witty remarks or banter between dueling gentlemen. Galadrath had fired the first volley into the warzone, drawn blood, and now his enemies returned in kind—with extreme prejudice. The room immediately descended into controlled chaos. Walls of stone shot from the ground around the throne and the seats adjacent, separating the lords and their servants from the gaze of Galadrath. The air hardened and iced over as defenses were prepared, and winds whipped in every direction, listening to the whispers of the voices that controlled them.

His own defenses rose up to meet the multifaceted onslaught. Barriers of ice and iron jutted from the floor in jagged rows that mimicked the massive, crooked jaws of ancient megalodons. Galadrath knew his own weaknesses and strengths. He was not adept at fighting so many different minds at once, but he could deftly outmaneuver a single one. He could not counter each attack with efficiency, nor did he have the time to. He could not spend all his resources defending.

Thus, he pushed the spikes out, the wall of ice and metal pressing closer to his attackers. Ball bearings and darts of iron flew at him, but he swatted them away with fuelless explosions of heat and flame. The projectiles redirected as shrapnel in every direction but his own.

One man who was so focused on his own attack got unlucky and caught an iron ball bearing in the face. Another faltered and froze, before being impaled by a slowly expanding spike of ice.

These were simple mistakes made by men who had never seen combat. Galadrath had expected the best to defend the throne, especially knowing now they had prepared for an ambush. Instead of the best, it seemed like the Many who surrounded him still belonged in the lectures hall of the Temple of Light, digging their toes into the sand of the sparring pits, learning the basics.

Then he learned his mistakes: His impatience and his pride had clouded his focus. They were trying to kill him at every moment, but their attacks were not meant as killing blows. They were testing his limits, knowing that he would eventually falter, even for just a moment, and it would be enough.

When he realized the strategy being used against him, there were already four Emissaries laying dead amongst the broken floor of the throne room. The walls were charred in spots, chunks of ice and clouds of whirling steam, tornadoes of rubble and flame ripped through the air around them. He felt the rhythm forming between his own onslaught and the blows launched against him.

It was a symphony of hammering, like a master smith striking with speed and skill against a preform of metal. He could not tell if he was the arm of the smith, the hammer, or the worked metal. The mind in charge of the chaos was not his; the vision of the smith and the design in mind was beyond him. Yet the stock was cold—the blows that were launched against him, and those he returned, were harsh, not meant to form and strengthen but to damage and destroy.

The power of the Emissaries grew as their own control solidified into a single fighting force, their focus honed itself together as they also found a synchronized rhythm. He felt the energy grow, static discharging in the air around them.

In response, he tapped into the collection of emblems, drawing in more of his own power. He felt two of the fingernail-sized stones disappear as he drained them completely, filling himself with their power. He had never tested the collective limits of the hundred odd trinkets he was carrying, and it was more than he could have ever imagined. He felt like every wave that would ever crash hung in motion between his shoulder blades—that every burning forest that blackened the horizon pooled their smoke and torrents of flames behind his eyes. Every storm and gale spun around in a churn, and at the center, he sat like a mountain whose peak rises above it all, silently bearing down its immense power.

He set his jaw as if to contain it—as if his next word held the power to release it all.

The two Emissaries closest to him sent a fusillade of missiles in his direction. Barbs, darts, and spear points conjured from their own energies and launched toward him, followed by lashing whips of metal and iron serpents slithering toward him in midair.

He opened his mouth and let out a breathless sigh, releasing the fury he held back. White light blinded the onlookers as the roar of thunder filled the room and cords of lightning shot toward the Emissaries. In the instant where the storm of sharp metal descended on him, the lightning climbed each one before jumping to the next.

As the volley of darts traversed across the space between the white-clad men and Galadrath's grim visage, they seemed to halt mid-flight. An intense surge of electricity superheated them and vaporized each projectile in succession. In an instant, both assailants lay smoldering, their bodies sizzling from the violent passage of lightning.

His attack and his focus on the two assailants had cost him his defenses, and he knew it was what the others had been waiting for. Razorlike jets of air cut toward him, some of them splashing harmlessly off sheets of ice and the residual barricades scattered around. The attacks were focused, burrowing through the obstacles between them and their target. He had been standing still, predictable, relying completely on strength and force of will to keep himself out of harm's way—but he did not need to stand still.

He Stepped out of the way. He felt the deadly air rushing toward him, and then the silence and idle mist replaced the roar of imminent death and relentless chaos. The stretch of time that spanned for days and hours and months and seconds in between the two sides of the same instant gave him a place to think. He turned to step to the other side of the room, where no one was looking, a place where he could launch his next attack from.

As he attempted to will himself through the wispy darkness of Tor Zuer, he encountered resistance. His body tugged sleepily at something, unwilling to move, as if his soul had been nailed down. Looking down, he saw the points of two blades protruding from his chest, red bubbles forming with each breath escaping from his punctured lungs. The red stained steel retracted, and his mind began to swim from shock. He stood for what felt like a lifetime, wobbling slowly from side to side, as the person who had killed him walked into view.

Diatara held the two swords at the ready, but the look on her face did not match her control of the weapons.

"I'm sorry Galadrath. I told you—you'd have to kill me. But you didn't. Now, I have done the deed. I had already betrayed you that day on the beach. I knew you were innocent, falsely accused. I was the traitor, the one that broke my vows—the one who swore my fealty to the lords," she said sadly.

He formed a reply, but his voice was softer than a whisper.

"You were the ambush," his lips moved.

"One of six," she said, glancing at dark shapes in his periphery. "They knew you'd come; they knew you'd show force; they knew you'd Step if you were pressed hard enough. They didn't want you destroying the whole throne room, and they didn't want you running. So, they picked us to stop you. When they told me this is where you would die, I begged them, Galadrath. I know how much you hate this place," she explained.

"Let me see my family. Let me die in the sunlight. Let me go," his words croaked softly.

He collapsed to his knees, his hands hanging idly by his sides, the immense power in his veins feeling insignificant in this place. The foamy blood pooled on his vest, seeping slowly from the wounds. He did not need to look around to feel the five other Accusers that stood around him. He felt no urge to remember their names or their faces, to hunt them down for their defiance of the oaths they all had taken as Pillars of the Lowest House.

There was no time to fix his failures, no need to make excuses for his actions, no spite left to hurl at his betrayers. No fury loitered in his bones; no poison floated between his teeth—not even fear of the terrible death that he faced in the endless and timeless halls of this dark place.

There was only sadness—only regret that he would not see his family again.

"I can't let you go," Diatara answered softly.

Her words carried into the distance. The soft tone and hushed syllables seemed to fade into the abstract darkness without losing their energy. The whisper continued into perpetuity, echoing somewhere far away, yet somehow at the same hushed volume as though spoken directly into each of their ears. Then, the silence followed the hush.

Galadrath's foggy mind sent a chill down his spine, as if a fever had boiled his thoughts and froze his bones. It felt like Diatara's words had fled from them in fear, trying to escape into the distance, while the invisible monster that pursued was the silence that followed—like a crushing wave.

"I can't let you go," the whisper returned.

One voice whispered it back a thousand times—the unison of the words each falling like raindrops in a thunderstorm. The tidal wave of silence that followed broke, and the whispers shattered into screams. The world around them seemed to have caught fire, roaring in agony, the same words, over and over.

I can't let you go.

For the first time Galadrath felt a warmth in this place. The endless banks of dull, barely lit black mists rumbled with a red glow. He could make out the silhouettes of volcanoes and calderas—fields and forests on fire—all obscured and choked out by the everpresent black vapor. The air grew hot and sour, reeking of soot and toxins—of molten slag and a burning world.

As the heat began to rise, he heard a yelp that was cut short. Galadrath watched as one of the Accusers that surrounded him came apart like brittle charcoal. The seams where he had broken apart glowed dark green for a moment before fading away again, and the petrified man crumbled into powdery ash. The others reacted immediately, vanishing from where they stood, disappearing back to the safety of reality. All except Diatara, who was transfixed on the pile of ash that had been a man.

"Go," Galadrath croaked.

A stiff warm wind gusted through the acrid smoke, parting it into neatly rolling puffs. Diatara turned to face the direction of the disturbance, as the new landscape came alive around them. A young woman emerged from the breath of wind, wearing a simple black wool dress with a modest neck, showing faultless white skin down to the collar bones. Her shoulders were wide, tapering to a small waist where the monotone fabric was held tight with a cloth belt, before the dress widened again until it reached the ground. Her hair was jet black, coiled around a ribbon of blue and bound around her head. A slim neck flowed seamlessly into a strong jaw. She smiled widely, and where her teeth should sit were, instead, the nubs of fingertips with long, dirty, broken fingernails—all covered in the same black ichor that coated her mouth. The fingers curled slowly, beckoning them methodically into the abyssal maw.

Galadrath's thoughts spun briefly as he took in the scene, then he focused on staying conscious as he continued dying. The young woman looked like she had been chopping vegetables before their interruption. She wrung her hands nonchalantly on her dress, despite the flecks of molten earth shooting from an eruption and cooling as they fell through the smoke in the distance behind her.

Staring blankly, Galadrath's eye locked on his former apprentice, who had stabbed him. He waited for her to acknowledge him, but Diatara's face was filled with fear, her glance flitting between him and the woman. She tried to Step away. However, when the black fog surrounded her before slowly blowing away, she was still standing there.

Diatara quivered under the latticework of glassy black brambles that constricted her. Her arms were bound by the long, thin cordage made of tendons and sinew, each glistening rope covered in twisted spines and hooks. Claws from cats and bears protruded from the vines and plucked at her skin; long acacia thorns dripping black ichor pierced her lips holding her mouth shut; and sharp edges of splintered bone dug at the clothing pressed tightly against her skin. Under the rumpled fabric, her thin form looked frail, and the bindings left her helpless. He could see the pain in her eyes, every movement causing a cut or puncture.

"My dear, Diatara. You can not run from me. You can not escape from my domain. You do not have my permission to return, unlike the others," the woman said plainly.

"Others?" Galadrath gurgled.

"The other Accusers—they've left. This one, however, she's got a special place in your heart. I'll keep her; I'll make her live."

The young woman walked briskly until she stood next to Galadrath, looking down at where he balanced on his knees.

"Mirrora," Galadrath mouthed.

"It's been so long, my dearest. But this just won't do—if only this woman had stabbed you in the heart instead. Maybe she has a soft spot for you, too," she smiled.

She came to a stop where he was kneeled, softly raising his chin upwards with slender fingers.

"When one is born, they cry as a sign of life. A simple instinct, calling for comfort, afraid of a new and vibrant reality. It is the purest song, announcing to the world, 'I am here.' But when one sits in silence, no longer able or willing to cry, drowning in sadness and shame, one is yearning for the grave. Sing for me, Gally—scream for me," the fingers between Mirrora's lips quivered as she articulated each word.

The pain in his chest had all but subsided as his consciousness began to fade, but it returned like a white-hot needle. His chest felt like it was being torn apart and burned from the inside; yet, his lungs filled with air and held the pressure, allowing him to exhale a scream of black fog tinged with a hint of glowing green. He coughed and choked on the smoke, the taste of charred flesh and burning coal on his tongue. The pain she inflicted had not merely stopped the bleeding, but had also closed his wounds. His mind was clear and sharp; the pain was no longer a vague throbbing but rather clean, vivid, and searing. The mental shock and numbness from blood loss had been replaced by vigor and suffering.

"How long has it been, Galadrath?" Her voice was strange, low and curious, yet high-pitched and demanding—conflicting with a placid and caring face.

She knelt next to him and traced the side of his head with her short clean fingernails, letting them catch on the strap of his eyepatch.

He blinked slowly and grunted in pain.

"Hm..." she hummed. "Yes, I agree. It's been a while. Too long. I just wished you'd asked me to visit sooner."

"I didn't," he said hoarsely.

"That's just the problem, Galadrath—you never have. You were so alone when I found you, and then you left, and I was all alone. You said you'd never let me go," she stated.

"I never said that," he answered painfully.

"I know. Wishful thinking, *mon amour*. You know I just saved your life. So how long has it been? How long since the first time I saved your life?" she said, her face blank and uncaring.

He stared at her and coughed slightly.

"How long has it been since the day you came here—when you came here and didn't want to go back? The day you came here—to this dark place to hide—to die? When this cold void was more comforting than the walls of your own world?" she asked.

"Almost thirty years," he said slowly.

He refused to look at her, staring forward at where Diatara was still bound standing, shaking ever so slightly under the pressure of the needles and claws burying themselves shallowly in her flesh.

"And I walked you personally back into the light. I gave you those thirty years; I made you live. You can walk the beaches and drag your feet through warm sand—sit in an autumn breeze and watch the bugs crawl along the bark of old trees. You can hear the birds sing and smell the roses. Now, you have a wonderful family and a beautiful home. I placed you in that field of flowers that day. I gave you everything you wanted—out of love," she said, her voice breaking between a sob and a chuckle.

She turned away from him and covered her mouth, pausing for a moment. She turned back with a grotesque smile, swinging her arms idly by her sides.

"Now I find you here again, on your knees again, ready to die, *again*," Mirrora said coyly. "Today, however, you didn't give up. You just failed and got yourself killed… almost. Failure can be forgiven. To fail is to find an obstacle stronger than oneself—it is natural. But to give up is to lose against oneself, and that is a contradiction. That is *unacceptable,* " she growled.

Her voice had become feral and distorted. There was anger in her eyes, and her jaw muscles balled up as they flexed. Mirrora grimaced at Diatara, showing the black mouth filled with fingers and bit down hard. The tips of fingers broke and splintered through the flesh. The nails bent and dislodged, and the black tar squirted out, dribbling down her chin. She closed her mouth and wiped her chin as she took a moment to chew and swallow.

"You were betrayed, my Gally," she continued.

Her voice was soft and pure, mirrored by a sweet smile, her mouth no longer black—the fingers consumed and replaced with shining white teeth.

"The people who you loved and cared for threw away your loyalty. They made you a monster, so you could be hunted—they asked for help so that they could prey on your kindness; they used the untarnished sheet of your honor to veil their own misdeeds. They tossed your family and your life aside like garbage. You protected them, made every hard choice for *them*, and were even willing to fail for them—and they were willing to let you," she said.

"Why did you break your oath?" he asked.

Mirrora looked at him and turned toward Diatara, to which his question was pointed.

"I guess I'd better let her speak," Mirrora said.

The large straight thorns that held Diatara's mouth shut began to move, not retracting back through the punctures they had caused, but pulling outwards, as if to forcefully open her mouth. They stretched away from her teeth pulling at the already bloodied lips and cheeks, until they tore their way free. Diatara screamed throughout the slow process.

"Should I let her go, as well?" Mirrora asked softly.

Galadrath watched as the hooks and barbs attached to the slippery black whips seemed to jitter with excitement, and he feared there wouldn't be much left of Diatara if she was freed. She agreed with him, speaking through torn lips and flayed cheeks.

"No. Please, no," Diatara mumbled.

"From the mouth of the traitor herself—then you can stay as long as I like," Mirrora smiled.

"Why, Diatara? Why did you break your oath? Why betray the Lowest House by selling out to Thainegom? How did they convince you to fight against me?" he asked with a raspy voice.

"I wasn't made for this, Galadrath. You know what it's like to live and train in the Lowest House. It is miserable, cold, and oppressive, keeping secrets and expecting unwavering loyalty as we kill and serve without explanation. The Court gave us a way out. They showed us what a life could be—they let us share in the greatness that we helped create," she babbled through broken lips.

"They gave you a way out?" he asked, unbelieving.

He breathed deeply, followed by a wheezing cough, and braced his hands against his knee as he painfully exerted himself to stand. He ran his fingers over the holes in his shirt, where he had so recently been run through by Diatara's swords. The skin was mended and perfect, but inside his lungs ached, as if he had breathed hot smoke.

"They gave you a taste of what we gave them—what we built for them. They've become greedy and arrogant, and they've muddled your mind and trampled on our ways. They turned against each other in weakness and pride, and now they've turned us against each other. Where is the trust that we shared? The Pillars hold up the roof that shelters us all. If they gave you a way out, then you've left us to be buried in the rubble!" he yelled.

"I was tired of the killing..." Diatara sobbed.

"And all they asked in return is to stab your mentor in the back. Now that you've sold your loyalty and your friends, what do you have?" Galadrath growled.

"As much as you," Diatara mumbled.

"Oof. Galadrath, you got burned," Mirrora chuckled.

He turned to face her, puzzled at the remark. His anger was wild, and his eyes tried to reconcile her statement with his own feelings.

"I've been betrayed, not burned," he corrected her.

"Never you mind, Galadrath," Mirrora sighed.

"Why aren't you afraid?" Diatara asked softly. Her tears sluggishly running down into the coagulating blood and fresh torn cuts. "You were always so afraid of her. I know I would be—I am."

"I am afraid of what I do not understand, of what my shame may cost me, of what she might do to others. I was afraid she'd hurt the people I care for—to call on me to return the favor I was given," he spat.

"You wound me, Gally. I am standing right here you know," Mirrora lamented sarcastically.

"Right now, you should be afraid of what I might do," Galadrath grumbled at Diatara.

"Yes, Galadrath. Unleash your wrath, wreak vengeance," Mirrora whispered.

Her voice echoed softly in the air around them, lingering like a sick smell in a poorly ventilated cage.

"Accuser Diatara Slaaterson you have been accused..." Galadrath began.

"Oh no, Gally, I meant the court. She's mine. I'll give her thirty years, just like I gave them to you," Mirrora said.

"You'll let her go?" he exclaimed.

"No, Gally, you know I'll never let her go. She'll keep me company here," Mirrora smiled.

He felt robbed once again of justice, and as his anger flared up so did a feeling of compassion. He deserved to kill Diatara, and she deserved to die, and neither of them would get what they were due.

"Come now, back into the light we go. There are so many people waiting for us," Mirrora said.

"You're coming with?" he asked.

"I've been cooped up here for so long; I think it's time I stretch my legs. And I wouldn't want you to go get yourself killed all alone again. That would be an embarrassment."

"Why are you here? Why are you helping me? Am I dreaming this? Have I died? Is this just another memory?" The questions spilled from him in his bewilderment.

"Why am I here?" she laughed. "This is my home, Galadrath. I invite you all here to keep me company, and all of you—all my children—just pass through. Now they have the audacity to kill you here. I've taught you many lessons, Gally, but you all must learn the consequences of your actions."

She held out her hand to him with a bright smile, but he refused to take it. She dropped her chin in a single sad nod of understanding, lowering her hand back to her side.

"Suit yourself. See you on the other side," she said.

Then in the most beautiful and pure pronunciation of the Sylan language he had ever heard, she uttered words he did not understand.

"*Je fais de mon mieux au soleil.*"

In a cloud of black, she vanished.

"I'm sorry, Galadrath," Diatara spittled.

"I'll never forgive you, but I fear you'll suffer a fate worse than you deserve," he replied.

"I fear I may deserve it. You should've killed me when I told you to."

"And maybe one day I'll have another chance."

He Stepped away, returning to the chaos of the throne room. His mind resembled the manifest forces in the room—whipping back and forth, teeming with violence and anger, caught up in confusion of the many moving parts.

29

THE SONG OF THE LOST

MIRRORA STOOD IN THE middle of the room, where Galadrath had vanished in an instant before. He watched her from his position at the side, as the rain of attacks descended on her. As the first razor-sharp blast of wind neared her unconcerned face, all motion ceased.

Galadrath could hear his own heartbeat—it was the only evidence that time did not stop. The room was completely silent. Explosions and flames, projectiles and flying rubble—all rigid, unmoving. She had exerted her influence over the space, and it was like nothing he'd ever felt before.

Usually, he could hear the chanting in the air—the praise being sung by every mote of dust, every fleck of moisture, every flick of flame. The elements listened to their masters, celebrated them, captivated by the mind that took control of them. Mirrora's influence was different. The elements were silent. No longer happily obeying her will, but instead they had been possessed. They had become a part of her.

Galadrath could not test her influence—because it wasn't just influence. She had absolute control.

Mirrora spread her arms slowly, palms facing the ceiling, and her fingers danced in the sunlight. She smiled widely, openly enjoying the sensation.

"This room seems to draw death to it. It is appropriate that it is a

345

tomb. Do what you came here to do," Mirrora said.

Her voice was soft and dull, as if struggling to cross the frozen expanse. Then, softly, she began to sing.

Your words choke you,
Or you choke them,
Which of you will die?
No one wants to die.
Do you sing or do you drown?
Do you sing or do you drown?

The iron grip that trapped the very energy in the room flowed around him. As he moved through her influence, he felt the resistance—but it did not bind him as it did the others. He walked forward toward the throne, where the makeshift walls of stone melted away into the floor before him. Wherever he stepped, his path cleared, the world bending to Mirrora's will to accommodate him.

He ascended the short steps to the throne and came face to face with King Dartan, offering a slight nod. The old man did not respond, but in his eyes, there was both understanding and fear.

Galadrath moved to one side, stopping in front of the chair where Lord Sigrol Braf sat.

"Sigrol Braf, you have been accused of treason, for taking part in a coup against King Dartan Thestus, and betraying your station in the Court of Lords. The trial is to be carried out by the court of King Thestus, 48th of his name. The accused, if found guilty, is sentenced to death," he said.

He drew one of the swords at his waist, leveled it at the lord's face—and the blade began to glow.

"Rihhi took an eye from me doing your bidding. Now, I'll take one from you," Galadrath rumbled.

Where does your day end?
Never is a long time.
There so many, You do send.
Ripping souls like threshing wheat,
In rows standing, ready and neat.

Do you sing or do you drown?

He slowly pushed the blade into the socket of Sigrol, and only stopped when the sizzling of the blade bubbled out the back of his skull. He had expected the man to thrash, to scream, to jerk his head away in agony. He had not just expected it—he craved it. He longed to feel the muscles in his arm tense against the vain attempts to escape. But Sigrol was held in the absolute grip of Mirrora, and even as he died, the only response Galadrath received was the slackening of Sigrol's remaining eye, going limp and unfocused.

"An eye for an eye leaves the whole world blind, Galadrath," Mirrora chuckled slyly.

"You're quoting the Brightcaller?" he replied.

"Hah! Yes, the Brightcaller said it, but she quoted it from a little old man. He was the worst kind of man, a *pacifist*," she spit the last word.

Galadrath watched as the smoke from the wound rolled around in the eye socket, trapped by the cocoon of Mirrora's grip, unable to escape into the influence she held.

Do you listen when you wear the crown?
Sing for them, hear the sound,
Blood or water, do you find?
What troubles your mind?
When you seek to find your death,
What is it that drinks your breath?
Do you sing or do you drown?
Fill your lungs with blood,
Sing so you can drown.

"There is no honor in this. They should have a chance, trial by combat," Galadrath said half-heartedly. He watched as the eyes of the Administrant sitting behind Sigrol's corpse rolled back into his head.

"What's wrong with him?" Galadrath asked.

"They can't breathe. Looks like he breathed out before I took control. The air is all mine—everything is mine," Mirrora said.

Galadrath realized that the concessions she had made for him, allowing him to move through the space of her influence, was not extended to the other living beings in the room. They could not breathe the air or move in the slightest—they could not even sweat without her permission.

"What? They'll die! Let them go!" he yelled in alarm.

"I thought that's what you wanted," she frowned.

The sound and movement in the room returned all at once. The chaos dissolved into mist, replaced by a soft, warm breeze. Each act of violence was snuffed out like a candle, the wick leaving behind a lazy trail of smoke that marked the departed heat of the flame. The roar of fire and cracking stone, the shattering of ice and the clanging of metal, gave way to moans and gasps as the court personnel caught their breaths.

The Emissaries readied themselves, unaffected by the need for breath, as the air in their veins sustained them. They attempted to prepare defenses, but Galadrath watched as each effort was quickly and relentlessly snuffed out.

"There. All better. Now they have a chance—just like fish in a barrel have a chance," Mirrora said, her voice dripping with dark amusement.

"Galadrath, stop this! Who is this that you've brought here?" Dartan commanded.

"I've only just begun," Galadrath whispered, with fury in his eyes. These men must be made accountable for their crimes. This is Mirrora—she has refused to let me die."

"That's my boy," Mirrora chuckled.

Galadrath moved down the line, speaking as he walked.

"Gresser Freid, you have been accused..."

The blade of his sword swept cleanly through the lord's neck, the power in his veins carried by the strength of the steel.

"...and sentenced to death."

A blast of flame shot from a corner of the room where one of the Emissaries stood, but went out as quickly as it came.

Mirrora looked toward the offender and unscrewed his head and spine from his body. His face contorted as the skin tore and bled.

"What are you doing?! Don't kill them!" Galadrath yelled.

"Gally, I'm getting some mixed signals here. You're killing people, why can't I? Should I forgive them instead? What do you want?" she pouted.

"Leave them alone—they are innocent!" he shouted.

She cocked her head to the side and smiled. She closed her eyes slowly and nodded. Fear bubbled up in him. She was unknown to him. Every move she made felt like a contradiction, yet he felt like he was being led in a dance. She was both the music and his partner. Every action he took was greeted by her knowing smile, as if she was teaching him the rhythm she had written long ago.

The energy in his veins threatened to spill out, but he managed to calm it somewhat, regaining control and refilling the emblems with their power. As he did, he watched her reaction—his outburst had affected her—and the look she gave him reminded him who he was speaking to. It was as if the darkness in the room had become corporeal, sentient, growing, and choking out the light in the magnificently illuminated room. He had been talking to her like a friend. Like an older sister that he hadn't seen for a few years. He acted toward her with the same familiar contempt one has when arguing with their mother.

The circumstances that he found himself in—the swirl of emotion and justification of his actions—the single-minded drive to redeem his name and his honor—had clouded his judgment. His brush with death and the latent pain that ached in every fiber of his body, the sharp stabs that sat like stinging insects in his beaten limbs had let him forget who he was talking to. In that moment it came back to him, and as he looked into her eyes, the fear ran from them into his head, where the feeling cooled into a rippling chill that ran down his amended spine. He was staring at something supernatural—and he had her attention.

"None of them are innocent." Her voice was soft, drawing inward, her words flowing from his ears into an unknown void.

He heard his own words, the words he spoke to Farrah at the Hercolid. He was unsure if she was mocking him. Her tone was a stark contrast to the hate with which he had spoken those same words. He felt like she was testing him, teaching him.

"That one there abducts people and traps them underground," she said, pointing at one of the Emissaries.

The man's eyes flicked back and forth between Mirrora and Galadrath. He began to float, and his alarm grew into mumbles and sobs.

"Gods forgive me," he said.

"I will," Mirrora replied.

As he hung in midair, his ribs peeled backward out of his chest, his arms bending until his wrists touched behind him as his body broke backwards. He gurgled softly—the muscles that would allow him to scream were already useless.

"That one burns her elderly mother with a fire poker," Mirrors pointed, her voice becoming rough.

The woman caught fire from the inside. The intense white flames instantly turned her body into crumbling charcoal, splitting at flamewreathed seams.

"I cannot unsee the things I have seen. No one is innocent—no one deserves to live. They are all tormented; they'll all be freed by death. I'll give them peace, then I'll never have to let them go," Mirrora said, coughing up black ichor.

She closed her eyes. Galadrath thought he could see the almost impermissible movement of her eyes darting back and forth under the eyelids. Something bulged underneath them, and then pried them open from the inside. Slick black fingers pushed their way out of her eyes, hands trying to fit through the narrow openings of her eye sockets, clawing themselves free from her head.

The plain, clean form of Mirrora was shed, revealing the grotesque form of a patchwork that climbed out of the husk of her body, accompanied with a choking black fog. The mist seemed to flow purposely onto the dead and dismembered bodies scattered around the room, haphazardly knitting the shapes back together with the syrupy black goo. Misplaced muscles heaped onto the figure that had replaced Mirrora, quivering and flexing as they bonded—the black tar oozing through sinews, gluing the horrific masterpiece together.

Galadrath could feel a change in the air, her complete control vanishing, and he took his own hold of it. He pushed his influence out, and as he did, the other Emissaries followed suit. The hellish beast at the center of the room had been the beautiful woman he had known so long ago—or perhaps it was the other way around; he was not sure.

Razors of air blasted against the slippery black form, immediately slashing pieces of flesh from its bulk. One of the Emissaries had restarted the assault with fresh vigor, now aiming at the patchwork in the center of the room. The freshly born abomination appeared to scream as injuries ripped across its body. The noise was muted under the howling wind, yet Galadrath could hear the sound of bones scraping together to mimic a voice, repurposed organs squeezed, releasing air through wounds like bloody flatulence to imitate a voice twisted in pain.

The monster pivoted toward the source of discomfort and rushed the man with blinding speed. The Emissary defended himself deftly, encasing himself in a solid block of stone.

The tonnage of reanimated corpses crashed against the pillar, shattering the newly formed sandstone into several large pieces. The geode protecting the man gave way under the force, trapped between the wall and the splattering, makeshift monster as it barreled onward. The patchwork surged through the pillar, slamming heavily into the wall like a lump of clay flung from a reed.

Galadrath felt the small sphere of influence fade from where the Emissary had stood, and gouts of light and flame cut from inside the point of impact. The flash bled out from beneath the edges between the mass of flesh and the solid wall, and then the explosion rang out, blowing limbs and pieces from the hulking mass.

He was holding so much power, and she crushed him like a bug—and yet she saved us from his destruction.

He poured the power from his veins into the floor around the beast, and massive spikes of stone shot upward in a ring. The spikes clashed against each other as they grew upwards, thickening at their bases, their points colliding as they closed into a jagged cone around their prisoner. The monster hammered with heavy blows from inside the ring along with the cracking of stone, but only tiny slivers of movement could be seen between the dense spikes. Except for a single hole at the base of the pyramid, where the spikes seemed to avoid, growing in at steeper angles to keep a tiny window open against the floor. Galadrath added another layer as quickly as the first, and another. The prison grew like a small mountain around the beast, fortifying itself against the attempts to escape from inside.

He drew on the fire emblem, and it feverishly listened, dissolving completely into his blood. The clawing and beating against the inside of the makeshift stone prison stopped. Mirrora likely sensed what he was doing. He heard a whimper from inside, the hollow space adding an eerie reverberation to it. For a moment, Galadrath hesitated. The frail sound unlocked some paternal instinct that he had not felt since his own children were infants. But the sound of suffering was not human—it was a dark mockery, the slick black flesh emulating the sound of pain and sadness.

Snapping from his hesitation, Galadrath lit the furnace that he had trapped the beast inside. A torrent of flame burst forward from him, funneling the corkscrew of air and flame into the small opening at the base. The room roared as the air around them attempted to fill the vacuum, while Galadrath pushed the jet of flame to a white-hot torch coursing into the center of the spiky dome. The flames burst out in vibrant blue streams from the cracks between the tightly formed spikes. The edges of the stone blackened and pops and cracks could be heard as the intense temperature caused the stone to break. The brightness of the heat, lapping through the air, painted stark, rippling shadows across the walls of the great room. Those who still lived shielded their eyes and faces from the heat and light, retreating to the outside walls as fast as they could. Nothing could be heard over the singular roar of intense flame.

Galadrath looked into the searing brightness at the entrance to the furnace, watching the fire pour out from around him into the hole, and the moment seemed to stretch forever. He saw the jets blasting from the sides into the room, the heat dissipating into a mirage. The deafening sound seemed to fade into what felt like the hushing of the ocean. The glow radiating from the floor as the stone was heated to its melting point, comforted his mind like warm, soft sheets on a cold morning. The light burned so brightly that it seemed to painlessly melt the hate from his mind. The feeling was peaceful and euphoric. Catharsis swept over him and embraced him, and he let the power in his veins pour out of him.

The heat intensified, the jets of flame wicked molten stone outward like drops of water being shaken from a shaggy dog. It was the last thing he saw before he closed his eyes, the light coming from the deteriorating furnace blinded the whole scene, washing it out to white. Even from behind his eyelids, he could see the brilliance etching itself on every surface.

Silence followed.

The majority of the energy he had held was spent, and the stifling heat of the room was barely kept at bay by the remainder of his power. There was a light sizzling in the air and a faint, irregular popping as the rapid heating and cooling played out its effects on the contents of the room. He held his influence for a while longer, searching for any sign of Mirrora. The room answered him softly, the chorus of voices humming in reverence as he exerted his influence over every piece. The only ones that did not answer were the few huddled shapes behind the stone wall that had been formed to protect the throne. There were survivors, but none of them were her.

Whatever Mirrora had become is no more.

He opened his eyes and looked around. There were pulsing after-images lurking in his vision, where the light had imprinted the evaporating furnace on his eyes. As that last sight followed him around the room wherever he looked, he saw a more permanent imprint on the walls surrounding him. He saw the shadows of the last Emissaries burned onto the walls, only their trinkets were left to signify that they had ever existed. The room was surprisingly clean, each surface altered by the heat. The furnace was gone, its remains speckling the walls where the molten stone had embedded itself and cooled. The floor was uneven, a mesmerizing pattern of waves cut into its surface as the ebb and flow of the released energy harmonized inside the cavity of the room. He stood quietly for a few minutes, taking in the scene completely.

Through the heavy mirage of heat still coming off the cooling surfaces, he could make out the wall that the Emissaries had put up. The massive, improvised stone slab in front of the throne was worn away at the edges, like a giant stick of butter that had been blasted by a blowtorch.

He breathed in quickly through his nose, nostrils flaring, then breathed out slowly through his mouth. He let the last of his energy flow back into the emblems, and he felt the familiar encumbrance of his body again. He felt the aches swimming back into the calm pool of his mind, like hungry eels searching for a meal. A fog of lethargy hung like mist over the pool, obscuring the waters beneath. He was exhausted mentally and physically, but he felt a calm like never before, and it carried him forward.

He pulled lightly on his influence, absorbing the wall between him and the throne. As it melted and vanished silently into his veins, depositing into the emblem, what was left of the court came into view. A crowd of lords and their entourages were huddled together, looking up and out over the room, taking in the view that had been previously obscured by the wall. A few Emissaries looked gaunt; one cradled a deformed hand and winced in pain. They had all exerted themselves as hard as Galadrath had, pouring their own power into the air around them, trying with all their might to succeed at repelling the onslaught. Now they showed no sign of fight, the last of their will and energy tapped and spent. The wall had taken the brunt of the explosion of light and heat, but the entire throne room had been heated to several times the intensity of the hottest oven. Even the air would have killed them if it had been given the chance.

At the edges of the line of chairs, Galadrath saw the proof of that. Where the wall had ended, charred bones lay unrecognizable. Based on their position in the semicircle of lords, Galadrath assumed one of them was Lord Pillus Souten, who would still have been loyal to the king—an unintended casualty among many. Farther beyond that, the wall had given little protection, and the influence and the defenses of the Emissaries had failed. The spot where Lord Jemat Ancient had sat was bare slag.

He had been wise to beg for his leave—almost too wise to see this coming.

Next to where the remains of Souten and his followers, Lord Willen Tireod lay on his side, stunned as Galadrath loomed over him.

"Lords Ostiphan, Braf, Freid, and Tireod," Galadrath mumbled, reciting Maxima's list. "Too bad you weren't sitting just one seat to the left, Willen," he added.

He looked up and down the man's person. Willen's purple wool jacket was finely embroidered, and now showed the black of flame-touched pigment, and carried the stench of a burned comrade. His face had not handled the heat as well as his clothing had. Some of his hair had curled up on one side, and his face was a taught, blistered red.

"It would have saved me the trouble of killing you," Galadrath continued.

"A trial, Accuser. Of course, give me my due," Willen said through stiff lips.

Even in the aftermath of a mad goddess and a rogue assassin, the man had the gumption to steer himself back to the land of the living. Galadrath was surprised. If wheat had the tenacity and cunning of a politician to preserve itself, the world would be covered in swaying fields of grain, and the people would starve.

Yet, the farmer's reaper does not hear the voice of the grain, and gods do not bother with politics.

"I made a promise that I intend to keep, but I'm too tired for the formalities," Galadrath mumbled.

He drew a sword and punched the blade shallowly into the chest of Willen. The man winced in pain and his eyes went wide, but he did not die. Galadrath grumbled and withdrew the point of the blade, poking it again with more accuracy and vigor, and the lord slumped to the floor, signifying his end.

"Lords Braf, Freid, Drumm, Ostiphan," he slurred, remembering his promise to Taroosa. He squinted at the huddling group, then yelled, "Drumm!"

Galadrath could not tell if the crowd was whispering or whimpering over the ringing in his ears.

"Listen, I'm tired, I'm hurting, and my business is unfinished. Somebody point out Lord Drumm to me, dead or alive," he said hoarsely.

Galadrath heard a throat clear behind him, and he looked in its direction. He saw the gaunt, sweaty face of a woman, the one who was holding her curled hand in her lap. She wore white and silver of an Emissary, now smudged with blood, soot, and sweat. The only thing about her that was not dulled was the five shining emblems that adorned the chain around her neck, and the shimmer in her eyes. She raised her injured hand slowly from her lap, and he saw the pearlescent sheen of fractal patterns, where emblem energy that had met the limits of her body. She had fought so hard to save them from his flames, that the power in her veins had burned her instead. She raised the hand and gestured with a curled finger toward where he would find Drumm.

"Thank you, High honor," Galadrath said to the woman.

He began to shuffle toward where she pointed, speaking as loudly enough as his scratchy voice allowed, so that everyone could hear him clearly.

"Lord Drumm, the information I have at my disposal suggests you are loyal to the king, and so, first and foremost, I would like to put your surely fluttering heart at rest. There is, however, a small issue I must personally attend to. You see, I made a promise to a woman named Taroosa Pix, a woman whom you exiled some years ago—an exile that I myself carried out. Fortunately, she was rightfully condemned to her fate, but I made a deal with a devil, so to speak. I promised her I'd make you suffer, and you know I am a man who takes his promises very seriously."

Lord Drumm sat on his haunches, his head low, looking up as the Accuser approached him. Galadrath watched as a few of the more zealous court pages clung to the fine clothes of the lord, as if they were ready to usher him to safety, to throw themselves in between the blades of the Grim Wreath and their master. He studied Drumm as he approached, noting how the man tried to calm the frantic nerves of his subordinates.

"I learned something new today. I learned a few things today, actually. That woman—that thing that we all witnessed—said some things that carry value."

"An eye for an eye leaves the whole world blind?" Lord Drumm said, his voice high, as if he were squeezing the air out of his lungs in an attempt to keep the fear from also escaping his lips.

"No one is innocent," Galadrath growled back.

The Lord shuddered at the intensity of the statement. Galadrath bounced the flat of the blade against the man's back, each light impact causing Lord Drumm and his collection of pages to wince. He paused for a moment, examining the blood on the tip of the blade as it began to dry, and he absentmindedly tried to wipe it off on the back of the hunched man while he began to explain.

"There is merit in both statements. No one is innocent. That one is simple—even as an absolute statement, it holds true. The whole eye thing, though, seems foolish at first. What kind of a place did this wrinkly old man live where everyone is running around plucking each other's eyes out? Did he have no faith in his fellow man? Wouldn't an eye for an eye only leave the victims and the transgressors short one eye each? The only way the whole world would go blind is if everyone were evil, and stupid enough to make the same mistake twice," Galadrath said, trailing off.

"I'm not sure the meaning is to be found in the literal elements of the metaphor," Lord Drumm answered.

"I wasn't actually asking you. I apologize—I'm more proficient at making people dead than making an argument. The point I'm trying to make is that I came here today for forgiveness, and because I was falsely accused of my crimes, I wanted to find forgiveness by sowing vengeance. So now, in this state of cathartic enlightenment, I extend forgiveness to you, Lord Drumm. You must still suffer, as I will uphold my promise, but the type of suffering is up to you. I'm sure someone in your station has the uncanny ability to choose an appropriate punishment," he said, waxing illustratively and flourishing with one hand.

Galadrath coughed hoarsely. The mortal injuries he had sustained and the horrible remedy that had saved him were aggravated by his speech.

"I'm pleased to hear my... crime... is forgiven. But I'm not sure what kind of suffering you have in mind?" Lord Drumm said, his voice now closer to its normal pitch.

"Thainegom suffers. Her people are hungry and tired. They have been neglected long enough. I think you could spend a lifetime giving back to them—that would be suffering enough."

"You want me to spend a lifetime in charity for carrying out a sentence against someone that you yourself just agreed was correct?" Lord Drumm exclaimed.

"Don't forget Drumm, no one is innocent. Should I begin a search to upend your freshly granted forgiveness?" Galadrath stated.

"No," Drumm answered immediately. "Please, I'll take the forgiveness and be on my way. It just hardly seems fair."

"You speak to an Accuser about fairness? I do not care for justice or fairness. The two hardly have anything to do with each other. An eye for an eye is lady justice; she is the lady who takes from those who have taken. We have not personified fairness because it does not exist," Galadrath spat.

"This lady justice you speak of... is that who was here with us. That thing?" Lord Drumm asked carefully.

"No—I'm not sure what she is or what she wants. I don't know what she was doing here, and I don't know what she wants from me or you. She is something else entirely," Galadrath said with annoyance.

"She, *is?* Did you not kill her?"

"Her name is Mirrora. I'm sure you've heard it whispered in stories and rumors. Now you know they are not just campfire myths. Call her by her name, and see if she is dead," Galadrath replied.

There was a short silence between them.

"I mean it. Call her name. Maybe she is justice, after all," Galadrath said as he sat on his haunches, his eye piercing with seriousness.

The calmness that had washed over him was brief. His interactions with the lords quickly grew tedious, and the exhausting and lingering pains were tugging at his serenity. He had become annoyed, and now a flash of insanity flickered across his face.

"I best leave instead. Thanks for sparing me, Accuser," Drumm said humbly.

"No. Call her name. Or should I?" Galadrath stated.

"I can't," Drumm said, shaking, a renewed state of fear washing over him.

"She saved my life. Do you think she'll save yours? Say her name—or I will," Galadrath whispered.

"Mirrora," Drumm squeaked.

Galadrath looked around while Drumm only bowed his head with his eyes closed. They waited for a moment, then Galadrath stood again. There was no answer, and the glimpse of insanity faded from Galadrath's face. He half-expected her to appear—for the Patchwork Haunt to claw its way back into their reality. He did not understand why she wanted his attention, but was transformed into the beast—why she saved his life but attempted to kill him.

"Make sure your life serves as your punishment for the crimes you did not commit. Make a point to suffer everyday, or I'll be forced to find you and rectify your errors," Galadrath said flatly.

Lord Drumm took the statement gravely, even with the tired nonchalance that it was delivered with.

"I'll speak to him now," Dartan mumbled to a page.

Galadrath turned on his heels to face the direction of the king.

Even in submission, a king commands—a king does not ask.

"The king demands your attention, Galadrath Yaralok," the page said as sternly as possible, the fear of death hanging in between each word.

"At your service, my king," Galadrath said, bowing in front of Dartan.

He fell back into the role of a trustworthy servant. He showed his submission even when everyone knew that he could not be made to submit.

"What is it you came here to do today, Galadrath?" the king asked.

"I came to destroy those who oppose you and your right to rule. To restore the honor of the crown and accuse those who blemish it," Galadrath stated.

Eyes narrowing, Dartan pressed, "What is it you really came here to do?"

"I came to crush a coup—a coup that was meant to usurp you and the great country of Thainegom. I came to hold those betrayers accountable and protect the people from their sinister plots," he answered.

"Yet, your old friend Teratos did not make it to court this morning? The man who damned you to your fate wasn't here to get his due. Did you warn him, or did someone else?" the king asked.

Galadrath was silent.

"It would seem I've let my trust of others trump my own judgment," Dartan mused. "I have spent too long in the convenience of the court, allowing these lords to decide the fate of this great kingdom on my behalf. I did not choose to be king, but I was burdened with it, and on my honor, it is my burden to carry alone. As of this moment, the court of Thainegom has been dissolved. The lords are welcome to attend, but their seats will be moved to the gallery. I am the son of Durium Thestus, and I am the ruler of this kingdom."

"My king," Galadrath bowed slightly.

"You say you're here to defend the throne in my name, but I'm afraid that what you came here to do was revenge, and it was in your own name. I owe you a debt, Galadrath. I can see that, and I do not refuse it. You've burned out the very weed of corruption from inside the throne room—at its root. But there is a considerable amount of egregious acts that you've committed to get here. Can you swear to me your work here is done?" Dartan spoke softly, his tone that of a father, not a king.

Galadrath sighed.

"You asked me about Teratos," he said, "if I warned him not to come today. I did. Now, I must ask you the same question. Who warned you that I would come? How did you know to expect me?"

"Maxima Callidron," Lord Drumm piped in.

Dartan and Galadrath both gazed toward him, the unexpected remark fouling the air of honesty. As their combined looks took effect, Lord Drumm bowed lightly, and without waiting to be excused, he scurried across the field of debris toward the exit.

Galadrath shook his head slowly, as if to carefully dislodge a pain there without amplifying it.

"The ones who hurt us most are the ones we try the hardest to protect," Dartan said.

Galadrath drooped his head.

"Can you swear to me?" Dartan asked again.

"Put Teratos and Maxima on trial. Exile them to Sijis. Do that, and I swear my vengeance is complete," Galadrath said.

"Done," Dartan replied. "Sijis is a beautiful place to raise a child."

Galadrath turned to leave, absentmindedly kicking at a chunk of burned debris.

"You'll be put on trial as well, Galadrath..." Dartan said.

Galadrath snapped his head to one side as far as he could, spinning on his heels, his good eye glaring over his shoulder at the king. Like the remains of a fire all but dead, kicked open to reveal smoldering hot coals beneath, Galadrath's anger flared in that moment.

"...to be absolved of your crimes," Dartan added.

The coals cooled.

"Understood," Galadrath replied.

He walked listlessly down the stairs of the throne and through the hole he had dissolved in the rock wall. There was hardly any sound in the expanse of the large room as he spent minutes crossing it, weaving between patches of scorched floor and smears of black soot where bodies and armor had been blasted into nothingness.

His arms were heavy, his eyelids tugging his head toward the ground, and his legs no longer felt solid. However, he managed to stay on his own two feet. He did not dare Step to take himself home because he did not know who he would find in the mists of Tor Zuer. A part of him felt like he could see Mirrora's knowing smile through the thin veil of reality, watching him from the place she called her domain.

30

THE SURVIVOR

THE DAY WAS STILL bright and shining. Galadrath hobbled out into it, and the few faces that waited awkwardly in the hallways and the gardens of the palace found him. The small huddles of people each had a purpose, a group to which they would report their findings. News of his arrival that morning and the evacuation of the throne room had spread like wildfire. The fact that he was still roaming the world of the living meant that he had earned his freedom one way or another. No one knew what had happened yet, and he was not about to set any minds at ease. For all they knew, their entire government had been put to the sword. But one thing was certain to them: Galadrath lived.

His clothes were dirtier than before, now stained with a second coat of sweat, soot, and dried blood. He walked slowly and painfully with stiff joints. His arms hung frozen at his sides, elbows bent, as if held immobile either to avoid aggravating an injury or to help keep him upright. His face was pale and damp, strain and exhaustion clinging to every eyelash, coating every tiny point of his fresh stubble.

Guards stayed rooted to their positions, watching as he passed them and walked through the courtyards, through the main palace gate, and into the city. The warmth of the day was dampened slightly by a sea breeze, and the people of Thainegom were busy conducting their business in haste.

Galadrath had traveled the wide road to the palace many times, but this was the first time that he had noticed the buzz of tension among the merchants. In the markets, he would expect it. The daylight hours could not be wasted in idleness when work and business needed to be conducted. But here, the stalls and rugs of the salesmen were covered by trinkets and luxuries. Each meant to attract the eye of tourists, dignitaries, and nobility who roamed back and forth between the palace and their points of origin.

Now the street was mostly empty, and the source of the restlessness between the hawkers of loot passed silently by their stalls. They stared as he limped by, waiting with bated breath for something to happen, clearly more afraid of what his presence meant than what he was capable of doing.

His pace was slow, and although he had plenty of time to peruse the collections of goods, he chose to lock his gaze forward. He concentrated on the short road ahead of him, where the slight slope descended into the strangely angled, narrow streets that wove together in the maze-like City of Light.

Even as he focused on the buildings ahead of him, a gust of wind rose, carrying the soft clinking of metals and the fluttering of light fabrics to his ears. A sparkle of light drew his attention toward one of the stalls. His sluggish pace shifted, veering toward the edge of the road where the vendor stood.

The man standing behind the booth was short and extremely old. The color in his eyes was faded, and his beard was wild with gray curls. His hands were crossed loosely in front of him—one bearing the telltale wrinkled, tanned brown of a man who had worked a long, hard life; the other was a pale white with stiff skin, like it had been badly burned and healed long ago. The rest of him was covered in dyed and embroidered silks, pristine fashion, contrasting his disheveled and worn appearance.

At his side, a younger woman sat. She alerted the old man with a soft tug at his sleeve. He blinked a few times, then his eyes searched aimlessly in front of him, as if willing his eyelids to scrape away the cataracts and restore, even for a moment, the fragile edge of his vision.

Galadrath thought he heard her whisper his own name under her breath, but his ears were still ringing, and the sea breeze swallowed the words in brine before he could make sense of them.

He stood closer, inspecting the piece of jewelry that was still swaying in the wind. The silver and gold shapes were deftly hammered into the shape of the gods, hanging from hooks as earrings—just as they hung in the sky. The set he admired had a myriad of tiny colored gemstones arranged around the broken gold core that dangled from the hook. It was exquisitely crafted, vividly capturing the sunrise over the Shattered Children.

"It's beautiful," Galadrath said.

"Who sits the throne?" The gruff voice of the old man asked.

"King Dartan Thestus."

"Good. Genev, help the Accuser with his selection," the man pointed at nothing while he spoke.

"I survived two wars, two kings, and two gods. I'd be disappointed if I had to make the tally uneven," the old man continued.

"I may have killed a god to spare a king," Galadrath said gravely.

"Bah. Stow your hubris along with your melancholy," the old man scoffed. "Beneath a crown is just a man. And yes, the man can be killed, but the title of king can be given and taken only by the people."

"And gods?" Galadrath asked.

"Gods can not be made or unmade by something as simple as a man. Neither shaking one's fist at the sky nor refusing to look up stops them from existing or shining their light down on us."

"Your philosophies are about as believable as your age, old man. If you've survived two kings, then you were alive when King Dartan Thestus's grandfather sat the throne. Do your patrons pay for your stories or your sundries? Or do you wrap one falsehood in the other to conceal their lack of value?" Galrath grumbled, his tone matching the remark's intent to injure.

The old man cleared his throat and sighed in a descending musical tone. His eyes were no longer searching aimlessly, having given up their attempt to regain their faculties. His expressionless stare made Galadrath wonder if he had found something in the distance, but when the old man began to speak again, he realized he had been searching for something within.

"When I was younger, still older than you are now, I sat on this very spot. I was a broken beggar with no future. I had nothing to offer but stories of the past. My life had already been lived, and all I did was trade a hoarse word for a sip of beer or discards of stale bread. My stories nourished me, provided for me. One day, I traded a simple tale for a second chance. What did I do, you ask? The same thing I did the first time. I went to war, and I lived when so many died. I was given another chance, and I took that one, too. Now I stand here, in the same place I once sat, a rich man instead of a beggar, surrounded by family with a full belly, instead of hungry and alone. So, Accuser, go take your chance—it would seem you've earned it."

"I have to get home," Galadrath said.

The attention he had given to the strange man and his jewelry was waning, and his pain-mulled exhaustion was once again making demands.

He walked onward, paying little attention to those who stared as he passed. Drifting toward Teratos' home, he moved through the shipyard docks, the fish markets, and shipping warehouses. He pushed his way through the bustling crowds until someone took notice of him. Their calls drew recognition, and the bodies parted around him like scattering pests.

Voices came at intervals from the crowded streets. Most of them had the tone of disbelief and fear; some carried excitement and surprise. None of it mattered to Galadrath. He heard them as if his head were submerged in a pool of water, the muffled words bubbling ineffectually through his mind.

Gods living and dead, here walks the Accuser! The Grim Wreath returns. I never thought I'd see the day that a man would defy a king and live.

He absentmindedly found himself at an intersection he did not recognize. Looking around to catch his bearings, he was amused that, after countless travels of the city, there was still a place he had yet to visit. He retraced his steps in his mind, trying to recall where he had come from, but for a moment, he could not reconcile his memory with the surroundings.

Then, realization struck. This place was all too familiar.

He looked up the street as it curved and widened up the hill to his left.

Frowning, his feet instinctively followed his glance up the hill. The small, winding street opened up—an unusual sight in a city renowned for its random, narrow streets and nonsensical labyrinth of passageways. The area felt different—open and fresh. Sunlight streamed freely into the courtyard, unhindered by the usual looming buildings. Benches dotted the space, and a few clusters of people lazed about.

A set of gardeners sat on a patch of dirt, chatting as they planted bulbs of flowers. Nearby, a barker shouted, his voice wavering somewhere between a loud plea and a soft yelp, as though self-conscious about disturbing the tranquility.

Galadrath spun his head around, surveying for a landmark to identify the space. His eye traced the smooth perimeter wall of the courtyard, looking for an inscription or a sign, but he found nothing.

Then it clicked. He was not searching for something; he was looking for its absence.

He was standing roughly where his own home had been—at the epicenter of the destruction caused by the lance that took the life of Larl Rihhi and his neighbors. Where the blast had hollowed out the hillside, leaving a glowing inferno in the dark of night, there was now only a smoothed-over wall. The rubble and the bodies—everything he had left behind—had been scraped up and repaved into this flat, pristine expanse. No doubt the court had summoned their architects by the dozen before the blood had even dried. The City of Light had too much pride to allow such a flagrant act of defiance to linger in memory.

No inscriptions. No statues.

And by the time the gardens grew and the bulbs flowered, the events that had unfolded here would be no more than whispers—soon to be forgotten.

He saw the face of the young woman who had served Larl his last drink.

He had not searched for survivors.

He had told himself that there was no time, but the truth was, he had been afraid—afraid of whose bodies he would find among the rubble of his actions. Larl had made it clear he had tried to take everything from Galadrath, and in the back of his mind, a question lingered: would Larl have been foolish enough to employ Raatel?

His greatest regret was not knowing.

Had the old man been there when the house ceased to exist? Galadrath could imagine the careful, callused hands steeping a pot of tea as the beam of light consumed the buildings.

He cleared his throat, forcing the vivid speculation from his mind. With a shuddering exhale, he purged his body of the last remnants of energy he had been holding to prop himself up, tossing aside the crutch of raw power. His body sagged under its own weight, and he hobbled home.

The door swung open as he approached Teratos' house. Mitte stood in the doorway, bowing low enough to avoid making any eye contact with Galadrath.

He limped his way into the house, heading directly for the smoking area, sunken into the floor of the opposite room.

"Galadrath!" Heladra yelled.

"I'm fine. I'm just tired. It's done," he mumbled.

As he reached the edge of the seating, he bent over and crawled a few feet on all fours before collapsing into the closest pile of pillows. He clawed at the puffy velvet shapes, shifting listlessly, trying in vain to make himself more comfortable. He closed his eye and began to mumble instructions.

"Mitte, can you bring me a glass of water? Then a glass of wine, please. Maybe two glasses of each. Can you have Krosse make me some of those little honeyed sausages? Something smells delightful—I'd like some of that too. And could you light this for me?" He pointed at the large smoking pipe, his face half buried in a pillow.

"Galadrath."

Heladra's voice, usually so measured, trembled as it carried across the room.

He looked up briefly and noticed the dining room table where his family and everyone else was sitting. Their faces were all stunned. Expectant. Unbelieving. For a moment, Galadrath tried to recoup some form of decorum. He rocked back and forth on the pillows to right himself, but managed only a half-lounging posture before giving up.

"I thought you all would have been out taking the day by now," Galadrath said as normally as he could.

"They said there was an explosion at the palace, so we brought the children home and decided to have an early lunch," Heladra said without emotion.

Galadrath nodded at her, looking back toward the servant.

"Mitte, all those things I asked for—please."

Heladra stood from the table, quickly excusing herself. Teratos and Maxima nodded approval, each party clinging to the pageantry of formality, giving the situation a familiar structure to lean on.

"Children, you may be excused to go play," Heladra said pleasantly.

"My lovely lily, you don't have to send them away," he replied.

"Are you alright? You'll tell us what happened, then?" Heladra asked.

She shed what was left of her formal dignities and plopped down on the pillows next to him, hastily trying to make him more comfortable, placing his head in her lap.

"Is this your blood?" she asked softly.

She plucked at his shirt, dried blood coming off in flecks. The wounds in his chest had drained much of it from him before they were miraculously closed.

"Yes, it's all mine this time. I'm fine though. Just tired. I'll tell you everything," he replied quietly.

Mitte approached with a glass in each hand, and Heladra took the first, handing it to Galadrath. He breathed in silently and began drinking, one quiet gulp at a time until the glass was empty. Then, he exhaled harshly.

"I think I need a doctor or two as well. Can you send for them?" Galadrath asked.

"What hurts?" Heladra asked, his previous statement adding panic to her words.

"My dearest, at this point, I don't think there is a part of me that isn't hurt," he smiled up at her.

"What happened?" she whispered hoarsely.

Galadrath placed the empty glass on the raised edge of the seating pit and reached for the glass of wine. He noticed that Mitte had poured him the Drunkard's Pour—the glass was filled to the brim. He grumbled in hesitation, and Heladra bent over, touching her lips to the surface of the liquid, sucking up just enough so he could pick up the glass without spilling.

Grasping the wine precariously, he moved it carefully in his half-laying, half-propped-up position and took a quick sip, setting the cup down quickly to avoid showing the wobble in his hand.

"They knew I was coming. Maxima had told them," he began.

"I must have sent the message before we had our conversation," Maxima said dismissively.

The room was a cloud of daggers as everyone stared at the hostess. Teratos began to speak, his face turning a brilliant red, but he was too slow. Impulse overtook the Accuser, his mind and his actions a coalescing fog.

Galadrath Stepped across the short distance of the room, the fog rolling to the ground from where he had vanished from his seat and reappeared, gripping Maxima firmly by the chin with one hand, his eye inches from hers. He was hunched over her where she sat.

"Maybe I should let you live out your days where they would have left me for dead. She would let you live, in the dark and shadows of Tor Zuer."

He held her tightly in his grip, and with his free hand, poked a fork laying by her plate. The utensil disappeared, the telltale black mist leaving its last trace. Then a spoon, and a knife, as his own hand crept closer to hers.

"Then, you'll know pain. Then, you will understand fear," he said sickly.

Maxima was struck with terror.

"Galadrath!" Heladra called sharply.

He snapped from his trance of insanity, stumbling back to the seating area.

"Doesn't really matter anymore. I confronted the king and the crooked court. They tried to kill me, and I returned the favor," he added, stopping to take another sip. "Then, they ambushed me, and I almost died. Mirrora saved my life by what I can only describe as the burning of my insides."

Teratos uttered a sound somewhere between a choke and a laugh, trying to stifle both.

"Yes, it sounds completely absurd," Galadrath drawled.

The wine was quickly thinning the remaining blood in his veins.

"We talked for a long time, and then, somehow, I unleashed her on the material world. Together, we proceeded to systematically execute the members of the court's coup. Then she got irritated that I was doing all the killing and wanted to share. So then she was eaten from the inside out by a patchwork, which in turn wreaked wanton destruction on the throne room. Then I trapped that thing in a cage and burned it to ash. Some of the court was still alive—the king and a few more of the dishonorable lords. So I finished executing them—"

"Don't you mean you put them to trial, my love?" Heladra interrupted, looking toward the children.

"No, my sweet flower, I put them to death. There were no trials, no farce in the name of justice. There was only life and death, and the choices made that placed us between those two points. She showed me that—and then I left," he said and took another sip. Finishing the next glass, he set it down and began to fumble with his pockets. "Oh,

I bought you a gift. A token to say I'm sorry for all this."

He held out a small, wrapped package.

She took it from him and carefully unwrapped it while he watched. Teratos stood from his seat and stepped a few feet closer.

"Galadrath. I'm not sure what to say. There are still so many questions," Teratos began.

"None you need to worry about, old friend. You and your lovely wife will be exiled. Once the smoke clears, I'm sure the court will send you a messenger to inform you of your trial. There is no need for you to trouble yourself with the comings and goings of Thainegom anymore."

Teratos grumbled and wrung his hands together.

"Fair," he finally said.

"You act as though your tongue is attached to your title. Do you mourn them both? I've never heard you with so little to say. I've given you your life and your wife, your wealth and your health, all of which can travel with you. It's hardly a punishment and much more than you and that snake deserve," Galadrath said.

"You dare insult me in my own home," Maxima said through gritted teeth.

"My home. This is my home now. Pack your things, woman, before I change my mind and bury you in it," Galadrath replied. His sharp words carried spittle stained with wine and blood.

The room fell silent except for the scraping of utensils. Like children trapped in the argument of their parents, they all sat around the table. Having nowhere to run away to, those not being scolded tried to be invisible, to camouflage themselves in normal acts.

Heladra looked down at Galadrath, stroking his hair where his head lay nestled in her lap as he commanded Maxima to leave. His children ate—or pretended to—and Teratos followed their lead.

He could feel the tension build, Maxima hesitating, making her final decision. Soon came the shuffling of her sandals as she retreated to pack her things.

He had won his final battle. The only one that did not require

bloodshed.
And he was relieved for it.
The campaign was over.
At last, he could rest.

31

THE IMPOSTER

HE WOKE UP WHERE he had lain down. A few pillows had been added to the awkward nest he had haphazardly cultivated for himself. He had turned over, and his shirt had been changed. It was a clean white shirt, bulky and loose—borrowed from Teratos—and it pulled across his back as he moved. The metal spines hidden by the fabric made him look like a hunchback.

Heladra had moved to the opposite side of the sunken circle of pillows. Her heavy perfume lingered close to him, and the room was dark except for a single candle burning. The curtains were drawn shut against the cool night air.

"Heladra," his voice creaked like an ancient door opening for the first time in centuries.

She stood and smiled, fetching a glass of water for him.

"And something for the pain, my sweet?" he asked.

She nodded and stood at the table, picking the petals from the deep purple flowers in a vase.

Galdrath rolled on his side and watched her, the candlelight illuminating her face as she worked.

"Fresh Nightbloom?" he asked, puzzled.

"Teratos went to pick them himself just a few hours ago. He said you deserve the best. I think he was feeling guilty—and sentimental, even.

375

He said the fields were in full bloom, like he'd never seen before, under a black sky without a sliver of moon in sight."

He grunted in response, unwilling to acknowledge the kind act.

"How are your injuries feeling?" she asked.

He took a moment to sincerely audit his aches and pains. His head was still swimming in vague discomfort, and fatigue clung to him, ever present. But the pain in his arm, face, and back—the throbbing pain—were all gone.

"Much better," he said.

"We had a lot of visitors while you were sleeping—messengers, court pages, and doctors. The doctors, Galadrath... they can not explain what's happened to you. They pulled the stitches from your back and your arm, surprised to find that they had been left in so long. They said the cuts had healed weeks ago—cuts that I saw still bleeding yesterday. They went to clean and cure the burns on your face and found only scars. And the blood—you'd lost a lot of blood. Your shirt was soaked red. But they couldn't find a single wound."

She paused and turned toward him.

"What happened?" she asked.

He sensed the concern and fear in her voice.

"Remember Diatara? She was at court today, along with five other Accusers. They had betrayed their vows and were sent to assassinate me. There was a fight with the court's Emissaries, and I Stepped away. When I did, Diatara and the others followed me. I did not expect it, and she got the best of me. She ran me through with her swords. I was dying—I had failed before I had even started. She had attacked me in the one place I had thought I was safe."

Heledra walked quickly to him, cradling the petals in a bowl, and sat down next to him. Even in the dark, he could feel the silent tears collecting at the corners of her eyes.

"Remember the day we met? And the things I told you about my studies while I was training in the Lowest House? How I was Wandering around the Tor Zuer when I found you?" he asked.

"Yes," she sniffled.

"That was the first and last time I saw Mirrora—until today in the courtroom. I was lost in that place. I had been there for what felt like years. It's been known to happen—Pillars losing their minds, unable to find their way back to the real.

"I was lost, but I didn't want to find my way back. I was ready to die there. I *wanted* to die there. But she found me, Heladra. She brought me back. She brought me to you.

"I've never admitted it. It's a secret I've even kept from you. I'm still ashamed to say it. When I appeared in that field and I saw your face—filled with fear, ready to beat me to death with that shovel—it was the first time in a long time I wanted to live."

"Then I should thank her," Heladra laughed through her tears.

"I never did," he said coldly.

"Maybe you should," she murmured, frowning.

"I should," he said, his voice softening. "I was filled with pride and shame. I always wanted to forget her. And over the years, that memory faded, twisting into something I was willing to believe. I changed the story in my mind so that I wouldn't feel so weak—so that I could forget I had given up. Until she stood before me and gave me my life back again, I believed my own truth. But now I'll admit. She saved me from myself back then. She *forced* me to live."

He stared at his dirty fingernails, picking at the dirt and soot underneath them. He shared the truth with his words, but he averted his eyes from hers to avoid sharing his pain.

"When I sat there dying, blood running from my chest with Diatara standing over me, all I wanted was to see you again. Mirrora healed me, she gave me another chance."

"I'm glad she did, but *why*?" Heladra asked.

"I think she likes me," he shrugged.

"Mirrora—*she*—is a ghost story. No one has ever seen her. She's just a legend, concocted to scare people. Old women whisper about a woman snatching children from beds, lurking behind the shadows, waiting to eat the souls of those she finds alone—" Heladra challenged him.

"What if all those stories are true? I've seen her, Heladra, and I've held her hand," he said.

Heladra crossed her arms and frowned.

"Are you jealous?" he asked.

"She can't have you," she stated flatly.

"I'm not sure what she wants. She stood there in the throne room, ready to kill everyone—right after she had saved my life. She said, *'No one is innocent,'* and then she turned into a *monster*. She turned inside out, a massive Patch clawing its way out of her, and began to fight.

"I stopped her. I put the beast down. She *made* me fight her. She *made* me fight for them. She *made* me save them. Does that sound like a ghost who steals children? I destroyed her, and she let me do it. She let me kill the monster. She allowed me to be the hero," he said, staring off into the darkness.

"Maybe she's not as bad as the stories make her out to be," Heladra said.

"She tore a man's spine out of his body. Then she crushed an Emissary against a wall and held him there as he detonated. She held an explosion at bay that should have turned the whole palace into rubble. She was toying with them. She was toying with me. She's been puppeting me since the day I met you," he added.

"I've been puppeting you since the day I met you," Heladra chuckled.

Galadrath's face went wild, staring in disbelief at his wife.

"It's a joke, Gally. I'm only joking. I'm sorry, I just meant to lighten the mood. This is all a lot to take in. I'm just grateful to have you back. I'm grateful you're here. Whatever she did, whatever she is, I'm in her debt," she said lovingly.

He nodded and squeezed her hand.

"I just hope it isn't a debt that will need to be repaid. I'm ready for a simpler life. I think it's time I retire," he sighed.

"You think you still have a job?" she laughed.

"Do you think they can stop me from having one?" he said playfully.

He meant his words to be light, but he could see she took them differently. The barber's razor she had been preparing in her mind to shave him clean with now bore other intent.

She looked hurt and turned her face away from him, her gaze landing on the pile of jewelry resting on the small table at the center of the sunken seating area. The treasure was heaped so high that the large glass base of the smoking pipe was hidden behind it. In the dim candlelight, the metal still shone between the smudges of blood and soot. The tears that had dried had left trails where they had wandered down her cheeks, and now they were freshly wet. She began to cry quietly, and soon her sobs could be heard.

"I didn't mean it," Galadrath apologized for something he didn't understand.

"I've spent my life standing by your side. I left my family and my simple life to join you here in this city. I made a home and a family. I watered the flowers that you picked when you went to work," she spoke as she cried, her words turning bitter.

"I nursed the wounds when you returned. I answered the children's questions when they asked where you were, when they wanted to know what their father was doing. They look up to you—the Great Grim Wreath, the icon of the power of Thainegom—not because of what you do, but because of what I tell them. You leave bodies on the doorstep. You track blood into the dining room on your boots and pull up a chair for dinner," she wept in anger.

"I'm sor—" he tried.

"They adore you! You are their father, and they look up to you! And you wander in here, on the brink of death, and you tell them plain as day that you are a murderer. You told them what you did. You sat there, covered in blood, and explained how you don't believe in justice—that you only believe in death. You told your own children you are a killer, and you did it without a single shred of remorse. Then you pass out and leave me to pick up the pieces."

"I am tired of washing the blood from your hands, Galadrath. I am tired of cleaning the death from your clothes. I am tired of asking you to be careful, tired of worrying whether you are still alive. When I look at you, I am tired of wondering if you are still alive. I'm afraid that the man I love no longer sits behind those eyes. I will never leave *his* side, but I am afraid he has died—piece by piece—and that some heartless horror has taken his place. I will not be married to a monster. I will not let my children grow up in reverence of an imposter charading as their father."

"I didn't—" he tried again.

"Yes, Galadrath! You're sorry, and you didn't—but what you did do is done. I sit here listening to you talk about having a simple life, and I see a glimpse of hope. I see the young man I fell in love with, full of life. And then you ask who can stop you. *No one can stop you*—you've made that apparent. You've stood before kings, gods dead and alive, and you ask who can stop you? It seems you can't even stop yourself!" she screamed.

She looked over toward the hallway, and he could see her come back to her senses for just a moment. She laughed softly between sobs.

"Even now I protect them from you. I'm their mother, and I will protect them until my heart stops. Not my love for you, not gods, not your mistress Mirrora—not even you—will stop me from trying to save them from what you've become," she spat, her face flushed with anger.

He sat in silence as she glared at him, shaking with a torrent of emotion as she waited for a response.

He glanced quickly at the pile of trinkets, and back at her. He recalled the names and faces of those he could remember, tallied the accused, and tried to picture those who had died at his hand. He tugged at the emblems laying among the trinkets, recalling the emotions locked in them—the memories that had been trapped in each one when they had been formed. The feeling of duty and honor, the grave seriousness of accusations and trials, and even the inkling of remorse that came with each death returned to him as the energy flowed into him. Feelings of calm and control, action and instinct, defense and offense, the throws of battle, the clang of victory, the power of destruction—all flooded into his mind. The wrath he had felt at the assault on the Hercolid, the unstoppable power that now surged through him again, and then the hopeless yearning for his family as he sat dying.

He let the feelings and the energy flow out of him, returning it to the emblems. Of all those memories and emotions he had felt, only at his death did he feel the shame of leaving his family behind. Buried in the memories was something else—something he understood for the first time.

"I'll never let you go," he said.

She closed her eyes and squeezed the last few tears onto her cheeks. Leaning forward, she grabbed his hands in hers and pressed her forehead into his chest. He could smell the sweet oils rubbed into her scalp as she answered him.

"I hope so, Galadrath. And will you let them go? Your spoils of war? The power you've amassed," she mumbled.

"No. But I will swear an oath. I swear I will use them to build what I have destroyed. I'll give back what I can to those who suffered their power. I will redeem myself in your eyes and the eyes of our children," he said.

Then he added, speaking for himself, "And we'll make memories together."

"We can plant flowers that don't get plucked," she offered softly.

"Whatever your heart desires, my rose. You will be my compass—point me where you will."

She picked up her head and met his gaze.

"I've heard your oath Galadrath Yaralok. With all my love, I swear to you: if you break this oath— if you stray from my side—I will find that shovel I held in my hands the day we met, and I will bury you with it," she said, with no hesitation in her voice.

He nodded gravely in understanding.

"And I won't stop you," he said.

She stood slowly, using him for balance, still holding his hands in hers, and pulled him to his feet, leading him down the hall.

32

THE SHADOWS OF THE LOWEST HOUSE

GALADRATH KNOCKED LIGHTLY ON the rickety wooden door. He stood wearing the loose loungewear left behind by Teratos. He had tied a belt in a knot at his waist, the leather lacking notches for his leaner figure. The baggy shirt proved useful to hide his metal spine.

He had nothing left for himself. The few things Heladra had rescued from their home—before Larl had moved in and before it had been leveled—were more sentimental than functional. Teratos and Maxima had been ousted from their home before he had woken, and the servants had been abuzz with the household's transition. Galadrath had not been ready to face the onslaught of couriers and messengers that the court had sent to his new residence. He was impressed at their ability to act so expeditiously.

He had grown used to seeing the grinding bureaucracy of politics interfere with progress. But his violent reordering of the court had been smoothed over and polished back into a functional unit—much like the hillside that had been reduced to slag by the Hercolid's cannon and then repaved into a park less than a day later. The court's workers had been busy creating order from the chaos.

He did not doubt that they would tell a story far removed from the truth, and he welcomed it. His actions—and the encounter with Mirrora—had been witnessed by so many and would surely be covered up. The court could not let such insanity and unspeakable acts harden into rumor—or worse, for the truth to surface. While they spun a more palatable narrative, he would do the same to reinvent himself.

Now he stood in front of a decrepit building in Threshook. The door opened, and the frail figure of the tailor, Randolph Kent, greeted him. Bright eyes peered up at Galadrath from behind the small spectacles.

"Vyhn, a pleasure to see you," Randolph said.

"I don't think we need to entertain that lie any longer," Galadrath said.

"Suit yourself, Accuser Yaralok," Randolph replied.

Galadrath laughed. "You've known me all along," he said.

"I've tailored for many a noble and their mistresses. It's likely I find myself in this wretched hole of a town because they also doubted my discretion," Randolph stated.

"I never doubted you. I could tell by your work—you take yourself very seriously," Galadrath replied, brushing off the admonishment.

Randolph smiled. "I was hoping you'd return—counting on it, even. I've taken a few liberties with your older styles, updated them to suit a more modern gentleman. Please step inside, and we'll get you dressed."

Galadrath was pleasantly surprised, but his excitement was quickly dimmed as he caught the tailor's gaze lingering on his eyepatch.

"I'm afraid my measurements have changed as well," Galadrath said.

He turned sideways to show the tailor his new profile.

"I see. We'll have to make some adjustments," Randolph sighed, before he turned in the doorway and hobbled inside.

Galadrath followed close behind, and Randolph pointed to a small stool in the corner of the room, urging him to sit.

"You'll have to take off your shirt. I'm not sure how to go about this," the tailor added.

It took some time for the alterations to be made, and Randolph worked quickly on the improvised changes. Galadrath sat still, his stiff back giving him no other comfortable option but to stare forward. He was shuffled into a shirt halfway and then back out, then a jacket, then the cloak. As each item was measured in turn, he could feel the tailor's pace begin to slow.

"Who did this to you?" Randolph asked.

"The injury or the remedy?" Galadrath responded.

"The... remedy."

"A mad woman Jeweler by the name of Taroosa Pix. Although, it didn't look this clean until I was subjected to a whole other set of horrors. I likely would have died from infection."

"How unfortunate. I don't mean to pry into personal matters—it's just that I haven't stood up straight since I was a very young boy."

Galadrath waited in silence for the rest of the story, but as the time passed, he realized the tailor's comment was the abrupt end to a fleeting hope. The cage that held his spine together could have opened to freedom for the tailor—freedom that he himself had taken for granted.

He ruminated on the idea as the man worked around him, and eventually his mind wandered onto other reflections as the hours passed.

"I'll wear this to my trial," Galadrath stated.

He stood and inspected himself in the tall, faded mirror on the wall once Randolph had finished and he was fully dressed. The fabric was light and pure, the floral designs bright and dense. Even the fins on his back shone more brightly where they extended through the fabric. They were no longer covered, but instead incorporated into the fit of the clothing—a large slit had been neatly formed around them. The cloak had been split at the top, the two halves hanging loosely and rejoining at the middle just below his waist, flowing into a lavish field of flowers that reached all the way to the floor.

"Just don't bring it back to me in tatters," Randolph said.

"Why don't you come along? I'll get you a seat."

Randolph's eyes shimmered with delight.

"To see my work stand before the king? I wouldn't miss it!" he said excitedly.

"I'll have an invitation delivered," Galadrath replied.

"Along with your payment." The tailor smiled up at him.

"Of course. I must go."

Without waiting for a reply, the pearlescent white silk—embroidered with a host of vibrant flowers—vanished in the contrast of black smoke.

He barely appeared for a second at his destination when he heard the voice of his mother.

"Galadrath! Come here!" Julera Yaralok screeched.

He had not appeared under the bed this time, but he still reflexively dusted himself off, as if the voice of his mother had unlocked some unconscious signal to his brain. A lifetime of being chastised for broken fingernails and dirty clothes had instilled some pathological sense of vanity.

"I was just coming in..." he said.

He pushed open the slightly ajar bedroom door and saw Brixby cock his head at him from where he was perched on a tall dining room chair. Galadrath turned to his mother—just in time to see her drop the plate she was holding. Her shudder was more jarring than the shattering plate. She did not deserve to see him like this. Even with new clothes and his name restored, he bore the scars of defeat. He had lived through his trials, but she could tell his injuries were not those of a man who had won every battle.

She held her hands to her mouth, her eyes locking on his face.

"Scar's depths. Sit so I can look at you," she whispered.

"I return victorious," he said with hollow words.

They were true, but he knew that his own opinion had never counted for anything. She still looked at him like he was a twelve-year-old boy in school—a mere initiate of the Lowest House. She still called him by his childhood nickname, and though she looked up at him as he walked toward the chair to sit, she made him feel small.

As he sat, she grabbed his face in her hands, inspecting him through squinted eyes.

"What's all the racket?" Vostranis said, entering the room.

Galadrath watched his old man slowly make his way into the room, his gaze fixed on the floor. Vostranis paused for a moment, and without a movement, the shards of the plate vanished along with the food scraps that had landed on the floor. He looked up, content with the restored order, and took in the sight of Galadrath and Julera.

"Galadrath, my son," Vostranis began.

He shuffled over and sat down next to the other two, carefully placing his hands in his lap and wearing a broad smile.

Galadrath braced himself for his father's disappointment.

"I heard you gave them quite a licking. Reminds me of the good old days. That's my boy," Vostranis chuckled.

Galadrath relaxed; he had expected to be chastised by them both.

"Yes, father, I gave better than I got."

"In my day, we didn't take as much as a scratch, but no matter."

Galadrath dropped his head. The blow he had expected had not been avoided, only delayed.

"No matter!? He's missing an eye, Vos! Look at this thing! He looks like some spined beast! Whoever did this to you will pay. You just give me a name and I'll have them buried—turning my beautiful boy into something grotesque," Julera screeched.

"She saved my life, Mother."

"Bah. Some woman? Give me a name! Vos! Get a paper and write down these names! Make the boy talk! Don't just sit there!"

"The important parts of him are still attached, my sweet carnation," Vostranis said.

"If your dear departed father were here, he'd already have heads rolling," Julera continued.

"I'm not dead yet—as much as you'd like me to be," the old man grumbled.

"I'm sure I'll have to do it myself! Vos! Get the plates out. Let me feed you two before I leave for the seat of the Archons! They'll hear about this!" Julera said, already shuffling aimlessly around the room.

Galadrath looked at her and back to his father, knowing she was beyond listening. He had learned early in his life that there was no sense arguing with her. He could only comply with her requests, and if they were too outlandish, she would have to be ignored. The fire of her anger could only be starved; anything thrown on it in an attempt to snuff it would be taken as fuel.

"Speaking of the Archons, they already know. One of the ambassadors of Thainegom sent a message in the night. It would seem there are traitors among us," Vostranis spoke softly.

"Four of them. Turncoats, or maybe just rogues now. I can't imagine the king would shelter them after what has happened, but I don't seem to have a knack for the infinite labyrinth of political skullduggery."

"Not five? Our reports give five names. Archon Kammul himself is currently roaming the streets of Thainegom, along with a horde of initiates."

"Diatara Slaaterson did not survive. Only four escaped. Archon Kammul? He's mobilized the initiates? Won't that create even more unrest?"

"He's not wearing a mask, my son. No one will recognize him. Today the streets of the City of Light will be slightly more crowded with the pattering feet of street children and urchins, as we search for those who have abandoned their positions as Pillars of the Lowest House."

Galadrath guffawed. He had been initiated into the Lowest House at the age of eight and could Step before he was nine. He could imagine the children running through the bright, bustling city, dodging into alleys only to disappear into thin air, then returning to the dark tunnels of their home with whatever scraps of information they could gather.

"Incredible. I should have expected nothing less. It's a great dishonor, and it will shake the foundation of our whole society," he added gravely.

"It is not the first time, nor will it be the last. Do you think the art of Stepping has been kept a secret for so long because we are bound by our unbreakable honor?" Vostranis asked.

"I've never heard of such a heinous act being committed by a Pillar. Running away is one thing, but defecting and swearing allegiance to another is unforgivable."

"You've been in the world too long, Gally. You've forgotten that we are its shadows—the keepers of its secrets. We'll root them out wherever they are hiding, and they'll be forgotten soon enough. "

Galadrath sat for a moment, taking in the words.

"Did Archon Kammul really send the message, 'Yield to none'?" he finally asked.

"Unofficially. We all know that Thainegom has been in tatters since the war. If they have some misplaced hubris that has hoodwinked them into believing they can subvert our own Pillars, they need to be shown their place. You put a lot of stress on the alliance between our nations, but I believe Archon Kammul secretly takes great pride in you. You've shown them that one Barkrillen can still break them, even if we have to remind them of that every seventy years or so."

Vostranis smiled and placed a hand on Galadrath's shoulder, patting it softly.

"Enough about the past. What does your future hold?" Vostranis asked.

Julera's misguided anguish had petered out for lack of attention, and she gracefully inserted herself back into the conversation.

"He's going to go back to work. They'd be fools to allow anything else. He's the court's Accuser, you know," she said.

"I've some small administrative things to take care of and some wrongs that need attention. I'll stand trial and be officially absolved of my transgressions. Then I'll retire. Heladra has made it clear I'm not going to return to my previous post," Galadrath said.

"That little farm girl has you by the short hairs. Talents wasted!" Julera added.

"That little farm girl is my wife."

"My son, the court's Accuser, tilling the earth like some scruffy laborer," Julera antagonised him.

Galadrath ignored her.

"Like you said, Thainegom is still in tatters. There are good people there who wish to carve out a simple life. Even the scruffy laborers deserve to eat in the safety of their own homes. I served them as an

Accuser, condemning their transgressors to death. Now, I'll serve them in a more constructive manner," he said, directly to Vostranis.

He saw the love return to his mother's eyes. Even her worst words were spawned from the best of intentions.

"Whatever you set your mind to, Galadrath. You'll succeed as a farmer, I'm sure. With less chance of losing another eye, I'm more than sure," Julera said.

He knew she was trying her best, even if it was only partially because she did not want to be ejected from the conversation a third time.

"Thanks, mother. I don't know if I actually said I was going to be a farmer, but I appreciate the kind words."

She smiled.

"I'll make something for us to eat. I'd like to hear all your stories, my dearest," she said.

Galadrath began slowly, tailoring the narrative of his adventures to best suit his mother. He deftly omitted names and brushed off her attempts to extract information he was unwilling to give. It pained him to lie outright—or to leave out details—but his father's words rang softly in his mind as he regaled them with his tales.

We are the shadows of this world, the keepers of its secrets... one Barkrillen can still break them...

After all, she was also a Pillar of the Lowest House and had served abroad. He could only imagine how many names and faces she had made vanish, how many of her own secrets she kept. In her misguided love, the old woman could bury his transgressors if she thought she was protecting her only son.

After hours of laughter and food, wine and worries, Galadrath was exhausted. It had been too long since he had spent an afternoon alone with his parents.

"I must go soon, but I have something you may want to pursue. I believe I may know who is currently in possession of the World's Edge," Galadrath said, leaning in with a smile.

His father raised his bushy eyebrows in a manner that would only mean one thing: Galadrath would not return home until the early hours of the morning.

33

THE DEBTOR

Days passed with the ease and nonchalance of trees changing their leaves. Weeks blew by on a careless wind, and before Galadrath knew it, the day of his trial had come. He had been in contact with the myriad of acquaintances he had made during his travels. The court had discreetly summoned him on several occasions to discuss anything from improvements that could be made to the Hercolid, down to the details of who could still be fomenting unrest in the court and in the countryside.

He hand delivered invitations to those he wished to see at the trial, and when he had nothing pressing to do, he made his presence known to the public of the city, wandering every narrow, curving street. Most people avoided him with a curt politeness. The merchants, however, could not pretend he did not exist while attending their stalls, so he visited each one of them until he knew them by name. He marked their absences when they were indisposed and informed them of places where their stalls might be better suited.

He had become oddly enthralled with the old man who peddled fine-crafted jewelry and spent many afternoons listening to stories of the past. He could never hear the man's voice waiver from truth, but the tales he told were of gods, men, valor, and destruction. They sounded like far-fetched legends, and had Galadrath not seen the absurdity of the truth for himself, he would have never believed them. Heladra had expressed her own concern at the amount of jewelry she had been gifted and had urged Galadrath to invite the old man and his family to join them for dinner. The old man had refused politely. As if rooted to the spot, he was never missing from behind his stall. Through rain and fog, scorching days and chilly nights, the man was a fixture on the road leading to the palace.

King Dartan had adopted unprecedented vigor and gave tireless attention to the state of affairs. He issued decrees almost daily—new laws, new positions, and new faces filling new seats of power. He appointed governors and allocated money and resources to neglected issues. Architects and Emissaries of the court were dispatched to corners of the kingdom, and in the tumult, Galadrath found peace in the unwavering old merchant and the stories he told.

Now, Galadrath trekked that same path leading up to the bluff on which the palace was poised. The route was crowded with people, the foot traffic barely shuffling forward. He carried his daughter on his shoulders, and her fingers fidgeted in excitement with the embroidery of his cloak's hood. She leaned back at intervals against the pillow he had wedged in between the top of his finned spine and her back. Looking up, he caught her staring off into the distance over the ocean, pointing and calling out the names of ships she recognized. He held tightly to Heladra's hand, who in turn had their son in tow.

He pushed through the crowd with as much civility as possible, and once people turned and recognized him, they quickly parted. He and his family made good progress, but the closer they got to the palace, the more the mass congregated. Even those who wished to yield space to allow them to pass, were already pressed against the bodies of other onlookers. Galadrath stretched out his arm in front of him and used his flattened hand as a wedge to manually move the crowd. The chains around his forearm glimmered in the bright light of the suns.

A woman took notice of his chains on the extended arm as he passed closely by. To his surprise, she raised her hand and stroked their surface. She whispered something between a curse and a prayer as he slipped beyond her grasp. Others took notice as they turned to identify who was parting the crowd, and as if she had revealed something previously unseen, outstretched hands emerged while a collective murmur built around them—each person adding their own quiet comment under their breath. They grazed the chains on his arms and the layers of trinkets that hung from his neck.

The Grim Wreath... gods living and dead... mercy... pass on by... Scar have you...

He made out single words and phrases as they floated through the air, the wave of hands like dense jungle foliage brushing against him but offering no resistance.

You killed my son...

Galadrath stopped where he stood and turned toward the crowd. The hands retracted reflexively as the crowd turned to see what had halted the slow march of the Court's Accuser.

He met the glistening eyes of a scruffy-faced man with heavily tanned skin. The man spoke again, his voice cracking—no longer a whisper.

"You killed my son," he managed to say.

Galadrath stared blankly at the bearded face as his mind traced the images of the countless men he had slain.

"I accuse you of killing my son," the man said, his voice wavering.

The words struck Galadrath like a hammer. It was a formal challenge that could be enforced under the old laws.

"How do you plead?" the man pressed.

Galadrath looked up the hill along the packed path. He could see the outer gates looming above the crowd. He was within a stone's throw of his own trial, and more importantly, his pardon.

"I'm on my way to my trial before the king," Galadrath tried to explain.

"State your plea," the man said on the verge of tears.

"I have my family with me—" Galadrath began.

"And mine is dead. How do you plead?" the man's anguish coated every word.

So this is how it feels.

He lowered his arm and rested his palm on the pommel of one of his swords.

"Not guilty," the Grim Wreath said.

He felt a blow on his shoulder blade from behind, not hard enough to injure him, but still unexpected.

"Galadrath, I swear—by the gods living and dead—we are not doing this right now," Heladra hissed at him with a balled fist.

Galadrath let his hand slip listlessly from the pommel it was resting on, then gathered his hands in front of him, flailing in small circles.

"I can't do this right now," he replied to the man. "I'm... I'm sorry."

He felt a churn inside of him that he could not explain. It was an emotional pain that shook his core. He had run, fled, strategically retreated from conflict, and regrouped for rebuttal; but he had never truly yielded. The Barkrillen slogan of arms had been a fiber of his being for so long: *Yield to none.* As he said the words, it was as if a tumor was painfully removed. He had seen many fall because of their pride—he himself had killed many men whose pride stood in their own way.

"I am sorry," he said, emphasizing each word.

He took a knee slowly, balancing his daughter on his rigid spine so her head was now at crowd level.

"Guilty," Galadrath muttered.

The crowd had parted slightly, leaving a small open space where Galadrath kneeled. The man made his way to the edge.

"Daddy, does this mean he has to kill you?" Radralia asked innocently from atop his shoulders.

"I guess so, my sweet bloom," Galadrath answered, struggling with his own emotions.

"Please don't, mister," she asked politely.

Galadrath bowed his head as far as he could and felt the trickle of energy filling his veins as he instinctively pulled on the emblems.

"Get up, Galadrath," Heladra hissed again.

He lifted his head just in time to see the crowd close behind the man as he simply walked away.

"Can we get out of here now?" his wife whispered to him, the angst in her tone replaced with concern.

"Yes, but I'm not walking another step. Hold on tight everyone," Galadrath grumbled.

Radralia instinctively wrapped her hands over his face, covering his good eye. He grabbed Heladra tightly by the waist, and she ushered Marcanus to hold onto both of them. They clung to each other as the wind whipped around them, and with a lurch, they floated above the crowd, through the air, and over the castle gate.

As they landed, Radralia was in a fit of giggles. Marcanus tried his best to maintain a brave face, and Heladra frowned playfully at Galadrath and reached up to adjust her windblown hair.

"I see your humility is fleeting, but it's a start," Heladra said. She paused, before adding more coarsely, "And don't ever do that again!"

"Which part? Flying or getting accused?" he asked genuinely.

"Throwing yourself at the mercy of a grieving man! In front of the children! Do you even have a brain in that hollow head of yours? Did Larl poke that out too?" she scolded.

"That's cruel," he replied.

She straightened her dress, wiggling her hips side to side, regaining her poise as she made the physical and mental adjustments.

"I'm sorry. The flying, and people talking about dying—it was just a bit of a moment. I really am surprised you have lived as long as you have without my constant supervision," she said, shaking her head at him.

He crafted a witty response in his mind, but it was drowned out by memories of his brushes with death.

"I'm sorry, Heladra," he managed.

He looked around to see if anyone was eavesdropping. The court-yard inside the walls was busy, but most of the city's denizens were held at bay by the gate guards. The huddles of people congregating there had given them ample space when he landed. Some hurried away to avoid the dust kicked up by the wind; others wandered off, wary of being associated with the most infamous figure in the kingdom.

"Galadrath! Galadrath! I know the Accuser! Let me in! Galadrath!" a familiar voice called from behind him.

His heart leapt. He turned toward the gate, straining to see if his ears had deceived him. The platoon of guards managing the crowd obscured his view, but above their ranks, he could make out the wild-eyed face of an old friend.

"He's right there! Ask him! Let me in! Galadrath! Galadrath, over here!" Raatel yelled.

He was waving his hands wildly, pushing against the shields and armor of the guards.

"Gods living..." Galadrath whispered in disbelief.

Then his voice boomed, strengthened by the power he still held.

"Let him in!"

The words rang from the hard walls of the courtyard, and before the last echo had died, the guards had received the message and complied with haste. Raatel scrambled through them as quickly as they parted and came to a standstill out in the open. His long, curly hair was no longer pulled into a tight, clean bun; it hung unkempt around his grimy face. His clothes were tattered and dirty—the same uniform he had worn every day in service to his employer.

"Galadrath! Mothers wept, Galadrath, this is the worst I've seen you yet! What's that on your back?" he exclaimed, crossing the distance between them.

Galadrath burst into tears. The edge he had held—the poise and control he had clung to—finally broke. The gravity of recent hours, days, and weeks came crashing down to a focal point. The lives lost and taken, the battles fought, and the spoils gained at such expense—all seemed to rest in the shallow wrinkles of the old man's face.

"I didn't mean to offend you, Galadrath..." Raatel ran forward, catching his employer.

"I thought I killed you. When Larl told me he had taken all of my things, I didn't see you there, but I thought you were in the house. I thought that when I sent the signal... I thought you were there. I saw the woman in the rubble—the other servant—but I couldn't bear looking for you. The house is gone. I thought I brought it down on your head. I couldn't bear to count you among the dead," Galadrath babbled through thick tears.

"Let's give these two a moment," Heladra said, pushing the children toward a fountain.

Raatel frowned deeply, not understanding.

"I killed Larl Rihhi. I demolished our home," Galadrath mumbled.

"Good riddance. I mean, it was a lovely home, Galadrath, but that man was a stain on it. I worked for him for no more than a few hours before I slipped away. I went north—my old ways. I figured he'd hunt me down, so I made myself scarce. When I heard you were back, when I heard the trial was on... Titans wept, Galadrath! These old bones jumped for joy! I couldn't miss it. I was just about ready to climb the walls if they wouldn't let me in," the old man said, waving wildly in excitement.

"I thought I killed you..." Galadrath sniffled.

Raatel shrugged and shook his head wildly, his curls flailing around in every direction.

"Dry your tears, you silly man. You cry for nothing. Don't you know me by now? I'm your shadow. You can try and stamp me out, but where you go, I follow," Raatel smiled.

He dragged Galadrath upright and wrapped his sinewy arms around him, pulling him into his chest.

"It's a happy day, Galadrath. It's so good to see you again. It seems you've made some... changes," Raatel laughed.

He pushed Galadrath out to arms length, let him go, and leaned in to flick the edge of one of the metal fins with a broken fingernail. The metal rang a faint tone.

Galadrath tried to mop his eyes with his forearms, but only managed to smear his tears onto the surface of the chains. He tried again with the edge of his cloak, with limited success.

"A lot has changed, old friend. We've got some catching up to do—over a nice pot of tea," Galadrath said.

"First, can you tell me how you dispatched that mongrel, Larl?" Raatel said, eyes bright.

"I shot him with a lance," Galadrath stated.

"Ohhh..." Raatel said, not quite understanding.

"I shot him with a cannon. A big lightning cannon, called a lance. I'm not actually sure what it shoots," Galadrath added.

"Very interesting," Raatel replied, still clearly confused.

"I'll tell you all about it later."

"Are you done crying, Accuser?" Farrah's voice interjected.

"Farrah! Did the whole courtyard just watch that spectacle?" Galadrath asked.

Farrah sauntered up to him with Tagger not far behind. Galadrath regained his formal demeanor and looked around properly for the first time. He made out the groups of travelers that he had invited for the event. Jack and Taroosa stood against the far wall, pointing at the Crown—a large, intricate array of mirrors that brought sunlight into the hole in the center of the throne room. No doubt they were debating its inner workings. Lucky sat on a marble bench near the fountain, his head buried in a book, Stars sitting upright next to him, shading the pages from the bright suns. Justus was excitedly babbling at Tibel, who was leaning against a pillar of the cloisters, staring out into the crowd. Emmett was meekly following Hester around as she caught up with various servants touting small delicacies and refreshments.

"You dropped out of the sky with your family in tow and then deafen the guards, and you expect some privacy? Yes, Galadrath, everyone just watched you cry," Farrah laughed.

Galadrath watched as Heladra's ears perked up at the mention of Farrah's name, and she marched over with the children.

"Umm... Farrah, Tagger—this is my wife, Heladra, and our son and daughter, Radralia and Marcanus," Galadrath introduced them.

"You're the one who kissed my husband?" Heladra asked, skipping the formalities.

Galadrath shook his head almost imperceptibly as Farrah glanced between him and Heladra.

"Technically, he kissed me," Farrah chuckled.

"That's… not helping," Galadrath sighed.

Farrah's playful demeanor cooled as he tried to counter the heat radiating off Heladra.

"He saved my life. Twice. The veil that lies behind this world is not something I would wish on anyone. We should all admire those who have walked there and managed to retain their sanity—and their humanity. The kiss was a noble act, Lady Heladra, and strictly professional. It saved me from the madness and darkness of that place. I would also advise against being crushed to death," Farrah stated frankly.

Heladra silently accepted the response, returning only a glare.

"And you—I hear you have a slippery tongue too," Heladra said, shooting a glance at Tagger.

"Heladra, please," Galadrath urged her.

"Slippery as it may be, my fair lady, I can assure you I keep it to myself." Tagger flashed a broad smile, before adding, "I can see why he ran off so quickly to be by your side, Madam Yaralok. He moved moor and mountainside to hold you again. Though, as you are such a formidable woman, I imagine he needed your safety more than you needed his."

"We're just glad to have him back," Heladra replied.

"Farrah, I'm about to crawl out of my skin with all these Emissaries and Keepers of the Peace around here. I feel like I'm in the belly of the beast. What if they know who we are?" Emmett said.

Hester sniggered through a mouth full of pastries. They had made their rounds collecting the savory snacks, and it would seem Emmett's paranoia had forced them to rejoin the group.

"I can assure you, they expect nothing of you. You're my guests. They wouldn't harm you," Galadrath said calmly.

"And what company do you keep, Accuser? Don't you think they know what we've been up to?" Emmett scolded him.

"I'll say it again, I can assure you of your safety. Trust me."

"I've not even a bludgeon to fend them off with, never mind a blade," Emmett grumbled in response.

Galadrath sighed.

"Marcanus, can you run and fetch that lady over there for me?" Galadrath asked, pointing at Taroosa.

He waited as the boy went to fetch the Jeweler, while introducing the others to the new additions. Hester quickly shared her pastries with Radralia, and they giggled together as the others talked.

"I expect you'll find certain absences in the court today, per our—" Galadrath began.

"Shushhhh," Taroosa interrupted.

"My name is Taroosa Pix. It is a pleasure to meet you all," she said with a small curtsy and a pleasant smile.

The introductions went around once more.

"Thank you for returning my husband to me," Heladra said sincerely.

"It's my pleasure, dear, but don't forget I almost shot him first. Not that it would have stopped him. It seems Galadrath here is tenacious in body and spirit. How did those stitches heal?" Taroosa asked warmly.

"I have one more favor to ask," Galadrath said quickly, afraid of being interrupted.

He gathered up a handful of the trinkets hanging around his neck. The brilliant metal shone, the blood and soot buffed from its surface. He weighed the items in his hand for a moment, judging their mass, but also taking stock of the actions by which he had earned them. He placed them softly in her hands as she cupped them.

"Can you please make me a blade? A knife if you could," he asked Taroosa.

"You know we don't make weapons from divine metal, for the same reasons we don't usually make chains. The metal does not bend, it does not break, it does not dull—" she stated.

"Where's the downside?" Emmett interjected.

Galadrath could see the conversation had stirred the red-haired man's fascination with sharp tools. Emmett hardly noticed the glare Taroosa shot at him when he interrupted her.

"A chain becomes a noose, a ring is a prison, a blade so keen that it is as dangerous to those who wield it as it is wielded against. Loose-fitting bangles, pendants, brooches—those are best," Taroosa said.

"Doesn't sound like you've ever held a sword if you think the handle is as dangerous as the pointy end," Emmett chuckled.

"A trinket *is* a weapon; it just doesn't have an edge. Please, Taroosa," Galadrath urged her.

She nodded. Her hands closed around the collection of jewelry, and immediately the metal began to flow from between her fingers. First, a frail stem appeared, and it thickened into a branch. The branch flattened into a slender leaf, the fine veins appearing on the surface. As the leaf blade grew in length and matured, Galadrath could make out the tiny serrations on the razor edge. The natural form of the leaf would make a formidable weapon. Smaller vines curled around the base of the blade, ending in smaller juvenile leaves. The curling leaves twisted, creating holes intended to fit a thumb and index finger, and the vines formed the hilt. The handle was rough, like bark from the branch that had been extruded into the blade. The blade continued to grow, and as it did, the flesh of the leaf was eaten away, as if diseased, leaving a few holes in patches between the veins.

"It seems I've gone too far. I've run out of material. Should I begin again?" Taroosa said sullenly.

The group stared at her in disbelief.

"It's perfect," Galadrath said.

"It seems brittle. Something meant for a lady," Emmett grumbled.

"Well, Emmett, it's yours, so it's fitting," Galadrath chuckled.

Now Taroosa was the one staring in disbelief, and Galadrath shrugged at her.

"I had a debt to pay," he added.

Taroosa turned to Emmett, hesitant to hand over the new creation.

"Unbending, unbreaking, and wickedly sharp," she restated the warning.

She turned the blade carefully in her hand and presented it to Emmett, handle first. He stood awestruck for a moment, and then gripped it slowly.

"It's lighter than I imagined," he said.

He chopped aimlessly at the air to test the weight, and Taroosa sprang backwards out of his way. He flipped the blade deftly in one hand, turning it over to inspect the other side, and instinctively ran his thumb along the edge to test its sharpness. The blade ran red immediately, his blood pooling against the veins of the leaf.

"Oh gods living, Emmett! Not even a whole minute!" Hester exclaimed.

"It's sharp," he replied.

Taroosa held her head in her hands.

"I told you it was sharp you fool!" she yelled.

"Scar be cursed! Emmett, it's deep! I think you cut down to the bone!" Hester said, grabbing the injured hand.

As Hester pressed against the wound, Emmett's face strobed between grimaces of pain and childlike delight.

"Thanks, Galadrath. It's a good one. Doesn't have the sentiment attached to the old one, but I'll manage," he forced out, sucking through his teeth.

"What's that all about?" Heladra asked.

"I melted down his last knife. I didn't think he'd ever forgive me," Galadrath replied.

"Look! Now everyone is beginning to file into court, and you're busy cutting off your fingers," Hester chastised him. "I'll have to give you stitches in the gallery. Look at me! The first time in my life I have an appropriate excuse to wear a dress, and you're going to bleed all over it! Let's go get our seats so I can handle this mess. I don't want to miss anything important!"

Galadrath had noticed they had all dressed the part. Tagger and Stars looked like they belonged, wearing their usual vests and gowns with nonchalance and elegance, but the others had traded their workwear for more formal attire. Even Farrah had abandoned her tan pants and drab shirts for colors and frills. The only person he had to imagine dressed up was Fingers, who was nowhere to be seen.

"Where's Fingers?" he asked Tagger.

"Off on business, I'm afraid. He does forward his apologies and regrets, I'm sure," Tagger smiled.

The others had begun to file toward the colonnades covering the front of the palace, making their way slowly to the throne room. As they pulled away, Tagger held Galadrath back.

"Speaking on business... and debts. I am now the one who must call on a favor. You'll be approached by a person of a certain prestige, and she'll ask you to deliver a message. It would please me if you didn't refuse her," Tagger said.

"Your first wish? You want me to deliver a message?" Galadrath asked.

"Simple as that," Tagger replied.

"Something tells me there will be nothing simple about it. How will I know this woman?"

"You'll know. She has a rather commanding presence," Tagger said with a menacing smile.

34

THE ACCUSED

THE THRONE ROOM WAS packed to the brim. The carved benches that made up the gallery had been squeezed in together and bolstered with small folding chairs, so when Galadrath passed along the tight rows, he could hear the nobility complaining about their lack of comfort. He kept a keen eye out, a small part of his subconscious requiring some sort of affirmation that he would not be betrayed in this room for a third time. The crowd helped to put him at ease. Surely, the king or those serpents still loyal to the Court of Lords would not try anything again with so many innocent lives at stake.

The collected whispers and conversations from amongst the seated citizens echoed off the hard walls of the vast circular room and mingled in a dull roar. The court's herald, Brixia, broke through the noise with a loud call to attention.

"Calling order to the court of King Dartan Thestus. On this first day of the seventh month, in the year seven-thousand ninety-six, the court is now in session!" Brixia proclaimed, her voice pure and unstrained by the volume at which she spoke.

The gallery became quiet, and King Dartan waited as the last of the whispers died, his presence demanding undivided attention. He stood slowly from the stone throne. The less permanent seats of the Court of Lords had been moved from the raised platform, and the army of pages and attendants, who usually crowded behind the seats, were hidden by the incline. The king stood alone as he addressed the court.

"I, King Dartan Thestus, stand before you today because of one man's brave actions. I've heard the whispers that travel the corridors and the streets of this great city. Thus, I have called this trial to lend truth to those that deserve it and to quash those that do not.

"Yes, there was an attempt to dethrone me. Yes, it did come from within the Court of Lords that shared this podium with me. The transgressors have been rooted out and tried. Lord Tallus Ostiphan, Lord Sigrol Braf, Lord Gresser Freid, and Lord Willen Tireod were found guilty and sentenced to death. The expanse of their treason was broad, but it was not deep. The full list of charges will now be read," Dartan said.

He sat back down on the throne, waved a hand over his shoulder, and summoned twenty servants carrying six rolls of parchments so long that they took three people to handily unravel. The first page began to read from the long list, detailing each transgression, what little evidence had been provided, and how each one ended with only one signature—that of the king. Each of the trials presented had already been carried out. Some had been held before a closed court, where the party was found innocent. Others were tried in the field by Accusers, where the accused was always found guilty.

Galadrath's mind quickly began to wander, not recognizing most of the names, but when he heard a shudder from Farrah after one particular name, he turned his attention back to the reading. He began to listen for the few names he knew: Green, Bartron, and the others he had met in Bracken village. Luckily, he did not recollect any of the names, but he could hear Farrah suck in her breath when a person she knew was called and hold it as she listened to the verdict. Soon, she made the connection: the few who had been tried before the court would be the only survivors—the rest were executed in the field.

He had not known the expanse of the insurgency that had formed against the throne, but as he listened to Farrah cry softly as the names of her dead friends were listed, he finally began to understand the scope of what he had been a part of. When the scribes and pages had finally reached the end of the second scroll, his back was already hurting, and he was happy to see the king stand up and address the gallery once more. He had been hoping for an intermission.

Galadrath made ready to stand when the king had finished speaking, but reclined slightly as he heard the words. The tension in his legs remained and spread to the rest of him as the king set the stage for the remainder of the reading.

"The following is the list of actions taken by Galadrath Yaralok and other followers loyal to the throne of Thainegom. It saddens my heart that so many good people have been caught up in the clutches of treason, and we honor the sacrifices made by those who fought brother against brother to uphold the great country that we all hold dear. Please, continue," Dartan said.

The page began reading.

"Galadrath Yaralok, hereby accused of theft of eight barrels of salt, a cart and oxen team, and arson resulting in the loss of three wagons, two teams of oxen, goods for export, and other sundries listed in Appendix 43. Damages incurred total an assessed value of fifty-four thousand gold pieces. The trial is to be carried out by the court of King Dartan Thestus, 48th of his name. The accused... is found not guilty."

Galadrath could hear the suppressed outrage as Emmett whispered to Farrah.

"Fifty thousand coins' worth of loot, and you had us stealing the salt?" he said, veins bubbling in his forehead.

"Emmett Brigborn, Justus Kennd, Tibel Morg, and Hester Karper, hereby accused of aiding and abetting in the previously stated crimes," the page continued reading, unaware of any outburst.

Emmett flashed a glare at Galadrath, and then looked to see if any guards were headed in his direction, but there was no movement.

"The witnesses are listed in the same appendix. The trial is to be carried out by the court of King Dartan Thestus, 48th of his name. The accused... is found not guilty."

The charges continued, each event chronicled in detail—the crimes listed and explained in no uncertain terms. Each time, Galadrath expected some other outcome, yet the verdict was the same.

"...The accused is found, not guilty."

"...The accused is found, not guilty."

"...The accused is found, not guilty."

The Accuser is found not guilty.

He listened attentively, placing each action in his mind inside its own time and place, giving the reading form—seeing the faces of those who had died. He recognized all the other accused names, those who had helped him. Even Taroosa was mentioned for lending aid, and her prior crimes from her youth were slipped in as an afterthought—pardoning her of all her crimes and reinstating her as a citizen of Thainegom.

As the litany of his actions continued to be read aloud for all to hear, he began to suspect that the remaining scrolls were all meant for him. His suspicions were slowly confirmed over the course of what felt like hours, as the scrolls came and went, the pages rolling them up neatly and carrying them away as the last length of parchment was unrolled and the scribe began to read.

He could feel nothing but guilt.

"Galadrath Yaralok, hereby accused of assaulting the fortress Hercolid. The trial is to be carried out by the court of King Dartan Thestus, 48th of his name. The accused is found not guilty."

Galadrath shifted in his seat, unsettled by the curt and vague description. He listened for the names of Tagger and his gang—to hear them mentioned as his accomplices, to hear their feats of disruption and the daring escape. He waited for the explanation of the attack on the city, when the lance incinerated Larl. But there were no details. Even in this moment of truth, the king could not admit that the fortress had been vulnerable, that their beloved city had been attacked by the very weapons meant to protect them.

What troubled him more deeply was that Tagger and his crew had been omitted from the record. They sat in view of the king and had not so much as received a glance. Jack, with his innocent smile and idle curiosities, had planted the bombs that leveled towers and buried soldiers. Every single one of them had taken a life without blinking an eye—and Galadrath was indentured to them.

"The following appendix will be read at the request of the king. Appendix 61: List of lives lost during the assault of the Hercolid, having taken place on the thirteenth day of the fifth month, year seven thousand ninety-six. Marcus Aberdeen, Keeper of the Peace—life lost in service of the king. Abigail Adina, servant to Larl Rihhi—life lost in service of the king. Jan Abser, Keeper of the Peace—life lost in service of the king..." the scribe continued.

The crowd was mostly silent. A few sniffles could be heard, and the king had bowed his head in respect for the dead, occasionally glancing up to make sure the people did not think he had fallen asleep. The minutes passed with more names as the reading continued.

Galadrath had lowered his head as well, trying to place the names with the faces he had remembered. There were so many that he did not know.

"Gods, living and dead," Heladra whispered under her breath.

He looked toward her, leaning his stiff body forward to try and see her face. Silent tears ran down her cheeks. He waited to catch her eye, but even his obvious attempts to get her to look at him, to show him something of what she felt, were ignored. She simply stared forward, and tears ran down her cheeks, dripping onto the front of her dress.

He had told her the stories of his victories and defeats, of glory won and honor restored. She had seen the spoils of his conquests laid in a glimmering, bloodstained heap when she had made her ultimatum. Now the list of names stripped all that away, and he could see in her trembling eyes that it left only a sense of needless death.

She had warned him that if he walked this path, he would become a monster—and now he wondered if she thought it was already too late.

Finally, his spiraling thoughts were interrupted by silence as the reading was completed.

"Let us hold a moment in silence to honor our countrymen who have sacrificed to save our great country," Dartan said solemnly.

Galadrath had never heard a congregation maintain such an eerie silence. In the Temple of Light, where a few citizens still worshiped the gods, the priests boasted that it was quiet enough to hear the gods speak. Even there, he had heard more than he heard now. Motes of dust wafted idly through the air, appearing and disappearing as they moved through the kaleidoscopic beams of light in the room. Those that wandered into the center beam above the tomb drifted upwards, as if ferrying the souls of the names read into the next life.

"With these events behind us, I would like to usher in a new age. Please help me rejoice in the appointment of the new Court's Accuser, High Honor Hector Rain!" Dartan continued.

The Custodians of the Temple of Light came forward and began the ritual of the sacred flame. Hector stood from his seat at the front of the gallery and moved forward to collect his new title and the trinkets that accompanied it.

"I, King Dartan Thestus, 48th of his name, grant thee, Hector Rain, the title of Court's Accuser. Henceforth you shall be known as the Court's Accuser. As granted by this title, you shall gain the benefits and the obligations as listed in the Laws of Thainegom, upheld by the throne. Rise, Accuser, and take this trinket fashioned in your style, as the thirty-sixth symbol of your title."

The ritual of the flame was quickly conducted, and the Jeweler added another trinket to the array that Hector wore around his neck. Thick links of gold dripped with the silver droplets of divine metal. His chest and neckline shimmered like a rainstorm held in stasis.

Galadrath watched, recognizing the man from his own past. They had both been in the Lowest House, though Hector was a few years older. They had both been children when they had met, and Hector had always been kind to the younger initiates. He had lacked the concentration and conviction to take his studies seriously and had played many pranks that earned him plenty of lonely hours in the dungeon under the halls of the Lowest House.

As Hector took his seat and the roar of the crowd died down, lines of Emissary Initiates formed to each side of the throne. None of them yet had trinkets of their own, and they would be receiving their first momentarily. Galadrath tried to count the heads to get an idea of how many of them there were, and he made out many faces of young men and women. Some were so fresh from the Temple of Light that he would not be surprised if one of them lost a hand to the ritual.

With the help of several other Jewelers, the procession moved quickly, and the roars and cheers of the crowd began to fade. The business of the court was completed, and the Herald dismissed the people. Galadrath waited in the gallery until it was almost empty, his children beginning to fidget restlessly.

He had meant to stand and address the people—to speak to the crimes he had committed, to plead for some form of absolution—but he could not bear to bring attention to himself once more. Every good memory of the awards he and others had received here in the throne room was soured by the recent past.

They stood and filed out of the room, returning to the sunshine of the courtyard. He met the gaze of Randolph as he passed by a group of nobles. He simply nodded to the tailor and smiled to himself.

The group gathered idly under an empty cloister at the edge of the open space, and they said their goodbyes. Tagger and his crew were headed to the islands on their airship. Taroosa was joining them, and it seemed to Galadrath that she was inseparable from Jack. He was happy to see that she had shed her exile so effortlessly, trading her hermitage for connection and purpose. Farrah and her group were headed back west to the hills, unsure if they would retain their old ways or convert to a more honest living.

"It seems we are right back at the beginning, Galadrath. The day you appeared in that tavern, I really thought we had a chance to change things. Now we've secured a steadfast monarchy, the remaining lords dismissed to govern their provinces, and all I've earned are the graves of my friends," Farrah said bitterly.

"You're still here. You can still make a difference," he tried.

"I'm not sure I can risk any more blood. The fight has left me, Galadrath. Maybe it's time to wait for someone else to pick up the banner," she shook her head.

"Maybe we shouldn't focus on molding the world as we see fit, but on changing the minds of the men and women that inhabit it," Galadrath said.

"And how do you propose we change the minds of the people—and the king? You saw them in there, cheering for the next wave of oppressors, forgetting the names of the dead as soon as they were read," she said, exasperated.

"I'm not sure. I've never had to negotiate much. I think I'm going to use my retirement to grow some flowers," he said with a shrug.

"Yes. No more insurrections. Just a quiet life for us," Heladra said, cementing the idea with her words.

"At least grow something we can eat." Farrah rolled her eyes.

35

THE MESSENGER

GALADRATH SAT ON A large stump by the side of the road, waiting for his crops to grow. He had forgotten about Tagger's cryptic message and rarely thought about the trial and the names that were read there anymore. Over the past months, he had spent many hours here, sitting and waiting for nothing in particular. He mostly stared into the distance toward the horizon, his view interrupted by the rows of trees that formed the edges of the partitioned land. His own fields sat at his back, waving grain and edged with flowers swaying softly in a warm breeze.

He had bought the land and worked the dirt. He had prepared, tilled, and planted miles of fields. When he had finished, he turned to help his neighbors. Many of them had more land than they could use and welcomed him. Dirt that had last been churned under the feet of the Tyrant's armies was turned over and used to grow wheat and vegetables. To his own reluctant agreement, his mother had been right—he had become a farmer. He had rarely seen one of the Many stoop to become a laborer, but it saddened him to see how much could be done with so little. The true honor was held by those who fed and clothed and created, not by those who held a title.

So he sat and waited. Not even the Many could will the plants to grow and ripen. When his eye grew tired of tracing the far edge of his vision, he would cast it downward and trace the edge of the stump with his hands, allowing his vision to unfocus and his mind to wander like an ant across the jagged cut surface of the stump. He had pondered the fate of the tree many times. The small dirt road neatly bisected the two fields that lay to either side of him, except where it curved ever so slightly around the stump.

He could imagine the surveyor who had plotted the straight road with painstaking precision—a man taking utmost pride in even the most rural of roads—only to find an obstinate tree partially in the way a few miles later. Instead of simply curving the road around the tree, it was cut down. Axes bit the skin and cut the flesh with the normal resistance of living wood. With sweaty brows and a half day spent, the girthy trunk heaved unceremoniously over, and the ground was covered in lush green as the smaller branches shatter on contact with the earth. The men of the survey team smile, victorious, and began to work at the stump.

But the stump did not move.

Even in death, the roots of the tree ran deep and maintained an immovable grip on the old clay. The men gave up, frustrated and behind schedule, and plotted the small bump where the road curved around the stump. The tree is dead—where it could have given shade to the passerby, where it could have continued to exist undisturbed for years to come. But it did not yield. It could not. Dead or alive, this was where it would stay.

Galadrath looked up, chuckling softly at the story he had conjured for himself from the tiny memories held in the dirt around him. In reality, he did not know when or why the tree was cut down, but he wanted to believe this story. He wanted to believe that the scars on this old wood meant something—that even as the tree stands shorter than it once had, it was not defeated. He patted the wood softly, and his eye caught movement in the distance.

At first, it looked like a carriage of sorts—a strange enough sight for the rural backroads. He squinted slightly, trying to make out the shape in the mild afternoon mirage. His mind worked tirelessly on the strange silhouette that approached. Minutes passed, and the bizarre vehicle became larger in the distance, until he finally came to a conclusion: it was two large, armored men carrying a grandiose palequin.

He was curious at the sight, but the curiosity stirred a latent fear in him. Time seemed to slow as the deliberate march of two sets of heavy feet approached the only imperfection on the straight road. When they were close enough for him to hear the heavy grinding of stone boots on the dry road, he could make out the details.

The two men were oddly shaped, the armor standing wider and taller than a normal suit would be. Their faces were obscured behind bulky helmets, pockmarked with small breathing holes and lacking any visor or slit for the wearer to peek out from. They stood at least a foot taller than a normal man, and while the armor was dull, barrel-chested and awkward, the palanquin they carried between them was sleek and ostentatious. Polished stone flowed like black waves around windows curtained with deep red silks. Each edge of the flowing form looked sharp enough to cut, and gold leaf was scattered in veins among the dull reflection of red rubies. The whole palanquin seemed to be cut from a single block of granite—as if a block had been cut from a rich vein of gold and gems, and then painstakingly carved into a vessel to carry something even more precious inside.

They walked in a wide arc in front of him without a trace of life between them, and no voice to sound an introduction—only the soft grinding of stone rubbing on stone, and the soft breeze causing the silks over the windows to ripple slightly.

Galadrath pushed out his influence and was instantly met with the overwhelming presence of an influence that was not his. The suits of metal and stone were inhabited, and he could not sense what lay inside them. His influence clashed at their surface against the will of another Many, and then, as he pressed into the palanquin, he felt a third.

For just an instant, he could feel the cotton of her shirt, the surface of her skin. Then his influence faltered. It was not the jarring rip of influence being wrenched free from the control of his mind—it was slow and methodical. There was no chorus of complicit voices from the air and the stones, only the same silence of pure obedience he had felt when Mirrora had exerted her will.

So he drew on the chains and pressed against this new threat. His efforts were in vain. His influence buckled as if it had not existed at all. He began to sweat, his concentration fixed on the force he was up against: the impenetrable, slowly advancing wall of influence expanding into the space that he controlled.

It halted, roughly halfway between the edge of the palanquin and Galadrath. The two armored bulks took a knee in unison, lowering the small set of steps leading from the side of the carved stone compartment closer to the ground. The top of the stairs were roughly at eye level with him, and the bottom step was still a few feet off the ground, leading Galadrath to believe the act was more ceremonial than functional.

The red curtain covering the doorway pulled back to reveal a young woman standing slightly hunched behind it. Her bright green eyes peered out at him from behind a few stray blonde hairs that had sprung loose from the rest of her mane, which was messily tucked up in a bun. The shirt he had briefly known was a simple red one in a loose-fitting style, paired with light brown pants that extended to just above the ankles of two bare feet that now perched at the top of the stepladder. He watched the toes curl over the edge of the precipice and noticed the heavy calluses along their bottoms.

"Can we reach some sort of a ceasefire so that we can begin with the formalities? I've traveled a long way, and I really would like to stretch," she said pleasantly.

Her hands waved outward toward the slightly crackling boundary between them. He saw her arms shimmer in the sunlight, the opalescent colors etched into her skin in patterns of fractal lightning. His own scars ached under his sleeves, and the weight of the chains that covered them. She had flirted with death just as he had—and just a moment ago, she had crushed his will like a potter softly flattening a ball of clay—yet he could not make out a single ounce of divine metal on her form.

"Of course," Galadrath said.

His voice was scratchy from disuse, and he cleared his throat into the dry air. Even with his arsenal of trinkets, it did not seem he had much of a choice.

"My thanks," she smiled.

She stepped quickly down the stairs, not stopping when she reached the end of them. He felt his reflexes tug at him, wanting to lurch forward and catch her as she stepped into midair—but her foot caught the edge of nothingness, and she finished her descent with grace, taking a few more steps down the invisible ladder into the dirt. He had not expected her to fly or float. The dry air of the day was still; there was no wind she had summoned to ride on. She simply walked on the air with the same ease she stepped onto the ground.

She stood straight, arching her back slightly and rolling her shoulders backwards. She was taller than him—even barefoot in the road, she looked down on him.

"You must be Galadrath Yaralok. It really is a pleasure to meet you. My name is Evelyn," she said warmly.

"Nice to meet you, Evelyn," Galadrath replied.

She studied him, her cheeks perking up as her smile widened. He grew uncomfortable standing there, his mind brewing more questions while the silence offered no answers.

"To what do I owe this pleasure?" he asked politely.

"Oh, yes. I'm sorry. I just thought you would be taller. I imagined someone—I don't know—a little more robust," she said.

His eyelid sunk in annoyance and welcomed the silence. Her face went blank, and she nodded toward him.

"I'm sorry. That wasn't exactly a polite way to introduce myself. You must excuse me—I've been traveling in this coffin for sometime now and probably should have gotten out and stretched my legs a bit more," she said.

"Gramma." An echoing voice came from beneath one of the helmets.

"Oh, I'm sorry, my dearest. Nadi, Gav, take a break. Help yourselves," she said loudly.

No more noise came from the suits. Instead, Galadrath watched as two young men appeared, each passing through the iron-fortified stone walls of the armor as if they were reemerging from a murky pool of water. They were Many, and they were well-trained.

They both turned toward Galadrath with an air of pageantry and bowed slightly. They turned again—this time toward the young woman—and bowed more deeply.

"Empress…" one man began.

"What did I say, Nadi? Don't call me that. You're family!" Evelyn scolded him.

"But he's…" Nadi attempted a rebuttal.

Even in the warmth of the midafternoon sun, Galadrath shivered when she spoke again. The relaxed skin on her neck grew taught around flexing muscles, and for a moment, he thought her eyes darkened from the bright green.

"You will not call me by my title, but you will not forget it when you speak to me," she said.

"Of course, Gram Gram," Nadi said, bowing more deeply.

Nadi and his counterpart took a few steps backwards, turned away, and walked quickly into the opposite field.

Galadrath's mind was stuttering under the weight of recent events. He had hardly realized that the suits of armor were now empty—each still taking a knee, the palanquin bolted to their shoulders, still suspended between them.

The two men were young but grown, dressed in fashionable clothes embroidered with the symbol of Irah. The woman looked to be their age, yet they had referred to her as their grandmother. His mind had sat empty at the edge of the stump for too long, and now his memories flooded in all at once, rushing to make sense of the scenario before him.

He bowed so low that he could only see her bare feet in his periphery.

"Queen Ancient. Timeless Mother. Forgive me for not recognizing you earlier," he said.

"It is actually *Empress* Ancient. My grandson did get that part right.

But Timeless Mother! Hah, that is just a silly name. I don't like silly nicknames. Please, stand up straight. You're short enough without folding yourself in half like that," she said, her playful tone returning.

Galadrath stood up, his eyes moving from where her toes were digging idly in the dirt up to her beaming face. He could not help but smile back.

"I, too, am not fond of nicknames," he replied.

She stared at him—her face still friendly and welcoming, but her eyes inquisitive, expecting more.

"That armor looks uncomfortable," he said, unsure how to continue.

"I wouldn't know. I've never been in it. No one has ever complained about it. Most wear it with honor. It's very outdated, but the kids really like the pomp of it—playing color guard soldier and all that," she mused.

"For a moment, I thought I was looking at hollow men—members of the Tyrant's army," Galadrath's mind wandered aloud.

"Nope. Not these two. Good old fashioned, man-filled armor here. 'Tyrant'—there's another silly nickname, if only you knew," she chuckled, squinting around her, shading her eyes from the sun and wrinkling her nose.

"Excuse me, but I'm having a hard time understanding why the Queen—I mean, *Empress* of Irah—would find me here, riding in *this*," Galadrath said, unbelieving of the whole situation.

"Would you rather have me swoop in with a host of angels and fall from the sky? What would your neighbors say? They'd think it was the end—might even think I've come to split open another god. Could you imagine?"

"You say 'another,' but you didn't destroy the Children," Galadrath corrected her.

Her expression grew colder, and he saw her eyes darken slightly. The bright green of her irises faded to a pale emerald for just a moment, as if a shadow had passed in front of her.

"My actions did not—you're right—but my words did. I need you to arrange a meeting. I need you to bring someone to me," she said sternly.

"Who? The Ashmaker?" Galadrath asked.

"Mirrora. I need you to bring Mirrora to me."

"I can't do that," he whispered.

"I know you can. Galadrath, my dear, the whole world knows what you did. You squashed a coup against an incompetent king. Thanks for undoing all my work there, by the way. You've successfully safeguarded the seat of a man who couldn't administrate a bakery—never mind a kingdom. You've singlehandedly undermined the immediate future of Thainegom. In the name of the institutions you serve, your country-men will continue to suffer. I would have said it was a masterstroke conceived by the Archons of Barkrill, but even they work with a heavier hand. Or a swifter sword, really," she said.

She had paced around idly as she spoke, eventually circling him until she stopped in front of the stump and sat down, crossing her legs tightly and tucking her fingers in between her knees.

"You planned the overthrow of King Dartan?" Galadrath asked.

"No. I just had some people in the right places who made me aware of an opportunity to end the reign of that little runt. So I spent some time—and a lot of money—making sure those people had the resources to bring about a new republic. Then you came along and killed those people.

"Not to worry—time and money I have plenty. Even if I just have to sit back and outlive Dartan, I will. I just feel terribly for all your poor countrymen—so many sacrifices made in vain," she said, frowning at the ground where she nudged at loose pebbles with her feet.

"You put the Court up to this? Jemat Ancient knew about the coup that day—I thought he was innocent. I thought he walked out of the throne room for the sake of peace. He was just cutting his losses—*your* losses. How many of your spies did he save? You instigated the killings? The trials that I was given to carry out? Sebattin, Diatara, the countless men and women that died defending the crown—all because of you? All for nothing?" he asked.

She pulled her slender fingers from where she had pinned them between her knees and began to bounce her foot listlessly for a moment. She wrinkled her nose, then scratched it with her freed hand.

"Galadrath," she paused, obviously trying to find softer words. "You killed those people. They died defending the crown from *you*. If you had done the right thing—and died for your country—none of them would have had to. Now, let's get back to business. Even though you made a proper mess of the whole coup, it was worth it, because I found you, and you found Mirrora. The whole world knows what you did for the king of Thainegom, but very few people know what you did in that throne room."

"I failed. I almost died," Galadrath grumbled.

"And Mirrora let you live—along with a few others."

"I haven't seen her since."

"Galadrath, Accuser Yaralok, you haven't seen her since because you haven't been looking. I know very well that you are a man who can find people—you could find a hermit in a snowstorm a world away. I want you to start looking."

"Mirrora isn't a person, and she doesn't want to be found," he stated.

"You're half wrong. In the old world, they called the gods *titans*. The titans are not as human as we like to make them—they are depicted as the wind, the waves, eruptions. Yes, Mirrora isn't a person. Mirrora is a god. A titan. And Mirrora does want to be found, by you."

Galadrath paused, having no clear rebuttal ready. He remembered when he was young, back in the dark rooms of the Lowest House. He remembered wandering in Tor Zuer—and getting lost. He remembered when Mirrora took his hand and led him back into the world. He had not known anything about who she was back then—not that he knew much more now.

"You've met her?" Galadrath asked.

"The day I met Mirrora I was given two gifts."

"And you want to meet this god once more? Maybe receive another gift?"

"I do. I must. This time, I'm the one who wants to give a gift."

"The old world, gods, titans… I'm not sure what this has to do with me. Why come to me? Why not find Mirrora yourself? You've seen the old world and saved the new one. Your power is uncontestable—as I've just experienced. Surely the Timeless Mother doesn't need the help of a humble Accuser," Galadrath mumbled.

"I don't appreciate your tone. And I also feel like I've already given you the answers to the questions you ask. So, Galadrath—ask me the questions I haven't answered," she said coolly.

He waved his hand toward an open section of the stump, and she immediately understood he was asking for a place to sit. She uncrossed her legs and made as if she was saving him a space on a seat without actually making any more room, then patted the rough wood beside her.

"Please, take a seat, my dear," she smiled.

There they sat for a moment in the soft sounds of the afternoon air, sharing the old wood as a seat, facing slightly away from each other, both staring off into the distance.

"Take your time. It's been a long time since I've been here. It is so beautiful now," she added.

He frowned and rolled his one eye upwards, knowing she could not see him. He was annoyed that she felt the need to give him permission to think. As much as he enjoyed the structure of royalty and government, those who held positions of power were often so tedious.

She laughed softly, stifling a chuckle, and then relaxed her posture, planting her palms behind her, rubbing a shoulder against the metal fins protruding from his back.

"No need to be mad. I mean it—take your time. I've got a long road ahead of me, and I'm quite enjoying the sunshine at the moment."

"You can feel my face? My expressions? I can't feel your influence."

"My dear, I'm eighty-four years old. I don't need to use my influence to know what your face is doing."

"The legends are true, then? That the first of the Few lived for hundreds of years? I always thought those were just stories—metaphors, hyperbole wrapped around a bit of truth. You'll live as long?" Galadrath asked.

"I can't speak for them, but I can live as long as I like," she said dreamily.

"So those two men are really your grandchildren?" he asked.

"Yes. I have a whole raft of children and grandchildren and their children. It's becoming hard to keep track of them all. They all look up to me and want something—power, respect, love, acceptance, attention, and authority."

"You look so young. Isn't it strange for you?"

"It is strange. My firstborn—my son—died last year. He was only sixty years old. His favorite horse got scared while he was cleaning his hooves. The horse kicked him in the head. He died instantly. There was nothing I could do. It was then that I realized—even though I have all the time in the world, others do not."

"I'm sorry, Empress. Surely this isn't the first time... you've dealt with... loss?" he prodded her shakily.

He could feel her head spin toward him but did not dare meet her gaze, afraid of what color her eyes would be, scared that she might turn him to stone.

"I've killed more men than you've laid eyes on, Galadrath—you know that. I've buried friends, a husband, a king, and three of the Few. I've watched countless graves get filled in—and filled as many myself. None of that prepared me to bury my son. A mother should never be allowed to survive her children," she said bitterly.

"I'm sorry," he croaked.

She sighed lightly, and he could hear her straighten herself and regain her composure. As she did, she brushed against the fins on his back again, and he could not help but feel like she was doing it on purpose.

"So, do you have a question for me?" she asked frankly.

"What happens when I find Mirrora?" he asked.

"I wish you to deliver a message. I wish to give Mirrora a gift."

"Dare I ask what the gift is?" he pried.

"You dare not. Speaking of gifts, though—I've brought you something," she said.

She stood quickly and took a few long, skipping steps toward the palanquin. The last few steps only touched the air, as she bridged the gap between the ground and the small ladder in the same way she had before. She tossed the red curtain aside, and he watched as she produced a beautiful set of garments.

"I know you have a thing for fashion. And what does one get a man who has everything? I, too, have a thing for fashion. I may not look the part, but I remember the first time I put on a dress. It was magical. I had these tailored after the style that you used to wear—back when you were still working. I took some liberties with the fit and the accessories," she said with excitement.

She held the pearlescent, shimmering white cloak and vest in her arms, spread wide so that the material would not touch the ground, as she descended back down the steps. The fine white was covered in fields of flowers of all different shapes and sizes—the vivid colors made from thousands of gemstones sewn to the fabric. The flowers were gilded in golden thread and set in precious metal. It was an extravagant, gaudy, and ostentatious ensemble, and he could see that even the fabric strained under the weight of the wealth incorporated into its surface.

"It's very nice," Galadrath smiled as genuinely as he could.

"We've had so many plays and retellings of your adventures in the theaters of Irah that I'm afraid the design might be a little... inflated. People do tend to stretch the truth when they try to entertain," she said, addressing his lack of excitement.

"You've had plays performed about me?"

"Of course, my dear! You're quite the modern romantic! The people love you. Tagger actually came up with the idea to make you this, when I told him I was coming to meet you."

Galadrath sat in shock at the mention of the charismatic thief.

"You remember Tagger, right? Him and his whole bunch? His retelling of your adventure together was actually the inspiration for several of those plays," she said, puzzled at his silence.

"Yea, yes. I do remember him. I just didn't think..."

"I understand. I'm not very fond of him to be honest—he talks too much. But Fingers is an old acquaintance of mine, and so he brings his cohorts by from time to time. Enough about them—please, do try this on," she said.

Galadrath mumbled to himself for a moment, searching the ground with his gaze, as if hoping to find something there that might make sense of the situation. He turned his eye back up toward her and shook his head slightly.

"I'm terribly sorry, but I'm afraid it won't fit," he said, hooking a thumb toward his back, pointing to the fins jutting from the loose shirt.

"Yes, and with that, I'd like to give you your second gift. After all, gifts are like people—better in pairs," she said, holding up a small green orb he did not recognize.

"What's that?"

She walked directly in front of him, bending forward slightly so she could reach behind him. She was so close to him that he could feel the heat of the day radiating from her neck as she whispered in his ear.

"Close your eye, and I'll show you," she said, almost too softly to hear.

He closed his eye, unsure if he should be excited or afraid. As he did, he felt a tug against the metal on his back. There was some pressure, and then the strange sensation of things moving under his skin—like a splinter being pulled from a place where it had long rested. The light tug on his back was steady, and when he ended, he rocked forward slightly as the pull ceased. He felt lighter, and his spine tingled, almost itching, like a limb awakening after being slept on, the feeling returning in a mixture of strange sensations. He focused on the bizarre feeling, his mind consumed by it, until the heavy clatter of metal sounded atop of the stump. His eyes shot open at the noise.

His world was half in darkness, his vision distorted. Then he realized it—he had opened his *eyes.* He pulled away the eye patch and felt his lashes scrape against it as the bright landscape came into view. He sat up, looking over Evelyn's shoulder into the distance. She stepped back.

"You'll have to start worrying about your posture again," she smiled.

He looked behind him and saw the strange contraption that had held his spine together lying there, the bent hooks that had once wrapped around his bones now exposed and clean. He realized he had turned without the stiff resistance he had grown accustomed to. His back was healed. His eye, somehow, restored. There was no latent pain, no aches or stiffness.

He was whole again.

He looked back and forth between the metal brace and the young woman a few times, unable to speak.

"How'd you think I stay this young?" she said with a smile, laughing lightly.

"How can I repay you?" he asked flatly.

"This is a gift my dear. Cherish it. Enjoy it. Oh—and see if *these* fit!" she said.

She pointed to the gaudy clothing still hovering in mid air.

He smiled back and nodded.

"Excellent. You can change in there. Some privacy," she said, pointing to her palanquin.

He emerged a few minutes later, pushing aside the red curtain. The bright sunlight caught the gems and shining fabric so sharply that he watched Evelyn squint as he emerged.

"You look magnificent, Galadrath!" she crooned.

"Thank you, Empress. Thank you for everything. A thousand times—I can't thank you enough," he said softly.

"My pleasure, dear," she nodded.

"This may seem forward... but would you join my family for dinner? I'm not sure I'd be able to explain any of this to my wife and children," he asked.

"Absolutely."

Galadrath nodded in excitement and began to look in the direction of the road.

"Don't forget your things," Evelyn said, gesturing at the brace and the old clothes he had discarded onto the stump.

"Ah, yes. I'll send them ahead," he replied.

He gathered the items up absentmindedly, and they vanished in a cloud of dripping black vapor.

"Don't you think your wife might worry when your spine shows up without you attached to it?" Evelyn said with a frown.

"Gods, living and dead," Galadrath groaned.

The black, rolling fog appeared again, and his old trappings reappeared exactly where they had vanished from. He scooped them into his arms listlessly.

"You don't think very far ahead, do you? I'm honestly surprised you've survived as long as you did. It's almost like someone is looking out for you," she stated with a wink.

"I stumbled through most of it," he grumbled, frowning at the insult.

"Hmmm. I wish I could *Step*. Could you teach me?" she asked.

"No," he said sternly.

"What if that is the wish Tagger wants granted?"

Galadrath had been afraid that she was the woman Tagger had inferred he would meet. The memory of the message he would have to deliver returned to his mind like an echo.

"You know of my deal with him, so you know I cannot refuse," he said.

The idea of teaching someone to Step as part of his dealings had never occurred to him. He had spent no time dreaming of the limitless, impossible things that could be asked of him. Better not dwell—it would merely cause him unrest.

"My thanks for that. However, that is not my wish. What I want is simpler than it seems. Find Mirrora for me and deliver my message."

He laughed. The absurdity of the request, the weight of what was expected, and the euphoria of his restored body all collided in his mind. "I don't think it will be so simple. I don't even really know what she is—*who* she is. You seem to know more than you're letting on."

"I'm sure of it, Galadrath. When you're ready, Mirrora will be too."

He looked back at her, knowing full well she had told him only part of the truth. There was an understanding in her words, a sadness in her tone that could not hide what she had seen.

"Let me tell you a story over dinner," she said gently. "And then I'll leave you be. Then one day, when you're ready, I'll be hearing from you."

She squinted at the suns, searching for something in the sky, and then back at him.

"Once you've talked to her—once you've called the titan," she whispered, like a secret shared with the wind.

DRADOFIR
PARK OF MARRETTE
WHITESPUR
NIGHTBLOOM
TOMB
SPRINGLETTER
VALLEY OF HEROES
THRESHOOK
HERCOLID
TIRV
AXEHEAD BAY
SILT
CITY OF LIGHT
THAINEGOM
BRACKEN
TREADFÖGS
IRAH
SYLAH
THE SCAR
BARKRILL

GLOSSARY

Accuser - A person who enforces the royal justice system. By law, any person can act as an Accuser. Any person can accuse any other person of a crime, and can then carry out a sentence, or trial by combat. The king has appointed the royal accusers, elite members of the Many who carry out these trials in the name of justice.

Ancients - A nickname given to the last surviving tribe of Irah by the Ashmaker. Members and descendants of the tribe use Ancient as their surname.

Architect - Job title given to Emissaries who specialize in civil engineering.

Archon - The title held by the leading oligarchs of Barkrill. The Archons of Barkrill are well educated in politics and warfare, while also trained in the use of divine metal and blackstone.

Ashmaker - The fourth member of the Few. Both the first and second Ashmakers were renowned for their destructive warfare and their vast knowledge of military tactics.

Barkrill - An island country far to the South of Thainegom that was split in half by the Scar. Almost ruined by the natural disaster, they rebuilt their society into a rigid, militaristic oligarchy that discovered blackstone and practiced Stepping in obscurity for almost 1600 years.

Brightcaller - The second member of the Few. The first was known as the King of Light, a religious man who fought relentlessly against the patchwork armies of the First Great War. The second was Delia King, remembered for her compassion, the aid she provided, and the asylum she granted for the people during the second great war.

Delia's Stretch - A very long and large road formed by Delia King, the second Brightcaller. The road was built early in the Second Great War to allow faster movement of people and goods to the port cities, during the mass exodus of refugees from Thainegom.

Divine metal - The metal alloy that made up a portion of the celestial bodies of the gods. Ranging from a light silver to a dark tungsten gray, it is virtually unbreakable and can only be smelted and smithed by the powers of the Many. Those who devote their life to this art are known as Jewelers.

Dradofir - Dradofir is the country north of Thainegom. With a cooler climate and temperamental weather, it is a more sparsely populated country than Thainegom, filled with tightknit villages instead of large city centers. The citizens are known for their red hair and fiery dispositions; they are often derogatorily referred to as "wild men". The "Sons of Dradofir" is used to refer to the citizens of the country, the lords of the lands that make up the country, and often the six sons of Warpriest Yeka. She united the families of Dradofir as a single fighting force in 7014, with her six sons serving as her generals during their brief invasion of Thainegom.

Draughtsman - The first member of the Few. Both the first and second were known for their ability to build and design things that fundamentally changed technology at that time in history.

Dusters - Slang term for people who have been in contact with divine metal and learned how to use its abilities without formal training. Many of the people who prospected for divine metal only found trace amounts, small pebbles of ore or flakes. Yet even a handful of divine dust could be used to channel the elements, which became the origin of the nickname. Dusters are not sanctioned by the Temple of Light to use divine metal in Thainegom, and so they are considered outlaws.

Earth Mother - The planet on which this story unfolds. Two large continents form around the north and south poles, with a single shallow ocean running the circumference of the equator.

Emblem - A pure, crystal-like form of energy and matter, coinciding with the last phase it remembers being in. If a user draws in energy in a certain form—such as absorbing a stone—and then deposits it in an emblem, the emblem takes on that identity. In the case of absorbing a stone, it would take the form of an *earth emblem,* and the matter it comprises would "remember" that it was once a stone. The more energized or "excited" the material, the higher it moves in the hierarchy of phases: solid, liquid, gas, plasma—or, in traditional terms, earth, water, air, and fire. Blackstone and its antithesis fit into this structure, but little is known about them. Emblems can be transitioned from one to another, but it requires immense effort. The user must "teach" the matter a new memory in order to adopt a new identity. Emblems tend to revert to their original form—so, for instance, an emblem made of granite would likely revert to granite unless the user exerts enough effort to "convince" the original matter to become something else. A user of exceptional willpower could turn stone into water, and with enough divine metal, even turn oxygen into gold.

Emissary - Members of the Many who have been sanctioned by the Temple of Light to work with divine metal. They are trained in many professions, but most of them are simply known as Emissaries, which is the generic name for soldiers who have access to divine metal.

Few - Five humans chosen to act as leaders for the human race. These humans are granted the ability of commanding matter and energy with their minds, and with time and training, grow in their power to do so. The Few have appeared at several occasions across history—the two most notable being concurrent with the two great wars. For this reason, they are often referred to as the "first" which arrived in 5414, or the "second" who arrived in 7032.

Influence - A zone brought under the control of one of the Many. All matter and energy have some level of sentience and contain their own memory. The larger or more complex the structure, the higher the level of sentience. Most inert objects like stones or air are simple minded, knowing they are stones or air and enjoy listening to more complex leaders. When a Many brings these objects into their own influence, they can manipulate them in almost any way. Divine metal acts as a conduit for this ability. The more divine metal—and the purer it is—the larger influence can be exerted by its controller. The more complex the sentience of a collection of matter (such as a plant or an animal), the more difficult it becomes to exert control over it. A human can not exert influence over another, unable to overpower the mind, soul, and free will of a being as complex as themselves.

Irah - The obscure island nation across the Scar from Sylah, deep in the ocean. Ruled by The Timeless Mother and completely revitalized from extinction during the Second Great War, this zealous nation is filled with mechanical technology. Emblem-powered machines and airships fill the streets and cities of skyscrapers and industrial complexes.

Lance - Desolator Lance, or simply *Lance* to the few who know of it, is a type of weapon that shoots a focused beam of plasma at a target, then uses the ionized medium as a conductor for a massive discharge of electricity. This combination of energies is powered by a fire emblem power source and is effective at defeating all but the most resilient of targets. These "lightning cannons" were designed and created by the Ashmaker and the Draughtsman of the Second Great War. *Dreadnought-class* refers to the largest size lance, which was originally mounted on the dreadnought airship named *Oppressor*.

Lowest House - The central governing body of Barkrillen society is known for its shadowy influence all over the globe and the strict order with which it functions. It safeguards the secrets of Stepping with utmost vigilance, recognizing it as a considerable strategic asset.

Many - Prior to the shattering, only the Few and some of their "disciples" had the ability to manipulate matter. When the pieces of gods rained down as meteorites, the divine metal ore was discovered, and some people who came into contact with it were able to use the metal as a conduit to emulate the powers of the Few in a very limited capacity.

Nightbloom - A purple flower that only blooms at night, known for its peppery-sweet scent and its strong intoxicating effects. It is used extensively for pain relief and sometimes recreationally, much like opium. The town of Nightbloom was named after the flower, which is indigenous to the northern area of Thainegom.

Park of Marrette - A park built on the site where the town of Marrette had existed. Marrette was one of the few official towns in the un-claimed territory between Thainegom and Dradofir after the Shat-tering. The cosmopolitan population of the town lived peacefully for decades before the greed of the two nations drove it to extinction.

Patchwork - Also called Patches, Patchwork, Patchwork haunts, Cents, Centonipes. The patchwork haunts, formally known as centonipes, are creatures of evil. They are created from reconstituted organic matter—corpses of animals, plants, and insects—reanimated with a tar-like black substance through a little understood process. They appeared in large numbers during the two great wars and are now found only sparsely. These creations are agile, strong, resilient, and relentless in their drive to multiply and destroy. Only the most elite warriors, or Many, have been known to be able to defeat these abom-inations.

Pillar - A title given to a person who has chosen to serve inside the governing body of Barkrill. With an emphasis on serving their coun-trymen, Pillars can be assigned an array of duties, ranging anywhere from farmers to soldiers to teachers.

Rat Catcher - A slang term for the Many tasked with catching and disposing of Patches. Due to their increased exposure to blackstone and its residue, they must be diligent in their own hygiene or risk becoming poisoned by the material—an affliction ultimately kills them and transforms them into Patchwork.

Scar - An incredibly deep ravine, hundreds of miles long, created by the immense energy released during the destruction of the Treadfögz. The Scar is the source of the mists that roll over much of the ocean, the islands, and prompted the construction of the Thaine-gom spires.

Shattered Children - A cluster of asteroids and debris forming a loose ring around the planet, composed of the remains of the two dead gods, Aster and Elgee. The Shattering refers to the event that broke apart these gods and sent their pieces raining down onto the surface, introducing divine metal to the human race.

Sijis - A country on the southern continent, renowned for its lush climate, rich flavors and fibrant colors. It is a strong trade partner of Thainegom.

Sisters - A pair of suns at the center of the solar system.

Sari - A red giant star, the older sister, known as the nurturer of mankind.

Seli - A yellow star, the younger sister, a symbol of fertility and promise of a bright future.

Stepping - The act of channeling and expending blackstone to teleport from any one space to another space the user can recall in their mind. Stepping places the user in Tor Zuer for an undefined period of time between their entry and exit. This movement expends blackstone, shedding it as waste around the user in the form of a heavy black gas. An object can be Stepped by itself—either retrieved from a location and brought to the user or sent to a far-off location. In either case, the object and its destination or location need to be well known.

Sturm - Also called *Sturmhund* or "Dogs of War," Sturms are dogs as large as horses. They were bred after the First Great War, serving both as a heavy cavalry against the Patches and as long-range messengers. They are strong, fast, bred for stamina, incredibly aggressive, and are often mounted in combat by veteran warriors. They were used extensively during the Second Great War, but after the appearance of the Many, the use of these dogs dwindled to ornamentation and became a symbol of wealth. The Thainegom coat of arms features a silver Sturm head on a background of white.

Sylah - An island nation to the south of Thainegom, notorious for lavish clothing, incredible naval prowess, and self-indulgent attitudes. The Sylan language is a dialect descended from French.

Temple of Light - The holy temple that was once dedicated to worshipping the Sisters, later repurposed as a training facility for the Many after the Shattering.

Thainegom - A large country on the northern continent, known for its proud military structure, power, and technological innovation.

Tirv - Originally a Thainegom port city, it was forgotten after the First Great War. Suffering a similar fate to Irah, it was abandoned by Thainegom when the Scar was formed. Covered in the encroaching mist and physically separated by the Scar, the people who chose to remain behind suffered for centuries, and the city fell into decline. Now it is a city-state under the fold of the Empire of Irah, revitalized and thriving.

Tomb - The ruins of a farming town destroyed by the formation of the Scar. Originally called *Tomme* (after the cheese), the name deteriorated and was forgotten, much like the town itself. It was briefly used as a dumping ground for exiles and people with incurable diseases.

Tor Zuer - The surreal realm made of shadowy memories, acting as a bridge between two points in reality. While Stepping and Wandering, the minds and bodies of those channeling blackstone move into and through this space. Without concrete indicators of distance, space, or elapsed time, any inhabitant can become disoriented. Along with this disorientation, memories that make up the real world and the landscape of Tor Zuer can interact more tangibly with other objects or persons, making it uniquely dangerous.

Treadfögz - Often shortened to "Tread," the large tube-like portal lies in the middle of the great ocean, between the islands of Sylah and Irah. It was created as a doorway for the Patchwork armies to attack from their own world. It suffered catastrophic damage at the end of the First Great War, at the hands of the Brightcaller and the Votary, and ceased to function. The immense release of energy at the moment of its destruction cracked the planet and resulted in the Scar—a large fissure hundreds of miles long—that the Tread straddles.

Trinket - A premeasured amount of divine metal, traditionally crafted into a piece of jewelry. These are given to Emissaries as symbols of their title. Like medals awarded for courageous acts, trinkets serve both a physical display of station and as a direct contributor to the power of the individual who holds them under their influence.

Tyrant - The General of the Hollow army. The Hollow army is composed of thousands of emblem-powered mechanical soldiers and supported by the original airships designed by the Ashmaker and the Draughtsman.

Votary - The fifth member of the Few. Ezidora, who was exalted as a martyr after being lost in the Tread when it was closed during the First Great War. She returned as the champion of evil during the second war and fought against the second set of the Few.

Wandering - The act of meditating, placing only the mind of the Wanderer in Tor Zuer, allowing them to discover places in reality they do not have a memory of.